The Stones Cry Out!

Josué Raúl Conte

Airleaf Publishing

airleaf.com

Library of Congress Control Number: 2006932960

ISBN: 1-60002-147-6

Front cover graphic ©2006
Jupiterimages corporation
www.clipart.com

This book is dedicated to all innocent priests who have suffered persecution from false allegations. "Blessed are you when they shall revile you, and persecute you, and speak all that is evil against you, untruly, for my sake. Be glad and rejoice, for your reward is very great in heaven. For so they persecuted the prophets that were before you." Mt 5:11-12

Any resemblance between real people living or dead is purely coincidental. No other archbishop could be as suave and virtuous as Marco's, no other clergy could be as circumspect as those surrounding him, nor could any other priest be as obedient to his archbishop as he, and certainly no other archdiocese could be as glorious as the mythical Archdiocese of Rosanada where life is always rosy.

1

Marco

"Marco Alexis Lamadrid!"

"Si, *Monseñor*." Laffy was after me again. When he called my name, my classmates Pompeo Dell'Anitra, Mínimo Tabrón, and Damian Babilonia all looked at me in alarm. What could old Laffy want now? Dead silence fell upon the study hall and all the seminarians there were staring at me, knowing that I was in trouble again.

"The bishop will see you now."

I feared the worst. God had called me to be a priest and now I was afraid the bishop had come to throw me out of the seminary. Taking a deep breath, I started down the long corridor that led to the library where he was waiting. Troubled and worried, I proceeded toward the fatal encounter, remembering my previous meeting with him. Laffy, Monsignor Raoul F. Lafayette, the rector of Pope Julius III Seminary of the Diocese of Rosanada, was motioning to me to hurry up. He had made it perfectly clear that he wanted me out of his institution. Ever since the first time he called me into his office and gave me holy hell, he had made my life miserable. Lafayette was a man after Pope Pius XII's own heart—self-righteous, meticulous in rubrics and liturgical matters, and obsessed with sex. Finding sin in everything, he was determined to root it completely out of the recently inaugurated seminary that was the pride of Bishop Lingam. Sex was the primary—the only sin—that Lafayette really cared about. Not only was masturbation an act deserving of eternal damnation, but even any sexual thought consented to would banish someone into a sizzling abyss in the deepest realms of hell, as all the serious and brainless moral theologians in the Church taught at the time. The abominable relationship of two seminarians who became intimate with one another was the worst of all possible sins. Such intimacy was grounds, not only for hell, but for a dishonorable expulsion from the seminary. For this reason, he would give frequent lectures inviting seminarians to avoid "particular friendships." How did he find out about sins of this kind? Seminary norms provided the solution by arranging it so that the seminary confessors could not grant absolution, if they were not given permission by the sinner to tell him about this deadly sin, or else the absolution was given *sub conditione*, meaning that the confessor gave the absolution under the condition that the penitent had to tell the rector himself or the absolution would not be valid.

Knowing who had committed a "grievous" sin was also very easy for Laffy. Instead of praying during communion, he observed the seminarians to see if any of them failed to receive the Sacred Wafer. If he noted that a seminarian did not receive communion, he knew immediately that the fellow had committed a "mortal sin"—for example, looking intently at a woman's breasts—because there was no other reason to skip the most important event of the day. Receiving the Eucharist when "fallen from grace" was the most atrocious, the most horrendous, and the most dreadful sin of all—it was…sacrilege! It was a sin that cried out to heaven for vengeance! Lafayette kept a good track of everything.

Early in the morning, the savviest seminarians ran to a nearby parish, and unloaded their sins onto some other, hopefully more benevolent priest, and then returned to the seminary triumphant that they had outwitted Laffy and the Catholic sacramental system. Catholics who know the catechism and the rubrics as dictated by the sacramentary have many ways to play games with the Church's regulations and laws.

According to Lafayette's gospel of darkness and gloom, women were the most despicable instruments of Satan, placed on earth just to make men sin. Every woman was a womb waiting to be impregnated. Womb—*hustera*—hysteria—woman, they were all the same. They were good only for cooking, cleaning or bringing up children conceived in the purest chastity. Matrimonial relationships needed to be regulated by certain rules that would prevent husbands from lusting after their own wives. After all, a man can get drunk at his own wine keg. So Laffy, following the Austrian Church tradition that he learned from his mother, recommended to the few wretched couples that came to him for advice that women should wear a long robe at night with a hole in the genital area that could be used to perform "the act," in absolute purity, allowing no room for all the new contraceptive methods that were becoming popular at the time. A husband should be much like a priest going to the altar of God, while the wife should be like an altar, ready to receive the ceremonial offering.

If Laffy found anything vaguely resembling pornography in the seminary, he immediately expelled the poor soul enmeshed in sin. If, by any unusual chance, he found a *Playboy* magazine in the dormitory, you could hear him scream from one end of the building to the other. I found it difficult to understand that this grouchy old man with the bulging eyes and pointing finger represented God in any way, and I felt sorry for the poor victims who ended up in his confessional, enduring his almost endless cross-examination. Now he was after me again. I could not understand why he did not believe me, when I told him the truth the first time that he called me into his office and pounced on me like a raging tiger about to devour a rabbit. The memory of this meeting was still very much alive. After calling me into his office about a year ago, he immediately attacked me.

"Where do you go at midnight? It has been reported to me that you leave the dormitory and go out every night. Where do you go? Who do you see?" He pounded his fist on the desk in front of him for emphasis. His eyes bulged and a vein in his forehead was pulsating from his anger.

"I just go to pray at the grotto of the Blessed Mother, *Monseñor*," I said softly.

"You expect me to believe that, eh? Ridiculous!" He stroked his thinning gray hair and glared at me in fury, while scratching his balls, a gesture that showed not only his poor manners, but also his total lack of respect for me.

"It is the truth, Monsignor," I replied with defiance in my voice. He was calling me a liar and I resented it. Ready to stand up for what I believe, I added: "Yes, Monsignor, I go there every night to pray the rosary." Expecting that he would commend me for my devotion to the Virgin

Mary and for my midnight prayers, I was dazed and flabbergasted, when he began to attack me relentlessly.

"You think I am an imbecile? No! You are lying. No! No! All lies." Leaning across the desk toward me, he stuck his face right in mine. "You go out there in the dark somewhere with your friends to read pornography and drink!" He glared at me with an expression of triumph believing he had found me out. "Or else you go to some girl's house in the neighborhood and crawl into her bed. I have had years of experience. That is the real truth, and you and I both know it!"

With his fat index finger almost touching my nose, beads of perspiration were forming on his forehead, as he continued pressing me to confess my guilt. Why had this so-called man of God completely misunderstood me? Why would he think all this evil about me? Trembling inside with anger and confusion, I knew I was in deep trouble, and there was nothing that I could say to vindicate myself. God had called me for a mission that I could not yet understand, and I was on the verge of being dismissed, before I even had a chance to try to accomplish it.

Faced with my silence, Monsignor Lafayette continued his tirade. "I am going to report you to the bishop, when he arrives here next month for his canonical visit. I will insist that he terminate your stay in my seminary and expel you. You have been arrogant and defiant ever since you came here. You violate this seminary with your presence! There is no room for people like you here! I will be rid of you once and for all!"

Seeing that nothing I could say would make him believe me, I maintained my silence. Fortunately, the bishop was extremely autocratic and would not permit Laffy to expel a seminarian without his specific consent

"Eh? What do you have to say to that, my friend?" he growled sarcastically while banging his fist impatiently on his desk.

"I am telling you the truth, *Monseñor*."

Shaking his head in disbelief, he stood in silence for a minute or two studying my face intently, before sitting down in his chair and saying in a softer tone. "Possibly I could be more lenient with you, if you tell me the names of your accomplices in sin. Who are the boys that go with you every night to enjoy sexual gratification? Tell me their names!" He was almost cajoling me to betray my friends.

I said nothing. I would never snitch on anyone. It is a code of honor among Cubans never to betray others. There was no way that I would ever tell him their names. Faced with my silence, he snorted, "Good! You go to the bishop! I am going to get rid of you! What do you have to say about that, eh?"

"I will be happy to have a discussion with him or anyone else about this matter, for I am telling the truth. I have absolutely nothing to hide. Every night at midnight, we go to the grotto of the Blessed Virgin and pray the rosary, because she is the guardian of our vocations." Folding my hands and placing them in my lap, unflinchingly I returned his gaze. As someone who came from a Protestant background my devotion for the Blessed Mother was very intense, something that he completely failed to comprehend. With his nose twitching furiously, he screamed irately, while pointing at the door, "Get out of here!" As I started to leave, he thundered at me, "You will clean all the bathrooms in the building

6

every day as long as you are here and that won't be very long, after I tell the bishop about you."

While cleaning bathrooms, I kept hoping that the bishop would be a benevolent man and would understand and believe me. Although I had seen him at ceremonies previously, I had no idea what kind of person he was. Arriving in a long black limo at his recently built seminary at 13 Misery Lane, he brought with him a strange entourage consisting of Monsignor Giuseppe Finolli, his personal secretary, Andrew Hollow, a seminarian who acted as his chauffeur, and an elegant, but aging, woman who leaned heavily on his arm after she descended from the car.

Pompeo, Mínimo, Damian, and I were watching from a dormitory window when this ecclesiastical circus came walking up to the seminary building, where they were greeted by Laffy, who could not do enough to welcome them. Inclining his head in a deep bow, he kissed the bishop's large ruby ring, and fawned obsequiously by making expansive gestures of welcome to the bishop and his guest.

His Excellency, the Most Reverend Priapus T. Lingam, D.D., Bishop of Rosanada, was a man of virile appearance. Although like most Catholic bishops, he wore a well-tailored black suit with a pectoral cross, hidden away in the inner left pocket of his jacket so people could only see its gold chain, he looked to me more like a businessman than a clergyman, with a stub of a cigar clenched between his teeth and a Panama hat perched jauntily on his head.

I could not believe that this man was a successor of the apostles. Elegant, proud and short, and looking like a pretentious chimpanzee, he was anything but inspiring, as he came up the walk with a sophisticated woman of the world on his arm.

"Who is the woman?" Damian asked as he crowded in front of me so he could get a better look. Babilonia was a good student, quite smart, bold, even pushy, but just dreadful.

"Yes, who is she," I asked not really expecting an answer.

"That's Aspasia Hetaira, of course," answered Pompeo who always seemed to know everything about everybody. He was the brainy one of the whole class. Reading books was his main entertainment and his mind was full of information thanks to his prodigious memory, but to tell the truth, even when he did not know something, he would still speak as an expert on the subject. He had the incredible ability of inventing things and then mixing them with what he did know to make them sound real. Always a peculiar person in appearance as well as behavior, he was very thin and had a protruding abdomen that made him resemble an olive on a toothpick. Because of his extremely thin, bony arms and legs some seminarians in their uncharitable tradition called him "Olive Oil," alluding to the physique of Popeye's wife in the comics. Although he was popular with some of the two hundred and fifty seminarians at Pope Julius III Seminary, others detested him and avoided him, because he never missed an opportunity to give unsolicited advice.

Emotionally unstable and with a strange way of distorting reality, Mínimo was a good student but his appearance was quite strange. Because of his crooked legs and his unbalanced walk, he seemed to be in a perennial state of inebriation. Moreover, he had the face of an Assyrian god as represented on monoliths near Baghdad or throughout Iran. Nevertheless, both he and Pompeo were devout at that time, although their faith was severely eroded in the years to come, and each had a good sense of humor, so I enjoyed their company occasionally.

"Who is *she?*" I asked, as the woman wearing a fur and lots of jewelry seemed to demand the bishop's entire attention. "She must be really rich and trying to impress us, since she is wearing a fur jacket in this warm weather."

"She is the bishop's lady friend," Pompeo replied with a knowing look. "I read in the *Rosanada News* that she owns an empire in the silk industry in the Principality of Salikistan, and she paid for the college seminary and is financing the building of the major seminary. She is a convert. After she got a divorce, she built a mansion for herself on the lakefront near the Wa'doli Country Club and another one next to hers as the bishop's residence. I heard a priest say that Wa'doli means penis in the language of the Cherokee Nation. Yep, she is the bishop's lady friend."

"I don't believe that," I replied. Just because she lives next door to him and holds on to his arm does not mean she is his lady friend. Bishops don't do that, Pompeo."

"Always so naïve, Marco," Mínimo commented, exchanging glances with Pompeo who shook his head in agreement. "Just look at the way she is eyeing him and the way he is enjoying it!"

Perhaps the most unusual member of the bishop's party was his secretary Monsignor Finolli who had the fine well-chiseled features of an American Indian princess. His Italian father had married a woman from the Lakota reservation. With his fine effeminate features, their son Giuseppe resembled the mother. He was tall and slender with a mysterious and sophisticated appearance, but he seemed to be the perfect clergyman with his luxurious flowing cassock and his tall Roman collar, even though he was not very manly. Later, I learned that he was typical of many seminarians.

"I hope when I am studying theology, they don't give me the job of driving the bishop around and waiting on him like his poor chauffeur does," commented Mínimo. "Look he is even carrying the luggage of the bishop and his lady."

I couldn't help thinking that any bishop would have to be out of his mind to let Mínimo drive him anywhere. He lacked all common sense.

"I would never do it," commented Damian. "When I get to be bishop, I will surely get one to drive me around though."

"They probably told him it was an honor to be the bishop's lackey," commented Pompeo. He brushed his thick curly hair back from his forehead. "Most bishops don't use seminarians that way, because they can leak information about the bishop's private life." Pompeo was even an expert on bishops and their ways.

"Well, it doesn't matter to me what they do around here," Damian said arrogantly. "I am determined to go to Rome to the Cuccaniensis Pontifical University to study canon law so I can become a bishop some day and tell you guys what to do." He was the only one laughing after this.

Watching Bishop Lingam and his entourage arrive was entertaining, but the show really began when he proceeded to the chapel where his frantic secretary, who was also his master of ceremonies, vested him with the sacred ornaments. I observed that Monsignor Finolli took his position very seriously as he jumped hither and yon, trying to put everything in perfect order, decking him out with amice, alb, cincture, maniple, stole, and finally chasuble.

"Look, I said to Pompeo who was sitting in the pew beside me waiting for the Mass to begin, "Lingam is wearing purple socks!"

"No," replied Pompeo with a condescending look, "they aren't socks, they are called buskins."

"They look like socks to me," Mínimo commented dryly.

Watching Monsignor Finolli was very entertaining. Obviously relishing his position, he arranged a special velvet kneeler with matching chair for Aspasia Hetaira, placing it below the huge picture on the wall bearing her portrait and the bishop's and right between Laffy and the rest of the faculty.

When the organ burst forth with *Ecce Sacerdos Magnus—Behold the Great Priest*—and with the choir singing to accompany it, the bishop, wearing a crested miter and flowing robes, resembled an enormous purple bird as he floated down the center aisle with his vestments billowing behind him taking his place in the sanctuary. Overwhelmed by all the pomp and ceremony of the seemingly never-ending Pontifical Mass, I was tortured by the thought that I had to face this web-footed and well-feathered purple fowl and perhaps be expelled from the seminary. I watched as they took the miter off the bishop and put it back on his head many times, not having the slightest understanding what it signified. Clouds of incense filled the sanctuary and floated out filling the entire chapel, making it difficult for me to breathe. The attending clergy were eminently delighted with the Latin chants, genuflections, bows to the bishop, washing of hands, the carrying of his crosier and miter, while the seminarians were blatantly suffering from boredom, as could be observed by their occasional yawns.

When Monsignor Finolli slipped and spilled the water and wine from the cruets, we seminarians could not help but laugh, as he blushed turning a deep scarlet. With a stern look from his cold blue eyes, the bishop silenced everyone and reprimanded Monsignor Finolli.

Waiting for the axe to fall and expel me from the seminary, I agonized with anxiety about my future. It was not until the next day that Monsignor Finolli came into the dormitory and, shrieking as loud as his high-pitched voice could manage, yelled out the names of the students who were to see the bishop, calling my name first. Terrified, I accompanied the monsignor down the long corridor to the library where the bishop was waiting. Softly Monsignor Finolli knocked on the library door, gently opened it, and announced.

"Marco Lamadrid, Your Excellency."

Quite literally shaking when I entered the library, I noticed at once that the windows and shades were closed, and that the bishop had placed a lamp so it would shine on the face of the person being interviewed, while he remained in the shadows. Although he no longer looked bizarre, he was still an imposing and frightening figure, for now he looked like a raven in his black cassock. His blue eyes were icy as he began to interrogate me.

"So you like to get away from the seminary at night?"

"To pray the rosary, Your Excellency. To pray the rosary." I was nervous and I could not conceal it.

His icy stare seemed to look right through me, as he sarcastically commented, "So we have a little saint in the seminary!"

"I would not say that, Your Excellency." My heart was pounding.

"And just what would you say then?"

"I have a great love for God, you see. I am a convert, and I believe God is calling me to be a priest."

Determined to put me in my place, the bishop was not to be distracted by anything I might say. Taking a big puff on his cigar, he spilled some ashes on Laffy's desk and continued: "Do you not understand that I have the authority to throw you out of the seminary immediately?"

Arrogantly I stared into his penetrating blue eyes and retorted: "You would not have it, if it had not been given to you from above!" I even startled myself by my boldness.

"You dare confront your bishop? Such a brave young man!" Whether he was mocking me or actually admiring my bravery, I could not determine.

"I am not confronting you, Bishop. I am just trying to answer your question."

"Where are you from?"

"Cuba, Bishop."

"What are you waiting for to get rid of your terrible Cuban accent?"

With a glimmer of hope, I replied: "For you to permit me to remain in the seminary."

After considering my response for a moment, he laughed, then asked: "Who do you go out with at night?" Beginning to perspire from the heat of the lamp on my face and from the pressure he was putting upon me, I said:

"Some friends, Sir."

He toyed with his plain silver pectoral cross momentarily and then said: "If you tell me their names, I will allow you to stay in the seminary." His eyes questioned mine intently, insisting upon an answer. If I had told him one of my friend's strange names, he would have gotten upset. His mother, knowing that she could not have any more children after he was born, gave him a baptismal name that encompassed every saint she was devoted to, including the names of three women.

"Your Excellency, I left Cuba after being arrested by the secret police when I was still practically a child. I did not reveal to them any names, and I will not do it today either." I waited for the axe to fall.

"Do you defy your bishop?"

"No, I do not. Ask the seminarians who go with me. They will tell you themselves. After all, the time we use for prayer does not detract from any of our duties, since it *is* our rest time." I refused to be intimidated.

The bishop smiled ever so slightly. "Your enthusiasm touches me, Marco, but I don't think you can remain here under the authority of Monsignor Lafayette. He really does not want you to be here." His eyes searched mine to see my reaction to his words. Carefully controlling my emotions to prevent him from seeing how upset I really was, I remained motionless waiting to hear the fatal news that my attempts to serve God in this way were at an end.

Chewing on his cigar with determination, he said: "However, I am going to order the monsignor to keep you one more year and at the end of that time we will decide what to do with you." Dismissing me he added: "Meanwhile, you and the others pray each in his own bed. No more midnight vigils. Have a good day."

I asked for his blessing and then ran from the room so fast that I bumped into Monsignor Finolli, knocking him almost off his feet, and frightening him out of his wits, so that he let out a ghastly shriek that echoed throughout the building.

At this early point in my life, I began to realize that in the Catholic Church how one appears to be is more important than what one really is. *"De internis non judicat ecclesiam,"* they used to repeat at the seminary. The Church does not judge your inner life. For this reason, I learned to follow the rules and the rites and to become an almost perfect seminarian, while keeping my spiritual life to myself, except for my spiritual director Spanish priest, Father Eduardo Moreno, who encouraged me greatly. I learned that the Church is a powerful institution and if you want to survive you disregard the unjustified anger of your superior, keep a low profile, and never complain. Above all you must never disagree with those in power. In the Catholic Church, the more mediocre you seem to be, the greater your chances are to get ahead. They might even make you a bishop, if they decide that you will never make waves.

So this second time, a year later, when Laffy summoned me to see the bishop, I determined not to offend the rector or disagree with him in anyway. As we walked together down the long corridor to the library where the bishop was waiting, Monsignor Lafayette took advantage of the opportunity to tell me just how he felt about me.

"Marco, I tell you frankly and honestly I have insisted to the bishop that he get rid of you. I intend to free myself of you. I have given him a full account of your behavior and I do not think he will be sympathetic with you again. In time, even you will thank me for this. It is for your own good that you leave this place." Monsignor Lafayette pointed to the library signaling for me to hurry to my doom.

Very quietly I entered the library expecting the worst.

"Good morning, Marco. Please have a seat."

After returning his greeting, I sat down and waited for him to explain the reason for our visit.

"I have examined your records and see that all your grades are excellent—that is with the exception of the C you got in conduct. You are not doing too well here with Monsignor Lafayette, so, well—to come right to the point, you cannot remain here." He observed me carefully with his penetrating icy eyes, waiting to see what reaction his words were having on me.

Learning to control my emotions, even though I was horribly pained and grieved to hear what he said, I did my best not to show it. No doubt he realized that his words had cut deep into my spirit. Suddenly, he smiled at me and said: "I have decided to send you to Rome to our seminary there—Casa San Sabastiano." As you may know, colleges in Rome are seminaries where you live to receive discipline and formation, while attending classes at the Pontifical Dionysian University, which is the very best in my opinion." He waited to see my reaction before continuing.

Thrilled and delighted, I repressed my feelings. However, a smile crept across my face, and I could not hide my happiness at receiving this news. He was not going to send me away! I was going to get away from Laffy and Pope Julius III Seminary and still continue studying for the priesthood! I was going to Rome!

When I ran to tell Pompeo Dell'Anitra, Mínimo Tabrón, and Damian Babilonia my good news, they did not share it with me. I could tell that they were envious of my good fortune. Damian was especially bitter and envious, because he had been so very sure that he would be the one chosen to study in Rome, never dreaming that instead I would get to go. Before the day was over Pompeo and Mínimo learned that they too were going to Rome to study at the same place. I thought that in time Damian would get over his feelings of bitterness and envy. Unfortunately his animosity toward me increased with the passing of time.

2
Damian

He had been so sure that the bishop was going to send him to Rome to study. Old Laffy had practically assured him of that. Instead Marco Lamadrid and those two clowns, Mínimo Tabrón and Pompeo Dell'Anitra, were going now instead. He had always been a bit envious of Marco because of his academic excellence and had competed with him for top honors, but the other two were misfits that would never make good priests no matter how much knowledge they accumulated in Rome. Both Mínimo and Pompeo would have benefited more from being sent to a good psychiatrist than to a Roman university. He actually felt sorry for Marco, for, no doubt, Mínimo and Pompeo would probably attach themselves to him, once they were in Rome, and give him no peace.

Mínimo was the worst of the two. He was emotionally unstable, seemed to be lacking in faith, was always criticizing the institutional Church, and seemed to have no respect for the magisterium. And Pompeo—he was an egghead and a gossip. He couldn't stand to listen to his chattering about everything and everyone.

As he was getting his things together to go to evening vespers, someone knocked on his door. It was Mínimo.

"Hello! I thought we could walk to the chapel for vespers together. I haven't talked with you for a while," he said waiting for Damian to welcome him.

"Congratulations on having been selected to study in Rome," Damian said without any enthusiasm.

"Oh, I heard you are not going! I was always sure you would be chosen. What happened? You must be very disappointed," Mínimo said gauchely.

"On the contrary, I don't want to go to Rome. I want to stay here and settle into the diocese and develop my relationships with the bishop and the priests in parishes and at the chancery. In due time, it will prove advantageous to me," he replied pretending great confidence. "I may end up being your boss someday, if you last that long."

"We still have a little time before vespers. Mind if I sit down and we can talk a little?" Mínimo threw himself down on the chair by the window without being invited to do so.

"What's on your mind?" inquired Damian.

"I'm not looking forward to going to Rome, especially since Pompeo is going. He makes fun of me all the time. He says I am ugly and clumsy, no good at sports, and have poor coordination. He forgets that I know perfectly well where he came from. His half-crazy mother had eight children with a variety of men, and then she converted, becoming a 'Latter Day Saint.' They allowed Pompeo to come to the seminary just to get rid of him, and he came just to get away from them." Obviously Mínimo was waiting for Damian to contradict Pompeo's assessment of him. Damian was not about to do that. He just kept quiet, waiting to see what else Mínimo would say.

"Pompeo says I am jealous, envious, and possessive, even daring to tell everyone that I am not in touch with reality—all of which are characteristics of him. Funny, but people always see their own faults in others and don't recognize that they are guilty of them also."

"Well, Marco Lamadrid is going too, I hear. He is your friend, isn't he?"

"No! He is not. Just because he is good looking and popular, he thinks the whole world should bow before him. I have tried to be his friend. I even got him a bouquet of roses for his birthday, but he did not seem to appreciate them. Pompeo always tries to monopolize his attention."

"Well, maybe you will find some friends in Rome."

"I hope so, because my life is a torment now. I hate this Julius III Seminary. It is like a jail and they try to brainwash you with all that stuff about the constant teachings of the Church. The only reason I am here, is because my mother insisted I become a priest. I am only child, and she has pestered me, since I was a little boy, with religion." Mínimo shook his head sadly, sighed deeply, and wrung his hands together in a gesture of despair.

"Maybe you should see a good psychiatrist," Damian suggested. Before Mínimo could respond, someone else knocked on his door.

"*Hola*!" he called. "Come in!"

It was Pompeo. "How are you, Damian." He pretended not to see Mínimo. "I am looking for Gorgeous. Have you seen him?"

"Who?" asked Damian. "Don't give me any of your crazy jokes!"

"He is looking for Marco—calls him Gorgeous!" Mínimo interposed, as he took a pill bottle from his pocket.

"Oh," said Pompeo pointedly, "I see you are still taking those pills for your nerves." Then to Damian he said, "Mínimo can't survive without those pills." If he meant to hurt Mínimo, he achieved that effect.

Damian thought Mínimo was actually going to break down and cry. Obviously he had very little control over his emotions. However, instead of breaking down, he lashed out at Pompeo saying, "You think you know everything! Living here is like living in a lunatic asylum and it will probably be worse in Rome. I hate people! I absolutely detest people!"

Pompeo was heartless. "Perhaps you should see a shrink?" He then proceeded to prattle on about the benefits of psychiatry, while Damian sat in bored silence, until he was hushed by the bell summoning them to vespers.

Thank God, thought Damian, as they started down the hall on their way to prayer. Thank God that I am not going to Rome with those two. When they reached the chapel, Mínimo and Pompeo spotted Marco kneeling in a pew at the rear of the chapel close to the statue of Saint Evita, patroness of the disenchanted, a devotion brought from Argentina in honor of dictator Juan Perón's wife, and hastened to sit with one on his left side and the other on his right, as close to him as they could get, while Marco pretended not to notice them.

No, Damian thought, he would not go to the university in Rome. He had better things to do. He would establish himself in Rosanada where he would climb the clerical ladder of success. He had something the others did not have. He had *savoir faire* and knew how to make the right moves and contacts to forge ahead. He had not told anyone that Old Laffy had chosen him to assist the bishop at public functions—a much better honor than going to Rome. His future in the diocese was assured. He was positive that he would be running things someday and telling Mínimo, Pompeo, and Marco what to do and where to go. They had not heard the last of Damian Babilonia.

3
Marco

Together with fifty other American seminarians I sailed on the Hindenburg, a German transatlantic liner, to Naples. We were the privileged few and we knew it, for studying in Rome is a path that often leads to advancement and a position of prominence in the Roman Catholllic Church. As for me and my future, I was young, very enthusiastic, and had great hopes of serving God.

Italy is glorious in the summer. The skies were deep blue and the weather warm and balmy that day in 1964 when our ship tied up at the dock in Naples. How proud I was to be wearing an immaculate collar and a well-pressed cassock that had three red buttons on the side of the chest near my shoulder, designating that I was a seminarian at Casa San Sabastiano. After we went through immigration, a bus swiftly hustled us away to Rome where two hundred and fifty more seminarians joined us.

Monsignor Thomas O'Leary, an Irishman with a bulbous red nose, and wearing a wrinkled cassock, welcomed us to Casa San Sabastiano. He looked like the typical Irishman that likes to tipple a bottle of spirits. This first impression of him turned out to be the true one. After leading us into a chapel, and before vesting for a very brief and hurried Mass, he tried to make us feel at home, but did not do a very good job of it.

"I'm most pleased to welcome you to Rome and to Casa San Sabastiano. I will try to help you in every way I can." Since he was heavyset and the day was quite warm, beads of perspiration were forming on his forehead, which he mopped with a white handkerchief before cramming it back into his cassock pocket. After briefly surveying us, he remarked bluntly:

"I lived for quite a long time in the United States. I know you Americans. Listen carefully. I don't stand on a lot of formal procedures. I always try to get right to the point. So I will give you the best advice I can to make your stay here successful. My Sons, always remember that in the Holy Roman Catholic Church the superior—I am your superior—the superior is like a rock and you—my subjects—are like hen's eggs. If the rock falls on the egg, the egg will break. If the egg falls on the rock, the egg will break. If you keep this in mind, you will never have any problems with me or the members of my staff. I believe I make myself clear." Having said that, he sped off to vest for Mass. That was a lesson for a lifetime.

Appalled by his words of welcome, I was discouraged and misunderstood, because I had come a long way since the Lord had called me to be his priest, and I had still further to go before reaching my destination. Nevertheless, I thought I liked Rome right from the start.

The seminary was magnificent and quite splendid, even grandiose. Located on the way to Porta Paolo IV, named after the first pope to publish the Index of forbidden books and to create a ghetto for the Jews in Rome, it was near St. Peter's Basilica, which I had seen briefly in passing and which I anxiously looked forward to visiting. The seminary, surrounded by a very high wall, had all the comforts of a good modern hotel. A football field, tennis, and basketball courts were all that a young man could desire in the way of sports. Because I was new, I did not get a room with a view of Rome, but it was very comfortable and really spacious.

Beckoning me to prayer, the tolling of the bells of St. Peter's awakened me early the next morning. Free to do as I wished after a session of orientation, I found my two classmates from Rosanada, Pompeo and Mínimo—one is Chilean, the other Panamanian—and together we decided to walk to St. Peter's to see the great church and visit the tomb of the Apostle Peter.

The weather had turned fresh over night. Proudly dressed in our new cassocks, we headed in the direction of the basilica, buying some chestnuts from an old man who was selling them just outside the wall of the seminary. Since Pompeo was six years older than I and a bookworm, he pretended to know everything. Having read a lot about Rome on the ship on the way over, he began telling us about St. Peter's, as if he had built it himself, and how collecting money to carry out its construction had been the cause of great tribulation in the Church.

"Actually the building of St. Peter's was one of the main causes of the Protestant reformation," Pompeo said very seriously as he glanced at his watch. Once he started talking it was impossible to stop him. Having trouble with a congenital hernia in my groin that I tried to hide from everyone, I was walking slowly, while Mínimo was rushing to keep up, since he was shorter and had to take longer strides.

"Pope Julius II," Pompeo explained, "needed money to build St. Peter's so he promulgated a Bull that a Dominican called Johannes Tetzel used to sell indulgences, as he traveled from town to town in Germany with a large chest, a huge cross draped with the papal banner, and the Bull of Indulgence on a velvet cushion. When he came to a town, he rang a lot of bells, waved a lot of flags, showed some relics, and put on quite a show in the local church, while selling indulgences to get people out of purgatory, even selling indulgences for people to use for sins they had not yet committed. He even had a little rhyme he chanted, and since English and German are both Germanic languages it rhymes in both of them. It goes, "When the coin in the coffer rings, the soul from purgatory springs."

In spite of the fact neither Mínimo nor I was listening, Pompeo kept on talking. "He sold indulgences for those already dead and no contrition was required on the part of the dead person. He was challenged by an Augustinian monk, Martin Luther, a Bible Scholar at the University of Wittenberg, to debate with him his famous Ninety-five Thesis," Pompeo explained with an air of smug self-satisfaction.

When we reached the Bernini colonnade at St. Peter's, we stared in sheer amazement at how grand the whole panorama was.

"That tall monument that stands like a big needle— the obelisk—came from Egypt and dates back to the times of the Pharaohs," Pompeo informed us to our great annoyance. We wanted to explore and enjoy on our own without his incessant lectures, but we had to put up with Pompeo's explanations. There was, however one important thing that he did not know, "*chiuso.*" Perhaps that was the first word I learned in Italian, for that is what the sign on the door of the basilica said. When we tried to open the door, we found it locked. It didn't take us long to realize that "*chiuso*" means closed. St. Peter's closed in the afternoons the same as many businesses. This also taught me a lesson in Italian culture. In those days in Rome, it was almost a sacred ritual for men to have lunch and take a nap afterwards, while the women washed the dishes.

That night I had my first Italian lesson. Since I spoke Spanish as my native language and had studied years of Latin, learning Italian was easy for me. Latin presented more of a challenge, because all classes were conducted in Latin, giving me the feeling that I was getting a medieval education.

The next day Pompeo, Mínimo and I returned to the basilica when it was open. I couldn't believe the size of the holy water fonts. They were enormous. Mínimo, who was interested in history, pointed out to us a plaque on the floor near the entrance to St. Peters that told us that it was the very spot on which Pope Leo III crowned Charlemagne Emperor on Christmas day in the year 800. I found it exciting to see so many things of historical significance.

We proceeded toward the main altar, lingering at the statue of St. Peter and marveling at how the metal foot of the statue had been worn down by all the kisses of the faithful who had passed by it over the centuries.

"Actually," said Mínimo, "it was the statue of a Roman senator. I think they pulled it out of the Tiber and then turned it into a statue of St. Peter." As we came to the heart of the basilica and stood under the great dome that bears the Latin inscription from Matthew 16:18, "*Tu es Petrus et super hanc petram aedificabo ecclesiam meam*; You are Peter and upon this rock I will build my Church," I felt that I had finally arrived in Rome and was proud that I had been chosen to come.

As we glanced around, Pompeo commented: "They say that Veronica's veil is kept up there." He pointed to a place high above our heads. "They say she wiped Jesus' face with her veil and as a result a portrait of him was imprinted on it, but I don't believe it. I am a skeptic basically." Mínimo nodded in agreement. "They also claim that chair up there was St. Peter's chair." With a very dubious expression of his face, he added: "I simply do not believe it!"

"I don't believe it either," replied Mínimo who was always very matter of fact. "And, I don't think Thomas Aquinas would believe it either. Anyone who could write his *Summa* wouldn't believe that chair was Peter's."

It occurred to me that Mínimo, not at all interested in the art objects in the basilica that I found so interesting, resembled a San Francisco hippie, because he was totally lost to this world—spaced out and living in a world of his own making.

"Well, why not? It *could* be his chair," I said expressing my feelings. I could see disbelief in Mínimo's dark brown eyes. "His tomb is here. Why not his chair?" I asked, taking a deep breath and trying to hide the pain that I was experiencing from the hernia in my groin, because it was especially bad that day.

"You are completely retarded, Marco. Be reasonable. A wooden chair would have deteriorated by now and there would be nothing left of it," Pompeo said. "You would believe anything, Marco. They say that in one church here in Rome you can see milk from the Blessed Virgin and even the foreskin of Jesus from his circumcision. I suppose you believe that too! I read that in my guide book coming over on the ship."

Mínimo laughed. "I heard someone say they even have the cloth that covered the Lord's private parts when he was being crucified." They looked at each other in agreement and laughed heartily about this."

"Do you think they are trying to deceive people?" I asked looking into Pompeo's skeptical and mocking eyes. He simply shook his head, and we moved up to the railing around St. Peter's tomb. I was overwhelmed when I looked down into the lower level where the apostle's tomb had actually been found and verified to be authentic. "Sometime I want to go down into the lower level and see for myself the excavations and what they reveal. However, what I really want to do is climb up the Santa Scala to get a plenary indulgence. We can't do that today though. It is too far from here."

"I pass on that," Pompeo remarked flatly. "So do I," Mínimo chimed in.

"But it *could* be real. They say St. Helena brought it back from the Holy Land when she found the true cross," I protested.

Because I did not want to go alone to climb the Santa Scala, I invited another seminarian, Christian Brown from Oklahoma, to go with me. His room was right down the hall from mine. He wasn't at all like Pompeo or Mínimo, rather he had very fair skin, gentle blue eyes, and was quite nervous. One thing he did have in common with me was the love of music. Actually I felt sorry for Christian and listened sympathetically as he told me his problems.

"I feel so depressed," he admitted.

"You are probably just homesick. You will get over it," I replied patting him on the arm.

"No, it is more than that. I went to see a psychiatrist a few times, but he wasn't able to do anything for my depression. Perhaps that was because I really did not feel I could trust him. I could not take him into my confidence." Christian looked unkempt with his cassock in wrinkles.

As we were approaching St. John Lateran Basilica and nearing our destination, I could not help but think of all the numerous people who had come to Rome over the centuries and climbed the steps on their knees. I was determined to do the same thing—all twenty-eight of them.

When I was making progress going up the stairs, I noticed that Christian had decided to quit going up on his knees and had taken the alternate and easier route. I don't think he was very strong. I finished the stairs on my knees, said the prescribed prayers, and was confident that I had done everything to gain the indulgence, since I had been to confession, only the day before.

As we were walking back to the seminary, Christian, his blue eyes filled with melancholy, confided in me that he felt very lonely at the seminary.

"Come on! I am your friend, Christian. You can tell me your troubles," I assured him. When I offered to be his friend, he seemed to perk up a bit and even smiled faintly.

Pompeo and Mínimo spotted me returning to the seminary with Christian, and as soon as Christian went to his room they began laughing at me.

"What's so funny?" I inquired as they followed me to my room.

"You went some place with that queer!" Pompeo gave Mínimo a knowing look.

"What do you mean queer? He is just a quiet fellow with nice manners," I replied.

"Sure he is! Didn't you see his limp wrist?" Mínimo snapped at me, while holding up his own wrist limply dangling in mid air.

A bit more patiently Pompeo explained, "He is a homo. You know—a homosexual."

"I don't believe that," I replied impatiently throwing myself down on my bed and turning my face to the wall.

"Well, believe it or not. Take our advice and stay away from him. If you associate with him, people will think you are a queer too. You don't have to go out with people like him. I would be very happy to go places with you anytime you want," Pompeo said, pushing Mínimo aside so that he could stand right in front of me.

"Me too," Mínimo exclaimed, shoving Pompeo with his elbow. "I'm always glad to go with you."

The next day, I decided to go visiting the holy places by myself, and continued doing so for the next two months. I had to slip quietly and quickly from the dorm, so that Pompeo and Mínimo would not be able to join me or follow me. By visiting the churches of Rome— there are over six hundred of them—I must have collected enough indulgences to set all the souls in purgatory free, but I did not experience God, which disappointed me greatly for I had imagined that He would be easy to find in the Eternal City. How could I become a priest and draw near to Him and bring others closer to Him, if I couldn't find Him?

A long time had passed since He called me. I wasn't even a Catholic at the time. My parents were Methodists and I was being reared in that tradition, attending a Protestant school in my home town of Mérida in Cuba. One afternoon when I was perhaps twelve years old, I went into an old Carmelite church to look at the Colonial-Baroque art treasures there. Something happened to me that day. I can't explain it. I had always believed in God and had a lot of faith. Well, I was in a corner of the Carmelite church looking at the various art objects, when suddenly I felt a Presence and in a bright light I saw a scroll. I guess you would call it a vision, because there was no scroll in the church. Yet, I could plainly see a scroll with these words emblazoned on it: "The Word of God." Then I heard a voice deep in my soul, very plainly and clearly, saying, "Take My Word and make it your own and preach it!" I was stirred in the very depths of my being, but I also felt really unworthy. How could God approach anyone as insignificant as I? Many thoughts ran through my head—first and foremost—"Does He want me to become a Catholic?"

After giving it a lot of thought, I decided that God in fact did want me to become Catholic, and despite my family's objections, I talked to a priest and some months later after getting the approval of my parents, I received the Sacrament of Baptism and made my first communion.

Now that I was in Rome studying to become a priest, trying to follow His command that I make His Word my own and preach it, I wondered why He did not reveal His Presence to me again. Although I visited many of the great basilicas, I did not find in them the Presence that I so much longed to experience. However, one afternoon I went in the seminary chapel where I was all alone with the Lord in the Reserved Eucharist, when suddenly His Presence was with me, filling me with light. I responded with all my heart, as I felt Him again calling me to preach His gospel and to renew His Church.

I continued visiting the churches and monuments of Rome by myself. However, the day I visited The *Foro Romano*, Pompeo and Mínimo spotted me leaving and I could not avoid their going with me. After viewing the Temple of Castor and Pollux, we approached the temple of the Vestal Virgins, where we saw scores of cats— permanent inhabitants of the forum that are still there to this day.

"Vesta was the Roman goddess of the hearth," I said.

"Yes, she was," Pompeo responded eager to show off his knowledge. "The Romans had a god or goddess for everything. They even had a goddess of the Cloaca Maxima, the sewer—Cloacina." We all laughed at the idea of having a sewer goddess.

Pompeo shielded his eyes from the afternoon sun and then began to speak seriously. "The Vestal Virgins made a thirty year commitment to remain chaste and keep the sacred fire burning in the temple there." He pointed to the ruins of the ancient temple of Vesta. "They started with two of two of them in the beginning and finally went to six. If one of them let the sacred fire go out, the Romans believed that she was impure, and they felt that Rome's security was threatened.

"A Vestal Virgins who lost her virginity was buried alive in the Campus Sceleratus—that is near the Colline gate. They led her down a flight of steps to a room with food, a lamp, and a bed. Once she was down there, they removed the steps and piled dirt on the entrance to her room, leaving her there to die."

"Wow! "What a way to go," Mínimo exclaimed.

"The Romans were pretty harsh people," Pompeo continued. "After the thirty year term was up, they were free to marry, but most of them did not."

"It sounds to me that perhaps they were dykes," Mínimo commented with a superior air and a wink.

Fortunately, it was time to go back, for I was not in the mood to continue the visit with them any longer.

When we returned to the seminary, I went to my room to study a little while before dinner. It wasn't long until someone knocked gently on my door. It was Christian, and he looked very troubled. We had become friends despite the jeering of Pompeo and Mínimo who seemed to be jealous of my friendship with the poor unfortunate fellow from Oklahoma.

"What's the problem, Christian?"

"I just felt lonely. I thought maybe we could talk."

"Sure, of course." I was beginning to feel like the savior of the world, because many seminarians came to me with their problems. I've always tried to help people, perhaps because many times I could sense what they were feeling and thinking. "What can I do for you?"

I offered him the chair and I sat down on the side of my bed. As he sat down nervously on the edge of the chair, he kept toying with the red buttons on his cassock.

"I thought maybe you could help me with my philosophy. You seem to be really good at it. You seem to be very knowledgeable." His skin seemed paler tonight than usual. I studied his soft and gentle face as his eyes avoided mine.

"Of course, what would you like to know?"

"What is Occam's razor?" He got up from the chair and came and sat beside me on the bed. As we talked, he wiggled closer to me, and I started to feel uncomfortable. Perhaps Pompeo and Mínimo were right about him. Maybe he was a homosexual. I moved gently away from him, by sliding farther down on the bed.

"*Pluralitas non est ponenda sine necessitate,*" I replied without hesitation. "It is really quite simple." I watched as he reached out and put his hand on my arm.

"What does it mean?" he asked squeezing my arm affectionately with a hungry and pitiful expression on his face. I shook my arm free from his grasp.

"It means you should not make any more assumptions than necessary." He seemed to be assuming that I would respond to his familiarity. He looked hurt when I said that.

I did not want to hurt him, so I rose to my feet and explained, "If something happens, the simplest explanation is the best." I was trying to come up with an explanation of his overly friendly behavior as well as Occam's razor. "Look if you see a tree in the forest that is broken and charred, you could think that an airplane struck it, but the simpler explanation that lightening hit it is to be preferred. That is what Occam's razor means." This said, I jumped to my feet, walked to the door, opened it and said, "I have a lot to study before dinner."

Christian looked as if the world had just caved in on him. "If there is anything I can do for you, just let me know. Would you like me to do your laundry? Do you need money? I would be happy to help you with anything!" I shook my head. Sadly he left. I will never forget the look of rejection on his face.

Later that evening after dinner when I returned to my room, I found a note had been slipped under my door. Quickly, I opened the envelope and read:

"Dear Marco, I feel awful the way you rejected me this afternoon. I would like to get to know you better. I have very deep feelings for you. What I am trying to tell you is that I love you and I think you love me too. I know you and Pompeo are friends. I want to be friends with you too. Could I possibly come and spend more time with you. I am very lonely here by myself.

Christian

Realizing at once that Pompeo and Mínimo were right about Christian, I really did not know how to handle this situation. For certain, I would not go to the rector and report him. Since Pompeo was older than I and had had a lot more experience, I decided to ask him for advice.

"What shall I do?" I asked distressed by the problem.

"I told you to stay away from him. Let me handle it," he offered. "With your permission I will confront him with this letter." Immediately Pompeo left for Christian's room. In five minutes he was back telling me that there was nothing to worry about.

"What did you do?"

"I showed him the letter and asked if he wrote it," replied Pompeo with an air of satisfaction that the matter was settled.

"What did he say?"

"He denied writing it, and asked what business was it of mine, if he did write it. I told him you are my friend and I want what is best for you and for him too." Pompeo seemed confident that the episode was over. "I returned the note to him, so he would know that we are not going to report him to the rector." Convinced that the matter was settled, I put it out of my mind. However, when I awakened the next morning, from my window I saw the pathetic figure of Christian up on the seminary rooftop, pacing back and forth. What was he doing up there? I watched a few minutes and to my horror he walked to the edge of the roof, looked down the six floors to the courtyard below, hesitated but a moment, and jumped before anyone could have stopped him, falling to the ground with a terrible thud. He died instantly.

I watched from my window as Onesimos, the doorman, rushed to get the rector who lived on the first floor of the building.

"Monsignor! Monsignor! Come out! Something awful has happened! We have a big tragedy!" Onesimos banged on the window of the rector's room.

O'Leary came rushing out instantly in his bathrobe and slippers, yelling at a frightened Onesimos: "All hell is going to break loose, because you woke me up! I have enough to do with all these seminarians and their bishops without your waking me at dawn! You are going to pay for this! What is wrong now?" O'Leary was livid and violently raging at the doorman.

"I'm sorry, Monsignor, but one of the seminarians is dead!" Onesimos cowered in front of the rector, waiting to see what he would do.

Then I heard the rector yell, "Just what I needed! One of the bastards is dead!" A father of several children the ages of the seminarians, Onesimus was sobbing, as he took O'Leary across the courtyard to where Christian's body lay broken and bleeding with his head split in two and his brains gushing out onto the courtyard tiles.

Frozen in horror, I watched as O'Leary gave Christian absolution, although it is not to be given to the dead. Then I saw him get a sheet and cover the body and bloody remains of the pale boy from Oklahoma that was so sad and lonely. He then sent Onesimos to fetch the Vatican guards to come and remove the body, before all the seminarians would awaken and see the ghastly mess. In a few minutes, they carried Christian Brown's frail, broken body away. Because I had an early class and did not want to be late, I did not have time to consider the matter anymore.

I got dressed quickly, and as I was getting ready to leave my room to go to Morning Prayer and breakfast, I noticed that an envelope had been pushed under my door sometime during the night. With trembling hands, I tore it open, already suspecting it was from Christian. It was a long rambling letter, blaming me for his death. Some of his words still burn in my mind: "Please pray for me and look on me with compassion. I am totally without hope. No one who commits suicide can enter eternal life—nor can anyone who commits sodomy. I am lost."

Later that morning I saw Pompeo and Mínimo in the corridor just before my morality class. They were bursting to tell me something.

"Did you hear that Christian died of a heart attack? asked Mínimo.

"Are you sure about that?" I asked dumbfounded.

"Yes, of course. A Vatican doctor certified that a cardiac infarction was the cause of death." Pompeo shook his head sadly.

"Now you two are the ones who are gullible and naïve. Christian jumped from the roof of the seminary and landed in the courtyard behind the building. I saw him do it!" The horror of the situation overwhelmed me, making me sick at my stomach. The two stooges looked shocked, as they heard the truth.

"Damage control," I added. "The seminary and the Vatican could just not take the negative publicity that one of the seminarians killed himself."

Although my confessor and some other friends did what they could to help me, I suffered in silence for months. The hardest thing for me to understand was the way the seminary handled the whole matter. Even though Monsignor O'Leary and his faculty celebrated a beautiful mass for Christian, I was totally disgusted with the preaching, the novenas, and everything about it, because the lies were more than I could endure. With complete duplicity, the homilist commented that it was a terrible tragedy that a heart attack carried Christian away at such a young age.

How could so much hypocrisy exist in the Church? This was a question that kept gnawing on me and one that I continued to ask the Lord in my daily visits to the chapel. The only explanation is His parable of the wheat and the tares. The enemy indeed has sewn weeds in the field of the Lord. With the passing of time, I came to believe that Christian Brown was a victim of circumstances, of his background, and may even have been a victim of his genes. If animals, such as some dogs, cats, and moneys, demonstrate homosexual behaveior, would not that indicate that it is genetic in origin? I also wondered exactly what Pompeo had said to him when he contronted him with the letter asking to spend time with me. Could something he said have possibly precipitated Christian's suicide?

Deeply depressed following Christian's death, I immersed myself in my studies and tried to keep up with all the Vatican II changes that were taking place in the Church. All the seminarians entered into long discussions about the pros and cons of the Vatican II reform and theological and moral renewal, with the arguments never ending.

"I think it is good that Protestants are now called 'our separated brethren,' and we no longer refer to them as heretics," I told Mínimo and Pompeo with enthusiasm, as we ventured out to see the sights of Rome. This time our destination was St. Paul's Outside the Walls. I was somewhat surprised that Pompeo and Mínimo were not wearing their cassocks on our outing, because Pompeo was wearing blue jeans and a T-shirt, while Mínimo was in bell bottoms and a tie dyed shirt.

"Get with it, Marco. You are still wearing a cassock! I thought you liked modern things. You look like someone out of the nineteenth century with your black cassock. No one is wearing cassocks any more," Pompeo insisted while pointing a finger at me and laughing.

Mínimo, always ready for a laugh, joined in, also pointing his finger at me. "Cassocks went out with the tonsure."

"Give me a break. Cassocks are a testimony of our calling." I replied walking with my head held high, proud to wear it.

"That's old fashioned. Clothes do not change a person's commitment," Pompeo retorted.

I chose not to continue the argument, since the bus was approaching us.

After a terribly crowded bus ride past the Pyramid of Cestius and out through the Porta San Paolo, the ancient Porta Ostiensis, we finally arrived at St. Paul's Basilica, which contains the tomb of the apostle who was martyred nearby at *Aquae Salviae,* now *Tre Fontane,* about two miles from the basilica—one of the most beautiful churches of Rome. As we approached it, the magnificent statue of Paul impressed me with the uplifted sword in his hands— the instrument of his martyrdom—bearing the inscription, "To the preacher of truth, the teacher of nations." When I saw this statue of the great apostle to the Gentiles, I recalled that the Word of God is like a two edged sword and that Paul wielded it throughout the ancient Roman world. I too longed to preach the Word of God. A fire burned within me for His holy Word and I desired nothing more than to preach Christ and Him crucified, as St. Paul expresses it.

Kneeling at the railing surrounding the tomb of the great apostle, I prayed that I too might proclaim Christ to the world. Pompeo and Mínimo took a quick tour around the basilica, while I lingered to look at the portraits of the popes that were high up on both sides of the walls above the colonnades of pillars. They were all there—everyone since and including Peter, but it looked like they were running out of room to add any more.

St. Paul's was fascinating and I could have spent the day looking at all the beautiful art, but Pompeo and Mínimo were hungry, and so we left, but I planned to return when I would have the leisure to see it all. We stopped in a *trattoria* in the heart of Rome, not far from the Vatican, for a light lunch. We saw that although there were many other seminarians there, I was the only one wearing a cassock. Some of them were even smoking cigarettes.

After ordering a large *capricciosa* pizza and a decanter of Frascati, we settled down to discussing the radical trends in the Church. Many theologians were questioning the ancient dogmas handed down from the apostles. There was a school of thinkers that even questioned the dogma of the Resurrection. It was shocking to the three of us that strange experimental Masses were taking place in which readings from oriental religions were included. Large numbers of priests and religious were asking for dispensations and leaving in droves. We heard that a commission had been set up to explore the question of birth control and it was expected that the Church would reverse its position on this controversial subject.

"It is good for the Church to change radically," Mínimo exclaimed as he nibbled on a crust of pizza. "Everyone is talking about peace and love, saying that creeds really do not matter. The world is making progress. If we could just do away with creeds and live together in peace!"

Pompeo held up his fingers and made the peace sign that was recognized worldwide among students.

"No, I disagree." I said taking a sip of the Frascati.

"How is it possible that a guy like you has become a Holy Roller, Marco?" Pompeo asked contemptuously.

"Jesus said that He *will* be with the Church until the end of time and that He is the way, the truth and the life and that no one comes to the Father except through Him." I stated my firm belief. My friends never seemed to understand how I really felt about things. I was often cut to the quick by their remarks and did not even try to explain what I meant. What they thought about me did not really matter.

A few days later I stopped at the entrance door of the seminary to talk to Onesimos Santini. He was a typical Italian doorman and we had very little in common, but he had a beautiful daughter, and she was there with him. Every time I talked with Angelica, I felt as if I came alive. One word from her and I would feel flustered, but yet I wanted to talk with her. This day I was bolder than ever and invited her to go for a walk with me. I ended up by taking her into the dormitory and into my room. Angelica—ah, she was angelic! I still remember her pretty smile. Since I only had one chair in my room, I sat down in it and pulled her down on to my lap. She put her arm around my shoulder and we were having a grand time just talking.

Unfortunately, because I was enjoying her companionship so very much, I had forgotten to lock my bedroom door, when we came in. Suddenly the door flew open and Pompeo entered, finding me with Angelica sitting on my lap with her arm around my shoulder. He began laughing hysterically and pointing at us.

"You better leave, Angelica," he ordered. The girl jumped up and fled out the door. Turning to me he fumed, "Have you gone crazy? What were you going to do with her? Kiss her? Make love to her here in the seminary?"

Speechless and annoyed that he had broken in on us, I glared at him in silence.

"Aren't you the holy one with all your talk about dedication? Too many prayers!" he yelled at me.

I had had enough! "You can go to hell!" I yelled at him. "Get out of here." That was the last I ever saw of Angelica.

About this time, I went alone to St. John Lateran one afternoon, and something very unusual happened to me. Since it was the oldest official place of Christian worship in the world, known as *Omnium urbis et orbis ecclesiarum mater et caput,* the mother and head of all churches in the world," I was especially attracted to this basilica. In 321, Emperor Constantine donated the house of the Lateran family to become a church worthy of Christianinty.

On this particular day, I was praying in the semi-darkness of the great old church, before the high altar where Pope Martin V is interred. The hernia in my groin was hurting as it shifted, changing shapes. Sometimes it bulged out causing people to stare, but fortunately my cassock covered it. As I watched the candles burning brightly before me, the Presence was suddenly with me! I held my breath and waited hoping to hear His Voice. His words welled up within me. This was a deeper revelation of the Presence than I had ever before experienced. Overwhelmed by His Loving Presence and an ardent desire to serve Him, I held very still, lest he suddenly leave me. Knowing that I would say yes to whatever he wanted me to do, I desired only to be with Him forever. How long I stayed there with Him, I have no idea. Time stopped and there was only He and I. When the prayer was finished, I realized that the hernia no longer pained me.

I slid my hand under my cassock and inside my slacks. The hernia was gone! Completely gone! God had performed a miracle on me! All my life, I had felt ashamed because of the hernia, and now it was gone! I had a hard time to believe that I was free of it. When I was little, I had asthma and my parents did not want me to have anesthesia and surgery for that reason.

The next day I went to see a doctor who confirmed my miracle. It was true. The hernia had completely disappeared! Now I felt closer to God than ever before in my life. This was the first great deed God performed for me. To me it was a portent of wonderful things to come.

The next great thing that happened to me was my first ordination. Feeling that I was at last making progress toward my calling, I received two of the minor orders, being ordained porter and lector, as a bishop wearing a tall miter sat before the altar in the seminary chapel. With a burning candle in my right hand, I went forward when they called my name and knelt before him, making the proper response. "*Adsum.*"

As the bishop explained what the duties of a porter are, I listened carefully. We were to ring the bells summoning the faithful to church, to open the church and the sacristy, and to open the book for the homilist. Standing near me were Pompeo and Mínimo, looking very devout. Very solemnly the bishop admonished that we were also to open the hearts of the faithful to the word of God. We then laid aside the candles and the bishop extended the keys of the church for each one of us to touch them. A deacon then took us to the back of the church and had us lock and unlock the entrance door and ring the tower bell. We then returned to the altar where the bishop was waiting to proceed with the ordination. After asking God to bless us, he laid aside his miter and turning to the altar intoned in deep voice:

"*Oremus.*"

"*Flectamus genua,*" the archdeacon sang, and we all knelt.

A few seconds later he sang: "*Levate,*" and we arose again.

Then as we again knelt before the bishop, he prayed for God to bless us. As soon as we had returned to our places and a Latin hymn was sung, the deacon called for those who were also to be ordained as lectors.

"*Idem,*" he called since we were the same ones who had been ordained porters.

Once again I went to the altar and knelt before the bishop with candle in hand with my classmates.

Very solemnly the bishop proceeded to perform the ritual, according to the Roman Pontifical.

This was a milestone for me. Having received two of the minor orders, I was free for the summer. In Stuttgart, I found a job working at the Mercedes Benz factory and was able to return there in future summers to earn some money to help with expenses during the school years. During all the summers I was in Europe, I had some time to travel and see most of Western Europe. I felt close to and even infatuated with different girls during my vacations, but I never doubted my calling, for the Presence was very real to me.

However, when that first summer was over and I returned to the seminary, I was only there for a short time when I found a letter from my father in my mailbox. Thunderstruck, I read that my mother had been arrested and put in prison for her protests and activities against the Castro regime. The pain I felt was awful, bringing uncontrollable tears to my eyes. Going to the chapel I sought for some consolation in the Presence, but I felt absolutely nothing—there were no voices, no lights, nothing! I was alone in faith before the absolute mystery of God.

Sharing my bad news with Pompeo and Mínimo who sympathized with me, I realized for the first time that no one can feel the pain of someone else's cross. We can help others, but each one of us has to face pain himself. I so much wanted to be with my father and help him find where they had taken my mother. Writing to him, I told him that I would come home at once, that all I wanted now was to be with them.

When I went to the Cuban consulate to ask for a return visa in order to spend some time with my family, they refused to give it to me, saying that, since I was a seminarian, I would have to see the Secretary of State Monsignor Ribelli to get one. When I went to see him, the only response I received was the typical Italian one, "Vediamo." We will see.

Next I approached Monsignor O'Leary, expecting him to help me, but instead he turned a cold shoulder to me, having absolutely no interest in helping me. Trying to find help, I visited everyone I could, only to learn that the Cuban government at that time was not willing to accommodate any desires of the Church or their clergy. As they saw it, I was just a seminarian from an institution that was opposed to the Cuban government.

Knowing that my mother was probably being tortured in a dirty Cuban prison was very traumatic and painful. I spent long hours in the chapel where the Presence again would console and encourage me toward a future filled with His power. I cannot even begin to express in words what I felt as His Presence lifted me up and embraced me. As St. Paul says eye has not seen, ear has not heard the wonderful things of God. Only the love of God and the marvelous moments, when I felt illumined, permitted me to go through the torment of being far from my family, while my mother was wretched and probably being tortured in a Cuban prison.

Her imprisonment lasted for years. How much I wished my parents could be present for my ordination as a deacon and then later as priest.

As the time came closer for my ordination to the deaconate, when I would embrace binding commitments forever, I began to consider the seriousness of the step I was taking. It is not easy for a man to give up any hope of having a wife and children. Women had always played an important part in my life.

When I got to know Maria, a young black girl with more experience than years, and had my first experience of intimacy with a woman, I was only about twelve or thirteen years old. She was the nanny for the family whose house was next to ours in Mérida and acted as if she were attracted to me, even though she was just looking for a little fun and a few Cuban pesos. Because I was friends with the young people in the home where she worked, I used to go to the movies with the oldest daughter of the Pérez family, Lisa, a girl about my age. In the movie theater, I would hold her hand and even give her a kiss on the cheek occasionally. Sometimes in the afternoons we would go for a stroll in one of the many parks of Mérida.

On one particular afternoon, after I said goodbye to Lisa, dropping her off at her house, I was walking behind her house to cross over to ours, when Maria, with black curly hair, bright eyes, and a winning smile, signaled to me. Walking over to where she was sitting on the front porch of the maids' quarters of the Pérez' house in which she lived, I asked:

"*Hola*, Maria, you want to talk to me?" My voice cracked when I spoke.

"Yes, come over here and visit with me for a little while."

"Ok, for a few minutes." I entered her house and sat down beside her on the sofa.

"You are getting to be quite a handsome fellow. Almost grown up."

I smiled and sat up straighter. I had grown quite a bit and was now as tall as my father.

"Soon you will be a man," she continued as she ran her hand over the muscles in my arm. She leaned over to me so that her face was close to my ear. "Come, let's go in my bedroom and take a nap," she invited.

"I am really not sleepy. I never take naps in the daytime."

She pulled her skirt above her knees and sprawled seductively.

Suddenly it dawned on me that she was not talking about sleeping. Then I understood, because some of my friends had told me of their experiences with maids and nannies.

"Come on," she coaxed. "It will make a man of you." Her face broke into a magical smile. "I know a handsome fellow like you is ready."

Debating whether to run home or go into her bedroom, I rose to my feet. The fact that we were of different races did not bother me, because among all my friends at the time such a relationship was considered normal, as long as it remained just an adventure.

She stood up and slowly started walking to the door of her bedrooom. Captivated by the enticing looks she gave me, I followed her into her room where she proceeded to undress me. When I left that afternoon, I considered myself a man.

As I walked out of her house, she whispered, "Come back tomorrow night. You can slip out of the house after your family has gone to bed. I will be watching for you to let you in." Flashing her magical smile at me again, she winked at me and smiled seductively.

Caught like a butterfly in a net, I occasionally went to see her. She was a good teacher, and soon I had the satisfaction of knowing that I could make a woman happy. An expert at sensual pleasure, she was, I learned, the mistress of Roberto Pérez, the man for whom she worked.

Developing an extreme ardor for what Maria had to offer, I spent brief moments once in a while in her arms, scaling the mountain tops of sexual desire and spiraling down again on the other side into the valleys. This went on for a couple months, until one day the secret police arrested me for my activities against the Castro government and I had to leave Cuba and go to the United States.

I hated to leave my family, and I hated to leave Maria, but my parents, knowing that I had no future in Castro's Cuba, arranged for me to go to stay with my Aunt Martha and Uncle Norberto Lamadrid in the United States. They were waiting for me when I got off the plane in Rosanada after a long flight.

Although Aunt Martha hugged me, she radiated a certain coldness and aloofness. I knew at once that my arrival in their home was going to be a problem. "Welcome, Marco, my son. You are now going to be our son, you know."

"Thank you, Tía Martha."

Norberto hugged me without saying a word.

As soon as we got in their car, Aunt Martha began snapping out orders to Norberto about which streets to take and how to drive.

"You are going too fast, Norberto. Slow down." She looked older than her years, with her face deeply furrowed with wrinkles. Slightly stooped, Norberto shuffled his feet when he walked. Obviously, life had not been kind to them in Rosanada. Although I knew they were the same ages as my parents, they looked ten years older. Our life in Mérida had been comfortable. My father, a surgeon with a large practice provided well for us.

"How is Luz?" Martha inquired.

"My mother is fine." I always remembered how beautiful she was when she got dressed up and went to play canasta with her friends. Recently, however, she had become a political activist, working to overthrow the Castro regime. Often times she would be entertaining other activists in one part of our house, while my father was being visited by prominent members of the communist government who came for medical consultations in another part of the house.

"My mother always keeps busy," I added.

As we drove to their apartment in the northwest section of Rosanada at some distance from Saint Sophia Church, Norberto was silent, merely grunting, when his wife issued commands.

When we arrived at their home, I learned just what I was in for. As we entered the small living room that was fitted out with a sofa, a couple of chairs, some lamps, and an old television set, Martha laid down the rules of the house to me.

"Put your suitcase under the sofa. The sofa is where you will sleep." Pursing her lips and frowning, she added,

"You must keep the living room clean at all times and in perfect order. Keep all your clothes in the suitcase."

I slid the suitcase under the sofa.

"There is a hamper in the bathroom that you can put your dirty laundry in, and then you can wash it every week." She studied me very seriously with her dark brown, sad eyes and said, "You can call me Mom and Norberto, Dad, if you want." I didn't want to.

When the house got quiet, I undressed and stretched out on the sofa, after I had spread the sheets that Martha had placed there for me. As soon as I turned out the light, tears began to flow. I fell asleep with my pillow wet from them.

The next morning things looked a little brighter, when Nancy, the baby sitter for the Lamadrid children, came to meet me.

"*Hola! Me llamo* Nancy." That was about the extent of her Spanish, but with the help of Martha, I discovered that Nancy, a very attractive woman about twenty-four, with skin like ivory, hair flowing down to her shoulders, and kindly eyes that crinkled when she smiled and laughed, was inviting me to go on a tour of Rosanada.

I was eager to get away from the apartment, but Martha caught me by the sleeve and said, "Wait a minute."

"How is Raúl, your husband, Nancy? I haven't seen him since your wedding last Spring." Then in Spanish Martha explained what she had just said to Nancy.

Before Nancy had a chance to answer, Martha lit into me.

"Wait, before you leave, pick up your clothes there on the chair and put them in your suitcase," she demanded, making an awful scene in front of Nancy. "We are poor, but we are clean and decent," she snorted. "We are not going to allow you to behave like a rich, spoiled brat." Shaking the broom she was carrying for emphasis, she added adamantly: "We don't have maids to pick up after you and do the cleaning." With a big huff, she stormed out of the room.

I enjoyed the day with Nancy. She did not speak much Spanish and I did not yet speak English very well, even though I had studied it in Cuba, but I had never had an opportunity to speak it. Although we used sign language and a few words to make ourselves understood, I had no trouble understanding her when she brought me back to the apartment and planted a big kiss on my lips.

As the days went by, Nancy continued coming for me and taking me for drives and sightseeing of the city. Her kisses became more impassioned the longer I knew her. My friendship with her seemed to invoke the wrath of Martha, because she always stormed around the apartment grumbling, when I returned from outings with Nancy.

One day when I came home, she announced to me that she was registering me in a school. Although, I had gone to a private school for boys in Cuba, I really liked the school she found for me, because there were girls in it, as well as boys. It was there that I met Cristina, a beautiful Cuban girl from Havana that I liked at once and who offered to help me learn English. A devout Catholic, she volunteered to take me to Mass every Sunday in the little red car her parents had given her for her birthday, when she learned I had no way to get there.

Cristina helped alleviate my loneliness and fill my emptiness. Really happy that I could go to Mass again, I enjoyed being with her immensely. We liked each other very much and she took me into her bed. Every Sunday before Mass we would go to confession and make a firm resolution to remain chaste, during the coming week, but our resolutions lasted only until Wednesday or Thursday, at the very latest. Very rarely would we reach Friday, without having lost our good intentions and our virtue.

Strangely, however, I continued to hear the voice of God calling me to serve Him, and I was beginning to believe that He wanted me to be a priest, which was difficult for me to fathom. How could God call someone who fell so easily into sin? I did not yet know the Bible and that many were called by God, not because of their virtues, but because of God's grace and goodness.

Too many people think of God's grace as being like a vending machine in which you insert your prayers and good intentions, and the favors you want come rolling out. Cristina and I felt that we were in God's grace and favor, as long as we went to confession and received absolution after we had been together. Our religion was intense, but without commitment. What a paradox! The sweet, domineering, and religious woman, who brought me closer to God, by taking me to Mass, was also the one who was keeping me away from Him. I was a puzzle to myself. God was calling me and at the same time, I was drawn to this woman. Some days I felt so close to God that I was willing to do anything for Him. Other days I was cold and indifferent to spiritual things. However, God's voice became more and more insistent, burning in my soul so fervently that I knew that I had to give Cristina up.

The day I told her, the sun was dancing on the river that meandered slowly down the mountain valley, as we were driving beside it on our way to the state park for a picnic. Since I could not find anyway to make the news palatable, I just blurted it out.

"In all truthfulness, I must tell you that I feel God is calling me to be a priest!" I held my breath waiting to hear what she would say.

Shaking her long black hair, she exploded. "What kind of priest are you going to be after all you have done with me?" She sighed deeply and bit her lower lip. "You think you can live without me? Every time you see me, you are going to desire to possess me. And if you never see me again, the passion that we shared will remain with you." A tear formed on her cheek and began to roll down toward her chin.

I was devastated. O God, I prayed, is it fair to ask me to give up the love of women? When I was a Methodist, I saw how pastors had wives and everything seemed to work well for them. The more I prayed, the more I realized that He was, in fact, asking me for a total consecration, which included giving up Cristina's love and all sexual activity.

I broke with her and was admitted to the diocesan seminary. From that time I have remained chaste. I have kept my commitments. And now I was fully determined to be ordained a deacon and embrace a celibate life. The Presence has become so strong in my spirit that I would give up anything, everything, even my very life for Him.

4
Marco

The great day finally arrived when I was to enter and ascend to Major and Sacred Orders. The Second Vatican Council led to the elimination of the sub-deaconate, so I was to be ordained a deacon. The language of the liturgy had changed, being in Italian, no longer Latin, as it had been for centuries. The seminary chapel was filled to overflowing, but, of course, my parents could not be there. Besides they were both Protestant and would not have understood the true significance of my vocation. I only wished that we could be reunited as a family around the altar of God. With all the pomp and ceremony that the Roman Catholic Church is famous for—chants, clouds of billowing incense, luxurious vestments, with the bishop wearing a very tall and brilliant golden miter, we celebrated my entrance and the entrance of Pompeo and all our other classmates into Major Orders. Mínimo was not ordained because he had decided to request a leave of absence due to his lack of faith and a desire to experience life in the world. That year he left for Hollland where he spent seven years as a member of a terrorist leftist group, having lost his desire to be part of the Church.

Addressing us solemnly, the bishop warned us that the obligation of perpetual continence is incumbent upon those who receive this ordination. Then he proceeded to perform the ritual ceremony that brought me to a deeper relationship with God in a ministry of service and love for others.

Time flew by. I was finishing the licentiate in sacred theology when one day Pompeo came bustling into my room.

"I just heard the most exciting news," he exclaimed.

I stopped what I was doing—studying for an exam—and waited for him to tell me what he heard."

"Pope Paul VI is going to ordain us in St. Peter's Basilica in May!" His face was flushed with enthusiasm.

That was news. The popes had not ordained priests for centuries. Because I was going to be one of the first to be so ordained, I regarded it as a sign of God's special favor.

A month before my ordination I went to a retreat designed especially for those who were to become priests. The first night I felt lonesome, gloomy and discouraged and spent most of the night in the chapel, considering celibacy and the many responsibilities of the priesthood. During that long night I also experienced my unworthiness to be so blessed by God. Then suddenly, the Presence appeared in all His magnificence and asked me, just like He asked Peter three times, "Do you love me?" Each time, I answered, "Yes, Lord." Three times the Presence told me "Feed My sheep." All doubts and misgivings vanished in the immensity of His love.

I barely slept the night before my ordination. It was very exciting. St. Peter's was filled to capacity and overflowing with many cardinals and bishops taking part in the celebration. As I knelt in prayer, I looked up at the stained glass window of the Holy Spirit in the far wall of the church behind the altar. The sunlight was streaming onto the amber glass and vivified the symbolic dove, making it appear to quiver gently in the air above and behind the altar. Then the Presence flooded my soul. I was entranced throughout the entire Mass and ordination, caught up in the embrace of God who received me as His own. I hardly remember the details of the ordination; I was so deeply united to God in prayer.

I remember the chanting of the *Veni Creator Spiritus.* His Holiness seated himself in the sanctuary before the high altar and waited for me and the other ordinands to come to kneel before him with outstretched hands, palms up and little fingers touching each other. I watched intently as he dipped his thumb into the holy oil and drew a line from the thumb of my right hand to the index finger of the left, and from the thumb of my left hand to the index finger of my right. After anointing my palms completely, he prayed:

"Vouchsafe, O Lord, to consecrate and sanctify these hands by this unction and our blessing."

Overcome by emotion, I could hardly answer, "Amen."

"That whatsoever they shall bless may be blessed, and whatsoever they shall consecrate be consecrated." Again, I answered, "Amen."

Then extending his right hand Pope Paul VI said: "Let us pray, dearly beloved brethren, to God, the Father Almighty, that He may multiply heavenly gifts upon these His servants whom He has chosen for the office of the priesthood. May they by His help accomplish what they undertake at His gracious call."

I was now a priest of Jesus Christ and would be for all eternity according to the order of Melchisedech. I waited to be vested. The pope placed the chasuble on me saying, "Receive the priestly vestment, by which charity is signified, for God is powerful to increase unto these charity and perfection of work."

Joyfully, I responded, "Thanks be to God."

After the offertory of the Mass, the pope again put on his miter and took his seat in front of the altar. Two by two, we ordinands approached and knelt before him, offering him our candles and kissing his ring.

As the pope continued, we concelebrated the Mass with him.

The next day I celebrated my first mass in the Catacombs of San Calixtus. From there, I went to the convent of the Maids of the Sacred Heart for a second Mass, finally the following day I had a solemn Mass with all my priest and lay friends in attendance at the seminary chapel followed by a simple, but moving reception. It was joy unspeakable and full of glory.

5
Renato

"Bless me, Father, for I have sinned," Renato Naburus Del'Ano mumbled in the darkness of the confessional in St. Peter's where he knew no one would recognize his voice.

"The Lord bless you, my son, and help you to know your sins. You may begin your confession," the anonymous priest on the other side of the grill said hurriedly.

Because his conscience tortured him about the emotional feelings—yes, he had to admit it—sexual feelings he felt for Father Lupo, Renato had come to St Peter's to confession, not daring to confess to one of the priests of his congregation, the Shepherds of the Lord that was dedicated to keeping the traditional practices of the Church.

Soon his studies at the Dionysian University would be over and he would be ordained a priest. Then he would return to Torricella in the mountains of Abruzzi and show Don Giorgio Bandi, his former pastor, that he did have a vocation to be a priest. He would show the old buzzard that he had been wrong about him.

Renato had always wanted to be a priest, having done everything he could to get Don Giorgio to help him get admitted to the seminary. He had been sacristan, taught catechism, and spent hours cleaning and decorating the village church, but nothing he did could persuade Don Giorgio to recommend him.

"You are not cut out to be a priest," the old pastor told him, as he was cleaning the sacristy one morning after Mass.

"I am determined to be a priest," Renato protested as he gathered the altar linen to take home to his mother to have it laundered. "I don't drink—I have never drunk a glass of beer. I have had small amounts of wine with dinner, but always in moderation. I don't play sports like the others my age. I will make a good priest." Taking off the cassock he had worn to serve Mass, he hung it up in the armoire. As he spoke, continuing his lament, his eyes avoided those of Don Giorgio. "I don't go out with girls. At least, to speak the truth, I have never gone out alone with one. I have never even been to a dance."

Don Giorgio spoke to him kindly. "Perhaps you should go to Naples, or Rome. There you will find people that are congenial. Your contacts in Torricella are very limited and so are your opportunities." He smiled and patted Renato on his arm to reassure him.

Renato felt that Don Giorgio had told the various vocation directors who had come to the parish, that he was not a good candidate for the priesthood. Nevertheless, he determined to talk to the new one who was coming to town from the Shepherds of the Lord. Perhaps he could persuade him to admit him to their seminary.

When the Reverend Father Virginio Lupo C.S.L arrived at San Solimano Church in Torricella, Renato attended every one of his weekend masses. Finally after the last Mass, Renato got up the courage to speak to the enthusiastic vocation director.

"I would like to join your congregation. I have heard a lot about the Shepherds of the Lord and the wonderful work they are doing to keep the traditions of the Church and stop the erosion of our faith with all the new ideas that are destroying it." Renato folded his well manicured hands on his chest and waited to see what would be the response of Father Lupo.

"My dear Renato, come have dinner with me and we will talk about it," the vocation director suggested.

"Very well, but first I have to run home and tell my mother that I will not be there for dinner."

"Fine, I'll drive you there."

Signora Juliana Del'Ano, a robust and domineering woman about forty who resembled a diva from the Milan opera, greeted Father Lupo with a warm welcome and gave Renato an affectionate embrace, as he explained why the priest had come to the house.

"My son—he's a good boy. I never have to worry about him. He is not like the others who chase girls and have nothing else on their minds."

"It is amazing how much your son looks like you, Signora. He has the same delicate face and graceful features." Father Lupo looked from mother to son and smiled in approval.

"He is my only son. It would make me happy, if he were to become a priest. When he was born, I took him to the village church and prayed before the statue of Madonna, telling her that I hoped he would be a priest some day." She reached over from where she was sitting and took one of Renato's hands in hers and patted it affecttionately.

"Vediamo—we'll see," replied Father Lupo. "If I decide that he is suitable for the Congregation of the Shepherds of the Lord, he will have to come to Rome— that is where our motherhouse is located. Would that be all right with you, Signora? Father Lupo flashed a winning smile at the woman.

"Of course, I would miss him. I lost my husband when Renato was just a little fellow." A look of sadness spread across Juliana's face.

"I'm sorry to hear that," Father Lupo said consolingly.

"I have raised my boy all by myself. I always felt sorry for him that he had no father. Perhaps in your congregation, he will find a father figure to help him. He is not very strong. The other boys here in Torricella don't welcome him into their activities," she confided, as she toyed with a cheap rosary that she had entwined around her fingers.

Renato went to dinner with Father Lupo who encouraged him to eat the antipasto consisting of prosciutto and figs. When the waiter brought the pasta, Father Lupo asked with a flourish of his arm that he bring him a bottle of Refosco dal Peduncolo Rosso—his very best.

Renato was impressed with the priest and ate heartily of the cannelloni. He also sensed that Father Lupo was drawn to him and that the two of them had much in common. With a careful and delicate motion, Renato picked up his glass and took a sip of the wine.

"Drink up," Father Lupo encouraged him with a big smile. "Here, waiter, bring us another bottle of this wine." He motioned expansively at the waiter who came to do his bidding.

As the wine coursed through his veins, Renato became talkative and told the vocation director of his longing to become a priest and of how he never went out with girls, or never went into sports, or dancing."

Father Lupo encouraged him to keep talking. "I think you will be very welcome in the Shepherds of the Lord," he murmured with satisfaction.

By the time the second bottle of Refosco was drained, they had become very close, and Renato felt tipsy and joyous. Deciding that Renato's joining their congregation was a very desirable idea, Father Lupo could not have been more pleased with him, or he with the priest. "Tomorrow," announced Father Lupo, "I will talk to Don Giorgio and tell him I am taking you with me back to Rome to our seminary. And then as soon as you have your things ready, we will drive to the City."

Renato had never been to Rome—in fact he had never left Torricella before—and he was exhilarated by what he saw—St Peter's, the Tiber—it wasn't nearly as nice or as big as he had imagined it to be—the Via del Corso and finally the simple and unpretentious motherhouse of the congregation.

Renato was well accepted by the seminarians, a small group of overweight, nerdlooking, shy males of different ages. They were mostly from United States where the congregation had been founded only a few years before in the Mid-West, which could explain why they were so white, except for a good looking and vociferous Puerto

Rican who was Father Lupo's best friend, or as he himself liked to call him "his little brother," a reminiscence of the Caribbean island where they address friends as brothers, but highly inappropriate for a priest and a seminarian.

They accepted Del'Ano's ways of behaving as the result of his Italian culture, being unfamiliar with the local customs and manners, for, to the average American, all Italians look somewhat feminine. So they did not give too much thought to Renato's voice or movements. For the first time in his life, other men did not mock him and find him unusual.

Renato loved Latin chants and the waves of incense that filled the chapel. In fact, he loved everything about the Shepherds of the Lord. Father Lupo became his mentor and introduced him to fasting and flagellation of his flesh. He really enjoyed taking the discipline by striking his back with the whip that the novice master gave him.

Although his spirit was willing, his flesh was very weak, especially in the presence of Father Lupo. He enjoyed it when Father Lupo came to visit him in his room, and always requested that the priest would whip him as penance for his sins, but he felt strange stirrings in his body that he had not experienced before. Because of these feelings, he felt guilty and that is what brought him to St. Peter's and confession.

"It has been one week since my last confession. Since that time I have been bothered by strong emotions and sexual feelings." He paused and took a deep breath.

"When do you have these feeling?" the priest asked.

"Every time a certain man comes to see me, I get sexually aroused. I fast and do penance, but I feel very guilty," Renato added contritely.

"Do you ever act on these feelings?"

"Not really, except for the fact that I ask him to discipline me with my whip, but I feel guilty"

"Do you get whipped on your back or on your butt?"

"On my butt, Father."

"Does he discipline you with your pants up or down?"

"Down, Father."

"How about your underwear?"

"No underwear, Father."

"Do you get an erection during the disciplining?"

"I always do."

"You should feel bad. These feelings come from the devil. If you act on them, you will go to hell! Do not see this man any more than you absolutely have to. When you feel emotionally attracted to him, go for a walk in the fresh air. And above all, pray for victory over the devil and his temptations! For your penance say fifteen mysteries of the rosary."

Try as hard as he could, Renato could not overcome his attraction for Father Lupo. Therefore, he determined to be an exemplary seminarian, devout and smiling, giving those he encountered the impression that he was pious and even holy.

It was shortly after his confession in St. Peter's that Renato met Marco Lamadrid for the first time, and developed an instant antipathy for him. Because he had heard that Marco was from Rosanada, he sought him out, since he had just learned that his congregation had decided to send him there upon the completion of his doctorate in liturgy at the Saladin's Pontifical Institute of Saint Desiderius Erasmus, the very best in the entire Church in liturgical matters. As an expert in rites and ceremonies, he had fully expected to continue working in Rome, developing there a solid career, and was disappointed that he was being sent elsewhere.

"Hello, you are Father Lamadrid, I believe," he said quizzically as he eyed him, studying him from head to toe.

"That is my name all right, and who are you?"

"Renato Del'Ano. My congregation, the Shepherds of the Lord, is opening a new house and it is going to be in Rosanada and I am assigned to go there in a very short time. I thought you could tell me a bit about the place."

"I'd be glad to, but to start with, let me be the first to welcome you to Rosanada," Marco replied. "What will you be doing for your congregation there?"

"I am going to teach liturgy in the college seminary there," Renato answered.

"Oh, I see you are a liturgist. Liturgy is an exciting field to be in now with all the changes that are being implemented. I am sure you must be very enthusiastic about the *Novus Ordo*."

Bristling slightly as he spoke, Renato said: "On the contrary, I support the Ottaviani Intervention wholeheartedly."

"Just exactly what is your objection to the new Mass?" Marco set down his plate of canapés and took a sip of wine.

"It goes against Catholic tradition—that is exactly what is wrong with it. The faithful never asked for the Mass to be changed. The language must be Latin. It has been the same for centuries. St. Pius V had the Roman Missal drawn up so that it would unite Catholics. The new Mass is causing nothing but division. St. Pius V clearly stated in 1570, at the end of the Bull that promulgated it, that if anyone were to tamper with the Mass, as he set it up in his Missal, that they would incur the wrath of Almighty God and that of the Apostles Peter and Paul." His voice had become strident and anger blazed in his eyes.

"I doubt it is as rigid as that. Times change," Marco responded, hoping that would end the conversation.

Renato was not about to be silenced. A nerve had been struck, and he would have his say. "The Mass now is very close to Protestant theology. The unbloody renewal of the sacrifice of Calvary is not affirmed. The Real Presence of Christ in the Eucharist is de-emphasized. When you go into a church, you can't even find the tabernacle. It is like going to visit someone and you can't find him until someone tells you he is out in the garage." Standing rigid and inflexible, Renato was beginning to fume.

"It is not that bad," Marco protested. "The presence of Jesus Christ is real in all apostolic traditions. I like the liturgy in the language of the people just like they have it in the sister churches, the Eastern Orthodox and the Old Catholics with their people taking an active part in participating, rather than saying the rosary all during the entire Mass as we used to do."

Abruptly Renato set down his wine glass on the table beside Marco's and without further ado said, "There is no point in continuing this conversation any further." With that he smoothed out an imaginary wrinkle from his habit, walked arrogantly across the room, and began conversing with someone else. Neither he nor Marco could have possibly realized the sinister part he would play in Marco's life as a priest.

6
Marco

Spending my first summer as a priest in a picturesque lakeside village near Rome, ministering to the local people while their pastor was on vacation, was a real joy for me. When summer ended, I returned to the seminary to pick up my belongings, including all my books, to ship them to the United States. I myself returned on TWA at the beginning of the seventies. Although Pompeo returned a little later, Mínimo did not come back to the states until ten years later, because he was delayed in finishing his studies in Rome, since he had gone to Holland where he took a job, first as a sacristan and later, after spending two years in a mental institution, as a domestic servant in a bordello in Amsterdam. Actually he was suffering from a crisis with his faith and ended up joining the communist party, after a very handsome young man induced him into swearing that there is no God. Then Mínimo, obediently and reverently stated that everything comes from matter and there is no such thing as spirit.

Although I felt my calling to the priesthood very strongly, my first assignment was most discouraging, because the parishioners of St. Ellen's parish did not receive me well. Perhaps it was the European ways that I had picked up over the years in Rome that they did not like. Perhaps I was a bit arrogant. Certainly my long hair did not help. Although I had finished my studies at the

Dionysian University with the highest grades possible, I felt that my marks that I was receiving in the University of Life were not so good. Although I always thought I would be ordained for a special and extraordinary mission, I felt rejected by the people I had come to serve.

During my stay in Rome, the Most Reverend Priapus T. Lingam, the same bishop who sent me to the university in Rome, had managed to elevate Rosanada to an archdiocese with the help of the large financial contributions that Mrs. Aspasia Hetaira made for him at the Vatican, scattering many donations at the Secretariat of State and the Congregation for Bishops, and crowning her efforts with a substantial check for the Holy Father's charities. In spite of the fact that other dioceses had better claims to this honor, Rosanada was placed among the archbishoprics.

My pastor at St. Ellen's was Monsignor Alfred G. Douglas, the secretary to Bishop Priapus T. Lingam D.D., the Ordiinary of Rosanada. At first, I thought it would be nice having the secretary of the archbishop as my pastor, especially since Monsignor Douglas was also in charge of media for the archdiocese. In a short time, however, I discovered that it was an extremely unpleasant assignment, because the monsignor treated me like I was a servant, making me walk his dog, pick up his clothes at the cleaners, and drive him around in his car.

When Monsignor asked me to drive him to a dinner party at the home of an affluent parish couple, Jennifer and Michael Casey, I had only been at St. Ellen's a short time. Although we arrived a half hour late for dinner, because Monsignor Douglas could not find his diamond studded cuff links for the French cuffs on his shirt,

Jennifer Casey welcomed us politely and ushered us into her opulent living room that was decorated with authentic and decadent French Rococo furniture.

Since the monsignor did not introduce me, I smiled to the Caseys and said, "Let me introduce myself. I am Father Marco Lamadrid."

"We have heard a lot about you, Father," Michael Casey said extending to me a vulgar "Sex on the Beach" cocktail. Handing a cocktail to Monsignor Douglas, he said: "You may have your "Sex on the Beach," as you always like it; however, it is safer in the rectory."

At this, Monsignor, clenched his teeth and grimaced, while Marco laughed softly to himself.

A petite blonde girl wearing a uniform like a French maid brought a plate of canapés and invited Monsignor Douglas to help himself. In disbelief, I watched as I saw him fill both hands with the canapés and stack them on the linen napkin the maid gave him, while I took one canapé and thanked her politely.

"Well, I hope you heard good things about me," I said returning his smile.

"We heard you were ordained by Pope Paul VI," Jennifer said between sips on her drink.

"Hrrmpf!" said Monsignor Douglas, not wishing to be ignored from the conversation and directing attention to himself. "Yes, he is a good priest. I find him very helpful and he is on call whenever I need him." The monsignor signaled for the maid to refill his cocktail glass. "I got a new batch of British Colonial stamps for my collection, Michael. Remind me to show them to you sometime."

"Sure, Monsignor, I'd love to see them. Perhaps sometime we can play golf, and I can stop by the rectory and take a look at them." Michael obviously was not interested in stamps and was simply trying to be polite.

"I don't like golf, but if you would like to go fishing—trout fishing—I'd take you up on that," the monsignor replied laconically.

When the French maid announced dinner, we went to the dining room and took our places, while Michael uncorked a bottle of French champagne. My hosts drank a toast to my success at St. Ellen's parish and wished me well.

"Oh, he will do just fine," the monsignor snapped churlishly. "He is learning to do what he is told. In the seminaries these days they get too much freedom." He yawned and scratched his thick salt and pepper hair causing a flurry of white flakes to fall on his black jacket.

During the dinner of delicately prepared roast duckling, I noticed that Monsignor Douglas quickly quaffed three glasses of champagne. When desert came, the maid filled his glass again and he quickly emptied it and waited for a refill. When we got up from the table to return to the living room, I noticed that Monsignor was having a bit of trouble trying to keep his balance. Even so, he accepted a vintage cognac from the tray the maid held out before him.

Sinking down in a deep armchair, he began to look very drowsy. When he drank the cognac, his eyes began to have a glazed look, causing me to fear that he was going to pass out. "Monsignor, I really think it is time for us to be going home now," I suggested softly.

"One for the road," he insisted.

When he finished the drink, he rose to his feet and began to totter. Grabbing his arm and supporting him, I managed to get him to the car, while thanking our host and hostess on the way.

When we got to the rectory, I got out of the car and went around and opened his door for him. When I helped him get out of the car, he threw his arm around my waist and leaned on me for support. "You are a nice man, Tiger. I really like you."

With that he threw both arms around me and proceeded to give me a big hug. Remembering Christian Brown, I quickly tried to break lose from his embrace, having learned to avoid giving all mixed signals to homosexuals. "Watch your step, Monsignor, there are two steps up to the porch," I cautioned.

A big man, more than six feet tall with a large body frame, he would have fallen on the concrete without my support, if he stumbled. Once I got him into the house, I guided him to the living room sofa and sat him down.

"Come, Tiger, sit here beside me so we can be close together."

As he tried to pull me down to be with him, I protested, knowing that I had to avoid him at all costs: "It is getting late, Monsignor. I have the 6:00 a.m. Mass in the morning. I really must go to bed now. Please excuse me." Determined to keep my distance, I started to leave the room.

"Wait!" he called after me. "Before you go, get me my bottle of Johnny Walker Black Label and a glass and bring it here." He began to undress, taking off his jacket, shirt, and trousers, standing there in his boxer shorts.

"I think you have had enough to drink for tonight, Monsignor."

This comment made him furious. "Hey, you do NOT tell me what to do!" His speech was slurred. "I'll get you for that." Before he could say another word he fell over on the sofa, and I made my getaway to my room.

After that evening, he did not speak to me for a week. In fact, I did not even see him for three days, for he was holed up in his room with Johnny Walker. When he finally came out, he totally ignored me for four days. I learned to expect this silent treatment from time to time when his anger would consume him. Such was his behaveior whenever he had to put up with the rigorous archbishop's tantrums. Perhaps he was not even gay, but he was certainly a very lonely man, desperate for any kind of consolation.

Although my life in the rectory was fraught with discord and unpleasantness, I loved the ministry that was assigned me. I was responsible for the women of the Legion of Mary and several groups of married couples, helped out at the Fátima Sanctuary, and, with the help of a religious sister, guided some wayward young people. I was also confessor to a convent of nuns, and the spiritual director of the nearby St. Ashera's High School. Although I had a very busy life, I found the ministry very rewarding and a source of strength to help me with my dysfunctional relationship with Monsignor Douglas. Years later his body was found decomposed at another rectory, after he spent four days of isolation, because of a heart attack, while the priests there thought he was having an alcoholic binge.

In time, I got to know the people of the parish and, with some of them, established friendships that have continued down through the years.

One of the most unusual experiences that I had my first year at St. Ellen's was having dinner with Orias Sodomat, a plump, vulgar, and ill-mannered social climber and her husband, Sitri, the owner of a third-rate Spanish television station—WSAP that had a rainbow as its logo.

If I had known what I was getting into by becoming acquainted with them, I would have said no emphatically to her invitation to visit their station and then have dinner, when she asked me one Sunday after the 11:00 am Mass.

When I entered the station with Orias, her husband, much older than she, a man with delicate features and long tapering fingers, was waiting for us. He took us into a studio where a talk show was in progress—a group of men of various ages were discussing how they were seduced or even raped by a good friend of their father and how they themselves had subsequently become homosexual. Forced to sit there during the entire show, I was thoroughly disgusted, while my host thought it was highly entertaining. After showing me around the station, we went to dinner in a nearby French restaurant. Sitri beckoned for the *maître d'* to come and seat us by throwing him a kiss in the air. I was perplexed by this gesture and he must have realized it because he quickly said, "That is a French gesture. That is how they do it in France." To me it seemed strange that he would summon the man by throwing him a kiss, but I decided that I was probably just ignorant of the ways of the world. I knew France well, but I had always visited simple restaurants and never places of elegance. Never in my life have I ever seen anyone else signal a *maître d'* in this fashion.

"Give us the best table in the house!" he ordered flamboyantly. We were escorted to a table close to a stage where a singer was crooning the latest popular song. A few couples were dancing on a small dance floor in the center of the room. Suddenly Sitri Sodomat rose to his feet and, climbing up on the stage, announced: "I want to dedicate the next song to our good friend, Father Marco Lamadrid. Stand up, Father!"

Slowly, I rose to my feet in embarrassment. I was glad it was so dark that probably no one could see me.

"Make yourself comfortable, Father," Orias invited, "and let us order the specialty of the house for you."

The specialty of the house turned out to be a very mediocre lobster thermidor drenched in butter. I do not care for butter; it just does not agree with me. I managed to shake off as much as I could and ate sparingly of the lobster. When the evening was over, I thanked Mr. and Mrs. Sodomat for their hospitality. They were trying to be friendly and helpful, and I appreciated their good will. During the three years that I remained at St. Ellen's, they invited me to their television station and out to dinner four or five times.

On one occasion, as we sat at table listening to an intolerable Mariachi band that I found boring, their only son, Frido who was sixteen years old and slightly overweight came and sat down at the table with us. His face was covered with acne bumps that had caused some scarring. In contrast with the redness of his face, his teeth were very white and set in an extremely large mouth where his braces sparkled every time he smiled. As he stared at me from across the table, I could not help but think that his eyes were malicious. He actually had a spaced out look in them like drug addicts have. I later learned that he had been using drugs for a while, and eventually they became part of his daily life. I recognized him as a youth who occasionally played the guitar at Mass on Sundays, and was a student at the High School, where I served as a spiritual director. He had the same delicate features and hands as his father. I sensed Frido was gay and I had a premonition that he meant trouble. I did not know exactly what kind of trouble, but I was put on my guard against him. However in the long run, I was unable to protect myself from his treachery and lies.

I had hoped in 1972 when Archbishop Lingam decided to demote Monsignor Douglas and assign him to leave St. Ellen's and go to the Pope Julius III Seminary Seminary, that life in the rectory would improve. Father Aurelio Toloso, a handsome, bright, and elegant middleaged priest of Spanish origin, famous for his sermons and his love of literature, moved into St. Ellen's parish and rectory. I soon learned, early one morning when I decided to go for a bicycle ride before the 6:00 am Mass, that he also had a great love for women.

Trying not to awaken my new pastor, I tiptoed out of my room and down the hall. Because I was trying to walk quietly, they did not hear me approach. The pastor, standing in the doorway of his room wearing nothing but a bath towel around his waist, was embracing and kissing a woman! Later I learned that she was Miss Trini, his mistress, who was trying to leave before I woke up.

Thunderstruck, I hurried past them. "Good Morning," I stammered in embarrassment.

When I returned after my bicycle ride, the woman was, of course, gone. Later that night, he sought me out.

"Marco," my pastor said gruffly, "Let's talk man to man."

Still bewildered by what I had seen, and very curious to find out how he would approach the matter of a woman leaving his bed at the break of dawn, I just stared at him in silence.

"You have seen nothing here. Do you understand?"

I nodded.

"If you get along with Trini and me, you will have no problems." He smoothed his rumpled hair. By now he had put on a white terrycloth bathrobe.

I said nothing. To my surprise he handed me an envelope and said, "Go out to dinner tonight and enjoy yourself." With that he turned and entered his room. Then I could hear the water in his shower running.

When I opened the door to my room and turned on the night light beside my bed, something really strange and frightening happened. It seemed as if a man were seated in the armchair by the window. Because the light was dim, I could not see his face clearly, but I could determine that he was dressed all in black. I also noticed a strange smell in the room. Although I saw him only for a brief instant, the nauseous odor lingered for some time after he vanished, with a haunting laugh that mocked me, and lingers in my memory.

Visibly shaken, I opened the envelope the pastor gave me and found that it contained a hundred dollar bill—almost half my salary, then. I was perplexed. Although, I did not like living with the knowledge of my pastor's sin, all I could do at that time was to ignore it. Who would have believed my word against his?

My duties at St. Ellen's reduced the amount of time I had for prayer, but, nevertheless, I felt the Presence occasionally while I was there. Although my longing for holiness had decreased, I still felt that God was calling me to do something special for Him, but I was still not sure what it was that He wanted of me.

My life in the rectory had been anything but what I had expected. Worse was yet to come. There is no way I could have prepared myself for what Father Aurelio did next.

7
Marco

Because he liked to go away every Sunday afternoon, staying until very late at night, Father Aurelio Toloso determined that I would have the Sunday evening Mass. As the celebration of this Mass became extremely popular, people flocked to it just to participate in a vibrant and dynamic service. Craving a deeper relationship with God, the people enjoyed the guitars, the sermon, and the meditation after communion with the lights dimmed—features Catholics had not enjoyed previously in their churches.

One Sunday evening when I arrived at the church, I found a sign on the door announcing that the Mass had been arbitrarily suspended indefinitely. I could not believe that I was being victimized for doing a good job. Because I had become their friend and the person they looked to when trouble came, a large group of agitated and angry parishioners that gathered on the steps welcomed me warmly. One of the men, Alfredo Altuna and his lovely wife, were standing on the top step addressing the people.

"Now that Father Marco is here with us, we will find out why our Mass has been suspended."

Because this was the first indication I had received that Father Aurelio was going to change the schedule, I was at a loss for words.

"I have no idea," I said almost inaudibly. I was about to learn the meaning of envy. Even though I had suffered it in the seminary and was driven crazy by my first pastor because of it, I had no idea that it would pursue me all my life.

Assessing the situation, Pedro Sánchez, a forceful businessman accustomed to taking charge, said to the people gathered on the steps below him, "Well, my friends, we will sign a petition and take it to the archbishop. We have certain rights under canon law, and I intend to see that they are upheld."

Immediately Manolo Ochoa, a golfing friend of Sánchez, handed him a notepad and a ball-point pen. "Here, Pedro, I have already signed my name to this petition."

"Thanks, Manolo. Anyone wishing to sign, just line up here." About seventy-five people rushed to put their names on the petition. Others walked out in disgust. Still others, a small minority, defended the pastor's decision, saying that the most important thing for a Catholic to do was to be obedient; they criticized the rest of us, as rebelling against the legitimately constituted authority! The nuns who worked in the parish were in full support of them.

The following two hours, I spent talking with my friends in the parish hall, where one of the women brewed a pot of coffee. I tried my best to soothe their troubled spirits and to make excuses for the pastor.

When I returned to the rectory, I was dumbfounded to find that Father Aurelio was sitting in his favorite chair with an empty bottle of Johnny Walker Black Label at his feet. He was fingering a high-powered Winchester rifle, a gun he used when he went deer hunting in the nearby mountains. I froze in terror as I saw him lift the gun, aim it at me, and cock it, so it was ready to fire. I stopped in my tracks and remained motionless, hardly even daring to breathe.

"You, son of a bitch, motherfucker, little shit! I am going to kill you!" he threatened with slurred speech. He stood up and started toward me. "You are trying to screw me, gathering signatures to make me look bad at the chancery. *My* parishioners called me right away informing me of your disobedience and bold attitude, pretending to be above my authority!"

"Calm down, Aurelio, there is no reason to get upset. We can work this whole thing out." I was not at all confident that we could.

Bounding toward me, still aiming the gun at my heart, he pressed it tight against my chest. I knew the shot from that gun would have blown me to pieces.

Shaking with fear, I stammered, "Father, you must think about what you are doing. It would be a horrible sin for you to shoot me, and you would wind up in jail."

"You have betrayed me, you, *hijo de la gran puta*." His eyes were bloodshot and the stench of liquor on his breath nauseated me. "You have your own parish inside of my parish! I won't tolerate that! Do you hear me?"

"Of course, Father," I quickly agreed and added: "There is only one boss at St. Ellen's, and you have proved that today."

I took a deep breath and sighed, as I watched him lower the gun.

"All right, be a good guy," he said flatly, "and go out in the kitchen and find me another bottle of Johnny Walker." I rushed to get it. The battle was over.

It was five in the morning when I finally got to sleep. When I woke up at about ten, I noticed that an envelope had been pushed under my door. It contained three one hundred dollar bills and a note that read: "Man to man— take three days off and go on a vacation. Don't be coy, ram somebody." Up to this moment, I have never before told anyone about this, for one simple reason—nobody would ever believe it. Eventually, he got cancer and repented. By that time, he had become a good friend of mine.

Life continued to be turbulent in the rectory of St. Ellen's. In mid-summer, shortly after the Fourth of July, Father Aurelio cornered me, as I was returning to my room one afternoon. My first thought was: "Thank God he is sober."

"I have something to tell you," he announced pushing his face up into mine. Although I am almost six feet tall, he was taller and used his physical presence to try to intimidate me. "I have something I want to tell you up close and personal."

I set down the package I was carrying and put it on the hall table and waited for him to speak.

"I tell you right out to your face. I have asked Archbishop Lingam to move you to another parish. You are dividing the parish. You have too many friends." His eyes, though bloodshot, bored into me like two bullets.

"Thank you," I said simply and picked up my package and walked quietly to my room.

I figured that it would be only a matter of time until I would get a notice from the vicar general—archbishops are always too busy to contact the clergy themselves—saying that I had a new assignment. Although it would have been welcome news, it never came. Instead a few weeks later, as I was getting ready to go to the nearby Fátima Sanctuary to hear confessions that afternoon, I noticed that Father Aurelio was busy packing up his belongings and carrying them to his car. Pretending that nothing unusual was happening, I left for the Fátima Sanctuary. When I returned to the rectory a few hours later his things were gone and so was he.

Later that night the Most Reverend Manuel Parente, auxiliary and right hand man of Archbishop Lingam, moved into the rectory. What a relief! Bishop Parente was a holy priest—a righteous man, diligent, and very demanding—in short an exemplary priest with whom I enjoyed working. Always considerate of my feelings, he treated me with respect, and I was grateful for the inspiration he provided me.

A few weeks after Bishop Parente moved into the rectory of St. Ellen's, I learned through the clerical grapevine that Father Aurelio had retired from the priesthood and had gone to live with Trini. Unfortunately, she passed away a few months later in a tragic accident, but he inherited a nice house.

I had a good year or so at St. Ellen's with Bishop Parente. One of the best things that happened to me then was my discovery of the Charismatic Renewal Movement. I attended a meeting one night with another priest, Father Matteo, whom I had met at a clergy conference. Very enthusiastically he phoned me and invited me to go with him: "I'm sure you will like it," he said. "The Spirit of God is very active in the meetings."

At first I found the meeting strange and different as it opened with the singing of "Alleluia, alleluia, alleluia," because I could not understand why they kept singing the same alleluia over and over again. Finally the singing stopped and the leader of the meeting, a deacon, invited people to come forth to the platform and give their testimonies. One by one they told of how their lives had changed, since they had received the baptism of the Holy Spirit. They recounted how they had been healed of illnesses or found jobs. I quickly realized that those financially deprived and poorly educated people knew more about God than I and most of my seminary professors did! "Only the children will enter into the Kingdom of God."

The music continued very prayerfully with the singing of songs that Protestant evangelists had made popular in the United States—"What a Friend We have in Jesus!" "There is a Fountain Filled with Blood," and "Sweet Hour of Prayer." Father Matteo was right. The Presence of God was really moving in our midst. When I felt a strange movement within my chest, words seemed to be trying to mount up in my mouth. At first, I tried to repress them, but then decided to let them flow. Strange sounds came unbidden to me. I began to speak words that I had never heard before. I looked at Father Matteo who smiled at me and said, "You are speaking in tongues. Bless God for His Grace!"

Continuing to attend meetings of the Charismatic Renewal Group where the gospel was preached in all its fullness, I began to witness the working of the Gifts and

Charismata of the Holy Spirit in the souls of the good people who came to the meetings. When I saw God at work in His people—a true Christian community of believers—I fell in love with the Church. So many people think the hierarchy is the Church. That is a very false belief. The Church is the people of God. I am glad that in the documents of the second Vatican Council, they made that very clear. It is very unfortunate that in the seminaries they do not teach seminarians to love the people that comprise the Church. Instead they instill fear and reverence into them for the institution and its hierarchy, creating replicas of their leaders, so that consequently the web of autocrats perpetuates itself in the name of a man from Galilee who rejected phylacteries and lengthy prayers two thousand years ago and who was neither a Levite nor a Jewish priest himself.

One day to my surprise I received a letter from a friend in Rome, Giuseppe Giordano, the secretary to the Cardinal Vicar of Rome—the pope being the Bishop of Rome cannot actually exercise that function, so he delegates that office to one of his cardinals—with an invitation that I come to "the City." The hierarchy refers to Rome as "the City," a very arrogant medieval Catholic tradition that ignores the existence of places like New York, Mexico City or Calcutta. Even to this day the pope always gives his blessing on special feast days *"Urbis et Orbis,"* to the City with a capital C, and to the world. I was invited to collaborate with the preparation and development of the Holy Year of 1975.

With the reluctant permission of Archbishop Lingam, I flew to Rome in the autumn of 1974 where I was assigned to St. John Lateran Basilica and what I incorrectly thought would be the exciting world of the Vatican.

8
Marco

Rome never ceases to deceive the multitude of visitors who travel miles to go there allured by a few old stones, over-decorated church buildings, and an audience with a Pope who for most people appears as a white speck far, far away, speaking with an accent that ranges from difficult to impossible to understand. Rome is like a very pretentious, highly educated, well-mannered grand dame who still wears the jewels of her youth, but her body is horribly deteriorated and decrepit. You can enjoy yourself and have a good time with her, but you would never dream of spending the night. Because I did not learn this lesson well, while a student there, I went back again arriving on November 14, 1974, when the days were getting shorter and darker and cold winds were beginning to blow. The tourists may spend their time mumbling a few prayers, eating, or staring at the sites. Most people, however, do not seem to be willing to pray, unless they are facing some kind of trouble. Rome has antiquities to explore, but as a city it is chaotic. Perhaps Mussolini had the right idea when he wanted to build a new Rome where today you find the Eur, because the old city simply cannot satisfy the needs of the present age.

My first assigned task in Rome was to attend a meeting of the pope's masters of ceremonies, as they planned the celebrations for the Holy Year. Immediately at a disadvantage, because I did not have the training to walk confidently in these circles, I soon learned that, in the high spheres of the Vatican, it is not important what is said, but rather what is implied, or hinted, or simply suggested. Even more, sometimes what you did not state may have had a greater significance than what you said. Obviously language is important, because if you change just one word in a document, you can modify the way people perceive the magisterium of the Church or the political views of the Vatican. Furthermore, the Italian language and mentality provide innumerable nuances and possibilities as you describe a fact or express a feeling. The Cuban ambassador at the time used to say that Vatican politics had to be measured in millimeters.

Since I was put in charge of the activities of St. John Lateran during the Holy Year, it seemed I was being given an impossible assignment, but I quickly learned that good manners and education could get me through almost any situation. In the course of the year, I met many interesting people, including Archbishop Woytila, Mother Teresa of Calcutta, the Prime Minister of Ireland, the President of France, and cardinals, bishops and many priests from various countries around the world, among others.

I was also an auxiliary for papal ceremonies—really nothing more than a glorified altar server—but I spent many golden moments that I keep in my memory. I loved the perfection of the choir in the Sistine Chapel. Also I never ceased being amazed at the throngs of pilgrims that came every day to see His Holiness Paul VI, a pope I loved and really admired for being open, honest, and liberal. Although he was coerced by the conservatives into signing the absurd encyclical *Humanae Vitae*, he reformed every aspect of the Church during his pontificate.

I enjoyed the Roman ceremonial, also known as *devotio romana*, which was the perfect execution of the rubrics. It spoke to me of the grandeur of the religious empire inherited from Constantine, even if his "donatio" was bogus, and now guaranteed by the word of Jesus: "I will be with you until the end of time." I felt that there was somebody still sitting on the throne of the Caesars. The popes with their magnificent regalia, their marble thrones, and their many aids made me feel that the Roman Empire still existed. When dressed for special occasions, many times they wear a splendid red cloak like a victorious Caesar, and John Paul II took the initiative to kiss the ground of the countries he visited, which was the sign of conquest for Roman emperors. Many moments were spiritually comforting, but I did not enjoy the Presence that I so much longed to experience, which came as a surprise to me, because I thought that by being in the center of Christianity, I would feel closer to Him. On the contrary, I felt far away from God, precisely because at no time had I asked Him, if it was His will for me to be in Rome, but had rather just assumed it was.

When I returned to my simple room in one of the many lodgings arranged for the Holy Year pilgrims in the outskirts of the city, I would be plunged into feelings of loneliness, because my friends were all so far away in Rosanada, and every new acquantaince I would make in Rome lasted only for a few days for they all had to return to their countries. I had one consolation—my father wrote me that he had become a Catholic, because he wanted to understand my vocation to the priesthood.

By chance I met a girl, Tiziana Ubaldi, who worked in the basilica taking care of the literature that was distributed to visitors. She took advantage of one of the weekly meetings I had with her to go over her accounts to invite me to have lunch with her. Because I was so lonely, I accepted her invitation. She was a lovely girl and meeting with her became a highpoint in my week. Although I did not do anything that was at all wrong, I began to feel uneasy about the time I spent with her.

Perhaps, I decided, the reason I did not feel the Presence was because of Tiziana. Little by little, I stopped seeing her and loneliness gripped me in its possession. I was dissatisfied with my life in Rome. The priests in the Vatican treated me kindly and I really had no complaint about any of them, but most of them were simply bureaucrats striving and competing for their next promotion. I found their jokes, outings, and their bachelor dinners extremely boring. I longed for the human warmth of the parish and the joys of the ministry. The Vatican was not the heavenly and holy city that I thought it would be. I had had a false vision of it. Actually it is a peculiar place since it is a society run by celibate men with a certain number of nuns to take care of minor jobs, and a good assortment of lay people. I do not think that any babies are born in that state.

What made my stay in Rome bearable was the large number of pilgrims from Rosanada who came for the Holy Year and had been given my name as someone they could contact. I enjoyed showing them Rome—the Colosseum, the Baths of Caracalla, the major basilicas, and the Spanish Steps, among other places. Our tours usually wound up in a restaurant where we would relax and talk about home and have something to eat and drink. The tourists usually wanted a demijohn of Chianti and would say: "Get us a bottle of wine with the basket around the bottle." The more sophisticated would order something from the wine list or ask me to recommend a wine. Psychologically I was continuing to live in Rosanada.

Near the end of September when I had been in Rome almost a year and I was having my evening prayer next to the main altar in the basilica, I again experienced the Divine Light. In His Presence, I clearly realized that I had made a big mistake in coming to Rome, because I had come for the wrong reasons—my own, and not to do the will of God and serve Him. I thought that I had made a decision always to obey God, but I knew now that I had never really tried to hear what God was telling me. I realized very clearly that my place in life was in a parish and not in the Vatican. Now I was more miserable than before and I determined to return to Rosanada, cost what it may, but I knew it would be difficult, because my superiors in Rome wanted me to continue there working for them.

Rome can be a nightmare if you are not very careful—streets filled with middle and low-class screaming Romans, pushing and shoving their way along, and extremely crowed busses. The subway was the preferred way to travel, but unfortunately it did not go everywhere. Ever present motorcycles and Lambrettas made almost unbearable noise. Numerous pickpockets, assailants, and thieves made life hazardous. One of the tourists I took on a tour of Rome kept her money in a brown paper bag, so that the pickpockets would think it was her lunch. One of the worst tricks of the thieves was to ride by a woman tourist and with a cane pull her purse off her arm and speed away with it. One woman was dragged about fifty feet before she got free. Another tourist that I took on a tour put her passport, money, and travelers checks in a purse that she wore underneath her shirt, making her look as if she were pregnant. "Everyone was so nice to me," she said.

Well, I was not so fortunate. Someone managed to steal my briefcase containing all my documents, causing me major difficulties and trouble. I had to file police reports, go to the American Consulate, and report my passport lost. I stood in long lines, waiting to take care of my problems, often only to have the clerk decide to close and take a break when it was my turn. I learned a lot of patience; I also learned that patience is a virtue that is infinitely perfectible. It is a virtue you can never really master, because just when you think you have it— surprise! You lose it again.

Needless to say, I was relieved when Pope Paul VI brought the Holy Year to an end with a Mass that was televised worldwide and closed the Holy Door to St. Peter's that is used only during Holy Years. It was with great joy that I receiver permission to fly home to Rosanada. I had no idea what was in store for me. If I had, I might not have been so eager to return.

9
Luz

"My dear, please, I ask you again, please don't bring those friends of yours into our home." Aurelio put his arms around his wife to reassure her of his love, because he had touched upon a sensitive issue. "One of the high ranking communists in the Castro regime is coming for a surgical consultation with me this afternoon. "It is dangerous for you to bring your freedom fighters here."

"We need to get out the truth about Castro and his regime. I have to distribute our newspaper. That is my job in the cell," Luz protested while kissing Aurelio gently on the cheek. Although his black hair was now graying and thinning at the temples, he was still the handsome fellow she had fallen in love with many years before. He was of pure Spanish descent—they both were. So many people in Cuba were a mixture of Indian and African blood, but they were from very old Spanish families from Castile that traced their ancestry back to *conversos*, Jews who converted to Christianity at the time of the Inquisition. Praying in Hebrew every day Luz's grandfather secretly remained a Jew his entire life. She could still remember his main prayer "*Shema Yisrael Adonai Elohenu Adonai Ehad.*"

"They are lining up people before firing squads and mowing them down. I worry about you." His kindly brown eyes became serious and filled with tension as he spoke. "I couldn't stand it, if something happened to you."

"Don't worry, dear, I am very careful All my friends that I used to play cards with are involved." She smoothed his hair caressingly.

"The *Commandante* will be here in a few minutes, I have to go to my office now." He headed for the part of their home that housed his medical practice.

Luz hated the Castro regime. It had taken Marco, her beloved and handsome young son, from her. Caught by the secret police and accused of anti-government activity, he had been arrested by the G2, when he was so young, just a child, because he was involved in organizing a student strike against the regime. Aurelio had been able to use his influence with his friend *Commandante* Diego Tacata and managed to keep Marco from going to prison. The Cuban prisons were almost a fate worse than death. They were just abominable. Because of this incident with the G2, the secret police, she and Aurelio decided that there was no future for the boy in Cuba. They obtained a visa and arranged for him to go to Rosanada to stay with Aurelio's brother Norberto and his wife Martha.

It was the worst day of her life—the day they drove Marco to the new modern glass and steel international terminal of the airport for the midnight flight to Rosanada. She was so proud of how Marco was trying to be brave. He had always been outstanding in every way—handsome like his father—tall with straight black hair that he kept neatly combed at all times. Although he excelled at sports, his academic record was still the very best. No mother could ask for a finer son.

"Mama, I don't want to go alone to the United States.

"You are a man now," Aurelio told him sternly, as they parked at the airport. "You are fifteen years old. Your mother and I have decided that it is best for you to go to the United States where you will have an opportunity for a great life. If you stay here in Cuba, you will wind up in one of the prisons for dissidents." Aurelio put his arm around his son's shoulders.

"Be brave!" Luz encouraged. "You will have a fine time with Tía Martha and Tío Norberto. They will enjoy having you with them. They have only three daughters."

"But Mama, I don't want to live away from you and papa."

"We hope to come to Rosanada and see you before long," Luz told him to make the parting easier.

"Here, Son, here is five dollars in American money. That is all the government will let you take out of the country." They had arrived at customs where an agent checked him carefully.

"Mama, when are you coming to be with me in the United States?" Luz could see that tears were beginning to well up in his eyes.

"Hurry now! Go through the gate," Luz replied, unable to restrain the tears that were rolling down her own cheeks. Looking through the window she saw Marco start down the runway to where a Cubana Airlines Clipper was waiting to take him away from her. Perhaps she would never see him again.

After Marco went to the United States, Luz busied herself with the distribution of an anti-Castro newspaper titled *Cuba Libre* that was printed in the house of one of her friend's right there in Mérida. This made her feel that she was doing everything she could to fight the Castro regime and hasten the day when Marco could be reunited with them. She understood that Aurelio was a very committed and dedicated surgeon and had been able to make the transition from providing medical care for generals and politicos in the Batista government to the *commandantes* and local chiefs in the communist regime. He was simply too much involved with his surgical practice to be interested in politics. His practice was flourishing and he provided a very good living for them with all the luxuries they had always been accustomed to enjoying.

It was unfortunate that Marco could not stay in Cuba and go to the university where his mother received her licentiate in philosophy and Aurelio his medical degree and specialization in surgery. Now Marco would grow up in a foreign country speaking a foreign tongue. She had studied English at the university and had tried to teach Marco a few words before his sudden departure.

One night when Luz went to her cell meeting, she learned that something really big was planned. That night Aurelio had gone to San Clemente hospital where one of his patients needed him. So she slipped unnoticed out of the house and drove in their old Chrysler—they refused to buy one of those cheap Russian cars—to the secret and hidden destination where the cell meeting was to take place. Continually moving from place to place so that no one would suspect they were anything but a group of casual friends who got together from time to time, they never met in the same home twice. She was shocked to hear their leader say:

"We are going to blow up the electric plant on the Bahía at Puerto Nuevo." Jorge, a heavyset middle-aged man of about fifty, was very enthusiastic as he looked around to see what effect his words were having on the cell members.

Another member, Roberto, a dentist by profession rose to his feet and asked, "Are we capable of doing this? Do we have the necessary knowledge? I think that is too much for us to do," he said emphatically looking around to get support for his opinion.

Obviously it was too much, but they decided to go through with it. Since Luz had a large car, it was decided that she would drive the people involved in the plot to Puerto Nuevo. After driving around in circles a few times, they finally found the electric plant. Jorge and the others managed to place the bomb in an open portico between two sections of the building. As soon as the bomb was put in place, they ran back to the car, and she drove them a few blocks away to where they planned to detonate it.

The bomb never went off. A small aircraft was flying over head, and it caused an alarm to sound. Suddenly a police car was gaining on them and was just two or three cars behind them. She slowed the car and stopped at a traffic light.

"Hurry, get out of the car, all of you, and run before the police catch you," Luz urged. They did not have to be asked twice, but disappeared into the twisted labyrinth of downtown Mérida, where they could quickly get lost.

Another police car was coming toward her. She was caught between the two.

"Get out of the car, the military policeman snapped.

"Stand beside the car with hands on your head," a second soldier commanded.

Although she was terrified, the thought that caused her the most concern was what Aurelio would think of this. She had not even left a note telling him where she had gone. He had warned her, begged her, so many times not to get involved with the resistance. Now all his worries had finally become a reality.

Frisking her to see if she carried a concealed weapon, the soldier began running his hands all over her body. Then they proceeded to drive her and her car to a police station.

"We saw your friends plant the bomb at the electric plant. Tell us their names and we will make it easy for you." The military policeman clipped his words as he spoke.

"Please call my husband," she asked politely. "He is Dr. Aurelio Lamadrid."

"Tells us the names."

She kept silent.

"We have ways to deal with people who won't talk," the man in charge sneered at her.

They put her in a small jail cell with a very bright light bulb hanging from the ceiling.

"Take off your clothes," the man in charge, a thin and wiry mulatto, commanded.

When she did not budge, but remained standing quietly in front of him, he struck her with the back of his hand on her face.

"I said, take off your clothes."

She remained unmoved.

He ripped her clothes from her slender frame. Leering at her naked body, he patted her on the rump and commented, "A good looking bitch for someone your age." He began to reach for her breasts.

"Stop," the other policeman commanded, "We don't have time for that now." His face twisted into a grinning smile. "That can come later. Now we have to search her."

What more could they do to humiliate and search her? Luz wondered. Then she remembered hearing about other women who had been strip-searched. They made them crouch down with their legs spread apart to see if they were possibly hiding anything up inside of them. "Please, God," she prayed, "not that."

Just then the policeman at the desk came into the cell. "You guys have to go right way there is an alarm at the Hotel Sevilla. They need back up."

The two policemen that were searching her immediately left the area.

"Thank, God," she whispered under her breath. Surveying the cell, she saw that it was about four meters by six in size. There was a concrete slab to serve as a bed. A guard came and handed her a bag of rags and told her to sleep on it. There were no curtains to provide privacy and some men in the cell across from hers were staring at her as she quickly put on her clothes. There was nothing in the cell except a hole of about eight inches in diameter in the pavement—that was the toilet—out of which were crawling a couple of large fat roaches. "God, help me," she prayed." Her parents, good Catholics had taught her to believe in God, but she had never really gotten to know Him. Now prayer was all she had to protect her. What would happen when the men returned?

10
Enrique Mutante

He was proud to be a Caraqueño. Even though they did live in one of the shantytowns south of Caracas, he could jump on a bus and in ten minutes be at the metro station and be whisked away into the city. He loved Caracas—the tall skyscrapers and the beautiful parks where he liked to go with Roxana after Mass on Sundays at the cathedral in the corner of Bolívar Plaza. He had been going out with Roxana for about two years, and his mother hoped that maybe they would get married, but the idea of marrying the girl and spending his life with her just did not appeal to him. Some essential ingredient was lacking in their relationship.

He wanted to be like his father Lino Alberto Mutante one of the respected local politicos. Although he had never met him, he was proud of his father. He had seen him a couple times at political rallies and heard him speak, but never actually talked to him. At least he had his father's name. His older brothers and sisters who had all left the home he shared with Encarna their mother did not even know who their fathers were, and they all shared their mother's last name.

His mother was a hard working woman, aged beyond her fifty years, and had never been fortunate enough to marry. She had been beautiful once, otherwise she would never have attracted the attention of Lino Mutante and bore his son. The long string of children she brought into the world had an assortment of fathers. That was also a way to get some money for daily living. No two of the six children resembled each other. He wondered if his mother even knew who fathered each child. But he knew who his father was, and he hoped in his heart that someday his father would acknowledge him and accept him as a son.

In spite of her somewhat loose life—she honestly thought some man would eventually marry her—she was a devout Catholic who never missed Mass on Sundays and had her house filled with all kinds of statues of saints. The largest one was the Virgen de Coromoto at the entrance of the small house. Inside the modest home there was a wide array of saints—St. Michael the Archangel, Saint Philomena, St. Rita, the patroness of the impossible, and more. She saw to it that all her children received the sacraments up through confirmation. She would never have sex with a man without first devoutly making the sign of the cross followed by the recitation of the Our Father, the Hail Mary and the Glory Be. Afterwards she carefully washed up while reciting the act of contrition.

Enki wanted to be the way he pictured his father to be and the way his mother described him—well-mannered, eloquent, and cosmopolitan. Once he had gone to the upscale Las Mercedes neighborhood just to look at the house where his father lived with his wife and daughters. Although his father did not acknowledge him, he had provided for his education and made it possible for Enrique to attend Central University and study economics, a field that held little interest for him. He studied it simply because Lino had insisted that he do so when he provided the money for the university. What really interested him was the Society for a Traditional Church, which he joined while a student there.

Encarna, his mother, would never have been able to provide him with an education. Although most people in Caracas were experiencing prosperity from the American dollars pouring in because of the oil boom, she was quite poor and no longer able to attract a man.

"What would you like to do with your life, Enki?" his mother asked, as she cleaned up the dishes from the supper of *Reinas Pepiadas, arepas,* corn pancakes, stuffed with chopped meat and avocado, that she cooked for them.

Before answering, he put on the shirt that she had ironed for him to wear to the meeting of the Society for a Traditional Church that night.

"I like preaching. I preach at the meetings of the Society and people say I am good at it," he replied while tying his shoelaces, as he got ready to go into the city.

"Enki, why don't you become a priest then?" Encarna urged. She handed him his shirt and patted him affectionately on the cheek that bore the long scar he got street fighting when he was a teen. "You would make a good priest," she commented, as she brushed back his straight black hair from his forehead "You have always been a good boy. And I would be so proud of you, if you became a priest."

"That is not the life for me," he said flatly and hurried to the door. "The bishops and priests are ruining the Church today—that is what the Blessed Virgin said at Garabandal." He knew that he could never become a priest, because he was a bastard—the illegitimate son of Lino Alberto Mutante! They don't ordain bastards, but he did not want to tell that to his mother. He was not aware that Church law had changed in that regard. Also, Canon Law has a peculiarity, it does not really matter what the rule dictates, because the "competent" authority can issue a "dispensation," an "annulment", an "abrogation," or simply a "decree" invalidating whatever is written. The clergy actually has plenty of bastards.

He rushed from the house and in twenty minutes he was in Plaza Bolívar, not far from the building where the Society held its meetings. Night was falling and the shadows were deepening as he arrived at the cathedral in the corner of the Plaza. He loved the old colonial church because it was a place of great traditions. With all the skyscrapers, posh hotels, and upscale restaurants, Caracas was losing its identity, but in the old cathedral he felt at home. As he glanced around the interior, he glimpsed a few people praying before the statue of the Blessed Virgin, and he noted some others praying in the Bolívar family chapel. Another group was waiting in line to go to confession. He knelt in the back of the church and sighed, as he took in the sight of the magnificent Baroque gilded altar.

Slowly Enrique crossed himself and began examining his conscience. Let's get the mortal sins out of the way first, he decided. He thought back over the experiences of the past few days. He had made love to Margot on the desk in his office after the Wednesday night prayer meeting. Then there was Elsa whom he gently seduced after the Sunday night meeting. She had come into his office to ask him a question and wound up on his desktop like Margot. Of course, they were starved for love and he was just trying to help them. He had learned at the university that many psychiatrists make love to their women patients for the same reason. But it was *wrong*, very wrong to go to that cheap dirty place and look at all that pornography on Thursday. He especially felt guilty about looking at the porn films of children. For some reason that he could not understand, and which his psychology courses at the university never explained, he was sexually attracted to children. Yes, it was wrong.

No one else was waiting to enter the confessional, so Enki crossed himself, rose from his pew, and entered the box. Hurriedly he confessed his sins, made an act of contrition, and ran out the door of the church, saying his penance of three Hail Marys on the way.

Because they were dissatisfied with the changes and turmoil the Second Vatican Council had caused, many people attended the meetings of the Society for a Traditional Church. Trying to hold on to their faith, they liked to come to the conventional meetings Enrique led, using the music and the ways of the Pentecostals to attract people to his services, but preaching the time-honored faith. The Council had downgraded the Blessed Virgin, not even giving her a separate document, but including her in the document on the Church. Enrique could not understand that, especially when the Mother of God kept appearing and calling people to repentance. It was so exciting—all the appearances of Mary at Garabandal! How he would like to go himself and visit San Sebastián de Garabandal and meet the young people to whom Our Lady of Mount Carmel appeared! He loved to preach and tell his little flock at the Society of the dire warnings that she prophesied will take place if the world does not change and of how the divine eye appeared above her, as if to emphasize the dreadful events to come. He also told them of how she warned that many cardinals, bishops and priests are on the road to perdition and are taking many souls with them. He knew that was true because the Second Vatican Council had undermined the ancient faith, and that is why the Society for the Traditional Church was founded.

After hurrying though the bustling streets of the great city, he reached the meeting place where a dozen people were already waiting for him to unlock the door and begin the singing and prayers. He had established a branch of the Society for people who were not affiliated with the university and would never have gone to the campus to attend meetings.

After opening the door, he rushed to his office, located in a room in back of the meeting hall, where the walls were lined with devotional books, mostly dealing with apparitions of the Blessed Mother, for he bought as many of them as he could. Besides his Marian collection, there were rows of musical books containing the popular music that the Pentecostals used so effectively to draw large crowds to their services. He had a good voice and his singing was the thing that most attracted people to his meetings.

Sitting down at his large desk that served him in so many ways, he thought briefly of Margot and Elsa who had recently benefited from it and smiled. Picking up some music and his guitar, he headed for the podium to begin the evening program.

Everything proceeded as usual. After handing out the words to the songs, he began with singing and inviting the congregation to join him. Something very unusual happened that night when he made the altar call for people to come forth and give their hearts to the Lord.

That is when he met Yo-Lin—Yo-Lin Sin. Hardly the type one would expect to see at such a service, she came forth and knelt with the others who had gathered before him. Older than most of the people there, a beautiful Chinese woman—of average height with hair the color of ebony held in place with ivory combs—she was dressed flamboyantly in an extremely short red oriental tunic that had a dragon embroidered across the front. The dress clung to her body in such a manner as to reveal all her amply padded curves. He couldn't believe his eyes—she had breasts like melons! He noticed that a few tears were trickling down her cheeks, as she daubed at her jade green eyes with a lace handkerchief.

As the meeting was ending, he decided to approach the woman and talk with her to learn more about what brought her to the Society.

"Buenas noches," he began.

"Hola!" she replied and flashed a big smile at him and fluttered her artificial eyelashes.

He welcomed her to the Society for a Traditional Church, and they continued making small talk, exchanging introductory information. He learned that she had been born in Shanghai, but had come to Caracus with her parents when she was a baby. Consequently she spoke Spanish like a native of Venezuela and her English, he later learned, was excellent. When he noticed that all the others had gone and they were alone, he inquired, "You gave your heart to the Lord tonight?"

"*Si*, and I have a confession to make to you," she said insistently.

"I am not a priest. I don't forgive sins," he replied, "but if you still want to tell me, I promise you that I will keep everything you say in the strictest confidence." He noticed that her eye makeup was smudged from her tears and from daubing her eyes, but her jade green eyes were sparkling and lively.

"I have been a boss in the Chinese drug cartel in its Venezuela branch for many years." She blurted it out, as if she were spitting out something very sour. Her mouth seemed to pucker around the words.

"I understand," he replied gently and softly, "but you really should think of ways to pay God for your sins and change your life."

"I simply cannot do that," she protested as she placed her hand on his arm. "I can't explain, but I can't do that," she replied with determination.

"Perhaps in time, you will be able to do it," he said doubting that it would ever happen." He noticed that she was wearing an emerald that must have cost a fortune. Her face took on a somber and downcast appearance, and her eyes avoided his. Suddenly, her expression brightened and she gave him a furtive glance and said, "I will give you large donations for your work here." She waited for his response.

He considered what she was offering and said invitingly,

"Come on back to my office; we can talk there privately and no one will disturb us."

As he made his way to the little room at the back of the meeting hall, she followed him eagerly. When he offered her a chair opposite his desk, he knew that he would have to go to confession again soon. The Lord would understand and forgive Him. That is what His business was—forgiving sins. What he did not know was to what depths his involvement with her would lead him in the years to come.

11
Renato

The thought of moving to Rosanada caused Renato great distress. Having written a superb dissertation, "The Uses of the Canopy and the Tintinabulum in the Medieval Liturgies," he had every right to expect to be granted an assignment in Rome where he could further his career. Nevertheless, he had been able to thank his superior for his new assignment and even pretended to be joyful about it. When he told Father Lupo he was leaving, he really did not seem to care.

He pushed his big-framed glasses that had slid down his nose back up where they belonged. In a few minutes his plane would be landing in Rosanada, so he drained the last few drops of his brandy, put his tray in the stowed away position, and made his chair upright. The captain's voice came over the loud speaker:

"Welcome to Rosanada. It is a clear day and the temperature is 98 degrees. We thank you for traveling with us and hope to see you again soon on another flight."

Renato also hoped he would be going on another flight soon—one that would take him back to Rome.

Two Brothers of the Shepherds of the Lord were waiting in the terminal to greet him and take him to the college seminary where he was to live. It was August, and he expected it to be hot. After all, Rome is hot in August, if you have to remain there, and he was accustomed to that.

He went through immigration and customs. Finally the automatic doors that led out of the terminal opened on to what some people described as "The Enchanted City where everything is possible." He was stunned. The suffocating heat and the excessive humidity astounded him. When a whiff of exhaust fumes from a bus hit him, he felt as if he were going to choke, causing a spasm to contract his entire slender body, shaking his slight frame. The two brothers sent to meet him took him by the arms and, almost carrying him, brought him to their car.

"I'm stifling," he groaned once inside the car. "The heat is unbearable!"

They turned on the car's air conditioning system. "You will get used to the heat, Father Renato," Brother Giovanni said. "It takes a little time though."

"*Io, qui non ce la faccio,*" was the thought that came to his mind, but out loud he said instead very piously, "I can do all things in Christ who strengthens me."

When they arrived at the seminary, Monsignor La Fayette greeted him with holy indifference, annoyed that he spoke English with a heavy Italian accent. He was pleased that the seminarians gathered around him and tried to talk to him and get acquainted.

The days went hurrying by and the students welcomed their new professor. They liked him and he liked them. They resembled him in many ways, and he fit into their idea of what a teacher of liturgy should be. Many of them looked and acted as he did when he was their age.

When he had been in Rosanada only a few months, Renato founded the Saint Thomas Restoration Movement, a group dedicated to the affirmation of Aristotelian-Thomistic theology, the promotion of the Latin Mass, and above all the encouragement of Marian devotions. He enjoyed his work with the St. Thomas Movement, for it provided him with him an opportunity to preach about the Marian apparitions that were so dear to his heart, and it gave him the chance to meet other people with similar interests. Some of them were devout wealthy women, a few others were ultra-conservative men and some seminarians, perhaps a number of whom were homosexuals, he imagined.

When he had only been in Rosanada six months, Archbishop Lingam made him a master of ceremonies, permitting him to serve at all the ceremonies at which he presided at the cathedral and also those elsewhere when the archbishop's private secretary and his regular master of ceremonies could not be present. When he received this position, Renato felt he was actually beginning to enjoy his life in Rosanada, in spite of having to speak English all the time and having to learn Spanish to communicate with the large Hispanic population of the archdiocese. He had no reason to believe that the future held anything for him except a good life. Soon, however he began to wonder about that.

12
Enki

Yo-Lin kept coming every Wednesday and Sunday night to his prayer meetings for the next month or so, even bringing with her once her two daughters, Tang Lang, a very unsightly woman, and Yin-Lu, whom Yo-Lin told him was a nymphomaniac. Enki soon learned that Yin-Lu took after her mother in that respect. And faithful to her word, Yo-Lin dropped large donations in the collection basket. With the contributions Yo-Lin gave him, Enki was able to buy a new guitar and an electronic organ to improve the music at the meetings. Continuing to linger after the services were over, Yo-Lin went with him to his office for their usual private session.

One night at one of their private encounters in his office, she was very nervous and seemed really upset.

"What's the trouble, Yo-Lin?" He asked as he sat down across his desk from her.

When she dug frantically through her large overly stuffed purse, he saw that she was carrying a revolver. Pulling out a piece of paper and a pen, she handed them to him, saying:

"Give me your phone number, so I can call you. I think the police are on to me. They arrested my boyfriend Lon Chiang and are holding him and trying to make him talk." Fear shone in her emerald green eyes. With her forehead deeply furrowed with wrinkles, worry and anxiety made her true age apparent. Enki figured she was well past fifty.

Enki wrote his phone number on the paper and handed it back to her. Grabbing it, she stuck it into her purse, stood up, and said: "I can't stay tonight for our usual evening together, I have to go. She took a handful of money from her purse. "I might not see you again for awhile. So I want to give you this."

It was a stack of one hundred dollar bills in US currency. Enrique looked at her, and she must have noticed the fear and doubt that he was experiencing, because she quickly added: "It's clean. It has been laundered. I wouldn't give you dirty money that would get you in trouble. You can trust me." She smiled and kissed him lightly on the lips and rushed out the door, with the fragrance of her jasmine perfume lingering in the room. "I'll call you, when I can."

A few days later, he read in the newspaper that she had been arrested. Her boyfriend who took the responsibility for their drug dealings got a ten-year sentence in a Venezuelan prison.

When Yo-Lin phoned him a few months later, he was surprised to learn that she was in Rosanada.

"Enki," she purred, "I want you to come up here."

"I'd love to come. I think it would help me get ahead with my career to be there," he replied, while waiting for her to explain.

"I am now an American resident and I have a job, working for myself and doing some other projects. I'm quite respectable now. I have an apartment on the river in Rosanada and a place where you can stay. I want you to come for a couple weeks and I'll introduce you to the leaders of some prayer meetings and I am sure you will be able to preach and sing for them. You will be a big success."

"Sure, Yo-Lin, I'd love to come and spend some time with you. But I don't have the money for the trip." He knew she would come through with the cash.

"Not to worry, Enki, I'll wire you money tonight."

A week later he landed at the Rosanada International Airport where Yo-Lin was waiting in a red convertible to pick him up.

"My place is in Willow Harbour," she said with pride. "It is the best address in all of Rosanada. The rich and famous live there, and so do the top socialites."

Having not yet learned that one's worth in the United States is determined by how much money one has, he could not imagine that they would accept her into their society.

As they sped up the river road to Willow Harbor, he was struck by the change in her appearance. She looked ten years younger. "What have you done to yourself?" he inquired. She looked thinner in some places and more padded in others.

"The grace of God and a little Botox can work wonders for a girl."

"You look great, Yo-Lin."

Before the day was over she told him that she was now a secret agent for the Venezuelan government, and they had made her a resident of the United States so that she could inform on the Drug Cartel and its operations. He was stunned to learn that she had fallen so low as to continue her work with the Caracas cartel and was even then working on a very big cocaine deal, her own "job" that was going to make her rich and bring millions to the Venezuelan government.

Enki had never seen such a luxurious apartment as the one to which she took him with its richly embroidered tapestries, black lacquered furniture, and very deep jade green carpets—all obviously imported from the Orient. He soaked for an hour in the hot tub in his private bathroom. Never had he seen such thick and absorbent towels, he mused, as he dried himself off and prepared to stretch out on the kingsize bed and take a nap, before he had to dress to go with her that very evening to a meeting of the church group that she attended.

As he climbed onto the bed, he discovered in the bookcase headboard that there were a lot of photos of children. Upon closer investigation, he saw that they were very erotic. Not in the least surprised to find such items in Yo-Lin's possession, he went to the door of his room and called,

"Hey, Yo-Lin, what's all this stuff in here?"

She came at once into his room to see what he was talking about."

"Oh that," she exclaimed, "is a sideline of mine. I make a good bit of money on it. If you are into that sort of thing, help yourself. Lon Chiang, my boyfriend, used to distribute it." She patted her ebony hair and rearranged one of the ivory combs that held it piled high upon her head. Pulling a long Egyptian cigarette from a gold case, she lit it with a matching gold lighter.

"Tell me about your boyfriend," Enki suggested.

"Which one? I've had a lot, but I have never married."

"Well, the last one."

"He is in prison. It was a question of either him or me. That did not leave me much choice, so I testified against him." She sat down beside him on the bed and blew a puff of smoke playfully in his face.

He studied her face carefully. It was hard and callous under layers of makeup. Although she used all the cosmetic arts she could, she reminded him of a cobra swaying before him the way they move back and forth just before striking their victim. There was nothing really womanly about her, and he knew for a fact that he could only trust her about as much as one could trust a snake.

She picked up a few of the photos that were on the bookcase headboard and said, "If you are into this sort of thing, I have lots of them. Top quality. And since you are my friend, I say, help yourself."

"Thanks, Yo-Lin, that is really great of you. Now tell me about this meeting we are going to tonight." He reached over and took one of the Egyptian cigarettes from her case and lit it with her lighter. Then he blew a puff of smoke in her face.

"I have been going to these meetings, because they are good for my image. They are a good cover and they give me an air of respectability." She kicked off her red sandals with spike heals and stretched out on the kingsize bed beside him. Because he knew she expected him to satisfy her sexually, he tried to comply, knowing that the woman was insatiable. He was also well aware that she tried to seduce every man she met and was not averse to having sex with women, including her maid.

After a light supper, fixed by Colette, the maid, who seemed to be devoted to Yo-Lin, they hurried off in her convertible with his guitar on the back seat, so that Enki could meet Renato and sing for the St. Thomas Restoration Movement. On the way down the river road, Enki asked her to tell him more about Renato.

"Oh, he likes to preach sermons about the apparitions of the Virgin. He especially likes to preach about Garabandal." She touched up her crimson lipstick in the mirror of her gold compact.

Perhaps he would find a kindred soul in Renato. "What else can you tell me about him?"

"He does not seem to be interested in sex." Yo-Lin sighed deeply. "I took him out for dinner at a very exclusive Russian restaurant in a *salon privé*. I gave him the best wine they had and got him really loaded, but I could not interest him in sex when I brought him home here. I think he is a queer." She shook her head. "Oh well, you win some and you lose some."

By this time, they had arrived at the auditorium where the St. Thomas Restoration Movement held its meetings. When Yo-Lin crawled out of her sporty convertible, Enki noticed that her jade green tunic was so short that it left practically nothing to the imagination.

When Enki saw the Reverend Renato Naburus Del'Ano, he noted his delicate facial features and his carefully manicured, long tapering fingers, and saw the way he walked and his various gestures and decided that Yo-Lin was right. Renato was a faggot. There was no doubt in his mind about that, but that did not matter to him. If Renato could help him get ahead in church ministry, he could play that game too.

Because he wanted to make a name for himself as a singer, he figured the easiest and the best way for him to achieve that goal was church ministry, because it was easy to break into. All you had to do was get a chance to sing to a group and you were on your way. Although he knew that the St. Thomas Restoration Society would not pay him, he was satisfied and expected nothing, because he simply wanted to use them as a springboard to better and more lucrative possibilities. Since he was good at preaching, he hoped to exercise his charm over them with one of his sermons, thinking that perhaps they might even give him an offering out of the collection if they liked him.

When he heard Renato preach, Enki became truly excited, because he told about some apparitions of the Virgin in Egypt that he had never before heard about.

From the podium, Renato signaled the approximately two hundred people to be silent, before he began speaking. Although he spoke Spanish with an Italian accent, Enki could follow him quite well as Renato switched back and forth from addressing the crowd for a few minutes in Spanish and then giving an English version of what he had just said.

"Tonight, I have a special treat for you. I want to share the appearances of the Blessed Mother in Egypt with you." A hum of approval and enthusiasm went through the room.

"The Virgin Mary appeared at Zaitun in Cairo on April 2, 1968 on the roof of a church," he began with enthusiasm. As these appearances continued every night for several hours and lasted for two and a half years, thousands of people saw her there with an angel standing behind her. There was a very strange phenomenon that took place during these apparitions. Although it was night, doves were flying around her, and doves never fly at night." The people murmured their amazement at the events he was relating to them.

He paused and looked at them all and his glance fell on Enki who fairly beamed his approval.

"At times she was dressed like a queen and wore a crown. Sometimes she brought the Christ child with her." Obviously delighted with the response his preaching was receiving, Renato continued: "Egyptian TV even broadcast the apparitions. Hundreds of photographers snapped photos of the Blessed Mother. Even the famous Egyptian President Gamal Abdel Nasser, a self-confessed Marxist, saw the Blessed Mother."

Seeing that he had truly captivated his audience, he headed for his favorite topic—returning the Church to the way it was during the days of Pius XII. "If we do not return to the traditional Church and the Latin Mass, we are in for calamitous and disastrous times. The Blessed Virgin warned us at Garabandal that bishops and priests would destroy Holy Mother Church. Now we are seeing it happen. She comes to warn us and no one seems to be paying attention, except for small groups like ours."

Mopping his face with his handkerchief, because the evening was quite warm and the building was not air conditioned, and with perspiration dripping down his soft effeminate cheeks, Renato concluded: "Now, if you have any questions or comments, I welcome them."

Realizing that this was the opportunity he had been awaiting, Enki rose to his feet and said, "With your permission, Father Del'Ano, I would like to tell the people about apparitions of Mary that have been occurring in my native Venezuela this very year."

Enki could see that he had touched a responsive cord in Renato's heart. They were going to be friends. Enki would see to that.

"Please do. Tell us." A murmur of voices around the room responded enthusiastically saying: "Yes, tell us."

Eagerly Enrique mounted the podium as, with hungry eyes and itching ears, the people waited eagerly for what he would say. "I am going to tell you the miraculous story of Maria Esperanza who was born in Barrancas in 1928 on the feast of St. Cecilia. I felt an immediate attraction to her as soon as I learned she was born on St. Cecilia's day, because this saint is the saint for musicians and I love music. After I finish telling you about Maria Esperanza, I will sing you a song, if you let me." As Renato shook his head in approval, the people in the audience applauded loudly.

Glancing at Yo-Lin, who was beaming with pride that the man she had brought to the meeting was becoming a real sensation, Enki launched into his story.

"Her birth was so very difficult that her mother offered her to Mary in exchange for a safe delivery. When the child was only five she saw a lady rise up out of the Orinoco River with a rose in her hand."

"Aaah," the crowd exclaimed.

"No, it was not the Blessed Mother," Enki explained, but rather St. Thérèse of Lisieux, and she threw a rose to Maria Esperanza. However, later when she was recovering from pneumonia, Maria Esperanza did see the Blessed Virgin. It was not a vision, but a real corporeal apparition." He waited for this to be assimilated by the astounded people in the auditorium. He was not disappointed, and as they waited in anticipation for him to continue his story, he brushed his shaggy black hair back off his face and daubed his forehead with a handkerchief.

"Later St. Thérèse, the Little Flower, appeared to her again and threw her another rose and, when she reached to catch it, she noticed that her hand was bloody—she had received the stigmata." So intently did they listen, the audience, unable to get enough of his story, were as hypnotized. "St. Thérèse told her to marry and have a family, and so she did. She had seven children."

After enumerating wonder after wonder about the incredible Maria Esperanza, he spoke of how Mary came to her. "The Blessed Virgin appeared to her this very year under the title of "Reconciler of Peoples and Nations." Warming up to his subject, he related the many warnings that the Virgin had given Maria Esperanza that either the world had to repent or suffer greatly. Looking at Renato for approval, he said, "We must restore the faith to the way it has always been." Concluding his talk so he could let them hear his beautiful singing voice, he said: "So I tell you, if we are going to have peace in this world, it will only come when we listen to the Mother of God and do what she tells us. Now if you let me, I will sing to you one of the most beautiful hymns in the world."

Picking up his guitar and strumming it softly, Enki sang in Latin: *Ave Maria, gratia plena, Dominus tecum; benedicta tu in mulieribus, et benedictus fructus ventris tui, Jesus. Sancta Maria, Mater Dei, ora pro nobis peccatoribus, nunc et in hora mortis nostrae. Amen.*

The applause he received was thunderous. When the people cried for more, he sang a popular Spanish religious song, *"Pon aceite en mi lámpara, Señor."* Although they liked the lively music and the lyrics and begged him to sing more, he decided he would make them wait for that. He knew he had won their hearts, made a friend of Renato Del'Ano, and had a future in Rosanada."

Before they left the meeting, Renato came over to them, shook his hand and welcomed Enki warmly to the St. Thomas Restoration Society. "I can see we are kindred spirits, Please come often to our meetings." Enki shook Renato's limp hand while thinking, "I can be AC/DC if that is what it takes to get ahead here." Aloud he said, "My pleasure. You can count on it. I will come often." He knew Renato would be an invaluable help in the future.

When they got back to Yo-Lin's apartment in Willow Harbor, he declined Yo-Lin's invitation to join her in smoking opium, when she settled down beside him in the kingsize bed and drifted off into opiate dreams. Enrique was content to enjoy his favorite entertainment—child pornography, a pastime that was bound to get him in deep trouble sooner or later.

13
Luz

Rats crawling up out of the sewage hole in the floor of the jail kept Luz awake much of the night. One even jumped up on the concrete slab where she was lying really frightening her so much that she was afraid to fall asleep. Because they would not phone her husband and let him know what had happened to her, she was frantic. Aurelio would be terribly worried.

At six in the morning a guard came and took away the bag of nylon rags that they had given her to put on the concrete slab that served as a bed. She had been able to use the makeshift toilet in the floor when the inmates across from her were all sound asleep.

In order to appear respectable, she tried to adjust her clothing that the guards had ripped from her the night before. About seven in the morning, a guard brought her a cup of tea and a piece of dry toast, which she refused, unable to eat or drink anything as she worried about what they would do to her.

She did not have long to wait. The guards came and put chains and shackles on her legs and handcuffs around her wrists.

"OK, *Puta*. Come with me" he snarled.

She followed him as he led her to a car in front of the police station.

"Get in!" he snapped and began to push her into the back seat.

They drove for hours on what she recognized was the highway leading westward. Hour after hour went by. She was puzzled by the way he drove. When they came to a hill, he turned the engine off and put the car in neutral, only to start it up again when they began to climb the next hill. It was his way of saving on gasoline.

As they got nearer to Havana, she began to realize that he was taking her to *Manto Negro*, one of the very worst of the more than one hundred prisons that Castro had built. When the tyrant came to power, there were only five prisons in all of Cuba; now you could barely count them all.

As they approached *Manto Negro*, she saw an impressive looking building in the distance that looked like a fortress with its few windows covered with iron bars. Upon closer inspection, she discovered that it was set on marshy ground, flooded with stagnant and fetid water that buzzed with flies and mosquitoes. Later she learned that the swamp was caused by sewage from the toilets and kitchen flowing into the prison yard.

Once inside the prison, she was horrified to see the deplorable living conditions of the prisoners. Although they put her in an extremely crowded ward with fifteen other women, she was fortunate to get a lower bed, because the former occupant had died during the previous night, leaving it vacant. The beds were bolted to the floor and could not be moved.

The ward had only a hole in the concrete floor for a toilet and a big stick to force the excrement into it. For some reason that she did not know, the other prisoners called the toilet "*el polaco.*" Coming from the ceiling there was a water pipe about two inches in diameter just above *el polaco.* As she was entering the ward, they turned the water on, and it came out with such force that it sprayed the entire cell, soaking everything and everybody.

Although there was a sink in the room for washing clothes, a woman was crouching on the floor laundering a few things in the water that came gushing out of the pipe.

"*Hola!*" Luz greeted the woman and sat down on her bed. She learned that the woman's name was Amalia and that she was in prison for buying a pig's foot on the black market.

"How long have you been here?" Luz inquired.

The woman who had a kindly face and was about twenty-four years old replied, "Four years."

"Four years for buying a pig's foot on the black market?"

"That is all I did." The woman picked up one of the garments she was washing and wrung it out. "I got the pig's foot for my son. It was his birthday and he wanted it very much. He is only eight year's old." Sadness came over the woman gentle features. She hung the garment over the iron bed frame to dry.

"Does your husband come here to visit you? Do they let him come to see you?" Luz was hoping she could find a way to get word to her husband that she was in *Manto Negro.*

"Yes, he is coming this weekend."

Since the other inmates in the ward were staring at them, Luz did not dare to give the woman her husband's phone number, but she knew she would find a way to do so. The occasion arose when the prisoners of her ward were led into the yard where they were told to take the sun for twenty minutes. This was a ritual that was done three times a week. Once they were outside, Luz walked beside Amalia and gave her the wristwatch she was wearing. The guards had overlooked it and let her continue wearing it.

"What's this for," Amalia asked suspiciously.

"I want you to ask your husband to phone mine and let him know where I am. He doesn't know what happened to me. And tell him to ask my husband to bring me some things. Would you do that?" Luz's eyes pleaded with Amalia for help.

"I can't give him a paper with your phone number. They will strip search me, even looking through my hair, before they let me see my husband. No. No, I cannot do it. They would put me in a solitary punishment cell if they caught me trying to sneak something out." Even though Amalia tried to walk away from her, Luz stayed close behind her.

"I will tell you my phone number and you can memorize it. No problem. It will be easy. There is no way they can know about it." Luz smiled her most reassuring and charming way at Amalia.

"I'll think about it? How much did the watch cost?" She examined the timepiece carefully. The gold glittered in the sunlight enticing the girl to accept it.

"It cost at least four thousand pesos. My husband gave it to me for my forty-fifth birthday." It is yours. I really would appreciate your help."

Amalia slipped the watch onto her wrist with delight. "Ok, I'll do it."

129

It was not long after that when Aurelio came to the prison. Although it was a long drive from Mérida to Havana and the Black Mantle, it was a drive he would continue to make once every week. Conjugal visits were permitted in a certain dimly lit room that afforded a small amount of privacy, but a guard was always within earshot.

When Luz saw Aurelio approaching the conjugal room, she broke into tears. "Oh, my darling, what have I done to us? I am so sorry." She felt his strong arms encircle her and pull her to himself.

"Sssh," he said, "just let me hold you for a few minutes. I thought I had lost you forever." "I couldn't live without you! Without you, I would have no reason to live anymore."

She looked up into his kindly brown eyes and pressed a kiss on his cheek. "Tell me about our son. Has there been any news from him recently?" Anxiety was written in her eyes as she spoke.

"He is fine. It won't be much longer before he is ordained a Catholic priest. He is going to be ordained by the pope!"

"Amazing! I did not think he would go through with it."

"Yes, it is amazing. I have decided I am going to learn something about the Catholic faith, since our son is going to be a priest. "Let's sit down on these chairs and talk." He pointed to a couple of metal folding chairs with badly chipped paint and opened them up.

"I have brought you some things. I hope I got everything you need. I brought a mosquito net to keep you from getting bitten when you sleep at night, some anti-malaria medication, and some antibiotics. I also brought you some tablets that you can put in the drinking water to make it pure."

"Thank God! The water is filthy. We have to catch it in plastic bottles whenever they turn it on. It has live larvae in it. It doesn't do any good to complain. One woman complained and they said they would look into it, but they never did." Her eyes were filled with love as she drank in the features of her husband's face. It was so good to see him. It had only been a week since she had been brought here, but it seemed like a year.

"I also brought you some food. Here is a complete dinner." He handed her a carton. "You have to eat it now. They won't let you keep anything that is prepared or will perish. I also brought you some other things to eat. They said I could bring you a *jaba* of crackers, powdered milk, and other things that don't spoil." He handed her a metal container that resembled a bread-basket in which the food lay. She would keep it under her bed. The metal container would keep out the bugs.

Because the prison did not even provide them with soap or a sheet, Aurelio had brought her sheets and some toilet articles. He had thought of everything.

"How is the food here?" he asked.

"Vile! They serve the same thing twice a day for about three days until they run out of it." She knew she had brought her suffering upon herself; what grieved her was how much her husband was suffering because of her. When he left, she thought she would die inside. She tried to be brave, kissed him, gave him a big hug and he was gone.

The weeks crawled by as she lived from one visit to the next. Fighting broke out frequently among the women prisoners, some of whom were quite violent. Some of them were lesbians and they tried to poach on the younger women. Thank God, they left her alone. Some of the guards also tried to get familiar with the women prisoners. She was so serious they also left her alone. She tried to keep a low profile and remain peacefully free of any encroachment upon her person.

Aurelio told her he had hoped to get a lawyer who could help get her out, but that all the lawyers supported Castro, and he could not find one who would help. Perhaps, he suggested, he could get one of the *commandantes* who came to him for consultations to help free her.

The nights were the worst times in the ward. Some of the women were mentally deranged by their stay at *Manto Negro* and they would scream in their sleep and wake everyone. At night rats and roaches roamed everywhere with the big brown insects flying though the air in the dark. One hit her face, and she swatted it with her hand, causing it to fall dead on her sheet. Actually the mosquito net prevented it from touching her skin, but she felt its impact as it struck the net. Fortunately, Aurelio had provided her with antibiotics, because a rat actually bit her foot one night when it had become uncovered by the sheet. Although the antibiotics prevented an infection, her foot would always bear the scar of the rat bite.

Every night at about eleven, a guard would bring her the sheets that Aurelio provided and a sack of nylon rags to serve as a mattress. Every morning at about six, he would come and take them away again.

Breakfast—a very watery coffee and a stale piece of bread—was served about seven. Because the cooks wanted to leave early, lunch was served about two hours later, followed by dinner, before one could digest the lunch bilge water they called soup. Five or six hours later, hunger pangs would begin to gnaw at the women who went to bed hungry, if their families had not brought them crackers or powdered milk.

Although Luz was old enough to be Amalia's mother, the young woman continued to befriend her and even confide in her.

"They told me, I could see my son. I got some little things together for him." Amalia began to cry, wiped away her tears, and explained the cruel trick they played her. "When he was supposed to come, they told me, he wasn't coming. They just did that to torture me. It is an old trick they employ to damage us psychologically. You can't believe anything they say." Luz watched as tears began to well up again in the younger woman's eyes. Noticing that Amalia seemed nauseated in the mornings, Luz inquired as she patted Amalia on the hand:

"You seem sick today. Do you need some antibiotics? I have some. My husband is a physician."

"No, I don't need any. I am pregnant. I got pregnant on one of the conjugal visits I had with my husband." She sighed and studied Luz's face. "They are trying to force me to have an abortion, but I have refused and keep refusing. They cannot make me do it!" She said with determination.

"What will they do?" Luz asked sympathetically.

"Oh, what they have done to other women. When I am about five months pregnant, they will move me to the infirmary and make me stay there until the baby is born.

My husband will be able to claim the baby when it is five months old and take it home."

From that time on, Luz began sharing the food that Aurelio brought with Amalia, because the prison food was not enough for a pregnant woman. Amalia was so greatful that Luz would give her all she could eat.

Once when Aurelio came and they huddled up close together in the conjugal room, he began to talk about Marco. Aurelio's presence was such a comfort to Luz. He was tall—over six feet—and he exuded strength and comfort. "It is truly a gift from God that He has called our son to His service. I know it came as a surprise that he is going to be a Catholic priest—a Methodist minister would have been easier to understand." He smoothed his straight black hair in place and searched her eyes to see how she was responding to his conversation.

Slowly he continued, "I have been reading about the Catholic faith, as I told you I would. I had discussions with the parish priest who has also been instructing me." He stammered a bit before blurting out what he had done. "I am going to be received into the Roman Catholic Church this week. I like what I have learned and I want to share it with Marco and with you, Luz." He squeezed her hand in his and waited for her to answer.

"I would really like to please you and follow in your footsteps." She smiled at him and leaned over and kissed his cheek.

"Here is a catechism book that I got you. You can read it and if you like it, I will arrange for a priest to come talk to you. I found out from the prison official that you are allowed to see a priest once every three months."

"My faith is what has kept me alive in this awful place. I will be very happy to talk to him. Please arrange it." Luz was about to embark on the greatest journey of her life.

14
Marco

Although my flight from Rome was two hours late, my old classmate Father Pompeo dell'Anitra met me at the Rosanada International Airport and drove me to St. Mary Tudor, Queen of England, Church where he was an assistant to the pastor, Father James Stalker, that they say makes the best Bloody Mary in the archdiocese. I graciously accepted Fr. Stalker's invitation to stay in his rectory, since I had nowhere else to go. Since St. Mary Tudor's was one of the largest and most prestigious parishes of the archdiocese with a membership composed of some of Rosanada's most influential and powerful families, this was an impressive assignment for Pompeo.

Mail was waiting for me at Bloody Mary's, the name Pompeo affectionately gave to his parish, because I had given my father Pompeo's address. I was overjoyed to learn that a priest who was permitted to visit her every three months had received my mother back into the Catholic Church. Since she was not able to make her confession, because the prison guards were always listening to the prisoners' conversations when they had visitors, the priest had her make an act of contrition and gave her absolution, insisting that, as soon as it would be possible, she would make a full confession to a priest. She was then able to receive communion when the priest brought it to her in prison, giving her great consolation.

My immediate family now had the same faith! My father had been received into the Church during the preceding summer when I was in Rome.

At dinner I was able to become better acquainted with Monsignor Stalker, a very distinguished looking man with a well-trimmed beard that he tugged on when he was considering something. He was a very genial host that set a fine table. The dinner was delicious—steak and mashed potatoes as the main course.

"We are glad to have you with us, Marco." Monsignor Stalker said, as he took a sip of a refreshing, cool white wine. "I am anxious to hear about your experiences in Rome." He looked at me in anticipation.

"There is really not much to tell. I met a lot of people—a few cardinals, such as one from Poland—I believe his name was Cardinal Woytila. I liked him even though he gave me a good going over with his frosty blue eyes, before he smiled at me and warmly gave me his blessing. You probably never heard of him."

"I have," interrupted Pompeo impatiently always eager to monopolize every conversation. "He is one of the minor cardinals. As a matter of fact he is only a cardinal-deacon, the lowest category with the title of Saint Cesareo *in Palatio*. Nobody has had that title before. Comes from Poland. He's not really significant in the scheme of things in Rome." Obviously, Pompeo did not want me to have anything up on him. In spite of his fiercely competitive nature, I considered him a friend.

"Who else did you meet?" Monsignor Stalker asked with interest as he put his fork into his Caesar salad.

"*Entonces*," I thought a moment, "*Madre Teresa de Calcutta*." Pompeo had no comments to make about her.

Silently he ate his steak, seemingly distracted and not paying attention to what I was saying.

"A good lady." Monsignor exclaimed. "I tell you they will canonize her for sure. Just mark my words. But not to change the subject, I understand you do not have an assignment." He looked at me waiting for me to confirm or deny what he had just said.

"That is true, Jim. I have not been assigned anywhere."

"Well, Marco," he said paternally without patronizing me, "go see the VG. He will find something for you to do."

The VG—the vicar general—was Umberto Martini. The reception I received two days later in his office was chilling. His secretary, a very prim nun, showed me into his grandiose office that had a view of the Rosanada River and the city skyline.

Monsignor Martini, seated at his desk behind a stack of papers, did not rise when I came into the room, nor did he shake my hand. Rather he called out to me as soon as I came in, "What are you doing here? You are supposed to be in Rome?" His face puckered up in a sour expression.

"The Holy Year has come to an end, Monsignor." I was left standing in front of his desk, because he did not invite me to sit down.

"So! What do you want from me?" He spoke in hostile tones.

"Just that you ask the archbishop to give me an assignment."

Picking up one of the papers from his desk, he perused it, while completely ignoring me. Suddenly, he tossed the paper on his desk. "Hrumph! You think we can come up with an assignment any time you want! The archbishop will not make any more assignments until May and that is several months from now." He picked up another paper from his desk and began reading it.

"What am I supposed to do meanwhile?" I asked softly. I felt like a grade school kid in the principal's office.

"That is your problem!" he shot back at me without raising his beady eyes to look at me.

"Who is going to pay my salary?" I was starting to get worried.

"You are young—dynamic. Go find some pastor that needs help."

He stood up, signifying that our meeting was ended. "Good day to you, Father Lamadrid."

When I got back to the rectory, Pompeo was waiting in the living room for me to return and tell him what had happened at the VG's office.

"That guy is insane, he enjoyed humiliating me. He was just plain heartless and cruel. He told me to go find a pastor somewhere and help him." I sat down on the very modern, cream colored sofa that blended nicely with the tropical style furniture Monsignor had chosen for the rectory. Pompeo sat on a rattan chair with a high back right across from me. Instantly upon hearing my news, he jumped to his feet.

"*Increíble!*" When he was agitated he tended to speak in Spanish. "You have to go to see the archbishop and complain. You have the right to get an assignment."

I was not about to protest to the archbishop. Because Pompeo flies off the handle very fast, he can make his situation worse by saying and doing things that he should not. I always am slower to react and think things through carefully first. Actually, it was not difficult to find a pastor who needed help. My friend Father Matteo who worked at the Fátima Sanctuary talked to the rector in charge there, and it was quickly arranged that I would help out there and make enough money to survive, since my room and board were taken care of by Monsignor Stalker and St. Mary Tudor's.

Because monsignor expected me to be at table every evening, I went to dinner the next day, even though I was not hungry and would have preferred just to stay in my room. Although Martha, the cook, had prepared a very good Hungarian goulash dinner, the smell of food was unpleasant for me.

"You are not eating, Marco," Pompeo protested, proceeding to give me a lecture about how one has to eat regular and well-balanced meals. "You will even sleep better if you eat a good meal. After you eat, you get an alkaline surge that makes you drowsy and relaxed." Pompeo was a pain in the neck—a stupid know-it-all.

I drank a sip of the wine, but I could not touch the food.

Monsignor Stalker decided to enter the conversation. "Pompeo, Marco doesn't look too well to me. His color is not too good." Turning to me he asked, "Do you have a fever, Marco?"

Why couldn't they just let me alone! "Yes, I do. Please, excuse me." I got up and went to my room.

The next day, I felt even worse. When I looked at my hands they had a yellowish tinge. When I went to the doctor, he told me that he thought I had hepatitis and put me at once in Divine Providence Catholic Hospital, drew blood for an Igm anti-HAV, which came back with a positive diagnosis of hepatis A.

Never had I been so sick in all my life! My energy drained from my body. The next day I could not even walk. Not even wanting to move a muscle, the following day I could not even get out of the small white hospital bed.

A couple days later Dr. Angelo appeared at my bedside, looking grim as he pushed his glasses up and shook his head slowly. "If there is no improvement in your case by tomorrow, I am going to have to start a more aggressive treatment." When I asked him how I got the disease and when I had picked it up, he replied, "It has an incubation period of about 28 days. Where were you 28 days ago?"

"In Rome."

"You probably picked it up in a restaurant from eating raw sea food. The Bay of Naples is seriously polluted and yet they take shellfish from it."

It did not make me feel any better to learn I had picked up hepatitis in Rome. When the doctor left my room, I prayed. I just opened my heart to the Lord and He filled it with His Presence. Wonder of wonders, the next day when the doctor returned, he commented, "You are doing better. Good! Whatever you are doing, keep it up!" He smiled and walked out.

The hospital spoke to me about death and was like a prison where many very sick people—most of whom were worse off than I—were suffering. I could hear their moans and some of them even screamed from pain. Because I spent every day listening and living their pain, it had a tremendous impact on me and made me more compassionate afterwards in dealing with people.

Because hepatitis was considered very infectious and anyone who came into my room had to wear gloves, a hospital gown, and a mask, very few of my former parishioners from St. Ellen's came to visit me. The ones who did come very rarely returned for a second visit. Some of the members of the youth group at St. Ellen's came to see me more than once, and there were several families who made repeat visits. Among them was the Gomorrahs and because some of Old Nick's children visited me frequently, I ended up befriending this strange and peculiar family.

Although the days were long and hard to endure, gradually I began to feel better. Praying often, I felt that life was pouring into my veins. I desired to live more than you can imagine. When one is only thirty, the desire for life is overwhelming. When I was able to get out of bed and sit by the window, I could see people driving up along the riverfront, and I longed to do the same or take a stroll in the pleasant Spring weather. I wanted to do anything I could to keep on living.

Recovery was very slow. I moved to the Fátima Sanctuary, where the rector welcomed me out of the goodness of his heart, and tried to resume a normal life. From time to time, I had dinner with Pompeo and Mínimo who now had a assignment at St. Inebrius Parish near Rosanada. Because my strength had not returned, I felt like a caged lion.

Finally at the end of August, my new assignment came with a letter from the archbishop. I was to go to St. Cassiel parish in the section of the Archdiocese of

Rosanada where many Latinos had taken up residence. Here, I learned, the Very Reverend Monsignor Camio Velvet was pastor.

"What can you tell me about my new pastor" I asked Pompeo one day when we met for dinner." I could always count on Pompeo for information.

Before answering Pompeo took a large slice of Cuban bread and without breaking it, buttered it and began biting into it with gusto. "It is well known that he is an alcoholic, they sent him years ago to a House of Affirmation for the recovery from addictions with two of his drinking priest friends, but it did not help him at all." Pompeo spoke with finality, giving me the impression he knew what he was saying.

"Who are his assistants?" I inquired wanting to hear what else I was going to have to endure. I laid my knife and fork down and waited expectantly for him to speak.

"Father Santiago Menor," he replied and took another mouthful of bread.

"You know him?"

"I met him once. He is a Cuban, about forty or forty-five. He is holy Joe. You and he will probably hit it off good together."

When I moved in to St. Cassiel's rectory, I found that there were two other priests assigned to the parish—Father Guy Hacker, an obviously and blatant gay weight lifter and Father Marcus Maloney who had been ordained four and a half years before and seemed to be walking around in a fog. Because he told me his intention was to be an ordained priest for only a five year time period, I found him really strange. When his fifth anniversary of ordination arrived, he left the parish with a girl, without anyone's permission, to go to work in a fast food restaurant where they specialized in fried chicken. The night before he left, he came to my room.

"Good evening," he said. He was wearing blue jeans and a western shirt.

I invited him to come in and take a seat.

"No, I can't stay. I'm leaving in the morning."

"Permanently?"

"Yes. I am leaving the priesthood and I want to give you my chalice. I won't be needing it any more." He handed me a leather case containing a chalice that I continued to use at daily mass down through the years, until some priest stole it from the sacristy.

I spent four years at St. Cassiel—four years of bewilderment, wondering where God was leading me. Monsignor would usually start drinking about ten in the morning. He would go to the refrigerator in the upstairs hall to get ice in order to fix his drinks. When we associate pastors heard him open the refrigerator door early in the day and the ice cubes were poured in a glass, we knew that we were going to have a good day, since this sound meant monsignor was going to be in a good mood. Because we had jalousies on our bedroom doors so that in summer the breeze could blow throughout the entire floor, we always knew when he started drinking. The days he abstained from drinking, we were careful to keep a good distance from him, because then he could be as mean as a junkyard dog.

Although he never touched a drop of alcoholic beverages, Father Hacker, the weight lifter, had a worse temper than the pastor. He was a health nut and all of us would have been glad if he could have found a way to sweeten his disposition. One day I ran up the stairs to my room faster than usual, and in my rush, I slammed my bedroom room. Instantly, Father Hacker was banging on my door. When I opened it, he menacingly said, "Why in hell do you have to make so much noise? I was asleep and you woke me up?"

From his belligerent look and angry voice, I thought he was going to take a swing at me. When he doubled up his fists, I ran and picked up my tennis racket, because I thought he was really going to attack me physically. I wondered why some people have the opinion that gays are weak and mellow!

Just then the pastor appeared in the hall. I was never so glad to see him! Whether he was sober or drunk didn't matter to me. He was a small man, very small, but with a temper quicker than Hacker's, and he got right up in his face. He did not say a word. He didn't have to. Hacker turned and silently went into his room.

Rectory living is difficult, when you have men from many different backgrounds, trying to live under the same roof. The simplest things can become explosive. The smoking zones, dirty dishes in the sink, disorder in the living room, even the way you fold the newspaper can start an argument. The relationship between a pastor and his assistant can also create a war zone. Pastors have basically three ways of dealing with assistants. They can let their vicars do whatever they want, but this usually brings chaos. An alternative is for the pastor to establish a schedule and make everyone adhere to it, but some vicars resent this, feeling they should be consulted about everything. A third way for a pastor to proceed is to be very strict—then he won't be able to find priests to work with him.

Monsignor Velvet was of the strict school. Although he drank, he was totally authoritarian in his approach with his priests. He decided when the air conditioning would be used. He determined the hours of the meals and what would be eaten. Dinner was mandatory and served promptly at 5:30 p.m. He used the mealtime to make plans for the parish, give orders, and even scold us.

Although I looked forward to being moved to another assignment, I tried as best as I could to do my duties at St. Cassiel. So far, I had had only one really good priest for a pastor. What would the future hold? More of the same? It turned out that I was in for much greater excitement and bewilderment than I had experienced thus far.

15
Luz

A new prisoner, an older woman—perhaps seventy—was brought into the ward. The guards handled her roughly, pushing her across the ward to the bunk bed above Luz's. When she had difficulty climbing up to the bed, the guard struck with a rubber cane, knocking the woman to the floor.

"Please," Luz begged, "let her have my bed. I can climb up to the top one." The guard offered no objection, so Luz helped the woman to her feet and invited her to sit on her bed as she began to move her own things to the upper bunk. The guard withdrew from the ward, snapping the large padlock shut so that the bars to the ward were locked.

"God bless you," the woman said fearfully. Her face was wrinkled and her glasses had become broken in her fall with one of the temples bent out of shape, and the screw that held it in place had fallen out.

"Here, let me fix it for you," Luz offered, searching the floor until she found the lost screw. With the nail file Aurelio had brought her on one of his visits, she put the screw back into the glasses. Smiling at the woman to try to help overcome her fears, she asked, "What is your name?"

"Marta," she replied softly. Trembling from fear, her small body with its slight frame was visibly shaken.

When Luz stretched out on her bed that night, she was hit in the face by foul smelling water that was dripping from the ceiling that she knew was coming from the toilet from the floor above. Because the bed was bolted to the floor and could not be moved, she turned herself around, so that her head was on the other end of the bed. Better to have it on my feet, than in my face, she thought.

With great anticipation, Luz looked forward to the visit from the priest Aurelio promised to send her. Father Jaime Moreno, an elderly priest with flowing white hair and a kindly face, greeted her in the visitors' room, quickly noting that there was no privacy, because the guards were always listening to the conversations of the prisoners. Consequently, they could not speak freely.

"Welcome, Father, it is so good of you to come here." She extended her hand in welcome.

"I believe your husband told me that you had been baptized Catholic in infancy. Is that correct?" He sat down on one of the folding metal chairs.

"Yes, Father, but I have not been confirmed." She glanced down at the floor and saw a roach making its way under his chair. "I have not really been a good Catholic, but I plan to change now."

"Why do you want to change, Luz?" His eyes questioned hers.

"Since I have been here, I have learned that I need God very much." She smiled at him faintly and added, "My son has recently been ordained a Catholic priest." She looked at him carefully trying to see what impact her words were having. "Then", she continued, "when I first came to this jail I was praying in desperation and I saw an angel with no wings waiting for me, and above him, I saw Our Lady of Guadalupe—she was inviting me to approach her, promising that she would lead me to her son Jesus Christ and to salvation. This was indeed a spiritual vision because I had never been a devotée of Guadalupe."

"You have a lot to be thankful for. God has really blessed you."

She was so proud of Marco—he was so handsome and bright and he had a special charisma about him. "He was ordained by Pope Paul VI."

"It is wonderful that you are returning to the Church. Your husband told me that you have been away for some years. God's grace is amazing that He would give your son a priestly vocation when his father was a Methodist and you…"

"Yes," she interrupted him. "He and I have always been very close. We can sometimes read one another's mind. He has *ashe*." When she said the word *ashe*, the priest became suddenly very serious.

"You say he has *ashe*?" he demanded in a harsh tone of voice. His face no longer seemed kindly, but rather fierce.

"Have you been involved with Santería?" he spoke very deliberately emphasizing each word distinctly.

"Very much so. Even though I was a baptized Catholic and went to the Methodist Church with my husband, I participated in it." She paused remembering past events. "When I was young I went to a Santería séance a number of times. That was when Marco—he's my son—was about five. The Santero told me that he had *ashe*. I returned to see the Babalawo a few times. I don't recall how many. I liked taking Marco with me. The Babalawo said Marco has charisma, power, and grace."

"Did Marco become a "saint" himself?

Luz thought a few moments trying to remember. Slowly the memories came back to her. "No, never. He said he could feel the spiritual power in Marco and begged me to let him instruct my child. He said Marco would be a powerful Santero. He said Marco had what he needed to communicate with the *Orishas*. When he asked if he could teach Marco, I agreed." She could see distress in the eyes of Father Moreno.

"So, did he teach him?"

"No, my husband never allowed it."

"Good, now you will have to renounce Satan and all his deceits.

"I will. However, I must tell you that I have always been attracted by the occult. I consulted mind readers, witches, and spiritualists. I have attempted to communicate with the dead; for years I have been involved with the Rosicrucians. It has been a long trek before I found myself as a Catholic."

"Luz", he said, "you have opened your lives to the Powers of Darkness. You must tell your son, because he must also repudiate any influences the Evil One might have on him."

Father Moreno gave her a rosary and encouraged her to be brave during her stay in prison. He was going to pray for her and her family.

"Now, I am going to give you absolution, but in order to receive it, you must make a full confession to a priest when you get out of here." He noted the presence of the guard who was listening, as he spoke.

He raised his hand in blessing and absolved her in the name of the Father, the Son and the Holy Spirit. She felt the weight of the sins of many, many years lift. Then he said, "For your penance, offer your painful stay in this prison for the freedom of our country."

Although Father Moreno could only visit her occasionally, each time he came, she felt closer to God and more at peace. Prayer became her constant occupation. She lived to pray and she prayed to live.

It was not long after this that Aurelio came to see her with the news that the *commandante* had been able to pull some strings and that he was going to take her home that very day.

Once they were in the Chrysler, heading down the highway for Mérida, she noticed that Aurelio did not seem well. "I have a pain in my abdomen," he explained. "I have been told that I am suffering from diverticulosis, I need to have an operation as soon as we get to Rosanada. I have a surprise for you." A big smile trailed across his face when he said this. "You are going to see Marco soon." Although he was driving, he reached over and took her by the hand.

"We are going to leave Cuba!" She could not believe it. Getting freed from prison was great, but to be freed from Castro and his vicious system was more than she could have ever imagined. "How soon do we go?" She could feel life flowing through her veins.

"Day after tomorrow! We are going to fly to Jamaica. Marco will meet us there and fly with us to Rosanada. He has already located a small apartment for us. Tears began to flow down Luz's cheeks. All the pent up emotions of the past years began to be released. Aurelio reached over and put his arm around her shoulders. "Everything is going to be all right now, Luz. Don't cry. Our future will be great. I have everything worked out."

Luz sighed deeply. How wonderful it was to be free at last. She couldn't wait to get home and take a real tub bath and soak off the dirt of *Manto Negro*. From now on, she could rely on Aurelio to take care of them. Unfortunately, there were some things he had not foreseen.

16
Marco

News that my parents were being permitted to leave Cuba and come to Rosanada inspired me with a new zest for living. Since they were flying first to Jamaica on their way from Cuba, I planned to fly down there to meet them and bring them back with me to the United States to the little apartment that I had found for them where they would feel at home with their many compatriots who had fled the Castro regime. A few days before they were due to arrive, I attended a clergy conference held at one of the hotels on the Rosanada Riverfront. Since they were the only occasions I had to share a time of fellowship and relaxation with various clergy friends, I looked forward to them and thoroughly enjoyed them.

Having just arrived at the hospitality desk for the conference and while putting on my badge with my name on it, I spotted Damian Babilonia, who pretended not to see me and walked passed me, while ostensibly reading the convocation schedule. I also saw Renato Del'Ano, whom I had met in Rome, standing alone on the other side of the lobby. Although my encounter with Renato had not been very friendly when we met in Rome, I walked across the room to where he was drinking a cup of coffee and greeted him.

"How do you like Rosanada?" I inquired.

"Great city! *Bellissima*! Teaching at the seminary is a very rewarding job." He was wearing a custom made cambric clergy shirt. "Even the most skeptical seminarians seem to listen, when I explain the messages of the Blessed Mother at Garabandal and tell them how the angel gave communion to a girl there. Here let me show you her picture." Opening his billfold, he pulled out a black and white photo of a very devout looking young girl. "The Holy Queen of Heaven told her that if we do not repent and do penance, we are in for serious trouble." Obviously, enjoying and savoring the threat of punishment that he claimed was hanging over humanity, he was eager to tell me more about the visionaries at Garabandal and their dire prophecies.

"Congratulations on your new St. Thomas Society," I said trying to change the subject.

Ignoring my remark and insisting on pursuing the subject further, he insisted, "I want you to read this little pamphlet containing some very good material."

I scanned through it quickly and found it repugnant and completely contrary to Christ's teaching on the love of God, because it promulgated the idea that the Virgin would stop the wrath of God against humanity. It spoke of a final warning and of the chastisements that would befall us, if we did not change. According to the visionaries, many cardinals, bishops, and priests were on the wide path that leads to hell and destruction, taking many of the laity with them. While that could even be the truth, these messages were completely contrary to the Bible teaching that God gave His only begotten Son that we could have life. No human being, not even the Blessed Mother, holy as she is, can love us more than God. Any message that proclaims that the Father is ready to destroy us and the Vrgin Mary will save us from His anger is contrary to the true Catholic-Christian dogma.

I thanked him for the brochure and stuck it in my pocket to be tossed in the nearest trash can, when he wasn't looking. Again, I congratulated him on the St. Thomas Society.

"Thank you, Marco. What is your assignment?" He set the empty coffee cup on a nearby table. Although, he smiled, his eyes were not friendly.

"I'm at St. Cassiel with a crusty old monsignor." I proceeded to tell him about Monsignor Velvet and the priest who had given me his chalice, when he left the priesthood. "Velvet drinks like a whale. He is well named—he is always giving us assistant pastors the steel treatment in a velvet glove—a real authoritarian of the old school."

"I hope you will come sometime to the meetings of the St. Thomas Society," he invited. "We have a nice group of people. Recently we got a great singer, Enki Mutante, from Caracas." Renato seemed genuinely interested in trying to get me to come to his meetings. "You would enjoy meeting him. Although he is a layman, he likes to preach at our meetings and people seem to like him. He flew up from Venezuela for a couple weeks. Now he is here permanently. Yo-Lin Sin brought him here. He is one of her good friends. Perhaps you know her?" He waited for me to answer.

"No, no, I have never heard of her or him," I said quite truthfully.

"Well, you will. She is a real mover, a great benefactor of the archdiocese, and an outstanding member of the

Hispanic community. Although she is Chinese, she grew up in Venezuela and feels she is *una verdadera criolla*—a pure native. She will be at our meeting tomorrow night and Enki will sing popular hymns in Spanish. I think you would enjoy it. I do hope you will be able to come." He gave me the address of where it was held.

"Perhaps I could come. I always enjoy meeting people."

Because it was time for the first session of our conference—a presentation by a bishop from a diocese in New York State on medical bio-ethics, a topic that did not particularly interest me—our conversation ended.

Although I, in fact, did attend the meeting of the St. Thomas Society, I left before it was finished, determined I would never do it again. The music was very nice. Without doubt, the young Venezuelan was talented and he sang the songs the Pentecostals used so effectively to draw people to their meetings, but there was something about him that did not appeal to me. In fact, I had very negative feelings about him right from the start. I was also repelled by his distributing "glitter from heaven", an organic matter that appeared miraculously around some statues of Mary in Venezuela.

As for Yo-Lin Sin, she was dressed in what I judged to be very expensive imported Chinese clothing. With her flamboyant appearance designed to attract men, she exuded exotic eroticism. Although she was past fifty, her flaming red silk tunic left nothing to the imagination as it clung tightly to her body and rode up when she crossed her long slim legs, a position which she maintained most of the evening. The olive skin of her face was taut and slightly wrinkled. Obviously, she was trying to reflect youthful ebullience, but she looked more like a faded lotus blossom. She sought me out before the meeting even started.

"*Hola*! I'm Yo-Lin!" Fluttering her eyelashes, she pushed herself right up in my face, as I stood by myself in the back of the room.

"What is a handsome fellow like you doing standing here all by yourself?"

I bristled, because I felt the woman was coming on to me. Later I learned that she did that with every man she met.

"I have to be leaving soon," I replied as I glanced at the exit.

"What kind of work do you do?"

"Mostly with youth groups," I replied trying to think of a way of escape.

"Oh, that's interesting, Father Del'Ano teaches in the seminary. He is such a brilliant man. I have learned so much from him, especially about the end times and the Virgin Mary. He says she is almost a fourth member of the Trinity, as daughter of the Father, mother of the Son and wife of the Holy Spirit." She reached out and laid her hand on my arm, while smiling flirtatiously at me and ogling me with her green eyes that resembled emeralds behind her long, and most likely false, black eyelashes.

That did it. I pulled away from her and said, "I really have to be leaving now." She winced, for her ego had been hurt by my slight rejection.

"Wait, I want to give you something for your young people." Fumbling through the large red purse, which matched her red outfit, she pulled out a wad of bills. "Here take these for your young people. Throw them a big party." As she thrust the bills into my hands, I murmured a quick thank you and rushed for the door. Later I learned she had a reputation for giving gifts to almost everyone, especially those in need, because of a great need she had to expiate her sins, which were grievous and manifold.

With reluctance Monsignor gave me permission to fly to Jamaica to meet my parents. Even though he granted me time to spend with them, he actually made it clear that he begrudged me every minute of it and lectured me about it.

"When you become a priest, the Church is your family. I put my family aside when I became a priest. You don't see me taking time off to visit them." What he said was true; monsignor was a solitary and friendless man who saw no need for warm personal relationships. He also had a basic antipathy towards Spanish speaking people, although his parents no doubt spoke English with an accent.

When my mother and father got off the plane that seventeenth day of October at Kingston airport, I never would have recognized them. My mother looked more like a skeleton than the vibrant woman I had known. Sick and in pain, my father walked very slowly and deliberately. Both of them looked much older than their years; my father was only sixty-two and my mother was ten years younger. Displaying a very wistful and sad air, she seemed to be withdrawn from what was going on about her. I knew it would take time for her to get adjusted to life outside prison.

Embracing my mother warmly, but gently, I held her close to my heart for a few minutes, thanking God that we had finally been reunited. I hugged my father and helped him into a taxi that took us to the hotel that I had booked for them.

Our reunion was bittersweet. Because I had been only about fourteen when we had last seen each other, I had changed as much as they. Now I was past thirty and had been separated from them longer than I had lived with them. We had a lot of catching up to do, but neither Castro, nor the separation, nor the prison had been able to destroy our unity and the love we had for each other.

The following morning, my parents went to the United States Consulate in Kingston. A week later, we joyfully flew to Rosanada. After many hugs, kisses, and tears we settled down to the serious business of getting caught up on what had happened to each of us over the years. We were the same people, but each of us was different and there was a certain indefinable quality that I could not put my finger on that was not the same anymore.

When I returned to St. Cassiel, I was met by a furious monsignor. No sooner was I unpacked, when he summoned me to his office, and I knew that some reprimand was coming. Sitting behind his gigantic desk that made him look even smaller than he actually was, but with the desk between him and me, he seemed to ooze power from every pore. He kept me standing in front of his desk and began to attack me.

"So I drink like a whale, do I?" he fumed.

I did not know what to respond so I kept silent. The Lord says that a soft word turns away wrath. I waited for his wrath to abate.

"That's the kind of garbage you spread about me around the archdiocese. A friend of mine heard it from Father Del'Ano, the Italian who teaches at Pope Julius III Seminary." Dredging up all the foul words he could muster from his ample vocabulary, he assaulted me with his ill temper. It was then that I began to realize that I had an enemy in Renato Del'Ano.

When he was finished, I said softly, "Please, Monsignor, may I have your permission to have the day off tomorrow? My father is having surgery at Divine Providence."

Grumbling he consented to my request.

Because, my father's condition had worsened, my mother phoned Martha, her sister-in-law, to see if she could recommend a surgeon. Being a physician himself, my father insisted he needed surgery, because he knew the seriousness of his condition. When Dr. Manuel Arroyo examined my father, he hospitalized him at once, saying that my father's condition necessitated immediate surgery. The consent forms were signed and the operating room scheduled for the very next day at 8:00 a.m.

During the surgery, which lasted four hours, my mother and I sat in the hospital waiting room until Dr. Arroyo came to tell us that my father's condition was guarded and that the next twenty-four hours would determine the outcome. We continued waiting for the next hour and a half for my father to leave the recovery room and go to a private room.

When I saw him, I was deeply concerned. He was ashen and in great pain even though they had him hooked up to a machine that put measured doses of morphine into his IV. My mother and I sat by his bedside and prayed. Along about nine o'clock that night he seemed to be having difficulty breathing.

"Mom, I will get the nurse. You stay with him."

Fortunately the nurse came immediately. After she took one look at him, she issued a Code Blue and called for the doctor to come STAT.

"Get the hospital chaplain," I ordered. I was very worried by this time, because I knew he needed the last rites of the Church. Since I was his son, I was not the one to hear his confession. When the chaplain came in the room, my father opened his eyes and then smiled faintly at my mother. She drew her chair closer to his bed and held his hand in hers and gently kissed his fingers.

"I am going to give him the last rites," the chaplain said compassionately, as he looked at me and saw by my Roman collar that I was a priest. "I'll take care of him, Father. Don't worry." While we waited in the corridor outside the room, he proceeded to anoint my father and listened to his very weak voice make his confession and an act of contrition. Summoning us, he said, "I will give you all communion."

In just a few minutes after the priest placed the Host on my father's tongue, he sighed deeply and breathed his last. My mother and I stayed by my father's bed in prayer until my mother finally spoke.

"We can go now, Marco. I saw his spirit leave his body and an angel of light coming to take him to God. And I felt a burst of energy coming from him as he departed." I saw how brave my mother was. She did not cry, but kept her pain to herself. Because she had had so much pain in prison, she had learned to control it, but above all she had learned to love God and trust in Him. I put my arm around her and led her to my car. She was only fifty-two and God still had much for her to do and I needed her, because I could not have faced my enemies without her prayers and her presence.

17
Renato

Renato welcomed the news that the Vatican was sending a co-adjutor with the right to succeed Archbishop Lingam who had fallen into disfavor with the people. When the Latinos protested that Lingam discriminated against them, various other groups took up the battle, crying, "Archbishop Lingam is a male chauvinist and a bigot." His arrogance, his friendship with Aspasia Hetaira, and his dislike for Latinos and non-whites gained him disfavor with the papal nuncio who ended up recommending a co-adjutor to take over running the archdiocese in his place.

Everyone did seem to welcome the arrival of His Excellency Eval Banshee Melusine M.S., D.D., everyone except the archbishop who was insulted that the apostolic nuncio had taken the side of the people against him and arranged for Melusine to come to Rosanada with the right to succeed him and the power to begin making changes immediately.

Melusine was the very representation of desolation. Because of his lack of coordination—he had the grace of an ostrich when he walked—he probably never practiced a sport in his life. Even though he was a puritan according to Catholic standards—no smoking, drinking alcohol, or secret sexual escapades—he gave the whole diocese the impression that the pope had punished us by sending us a moronic bishop. He had the tendency to stutter a bit, and not only was he good at belching, his flatulence became a legend around the archdiocese. No priest could produce a smellier, noisier and more prolonged fart than he. Around the chancery and the archdiocese, he was known as "Windy" by some, while others called him "Hurricane," because of his proclivities.

Melusine was of Caribe Indian descent, had dark skin, and curly salt and pepper hair. His family settled in Trinidad at the beginning of the twentieth century. The archbishop's father, the oldest son of the family, moved to the United States, and married an American woman. Their son, Eval, was ordained a priest and worked his way up in one of the Western dioceses to the episcopacy and was finally sent to Rosanada to replace Lingam.

Melusine's suits always had a veil of dandruff on the shoulders. The seat of his pants was always baggy, and even shiny, from sitting so long at his desk. He couldn't remember names, people seemed to intimidate him, and he had trouble working with them, always avoiding all confrontation. He reminded Renato of a character he had seen recently, when he went to Orlando and visited the Magic Kingdom—Goofy.

Melusine had not been in Rosanada very long when Archbishop Lingam died. Renato heard the bells of the cathedral tolling, announcing that the number one man of the Catholic community had passed into eternal life. Soon all the churches of the archdiocese began tolling the passing of Archbishop Priapus T. Lingam. Although many people were sad, Renato saw it as an opportunity to advance his career. As a matter of fact, he was very happy that the old bag of bones had finally died. New and better things were bound to happen. No one was really sad—except for a couple relatives, while the rest of them were wondering how much money they would inherit. Most priests rejoiced, because finally the cruel and wealthy dictator was gone. However, everyone said the usual polite clichés that were expected of them. The old pastors—the old timers—had plenty of folkloric stories to narrate about the "good ol' times" when priests were priests, and nuns were nuns, and sins were kept clandestine, but Renato was delighted as he dreamed of a better future for himself.

Very visibly and with a high profile, Renato visited the cathedral where the archbishop's body rested in full pontifical regalia in a coffin of pure cedar encased in bronze with tall candles burning continually, during the twenty-four hour vigil, making this follower of Jesus Messiah look like a monarch laying in state.

Everyone who was important in the archdiocese was there. The Order of Malta, the Knights of Columbus, and the Knights of Saint George were taking turns guarding the mortal remains. Why adult members of the laity and prominent members of the community like to lay aside their business suits and dress up in such out of date and ridiculous costumes is a mystery without explanation. Most of the clergy stayed only long enough to say a brief prayer of thanksgiving, while soaking his corpse with Holy Water, making sure the bastard was dead, and then depart. Renato saw many of them that he knew, for he had made it his business in the short time he had been in Rosanada to get to know as many of the clergy as possible. He saw Marco Lamadrid there kneeling in prayer and tried his best to avoid him.

None of the visitors seemed to shed a tear for the dead archbishop, including Marco, honoring the ancient Spanish saying, *"Se reúnen sin conocerse, viven sin amarse, y mueren sin llorarse."* They come together, not knowing each other, live, not loving each other, and die, not crying for each other. Priests care for practically no one beyond themselves and their little circle of friends. That is the first lesson they teach you in the seminary in order to remain chaste. As soon as the vicar general and the chancellor saw that Renato was present, he left, for he only wanted to be seen.

Returning to the cathedral for the Pontifical Mass presided over by the Apostolic Delegate, Archbishop Panza del Vecchio, with two cardinals and some bishops in the sanctuary concelebrating, Renato, whose specialty was liturgy, was impressed by the ceremony for the dead archbishop. He liked the sound of all the silver trumpets that echoed throughout the cathedral. Although he really preferred the tolling of the bells to the trumpets, the choir of a hundred voices singing *"Dies irae, dies illa"* made his heart skip a beat, even though he thought it would have been more appropiate to sing the lyrics *"In taberna quando sumus, non curamus quid sit humus"* from *Carmina Burana.* (When to the tavern we go, we do not care about death). Someday, he was determined they would sing the *"Ecce sacerdos magnus"* when he entered a church.

Directed by the master of ceremonies of the Archdiocese of Rosanada, an overweight young priest who looked like an Italian sausage in his cassock, the ceremony lasted a full two hours. Contrary to his opinion, the M.C. was the laughing stock of the clergy as he cavorted around the altar with scores of altar servers who had no idea what the Catholic ceremonial intended with all the bowing, incense and reverence. Renato timed it on his watch, because he was anxious for it to be over so he could get ready for his meeting of the St. Thomas Society that night. When the church funeral was over, the body was taken to the archdiocesan cemetery where Bishop Melusine, who would soon be the archbishop, assisted the Nuncio. When people came up to him as the representative of the archdiocese to render their condolences, Melusine frequently displayed a nervous laugh, while staring at the horizon, like someone who is about to receive a divine revelation. When some people came to greet him, the sad expression on his rugged, old Caribe face did not correspond to the slight smile that flitted at the corners of his mouth.

Renato, too, went to greet Archbishop Melusine and offer his condolences, for he was soon to be the only pastor, judge, and educator of the Archdiocese of Rosanada. Because he knew that first impressions are important, he very deliberately kissed the bishop's ring that he had bought at some West Indies duty-free store— an ugly and cheap tiger's eye cabochon ring, resembling a large brownish snake egg.

About a week later, Renato received the news that Melusine had appointed Father Damian Babilonia as Moderator of the Curia, Chancellor of the Diocese, Vicar General, and supervisor and director of an endless number of committees. Immediately, Renato realized that it was to his best interest to cultivate Damian's friendship.

According to a story circulating among the clergy, Melusine never touched a drop of alcohol, and because he was opposed to living in the luxurious residence that

Lingam enjoyed, the mansion was up for sale. It wasn't long before Renato heard that a Mafia don had bought it.

The meeting of the St. Thomas Society that evening after the funeral turned out to be quite exciting with Enki preaching on his favorite topic, the dire warnings of the destruction to come when God's wrath would lash out against sinful humanity. Renato enjoyed Enki's music and his preaching. The two were becoming good friends; they understood each other and they both had a basic antipathy toward Marco Lamadrid.

Lingering after the meeting, Yo-Lin Sin told him a fantastic tale. When she also tried openly to seduce him, he gently repulsed her saying the words of Maria Goretti: "I would rather die than commit a sin." Actually, because his interests lay elsewhere, he found her repulsive.

Dumbfounded by her story, he did not know what to make of it. She claimed that she was kidnapped by an old enemy, Pepe Villanueva, of the Bolivian Mafia, who grabbed her, threw her in a limo, and took her to an abandoned old house in a ghetto, and locked her up in a small room, where she watched television all day. Pepe had guessed that she was an informant on the Bolivian Mafia for the Venezuelan government and demanded a two million dollars ransom for her release. If her story can be believed, they must have paid, for there she was, more flamboyant than ever, wearing a fortune in emeralds and jade. She told Renato that she was so thankful to the Blessed Mother for her safety and release that she wanted to give him an offering of five thousand dollars.

"Please come to my new house on the river. I'm having a party. Bring some of your clergy friends with you. Enki will be there."

"You can count on me." He wouldn't miss an opportunity to socialize with top society, with people who had money and could help him climb the career ladder. That night he dreamed he was a bishop with a tall miter and a big amethyst—no cheap tiger's eye for him.

Because the seminarians were receptive to him and his ideas, he enjoyed working with them at Pope Julius III Seminary. He actually made close friends with some of them—perhaps too close. Well, he decided, he really could not help the attraction he had for other men. That is the way God made him. Nevertheless, he felt guilty and tried to repress his sexual feelings toward them. For this reason, on the following Saturday afternoon, he sought out the confessional of a priest in a parish where no one would recognize him, because he drove up to the next diocese to be sure to find a priest who would not know who he was. Avoiding the reconciliation room where he would have to face the priest, he slipped quickly into the anonymity of an old fashioned confessional box. When the priest opened the shutter, he sighed with relief to see that the little window was covered with cloth, so that there was no possibility that the priest would see him.

"Bless me, Father, for I have sinned."

The priest mumbled a blessing and told him to continue.

"I am a priest and I was unchaste six times."

"Was the woman married?"

"It was not a woman, Father."

"Oh, my God! Homosexuality is a serious problem. You cannot yield to it. It is a deadly sin and claims its vengeance from heaven. If you had died before making this confession, just consider what would have become of you." The priest paused momentarily before continuing. "How old were the men you had sex with?"

"They were young. One was a boy about 14." Renato felt great relief flood his mind and soul.

The priest must have heard the same story many times because he did not appear to be shocked.

"Anything else?"

"I had several masturbatory fantasies about other men."

"And you have continued saying Mass everyday with these sins on your soul?"

Very softly and shamefully, Renato admitted that he had.

"Every one of those Masses is a sacrilege, Father. Do you understand that?"

"Yes, I do"

"Are you sorry for your sins?"

"Yes, I am, I feel so guilty and dirty and horrible."

"Do you make a firm commitment to amend your life and sin no more?"

"I do."

"Make an act of contrition and ask God to give you the strength to avoid committing these sins in the future. As your penance, say three Our Fathers."

Renato did as he was told, but he did not feel that he would be able to follow through with a commitment to avoid his erotic fantasies.

That night he was going to make new friends and have some fun at Yo-Lin Sin's gala that he knew would be a tremendous success. He took with him Father Damian Babilonia who was impressed with all the French Champagne that flowed freely from a fountain that was placed in the center of the reception room. He was also obviously observing the ostentatious show of wealth of the men and women at the party.

The high point of the evening was when Yo-Lin related the whole story of her kidnapping to a room full of people—her best friends in the Mafia.

"My chauffer was going to drop me off at a jewelry store on the Boulevard where I had seen a ring I really liked and wanted to buy. Suddenly a car pulled ahead of us and another pulled up close behind our rear bumper." As she related how two armed men grabbed her and forced her into the front car, everyone's attention was on her. "Then a third man drove off with me. I couldn't see where he took me, because he put a blindfold over my eyes. When he removed it, we were in a garage with the door shut. They locked me up—I think it was Pepe."

When she said his name a murmur of contempt sounded from the guests who obviously knew who he was and detested him.

"I had to ask permission to go to the bathroom, she lamented with a hardened look stealing across her face. "Fortunately no man took any liberties with me."

Knowing her, Renato and probably most of the listeners thought to themselves: "That must have been a major disappointment." Out loud Renato said, very hypocritically: "I am thankful that nothing happened to you."

Renato enjoyed the party, especially since he had brought Father Damian Babilonia, the chancellor of the archdiocese with him. He could see that Damian was eyeing the diamonds and emeralds the women were wearing and the elegance of the men in white tuxedos who wore dazzling gem-studded gold rings and diamond tie pins. Damian was also responding favorably to the enticing glances that Yo-Lin was giving him.

After the dinner, the hostess served Dom Perignon and Louis XIII Cognac. Since Renato hardly ever drank, the beverages did not impress him. Because he had brought with him the chancellor of the archdiocese, every one treated him as a very special person. Although Renato knew that the other guests were Mafia members—it was no secret to him—but Damian was unaware just who the other guests were. Renato understood that Mafia people like to have priests at their parties, because they feel that God will help them carry on their "business," if they are friendly to the Church and its priests.

"I think, Renato," Damian suggested, "that we can get some good contributions from these people to help with the archdiocesan funds." Eager to approach Yo-Lin about financial contributions, he sauntered over to her with Renato trailing at his heals and enticed her away from the people who were surrounding her.

"I am wondering if you would like to help with the present financial needs of the archdiocese." He gave her an ingratiating smile, appearing to respond to her flirtatious glances.

"Giving to the Church is always a source of happiness for me!" she purred while stroking the emerald choker that encircled her neck.

"Perhaps your friends could join you; I think they will be able to help greatly." Circling his arm around her waist, he continued smiling at her from closer range. In amusement, Renato watched as Yo-Lin drew closer to Damian and flirted with him brazenly.

"You can count on us!"

Renato could see that Damian was pleased with him and Yo-Lin and her wealthy friends and that the evening was a smashing success. He was not about to tell him they were Mafiosi.

The next day, Damian phoned Renato with much enthusiasm and gusto.

"I have good news for you. I have just talked it over with Archbishop Melusine and you are now the head of fund raising for the archdiocese."

"Thank you very much, Damian. I accept. Please make me an appointment to come to discuss fund raising with you and my new position." Renato knew that his future was looking brighter now that he had Damian on his side. He would go far—as far as his driving ambition would take him. No one was going to stand between him and a great career, or so he thought, for he had become, as other priests would call him, one of "Damian's Boys."

To get started on his new career as fund raiser, he visited his new office in the chancery and met his secretary Mary Ann Maguire and his assistant Giovanni Rotelli. His office was not as large as Damian's, but he had a suite of rooms so that his office was private, with his assistant and secretary having their own facilities. He did not have the view of Rosanada River that Damian had, for his office faced on the parking lot, but this did give him the advantage in that he could see everyone who came in and out of the chancery.

To kick off his new career as fund raiser, he phoned Yo-Lin Sin inviting her to come to visit him in his new office, figuring that she would make a sizeable contribution to get the campaign rolling. As he waited for her to arrive, he thought about how he would induce her to persuade her friends in the Mafia to contribute also.

Now that he had an office in the chancery, Renato felt that he had really arrived. He had bought a new suit, an Italian import from a top designer, "Dress for Success"—after all he had to look the part, if he were going to be a successful money man. To go with the suit, he had his mother in Italy send him a dozen clergy shirts made of the finest linen with nacre buttons. Anxious to get Yo-Lin's reaction to his appearance, he watched for her and finally spotted her getting out of her car and heading into the chancery. When Ms. Maguire announced Yo-Lin's arrival, Renato went to the door of his office to greet her.

"Ah, Renato, you look so handsome, and what a beautiful office! She kissed him on the cheek, which, although it repulsed him, he pretended to enjoy. Her perfume—a sickly sweet oriental jasmine fragrance— almost stifled him. "You deserve this and so much more. You are a true priest. There are so few like you."

Renato observed that she had put a blue tint on her black hair and was wearing a dark purple outfit that had a low plunging neckline so that the cleavage of her breasts was very visible. On her feet she was wearing a pair of open shoes—studded with rhine-stones and decorated with marcasite—the heels of which must have been four inches high. Her toenails were painted a deep purple and so were her fingernails. Renato looked at her closely, as she pulled an oval Egyptian cigarette from her bulging purple handbag, offered him one, which he politely refused, and, with a gold lighter, lit up, crossed her long lanky legs, and sat back in one of the white leather chairs that graced his office.

Renato continued trying to figure her out. If she thought she was going to seduce him, she was badly mistaken. All he wanted from her was money. He knew what she wanted from him, but he also knew he would never give it to her. He decided to come right to the point.

"Yo-Lin, I must ask a great favor of you. I need you to help me organize a ten million dollar campaign to finance the future growth of the archdiocese." Smiling at her, as if he believed she were the most desirable woman in the world, he even winked at her audaciously and flirtatiously.

"Oh, Renato, of course, I will be glad to. Just what can I do?"

"I was hoping you could get some of your friends to contribute. They are such fine people." He remembered the ostentatious wealth he had seen the night he took Damian to her house for the party.

"Of course, of course! You can count on us. Let me be the first one to contribute." She fumbled though her purple bag, decorated to match her shoes with rhinestones and marcasite, pulled out a checkbook, and proceed to write a check for twenty-five thousand dollars. She handed it to him, saying, "Here is a little something to help you get started."

The following evening at the meeting of the St. Thomas Society, Renato took the opportunity to tell the group of his promotion. Because he was tired and really had nothing to say to them, he cleared his throat as he stood at the lectern.

"I want to give you my testimony tonight. I am now the head of fund raising for the archdiocese, because God chooses humble and simple men like me and trusts them with the finances of a giant institution."

Well, he knew he was exaggerating, when he said this, because he was not the administrator of the money, but simply the person in charge of finding new financial resources. Nevertheless, the members of the Society of St. Thomas responded with congratulations, hugs, and kisses. He was proud of his success and enjoyed basking in their admiration.

Caught up in self-admiration, he barely listened to Enki's sermon of avoiding the evils and pitfalls of daily life. To Enki everything that was in any way pleasurable was a sin. Dancing was wicked, gambling an abomination, and movies of all kinds were to be avoided. God's wrath was soon to fall on all unrepentant sinners, just as the Blessed Virgin, bored with her inactivity in Heaven, continued to announce during many of her apparitions.

After the meeting, Yo-Lin phoned him with promises of donations from many of her friends. He felt privileged that such a prominent and influential woman would phone him, assuring him that he was going to be a big success. That night he had a wonderful dream that he believed was a prophecy of things to come. In it, he was a bishop, wearing a tall jeweled miter and a big amethyst ring that everyone was kissing. He still did not realize that Yo-Lin was a powerful and dangerous woman who would kill, without regret, anyone who got in her way.

18
Marco

Despite all the changes that were taking place in the archdiocese, I kept busy at St. Cassiel where changes were also occurring. Monsignor's fits of temper and bouts of drinking were the only constants. Not long after Marcus Maloney gave me his chalice, before leaving to marry and work in a fast food restaurant, I read in the *Rosanada News* that Father Gus Hacker, the weight lifter at St. Cassiel, had vanished one day. Although Monsignor never alluded to his disappearance, I read in the Rosanada News that he had fallen in love with a city councilman. Of course Hacker, who disliked me intensely, ever since the day he confronted me for making noise coming up the steps and awakening him from a nap, did not tell me he was leaving. Another priest was sent to fill in for him, but in a short time he fell in love with one of the girls in the choir and left to marry. Later, I heard that they had two children. The priest that replaced him also soon left the ministry with a divorced woman.

Observing so many priests lose their vocations, I began to search my soul to examine my call to serve God and to speak for Him in such a troubled archdiocese and confused world, but everything seemed to be silencing God's call. Fearing that I would become like many priests I had known and compromise on my calling and opt for a life of debauchery, I recalled all the visions I had had in times gone by, the Divine Light that had infused me, and the gift of speaking in tongues that I had received. Having not yet learned that there is nothing we can do to receive God's special graces that He gives to whom He wishes and only when He wishes, I tried to recapture these experiences. I did not understand why God had stopped pouring His graces into me, not realizing until much later that God was looking for my brokenness. God loves a humble heart and a broken wick He will not extinguish. In time I learned to cultivate the humble heart.

One day, most unexpectedly, Monsignor, who was head of personnel for the archdiocese, informed me that Archbishop Melusine had assigned me to Saint Priscillianus Parish in the southern part of the archdiocese. Reluctantly, I packed my belongings, said good bye to the friends I had made at St. Cassiel, moved far away from where my mother was living, and settled in Saint Priscillianus to begin a new life in a parish I did not like.

Since I was the new priest in the parish, the pastor assigned me to the only difficult job they had—I was appointed chaplain of a nearby hospital where I attended the sick and injured, at any time of the day or night, six days of the week, visiting all the Catholics there daily. This rather small hospital was owned by a group of doctors that were more interested in their bank accounts than they were in the health and well-being of their patients. Because the nursing staff was not attentive to the sick, I often heard a patient screaming to get a nurse. Some people in intensive care actually got out of bed and walked to the lobby to find a cab, while protesting that the hospital was robbing them. That place was only a money factory for the owners. And the staff did not care, if they did not receive the consolation that only faith can grant.

In addition to my hospital duties, I was also in charge of the youth group and altar servers. Although my stay at this parish was rather brief, I learned a lot more English and gained some appreciation in understanding non-Hispanic American culture.

Although most of my priest friends did not like hearing confessions, it was one of the duties that I enjoyed on Saturday afternoons, because I loved the idea that I could share the ministry of reconciliation with Jesus.

One Saturday afternoon I sat in the reconciliation room waiting for penitents to come while doing some spiritual reading—a book by Jean-Pierre de Caussade, *The Sacrament of the Present Moment,* when the first one came in and sat in the chair opposite to me. The room was devoid of all furniture except for two chairs and a large crucifix on the wall. The first penitent was a man who repented for his sin of adultery. He seemed genuinely contrite and a tear seemed to form in his eyes, when I gave him absolution. Several children, who were having problems growing up, followed him. The next penitent was a nun— a religious sister whom I immediately recognized as Sister Ethel, who seemed agitated and furtively glanced at me. Wearing one of those new modern habits that resemble the clothing of lay women with poor taste, I could not have told by her garb that she was called to serve God in a special way.

As soon as she sat down, I said, "How long has it been since your last confession?" I waited expecting to hear the usual catalog of nun sins—I have been envious of others—or I disobeyed my superior—or I was impatient many times—or I lost my temper with a pupil. Was I in for a surprise!

"Bless me, Father, I have sinned. It has been two months since my last confession." Hesitating as if she did not know how to begin, she seemed even more nervous than when she entered my confessional.

"Bless you, Daughter, tell me your sins."

"I am in anguish and torment twenty-four hours a day." She paused, apparently finding it difficult to speak of her problem.

"Yes? Go ahead." I tried to be patient and gentle with her.

"I am madly in love with a priest," she confessed in almost a whisper.

"Does he return your love?"

"I am not sure. He doesn't even seem to know I exist."

"You should not see him or be with him," I counseled.

"The only time I see him is at Mass in our convent or occasionally in the churchyard." Sensing that there was something that she was not telling me, I prompted, "And what else?"

"I am madly in love with you, Father."

I was totally speechless for a few moments. When I regained my composure, I said, "I am sorry, Sister, but I cannot hear your confession. You will have to find another priest to counsel you." I raised my hand in blessing.

"God bless you always!"

She crossed herself and left. From that time forward, I had to brace myself every time I said Mass in their convent or encountered her in the churchyard, because I was determined to make sure that nothing about me would reflect either with my eyes, my handshake, or conversation what I had heard in the confessional. This was very difficult, because Sister Ethel, with her half closed eyes, her elusive smile, and her soft hands, continually reminded me of the tragedy she was living. After all, it was not her fault that she liked a man. However, it was her fault that she approached me with it. Realizing that she was trying to establish some sort of liaison between us, I determined to avoid her, because I knew for a fact that many priests and nuns were yielding to amorous relationships.

Before the year ended a new pastor, Father Rowland Stratford, took over St. Priscillianus and the administrator left in the midst of rumors about a liaison between him and the nun who directed the catechism for children.

In July, I flew to Spain for my vacation. At two a.m. on the morning of July 25, I received a phone call from Father Stratford at the hotel in Santiago de Compostella where I was sound asleep. He obviously did not take into account the time differences between Rosanada and Santiago.

"Congratulations, Father Marco."

"On what?" I was still half asleep.

"The archbishop has made you a pastor."

"Where?"

"At Santiago Mission in Gas'du Hills."

I had never heard of the place. I learned later that Gas'du meant ashes in the Cherokee Indian language.

Deciding that perhaps Pompeo would know about the place, I phoned him in Madrid where he was vacationing. "I can't understand it. The archbishop is sending me to some unheard of mission in Gas'du Hills. I have a Licentiate in Sacred Theology from the Dionysian Pontifical University and I spent a year serving the Holy See in Rome. Why would they do this to me?" As I talked to him, realization dawned on me that Damian Babilonia was the one behind this appointment. His animosity toward me went all the way back to our days as students at Julius III seminary. Now, he had been given the authority to rule the archdiocese on behalf of Melusine.

"Don't worry," Pompeo advised, "just go embrace the statue of St. James, the Apostle, at his tomb there in Santiago and you will feel better. The only thing that matters is to have fun in life and you can have fun anywhere!" That was Pompeo all right.

Before I could get anywhere near the apostle's statue, I had to wait for half an hour. After following the ritual of embracing it, I prayed during two Masses, but unfortunately I was not able to concelebrate, because of the large numbers that had come to visit the Sanctuary of St. James, famous since the Middle Ages as a place of pilgrimage. I could not help but wonder what awaited me at Santiago Mission.

When I arrived in Rosanada, my heart was beating a bit faster, because I was going to be a pastor for the first time, but I felt humiliated that Damian was sending me to an unknown mission, miles away from the Spanish-speaking area where I had lived and moved with familiarity.

When I actually saw Santiago Mission for the first time, I was terribly depressed, because it was far worse than I had imagined in my most depressing thoughts. Since we were in the middle of the rainy season, the ground was covered with puddles, forcing me to take my shoes off and wade ankle deep to the old trailer that severed as a rectory. As a consequence of this, I developed creeping eruption on my feet a few days later and had to go to a doctor and have it frozen to get rid of it. I got it no doubt from Father José's dog, Molly, that he left behind when he moved out.

Because one of the windows on the front of the trailer had a large crack, it was taped with duct tape to keep the glass pane from falling out. The inside of the rectory trailer was worse that the outside. I found a note from Father José saying there was no money in the mission's account and that the archdiocesan subsidy was being cut twenty percent in the new fiscal year. Worst of all, the place was filthy.

As soon as I walked in the door, Molly's fleas that were all over the place, jumped on my legs, biting me fiercely. About ten inches from the floor, every wall in the rectory had a black smudge where Molly had pressed against it when she was dirty and muddy. The whole place reeked. Dog odor was bad enough, but the real cause of the awful smell that permeated the entire rectory was Papo, an indigent and homeless old man that Father José had invited into the rectory to share the room next to his. Because Papo had an aversion to soap and water, his bed, his clothing, and his body all reeked with an abominable stench.

After finding a good home for Papo, I proceeded to clean up the rectory, seeking donations from friends at previous parishes to refurbish the house. Both inside and out, I painted the trailer myself. Pulling up and discarding the carpet that was stained by the dog's urine and accretions of many years was the most difficult job. Having found some inexpensive carpeting in Gas'du Hills, I had a friend help me put it in place. Fortunately, I was able to buy new beds and a few other pieces of furniture.

The few parishioners, who came to see me, more out of curiosity than a desire to welcome me, decided I had pretensions and what was good enough for Father José should be good enough for me. To make matters worse, I soon discovered that the old dilapidated church building was full of termites. There was only one bright spot on the horizon and that was Pedro, the church musician, a guitar player from Argentina, who offered me his complete support.

Pedro Gutierrez, brimming with desire to succeed in life, worked as a mechanic, but hoped to be able to go to school. Blessed with a lot of musical talent with the guitar, and anxious to help me in every way he could, he stopped by the rectory frequently to ask if there was anything he could do for me. I mostly needed information.

"Why are there so many cars in the parking lot of the mission every afternoon?" I could not understand why there were so many people coming and going all the time.

Pedro told me straight out. "Prostitutes, Father, prostitutes."

"And the parking lot is crowded at night because they return to drop them off?" I couldn't believe what I was hearing. When I invited Pedro to have a cup of coffee, he asked if I had a beer, so I opened a can and gave it to him. His information and help were worth far more than the price of a can of beer.

"No, they don't come here at night. They go elsewhere. The people who come here at night are drug dealers selling perico, pot, and crack, or whatever people want."

From Pedro, I learned that the mission was located in one of the worst crime areas in the state, and neither the church nor the rectory had an alarm system. Knowing that some addict, looking for a fix, could break in and kill me in my sleep, every night after my prayers, I made an act of faith in God's Providence to protect me during the night.

Because I wanted to be a pastor to these people who rejected me, I lay awake on long sleepless nights vexed by feelings of inadequacy. My great desire was to turn the mission into an exemplary Vatican II church, and all I got was opposition from my parishioners and even from Luisa, the housekeeper, who came in during the days to cook and clean. What could the future possibly bring? Although I felt extremely competent for any relevant position in the Church, I had been sent through no fault of mine to one of the worst places in Rosanada, where I was surrounded by criminals and prostitutes who continued trafficking in the parking lot. The bishops only did that to priests they wanted to punish. What could I do? What could I possibly do?

19
Luz

Aurelio was gone and Luz was devastated. Perhaps, she reasoned, if they had stayed in Cuba and he could have had his surgery sooner, he would not have died. Instead, he sacrificed himself, while in so much pain to bring her to Rosanada and Marco. She knew it was love for her that motivated him to do that.

The funeral was simply beautiful. She was amazed that the archbishop, the auxiliary bishops, and very many priests were in the sanctuary at St. Cassiel, concelebrating the Mass of the Resurrection for her husband. Marco's friend, Father Pompeo, preached a homily that was truly worthy of her husband. Surprised how many of the people who were at the Mass also came to the cemetery where Father Pompeo gave Aurelio a last eulogy, she watched as he touched the casket three times and the words he spoke still echoed in her memory: "This is not the end, but the beginning, for we will soon meet again in the Kingdom." Turning to the mourners, he said: "Aurelio is not dead! He lives forever!" When he said this, all those gathered around the grave broke out in applause. Although some were crying, Martha was stone faced as usual, but Luz saw Norberto wipe a tear from his eye.

Deeply grateful for the young priest's ministry, Luz, feeling weak and faint, leaned on Marco's arm as they made their way back to his car. Father Mínimo insisted on taking them out to lunch at a restaurant near his parish.

"Not now, Mínimo," Marco protested. "Can't you see my mother is not well?"

"Well, I thought it would nice—take her mind off things," he said thoughtlessly.

Marco drove her back to the little apartment he had found for her and Aurelio. How empty it was now that Aurelio was no longer there. He was the love of her life and now he was gone. She really wanted to be alone, she explained to Marco, and so he left her to return to Santiago Mission.

The next few days were the hardest. Going to the closet where Aurelio kept his things, she would pull out one of his garments, embrace it tightly in her arms, breathing in the scent of her husband that lingered on it. Their bed constantly reminded her of her husband. When she lay down in it at night, its emptiness cried out to her. How could she go on living without him! In her misery she cried out to *Ochún, Nuestra Señora de la Caridad del Cobre,* the Santerian patroness saint of Cuba for help. Finding a *caracol,* a sacred seashell that a previous tenant had left behind, she pressed it to her ear, hoping to hear what Ochún would say to her. Remembering her promise to Father Moreno back at Manta Negra that she would reject all involvement with Santería, she tossed the *caracol* in the garbage, deciding to tell Marco what she had done as soon as she saw him.

Although it was difficult for Marco to get time off, he came to see her as often as he could. When he came the next day, she immediately told him about the *caracol* and how she had been involved in Santería.

187

"I promised Father Moreno and God that I would give up all connection with Santería and now I found myself praying to Ochún. I am truly sorry. It is just that I felt so confused and alone without your father." She felt Marco's strong arms around her as he tenderly kissed her on the forehead."

"Don't worry, Mom, we will take care of it. Make an act of contrition and I will bless you."

"Oh, my God I am heartily sorry…" She continued the prayer in whispers, crossing herself as Marco blessed her. When he walked though the apartment, sprinkling holy water everywhere, reciting prayers of blessing, she sighed deeply and resolved that she would never again turn to Ochún.

Suddenly a terrifying thought crossed her mind. "I hope I will not experience the wrath of Ochún now that I have done this." Her eyes, the color of dark amber were filled with fear.

"No! Mother no! "Don't worry, Jesus will protect you from all harm."

As they sat down in the kitchen of the small apartment where Luz made a pot of coffee and offered him a dish of flan, he said: "I have something I want to tell you." Even though she had never cooked anything in her life before they came to Rosanada, she knew she had to learn, because she would not have four maids to wait on her as she always had in Mérida. Purchasing a box of Goya flan mix at the small mercado on the ground floor of her apartment building, she had managed to prepare it—the first food she had ever fixed for him in her life.

"What do you want to tell me?" she asked with mild curiosity, having lost interest in life since Aurelio was gone.

"One of my parishioners has a bookstore and has offered you a job. I think it would be good for you to have something to do to keep busy. What do you think?"

"Well, I guess I could try it." It would be a completely new experience for her, and she did need the money, because they had not been able to bring any of their wealth out of Cuba.

Because she did not like working in a public place serving customers, she quit after only a few days on the job. When she explained to Marco that she wanted to live a more private and secluded life, he came up with a solution that appealed to her. One of Marco's priest friends offered her the position as housekeeper for a large rectory that housed five priests. She jumped at the offer, feeling that working for the Church would make her feel protected and secure. The fact that she could not cook did not matter, for the parish had a full-time cook. Her duties would include answering the door and the phone and keeping the house clean and in order.

With Marco's help, she packed up her few things and moved into St. Mary Tudor the very next day where Father Pompeo made her feel welcome by bringing up her luggage to a nice sized room on the third floor of the relatively new and large colonial style brick house. She liked the room that was simply furnished, such as a room in a convent might be—there was single bed, a dresser, two wooden armchairs, and a large crucifix on the wall above the bed. There was also a private bathroom with both a large shower and tub *en suite.*

Although Father Pompeo was especially nice to her, she soon observed that he often acted in strange ways, doing crazy things that she found difficult to comprehend. For example, if she wanted to tell him something, he just wouldn't listen. Before she had a chance to speak to him, he would start talking and continue talking incessantly. Then before she had a chance to say a word, he would say goodbye and leave. Half the time, he seemed to be absolutely out of touch with the real world.

Quickly settling in to life at St. Mary Tudor rectory, she was at peace and her soul was beginning to heal from the trauma of years in prison and the loss of Aurelio. Surely she thought Ochún could not do anything wrathful or revengeful against her here in the house of God. Little did she realize that the Evil One is more apt to prowl among the people of God than he is among sinners who are already in his possession.

20
Marco

I tried everything to make the mission a success. When I found a list that Father José had compiled of the parishioners of Santiago, I phoned them all and greeted them as their new pastor, telling them that I was looking forward to meeting each one of them. The response was poor. Some were very busy, and others had many obligations. They simply thanked me in a matter of fact manner and had very little else to say. There were really very few remaining in the mission, so I deepened my resolve to work at evangelization. When I discovered there was a group of Venezuelans living in a nearby development, I determined to try to bring them into the mission, but God was not moving in the souls of these people. As the Scripture says, "Unless the Lord build the house, they struggle in vain who try to do so." However, I had not yet learned that basic truth.

During the Christmas season I arranged an ice skating party for the young people on a local pond after Mass and served them hot chocolate and pastries. This was a pastoral effort beyond what anyone anticipated, because I had long hours of work ministering to the souls who were seeking spiritual help, setting up an operational system for the mission, and developing a pastoral organization of lay people to help reach all who would come to Santiago.

Absolutely convinced that I could do something marvelous for God, I strove to expand His kingdom. I still had not learned that we do not do God's work, but, rather, He works through us. For His part, God has had many surprises for me throughout my entire priestly life.

Perhaps, I figured, if I could start a bingo game, it would draw people to Santiago and then to God. I talked to some friends about it, hoping to get some used equipment that could be used for that purpose. Nothing ever came of it.

During the course of one year, I tried everything I could think of—festivals, dances, raffles, all kinds of activities that served only to exhaust me and my helpers. Everything I tried was a failure, netting just a few miserable coins and making no spiritual progress for the mission. Heartbroken, I kept wondering what I was doing in such an apparently God forsaken place. Archbishop Melusine and Monsignor Damian, miles away in the magnificent chancery building, had absolutely no conception or interest in finding out of what I was going through. I made no attempt to tell them.

One day when I went to start my car to go shopping for food, it would not start—the engine simply would not turn over. Throwing up the hood, I saw at once that the battery was missing. Someone had stolen it. Well, God bless them—perhaps they needed it more than I. A few days later the tires were taken from my car where it stood in the parking lot next to my trailer rectory.

Prowlers broke the church windows and ransacked the building, looking for something of value to steal. One thing after another like this occurred, causing me to feel helpless and weary. Some days I felt very weak.

Nevertheless, in spite of all these adverse happenings, I managed to buy a second-hand mimeograph machine and began printing out a church bulletin each week. I was able to work on the accounting system and get it in good shape. What I liked doing most was helping the poor who came to the mission everyday, when I passed out food to them.

As the Lord said, we always have the poor with us. Since I was inexperienced, I got the idea of creating a store where it would not be necessary to pay—everything would be free to those in need. Setting up a room petitioned off from the rest of the church, I put in a stock of clothing and food with the idea being that those in need would come, take what they needed, and leave without paying. An angelic, heavenly idea—it was a dismal failure. People came, took what they wanted, and then sold it for what little money it would bring. I had a lot to learn about human nature and our sinful condition.

Deciding to combat the practice of selling what the mission gave them, I had people sign for whatever they took, permitting them to come only once a week, but when that did not work either, I tried making them pay a little something for what they got. Nothing I could think of worked, because with their cupidity they always outwitted me, forcing me in utter frustration to close the store.

Some of the women that came to the mission also proved to be a challenge. While some of them had holy intentions, others did not, causing me to deal with them as tactfully as I could, politely, but firmly sending them on their way. I was confronted with many appointments, requests for home visits, and all kinds of problems—often frivolous—for which women wanted counsel.

Although at night during my prayer time, I sought the Presence, I could not find Him, but deeply desiring to experience Him again, I persisted in prayer, longing to hear His voice as I had in the past, because I so much wanted to hear Him speaking in the depths of my heart. Nothing! Constantly I asked God, "What am I doing here?" My prayers seemed to go no higher than the ceiling of my room.

No matter how much I prayed and meditated on my problems, I did not know what to do to make the Santiago Mission grow. Even though I really wanted to make it develop and prosper and give God to people, nothing I did seemed to work.

A year passed, and I still had not been able to build a fence to protect my home from the various strange characters—often criminals—who roamed the street where the rectory and church were located. Nor had I been able to install an alarm in the house or church. Furthermore, there was no neighbor nearby that I could call out to for help, if I needed it.

One night I got a frightful scare. I can still remember the terror that I felt. It was about eleven o'clock at night, when suddenly the power went off, leaving the entire area plunged in a turbulent sea of darkness. I knew that under the cover of the blackout, thieves and muggers would prowl everywhere trying to ply their trades. I heard a gunshot—a loud blast—quite close by. Then I heard another shot, and still another. Terrified, I knelt, praying fervently. Why Lord, I asked, am I here? Nothing I do seems to work. Why am I here where anyone could break into the house and kill me for a few dollars to buy drugs?

Suddenly, the Presence of the Lord was upon me, lifting me up in an embrace of ecstatic love, and giving me an infusion of Divine Light. Time stopped and nothing mattered except to respond to His Love. Like a tremendous cascade, He inundated me with His grace, and I felt transformed and reaffirmed. I couldn't even move. I felt secure, protected. I was caught up in this experience of intense ecstasy for at least an hour, when I heard His voice speaking in my soul. "I know you are making a great effort for me. I know all your deeds, but you are missing the most important thing. You must return to your first love for me." In my soul the words sprang forth: "I will do anything for You!' When one is in the embrace of His tremendous love, one can refuse Him nothing. Slowly after about another hour, the Presence slipped away, leaving me filled with peace.

The words He had spoken to me reminded me of the third chapter of the book of Revelation in the message to the Church of Ephesus. I found a candle and a match, and by candlelight, I read the entire book of Revelation. Filled with fervor that the Lord was speaking to me again, I lay awake in my bed, praising God, feeling secure and safe, although the blackout continued many hours.

As I lay there in the night, thinking about my life, I realized that the flurry of all my fruitless activities had gradually eroded my relationship with God—a relationship of love. Many times I begged His forgiveness and each time the Presence again took possession of me, each time more powerfully than before. Finally at daybreak, He spoke to me again:" You are my beloved son, do not be afraid, because I will always be with you." With these words, all fear vanished.

I awoke that morning full of life and energy, willing to do everything God wanted, but I did not know where to begin. It was not until later that I understood that what God was asking of me was simply a deeper surrender to Him and His will. Then I forgave all those who had in any way harmed me and placed myself completely in the hands of God. Then I felt I was truly returning to my first Love.

Although my inner life and my union with God had intensified, still nothing was happening at Santiago. Feeling God's call on my life more strongly now than ever before, I wanted to carry His gospel to the ends of the earth—to speak for Him in the darkness of this world, carrying His message of faith, hope, and love to those who were lost in the snares of sin, but when I surveyed the poverty of the mission church and that of the neighborhood filled with thieves, muggers, drug dealers, and prostitutes, it all seemed like an impossible dream.

One evening, I watched a famous Protestant evangelist on television preaching to one hundred thousand people in a stadium in Buenos Aires, criticizing our holy faith and derogating it. Inspired to kneel down and pray, I repeated the words of one of the Old Testament prophets: "Lord, I am willing to take Your Word wherever You want."

Up until this time, I had not been able to communicate God to my parishioners, but that soon changed, because of something that happened during the monthly Mass for the sick in the poor little mission church that was dilapidated, but spotlessly clean. When the Mass had just ended and the candles were still burning on the altar, Pedro was strumming his guitar, leading the congregation in the hymn "Rise and be healed in the name of Jesus." Praying in general for all the people to be healed, I was at the ambo, when a man in a wheelchair came slowly down the aisle and stopped before the altar. Shrunken, frail, up in years, and obviously quite ill, and with pathos in his eyes, he called out to me: "Pray for me, Father!"

As I left the ambo and walked to where he was, the Presence came over me, urging me to tell the invalid that he had been healed, that he should get up and walk. Since I had promised Him that I would do whatever He wished, I placed my hands firmly on the old man's head and timorously, but in a loud voice said authoritatively, "In the name of Jesus, get up and walk!"

Suddenly, the man bolted from his chair, began walking, and then pushing his wheelchair down the aisle toward the back of the church. The dead silence of the congregation gave way to raucous applause and shouting.

I was dumbfounded! No one was more amazed than I. I knew miracles took place at Lourdes and Fátima and other sanctuaries, but to see one happen in a poor little mission church staggered the mind and the senses. I knew that all things are possible with God, but I never dreamed He would do such wonders through my intercession and ministry.

Immediately, other people were rushing down the aisle for me to pray for them. There were no medical explanations for the many healings that occurred. Right away, attendance at Mass increased dramatically. People who had seemed indifferent to learning about God now could not seem to hear enough about Him. And I? I was joyful, because finally, at last, I was speaking for God and He was working though me.

A man who had no faith brought his twelve-year-old son to me in desperation. For three hours I had been praying individually over the many sick who gathered waiting for prayers. When it finally came time for me to pray for the lad whose optic nerves had been destroyed, I laid my hands on him—instantly the boy fell to the floor and lay in an ecstatic trance. In total amazement, I looked at the happy smile that was on his face as he rested in the Presence, thanking God for His ministry to the child. When the boy arose after about fifteen minutes, he cried, "I can see! I can see!" The applause was thunderous. People were even peering through the open windows of the church to get a glimpse of what God was doing at Santiago.

When the healing service finally ended that evening, I returned to the trailer rectory with my heart overflowing with joy. God was answering my prayers. I thanked Him with all my heart for blessing his people and me so wonderfully.

Two days later the phone range.

"This is Monsignor Damian's secretary. The chancellor wishes to speak with you now." Her voice was like icicles and imperious to boot. After I waited about three minutes, Damian finally came to the phone.

Without any greeting or preamble, he yelled. "What the hell are you doing out there?" He did not wait for me to answer, but continued: "Someone told me that you are delving into the magic arts and healing the sick."

"I don't know what you are talking about, Damian. I just pray for the sick."

"Oh, so now we have another Padre Pio in the archdiocese!" His words were venomous and mordant. "Next I suppose you will be getting the stigmata!"

"Give me a break, Damian; I am not doing anything wrong! I just pray for the sick, like Jesus told us to do," I said softly trying to bring some calm to the conversation.

"Of course, but do it without hysteria or cheap miracles. Sentimentalism is also out of place." His voice was overbearing and oppressive in my ear.

"I will speak to the archbishop about it," I said gently, trying to assuage his wrath."

"That won't be necessary. I already have. We insist that you proceed very carefully, when you pray for the sick. Do you understand?" He clipped his words and spoke very harshly.

"Yes, of course. I understand completely." I understood very well that the language of the chancery was money and that they did not care about Christ's ministry. This was the first time I had heard from the chancery, since I had come to Santiago over a year earlier—a phone call to reprimand me for praying for the sick. What a Church we had!

Two weeks later, I had an appointment with the archbishop. The meeting was inane. Melusine, pale, thin, and remote, seemed lost behind the archiepiscopal desk. Although he smiled at me attentively during the entire interview, he seemed to have his mind on something else. Avoiding looking directly at me, he spoke in vague generalities. As usual his dingy black suit lacked a good dry-cleaning and the room had that strange sulfurous odor that I always associated with him.

Picking up a piece of paper from his desk, he read it and said, "Marco Lamadrid, I believe," taking my name from the paper his secretary had given him. Remembering names was an impossibility for him, for he immediately asked me: "What is the name of your mission?"

"Santiago, Archbishop." I replied without emotion.

"Yes, yes, of course, Santiago. Well, Father," he said patronizingly, "you must be very prudent out there. Prudence is a very great virtue. You must learn to cultivate it."

"I'll try, Archbishop," I responded politely. While I peered at him intently, his slate blue eyes avoided mine.

"In the Catholic Church, we have to make room for everyone. Yes, everyone—that is what it means to be Catholic. Even though people do not like your style, you have to make room for them too so that they also feel they are part of the community."

This did not make any sense to me. If people don't like my style, there is nothing I can do to make them feel at home at Santiago and with me. These were my thoughts, but I simply said, "I will do my best, Archbishop."

As I was leaving the chancery, I ran into Renato and Enki Mutante coming out of Del'Ano's office on the first floor. As soon as Renato spotted me, he at once stuck out his slender and limp hand for me to shake.

"There is nothing but talk about your miracles these past several days," he said leering at me with evident distaste. Obviously his dislike for me was intensifying.

Since I did not know what to respond to his insidious look of triumph that proclaimed he had caught me in an unsavory situation, I simply said: "You are invited to visit Santiago any day you wish." I stared him down.

Surprisingly Enki said, "I would like to come to one of your services." Because I pictured him as a loyal sycophant of Renato and Damian, fawning on them continually, and spouting obsequious and flattering words of praise, I was surprised to hear him say he would like to visit Santiago. How I could help advance his career and why he wanted to come to visit Santiago, I could not understand, because I still had a lot to learn about Enki and his ambitions. I also learned that Renato had humiliated him and he found it distasteful to be associated with his society any longer. O how I wish I had never issued him that invitation! The results were disastrous.

21
Enki

What a stroke of luck to run into Marco Lamadrid at Damian's office! Because he felt horribly oppressed and constrained in the St. Thomas Society, Enki decided that Marco might be the way for him to escape Renato and his domination and get away from Damian too, even though he detested Marco. True, the St. Thomas Society let him sing and preach, but he could not open his heart and preach against all the evils of society that need to be denounced, because Renato held him back, saying he did not want to offend anyone. He absolutely forbade him to talk about drug addiction, drug dealing and prostitution! On top of that, Renato had offended him! He had offended him by parading his doctorate and reminding Enki that he had not earned his degree at the university, but had dropped out after three years, and had even raised questions about his parentage. So he decided that the best strategy would be to take Yo-Lin Sin with him to visit the Santiago Mission to see if he could possibly find a better niche for himself there, where he would be able to do as he pleased. He felt confident that he could manipulate Marco; everyone knew how naïve he was.

At six o'clock the next day Enki and Yo-Lin arrived in the stifling August heat at Santiago in Gas'du Hills. Opening the cheap wooden door of the mission, he escorted Yo-Lin into the dilapidated old building. He noted that the linoleum on the floor was worn and the printed designs had worn off in places.

"Come, Yo-Lin, let's sit in the front where we can see everything."

She followed him as they made their way down the aisle and took a seat in what he considered to be the poorest church he had ever seen in the United States.

They knelt on a padded wooden kneeler and looked at the altar—a plain wooden altar, bearing an immaculately clean and starched altar cloth. The candlesticks were of silver, but not as fancy as they were in Caracas. A red sanctuary lamp burned dimly in the shadows.

He had to admit he was a bit embarrassed, because Yo-Lin was so inappropriately dressed in a bright green tunic that showed far too much of her long lank legs. Obviously she was not wearing anything underneath it, because the nipples of her breasts protruded boldly through the fabric. Apparently she had dressed to seduce him. Well, he would see about that when he took her home later that evening. Nevertheless, he felt uncomfortable about her tawdry and seductive appearance.

After a few minutes, Marco emerged from the sacristy and when he noticed the two of them kneeling devoutly in the front pew, Enki raised his hand in greeting. Marco responded by coming to greet them.

"Your Reverence, "Enki exclaimed, "It's a pleasure to see you. Your Mission is a beautiful place," he lied, "and it is an honor for me to bring my good friend Yo-Lin Sin and introduce you to her."

Enki watched as Yo-Lin immediately turned her charm on Marco. If he noticed how inappropriately she was dressed, he made no indication of it.

"I hope that the service tonight will be a blessing to you both. Now I have to continue with my preparations for it." Marco excused himself and returned to the sacristy.

Soon Pedro, the guitarist, started the music to announce the beginning of the healing service, as the people stood and sang the Pentecostal songs that Enki loved, although he could not endure their speaking in tongues and their other antics.

When Marco appeared at the altar, Enki thought, "I guess the show will begin now. I wonder what kind of a crude miracle he is going to invent this evening." He glanced over at Yo-Lin who looked utterly devout.

After welcoming the people to Santiago and inviting them to come forward to receive prayer for healing, Marco began talking in a strange unintelligible language. "A tongue talker!" thought Enki, totally repulsed by everything he had seen so far this evening.

"What's he saying? What's he saying?" Yo-Lin nudged him on his arm.

Before he could explain, people began to line up and approach Marco, where he stood before the altar. When Marco prayed for the first woman, laying his hands on her head, she screamed, "Hallelujah!" returning to her seat claiming to be healed.

One after another the people came forward and they returned to their places, claiming healing.

"Would any of you like to testify to what God has done for you?" Marco asked looking expectantly at the worshipers for someone to volunteer.

One woman got up, stood beside Marco, facing the people in the pews and said, "I had a terrible pain in my leg. And now it is gone." Shouts of "Praise God!" came ringing from the pews.

Another woman claimed she had been healed of migraines. Still another told of how the pain around her heart was gone.

More and more testimonies of healing followed. Still Enki was very incredulous, especially when Yo-Lin rose to her feet, walked up and stood beside Father Marco and told of how she had been healed from a severely prolapsed vagina and extreme discomfort of the vulva. After all she was a woman of the world. She basked in the applause that followed the account of her healing. After watching the proceedings, Enki decided that he himself could run a healing service. However, something happened that changed his opinion.

A man in a wheelchair, who was completely unable to walk, slowly wheeled his way down the aisle to where Marco was standing.

"What is you trouble?" Marco asked the man with evident compassion.

"I have been suffering with a hernia of the spine for the past ten years," the man responded almost timidly.

"Do you believe that Jesus can heal you right now?" Marco asked.

"I know He can," the man replied. I have seen others healed here in this prayer line."

Enki watched as Marco laid his hands on the man's head, causing him to shriek. Deep intense silence fell upon the congregation. Utterly amazed, Enki carefully watched as the man rose from his wheel chair and began to walk—at first with a few unsteady steps. Then he began to run down the aisle and all around the church, shouting at the top of his lungs, "I'm healed! I'm healed!" Going to his wife, he embraced her, as she incredulously watched her husband walk for the first time in ten years. Enki was completely awed by this miracle that he saw take place in the shabby little mission church.

When the healing service ended, Marco stood in the vestibule of the church, shaking the hands of those who were leaving. He was obviously surprised when Yo-Lin approached him.

"Father Marco," Yo-Lin said, "I would like to become a member of Santiago. I really love your church. Would you please give me a registration card?" Enki watched as Marco picked up a card from a table by the door and handed it to Yo-Lin who immediately filled it out and returned it to Marco together with her personal check for five thousand dollars. Enki could see that Marco was impressed by the devout Yo-Lin.

Once they were in Yo-Lin's Mercedes, she kicked off her neon green shoes, sat back and relaxed, letting Enki do the driving.

"That was a real laugh, wasn't it?" She lit up one of her oval Egyptian cigarettes and blew a puff of smoke in his face.

"Well, I was pretty impressed by the one who jumped up out of the wheelchair and began running around. It looked pretty genuine to me. And you, why did you register in the mission?"

"Oh that," Yo-Lin replied with a hollow laugh. "It will be good for my reputation. No one would ever expect to find someone with my connections, if you know what I mean, in a dump like that." She inhaled a cloud of smoke and blew it out again. Besides, I have a lot of guilt for things I have done in the past and at Santiago there are so many people that I can help. I am sure God will forgive me for my past, if I make up for it by doing good to people who are unfortunate. I have really done some very bad things."

She sat in silence for a few minutes and then continued. "You tell me about how Renato mistreats you. Why don't you ask Marco for a job at Santiago. You could get away from Renato and I am sure Marco could use you. You would be a very good assistant for him. Most importantly, I think he would give you the freedom to do as you please. Then you won't always be complaining to me about how Renato is controlling you."

When they arrived at her condo on the river, Yo-Lin told Enki that she was going to change into something more comfortable. Before she left the room, she tossed him a big stack of erotic photos of children, saying, "Here Enki! I believe this is your thing!"

No doubt about it, Yo-Lin knew what it took to arouse a man. After carefully considering what Yo-Lin had suggested about his getting a job at the Santiago mission and since it agreed with his own opinions, Enki phoned Marco the next day making an appointment to see him the following day.

During his interview with Marco, Enki told him about his life and his desire to minister in a community such as Santiago, and about his imagined spiritual experiences, and of how he wanted to convert people and get them to stop sinning. Seeing that Marco believed his every word, Enki decided that Marco was the kind of priest that never thought evil of anyone, taking everything they told him at face value. When he had finished recounting his story, Father Marco asked him:

"Why do you not want to continue with Father Renato and the St. Thomas Restoration Society? You seemed to be well established there. Father Renato has a strong community with great financial means and can compensate you much better than we can here at Santiago." Marco eyes probed his.

"The thing is, Father, that I feel a call to work with simple people. I'm not worried about money. I don't need much to live on," Enki lied, because he knew that Yo-Lin would provide for his needs. What he wanted was freedom to do as he pleased.

Finally after a long conversation, Enki sensed that he had convinced Marco of his desire to serve God.

"We can use a dedicated laymen here at Santiago," Marco told him, as they shook hands sealing their negotiations. "I need an administrative assistant. Would you be interested in the job?"

"If I can sing and maybe preach a sermon every so often."

"I think that can be arranged."

"How many employees do you have here?" Enki asked as he took a sip of the rich Cuban coffee and nibbled on a cookie that Marco served him.

"There is just the secretary and the housekeeper—and now you. You can live in the housekeeper's apartment nearby. It is small but adequate."

Later that evening when Enki told Yo-Lin what had happened, she laughed and found it hilarious that Enki was going to live in the housekeeper's apartment. "You can't live in that dump, she said as she offered him a plate of almond cookies and a Svaroski flute of champagne. "Let's drink to your new life. I know you will be glad to get out from under Renato's thumb, but live here with me." She drained her champagne flute and poured another.

"I can't do that, Yo-Lin. I will be working for the Church and I can't live with anyone that I am not married to. I will stay with the old lady until I can get something of my own." He drained his champagne and set the glass on the cocktail table in front of the sofa, where they were sitting side by side. "I, at least hope you will continue helping me out, like you have been." She had always been generous with money, and it did not make the slightest difference to him that it was Mafia money, acquired from the selling of drugs. He simply just didn't care.

When he leaned over to kiss her lightly on the lips, she drew him closer to her, holding him fast, and gazing deep into his eyes.

"You know you can count on me, Enki, for anything."

That is what he had been waiting for her to say. She handed him a stack of pornographic photos and said seductively, "Get ready for bed, Enki"

The next morning, Enki went eagerly to see Renato in his office at the chancery to break the news to him that he was now the administrative assistant at Santiago Mission and would no longer be ministering at the St. Thomas Society.

"Your Reverence, how nice it is to see you," Enki said as he sat down in the white leather chair across the desk from Renato.

"I am also glad to see you. What brings you to the chancery?"

"I have some good news to share with you. Yo-Lin has gotten me a job working at the Santiago Mission," Enki lied, taking the approach that he felt would most appeal to Renato.

"Don't tell me that Yo-Lin has become friends with Father Marco?" Renato seemed incredulous.

"You know very well, Father, that Yo-Lin is friends with all the priests."

"Then, you are going to sever relations with the St. Thomas Society and me?"

"On the contrary, Father, I think that as of now I will be able to serve you even better than before."

Enki could see that Renato was not convinced. "Yo-Lin thinks it's a great idea! She is all in favor of my working at the mission." He knew that bit of news would silence any opposition that Renato felt about the change, because Renato liked the large checks that she gave him.

Enki could see that Father Renato was still not convinced and even felt annoyed about Yo-Lin's intervention, but Enki knew there was nothing he could do about it. He also knew that Renato would never cross Yo-Lin and offend her in the slightest way. Laughing nervously, Renato extended his pale hand and congratulated him on his job at the mission.

Because he had to go through immigration proceedings and obtain a work permit, months passed before Enki was able to assume his position as administrative assistant at Santiago. Meanwhile he stayed at Yo-Lin's home, working at the mission every day, as well as attending various evening meetings during the week. Providing him with all the inventions that her sick mind dedicated to sexual pleasure could devise, Yo-Lin even occasionally invited her maid to share the bed with them and video taped the whole intercourse with a paid cameraman that ended up joining them. Her creativity allowed every part of her body to be used at the same time. And as she used to say: "This is just for fun! God does not care about the way you use your ass!"

Enrique Mutante liked being at the mission. He knew he was a born leader and people responded to his gentle ways. Always careful to speak gently not to offend anyone when he preached, he knew that with his pleasant voice and words taken from Scripture he had the power to enchant his listeners. Only Pedro, the guitar player opposed him, but he knew he could get rid of Pedro who had complained to Marco pointing out his flaws. Fortunately, Marco simply did not believe Pedro when he told him bad things about him. It wasn't long until Pedro quit directing the choirs and was replaced by Bastits Koldwall, a woman Marco hired, because she was needy like a stray cat, and he felt sorry for her. She could not help her looks or behavior, coming as she did from a dysfunctional family where the father had nothing on his mind but church activities. Every night of the week, he found a reason not to be at home, but rather occupied himself at the parish church. Her mother was a gossip, who spent her days on the phone with her friends talking about everyone's sex life, since she did not have one of her own. Never at home at night, she went out to play bridge or canasta with her crowd. Bastits learned from a tender age to cook pizzas in the oven. Her greatest problem was jealously, because her sister Honda Koldwall was extremely beautiful and popular with men. Although she did a good job of directing the choirs, her voice was actually unpleasant—she sounded like a fog horn—and so she left the singing of solos to various choir members, one of which, Augustas Mc Neith, led the praise at the Sunday Masses and the evening prayer meeting on Wednesday nights.

When he began working at the mission, Enki had a complete agenda ready with Yo-Lin standing behind him to ensure that it was carried out. Now nothing could stop him! He was in the United States, the land of opportunity, the friend of a powerful woman, and was working for a priest with the growing reputation of being holy. How could he lose!

22
Yo-Lin

Pleased with the results of her cosmetic endeavors and Botox injections, Yo-Lin looked in the gold hand mirror at her face, noting that her wrinkles were gone. Placing the mirror back on the white French provincial dresser in her bedroom, she let her silky back Naomi Campbell nightie fall to the floor where she left it lying for Colette to pick up. She reached for her robe that was lying on the gold brocaded chaise next to the bed and slipped it on, just as Enki was waking up.

Watching him sit up in the kingsize bed she shared with him, she chortled blithely: "*Querido*, what a sleepy head! It is almost ten and you are still not up. Father Marco will be displeased that you are arriving so late for work." She rumpled his black straight hair with her left hand and patted him on his scarred cheek with her right.

"I'm not worried about him. I got him wrapped around my little finger. By the way, I won't be home tonight, because I am moving my stuff to the housekeeper's apartment near Santiago today. I guess you will have to be satisfied with sleeping with Colette." He rose from the bed and went to shower. When he returned and began dressing, he said, "Well, you are all dressed up today. Special plans?"

"Yes, I am working on a ten million dollar deal with a Colombian outfit. I'll make enough off this one to keep you in style. And don't worry about me. Since you are moving out, I'll probably bring the Colombian boss here for the night."

She put the finishing touches on her grooming. Her black velvet Versace original, made especially for her, was simply a dream. She studied her appearance carefully in the wall mirror. The blue rinse was gone now from her hair. She really preferred it ebony, but she could see in the mirror that gray roots were beginning to show again. She would simply have to find time to go to the beauty salon and have it done as soon as she could possibly manage.

Rushing to the kitchen where Colette had coffee and juice waiting for her, she found that her daughter Yin-Lu and the Puerto Rican doorman of their condo building were at table. Yin-Lu was disgusting! There she was sitting on the lap of the doorman, a man with big muscles and no brain! Why couldn't the girl find someone with more class to sleep with!

Quickly she drank the orange juice and coffee and rushed out the door. Today she decided she would take her big white Cadillac sedan—it was more prestigious than the sports car she drove to places like Santiago. Thoughts of the mission came to her as she drove down the river road toward her appointed meeting with the big man of Atocha. Father Marco was nice, but naïve. She would have no trouble pulling the wool over his eyes. The next time she saw him she would drop another five thousand dollar check into the collection. What a wonderful cover the mission and Father Marco would be. She could put on a good act and he would think she was a saint!

23
Marco

Slowly, I was beginning to make a little progress in the mission. Because I wanted everyone who came to find a second home at Santiago, I put up partitions and made separate places for various events and groups in one part of the church building, Although I had never painted before, I managed to paint the entire church and rectory inside and out.

Most wonderfully the Lord continued to manifest Himself at our services with many people being healed. When I was praying over the people, I felt inspired to say that a certain person was being healed of problems with the eyes, or the heart, or the lungs, or other parts of the body. I told a childless couple that they would become parents and they did—a year later! I was able to tell the people many things—for example, I told one man that he was going to receive a financial blessing, and his employer gave him a big bonus and a salary increase shortly thereafter. It was a deeply spiritual and supernatural experience for me and for all the people who beheld the work of God in amazement.

When the ministry of healing was over for the evening, I invited everyone to accept Jesus Christ as Lord and Savior with a simple prayer of surrender. After these healing sessions, I was always very tired, but I could see that God was calling me in a special way to proclaim His Word.

When he approached me one day, Enzo Ciccio, one of the English speaking members and a businessman with a large successful delivery corporation, took me by great surprise. Because he took time off from work to come to see me, I knew he had something important and serious on his mind.

"Look, Pastor, I won't waste your time or mine. I'll come right to the point. I have talked to some of the other men of our parish, and we are convinced that we should expand and extend our mission. We feel that God is calling you to reach more people." His honest brown eyes met mine unflinchingly.

I nodded. "What do you suggest?"

He fidgeted in his chair, thought a moment before continuing. "I say we move to another address. The neighborhood is very bad. We should get out of it."

"I only wish we could, Enzo. I cannot set up a church where I would like to. A pastor in the Catholic Church cannot do that. He has to stay where the archbishop has put him."

"Ok, Padre, don't say that. Are we stuck with the place?" He seemed very disappointed to hear this.

"But," I explained "we could rent a building somewhere and use it for meetings and retreats. Perhaps that would be the answer."

His face lit up. "Great, we'll look into it."

A few weeks later, Enzo came back to see me again.

"We can't find a suitable building for rent that we can afford."

"I knew it would be difficult, Enzo. At least, you tried. The Lord will reward you for your good intentions." I stood up from the kitchen table where we sat talking, thinking our conversation was over.

"But wait, Padre, we have another suggestion." He smiled at me and had an enthusiastic twinkle in his eyes.

"Yes?"

"Since we cannot leave our present location, we want to start a television ministry and take the gospel to the ends of the earth, Lord willing!" Joy was written on his face.

"Television ministry?" I couldn't believe what I was hearing, because I speak English with a Cuban accent. "I can't picture myself going on television. Besides, I am basically shy."

"Padre, your accent is no problem. People will just have to pay closer attention to what you are saying." Because he was so positive and so filled with enthusiasm, I hated to throw cold water on his ideas.

"Well, it would cost a lot money," I said pointing out the obvious for his consideration.

"We'll get the money, Father Marco." He could see I was still not convinced. "If we can raise the money, Father, can we do it?" he asked with determination.

"If you get the money, I am willing to give it a try."

Enthusiastically Enzo shook my hand. "We will get it. You'll see, Father, that this is what God wants of us." He rose to his feet. "I want to go right now and tell the others." With that he ran out the door of the trailer, jumped in his Mercedes, and drove off.

Shortly thereafter I learned that they decided they needed to raise eighty thousand dollars for equipment and supplies. I never thought that they would reach their goal. No one was more surprised than I, when the community generously donated the money to support a television ministry. With deep emotion, I realized that God was moving in our midst and that He was blessing my ministry more than I had imagined He would in the poor little mission church of Santiago.

With a great desire to extend the Kingdom of God, Enzo and his wife Lillian Ciccio took charge of finding a group of friends and faithful people to form the first board of directors. As my television director, I hired Pazuso Masterna, a middle-aged Argentinian with a Canadian wife, Jennifer—his second wife, the first one having died in childbirth. A capable man, he had a degree in communications from a university in Buenos Aires. A bit of a bleeding heart liberal, in his faded and worn jeans, he reminded me of a holy beggar, because he was always ready to champion and fight for the less fortunate.

From the very first day of the television ministry, it was as if a legion of demons had arrived at Santiago determined to destroy the work of God. Extraordinary things were happening—the Gospel of Jesus was being lived, the sick and the prisoners were being visited, the hungry were being fed, and all those who had hunger and thirst for justice were being taught, sinners were being convertied, the sick were being healed, and the people were receiving consolation from God, but I endured vicious attacks from the powers of darkness.

In my theology classes at the Dionysian University in Rome, I learned that the existence of the demonic world and even the existence of Satan were seriously questioned. Many theologians simply denied it. For these reasons, when people kept showing up at the healing services, asking me to deliver them from the oppression of demons, I simply sprinkled them with holy water and gave them some good advice, which seemed to satisfy them, until one evening something very unusual occurred.

I had been praying for the people for about an hour, when a young woman about twenty years old, accompanied by two young men, approached me. As she stood before me wringing her hands, her hair was disheveled, she had a wild look in her eyes, and scratch marks on her face and arms. I also noticed that one of the men also had scratch marks on his face and arms. When I started to place my hands on her head, she let out a blood-curling shriek that sounded more like the howl of a wolf than anything human.

"False prophet! False prophet! She screamed. Instantly, with amazing strength her hands were around my throat trying to strangle me. The men who had brought her pulled her away from me and restrained her arms.

Flabbergasted, I watched as the girl fell to the floor and lay there at my feet, rolling frenetically around and twisting into all kinds of violent contortions. I had never seen anything like that before. Since I did not know what to do, I asked the men to bring her back the following evening. Although I did not tell them, I needed to do some research before I proceeded with her.

The following morning, I phoned the chancery and talked to a couple of priests, telling them what had happened, and inquired about an exorcist. Scornfully they laughed at me, saying: "We are not in the Middle Ages!

This is the twentieth century! Tell the people to take her to a psychiatrist. Demons do NOT exist."

I phoned a Protestant pastor that I had met at the Ministerial Association and asked him for advice and prepared to carry it out.

All day long I fasted and prayed, in preparation for the arrival of the family privately at my office, so there would be no great public display, while arranging for two men of the parish that I knew to be men of strong faith and virtue to be present.

As soon as the girl and the two men who accompanied her arrived and were seated opposite my desk with the girl between them, I began prayers of deliverance. Calling upon the name of Jesus, and asking for the intercession of the Blessed Virgin Mother and all the saints, I sprinkled her with holy water. When the holy water touched her skin, she shrieked viciously in a strange guttural voice and snarled, "You are about to die, Priest!"

Following the advice of my Protestant friend, I made no response, but instead asked her: "What is your name?"

My question seemed to increase her fury as the men, later I learned they were her brothers, restrained her as she struggled to free herself and attack me again.

"I will not tell you my name, lying Priest!" Then it seemed as if the demon took complete possession of her. Contorting fiercely, she fell to the floor, shaking and twisting.

I fell to my knees, and the two men I had arranged to help me knelt with me beside the girl who was wildly thrashing about, and they held her as best as they could.

"I command you in the name of Jesus Christ of Nazareth to leave!" I spoke as authoritatively as possible.

However, I really did not know what to do in this frightening situation, but I had no alternative but to continue, once I had started.

Vehemently, the girl yelled in Latin in a deep and husky voice that was not her own: "*O superbe, quid superest tuae superbiae?*"

Her Latin was clear and precise and I had no trouble understanding what she said, "O conceited man, nothing is greater than your arrogance." This was followed by a tirade of vile obscenities and curses.

"Stupid Priest," the strange voice continued, "I laugh at you!"

Insane laughter rolled thunderously from the girl's mouth.

"Silence! I command you in the name of Jesus Christ."

She was silent for a few minutes and then began taunting me.

"You can't make me leave. I'm stronger than you."

"You are a liar!"

"Just make me leave, you'll see." More obscenities and curses rang through the room.

"Silence! You will not say those things here! This is the house of God!"

Shrill raucous laughter pierced my ears, followed by absolute silence. Then the girl began reciting in that strange voice one of the Psalms. "Make a joyful noise unto the Lord. With my joyful noise, I am rejoicing over your failure, lying Priest." She laughed insanely and tauntingly.

Because of my lack of experience, the attempted exorcism dragged on for four hours.

"Excuse me a minute," I finally said to them all and walked out of my office, stepping outside into the moonlight, where I cried out to the Lord that I desperately needed His help. The Presence instantly flooded my being and He spoke to me in the depths of my spirit, telling me that I had to break down the door through which the demon had entered into the girl— Santería. She had to free herself from all the good luck charms and unearth the statue of the African god that she had buried in their backyard.

When I returned inside, they looked very discouraged and defeated. The girl had gotten up off the floor and was seated in the chair again.

Very calmly I said, "I have heard from the Lord. Here is what you must do." I glanced at them to see if they were willing to cooperate.

"Has she been involved in Santería?"

"Yes," they acknowledged, we all have.

"You must renounce your involvement with Santería and all of the occult. Will you do that?'

When they agreed, I led them in a prayer of renunciation.

The following evening, I commanded the evil spirit to leave in the name of Jesus Christ. It was all done very calmly and the girl was freed.

More people continued coming to me, asking me to free them from the forces of evil that oppressed them. Although I proceeded with the deliverance ministry with great caution, the attacks of the evil one seemed more and more directed at me.

Someone at the chancery must have heard my plea for help for delivering the girl, because the archbishop appointed an assistant priest to come to Santiago. Since he had participated in many deliverances in South America before coming to the United States, Father Chogui Rosa had a reputation for being an expert in things of that nature. I looked forward to having another priest in the mission and felt that it would be a great support for what I was doing.

When Father Chogui arrived, he came with great ceremony and a company of followers who always sat in the front row when he was ministering. Although he was a small man, short in stature, he was extremely self-confident and quite eloquent. Even though his sermons never lasted less than an hour and a half, he had a willing and eager audience who listened to every word, almost in a trance-like state.

During the year and a half that Father Chogui was assigned to Santiago, the deliverance ministry grew. At almost every healing service, you could hear the screams of those of the oppressed that were being released.

Unfortunately, Father Chogui had other interests too. Because he organized a folkloric dance group and a number of theatrical plays, he had no time left for doing anything else, as he monopolized people that I had organized to help with various ministries of the parish, overwhelming me with rehearsals, costumes, and theatrical paraphernalia. To make matters worse Father Chogui never went to bed before three in the morning and never appeared again until one the following afternoon. Since he was a much better choreographer, hair-stylist and decorator than he was a priest, he was more of a hindrance than a help.

I couldn't help but notice that Enki had become quite friendly with Father Chogui and was trying to use him to undermine my spiritual authority as pastor. If Father Chogui had not left Santiago when he did, I might have taken some kind of action against Enki. Although his presence at the mission forebode trouble, I did not perceive it quickly enough, because I have always made it a policy to think the best of people and overlook their flaws. In the case of Enki, I made a big mistake, and I would live to regret it.

24
Marco

What an experience! Preaching to a television camera for twenty-seven minutes without a congregation was a disaster—at first. We lacked the know-how to make coherent programs. When we finally arranged to have people come to listen to me preach, while they filmed me, it worked a lot better. Although we were able to present the program on several local commercial channels, it was a big disappointment when Trent Television Network turned us down and rejected our program for their stations. Therefore I was very much surprised, when Living Gospel Television welcomed me, for the simple reason that the first one is Catholic and the other Protestant. LGT has always supported me greatly.

Everything was going well for me, and there were no dark clouds on my horizon. Because LGT had state of the art and well-maintained equipment, gone were the days of taping in our small and poor studio. Everything in their studio was always in perfect taste. The girls that worked at LGT all looked like they had just stepped out of a fashion magazine.

One day I got a phone call from Renato. He seemed hostile, as he asked his usual question: "What the hell *are* you doing out there? Enki tells me you are more Protestant than Catholic with your television ministry. What are you doing on a Protestant channel?" he snorted.

"You can watch our program any time. Just click on the TV. I have nothing to hide."

"Damian doesn't like it. I was talking to him about it. You are too much involved in making changes that should never have been considered in the first place."

Renato wanted to return the Church to the days of Pius XII. "You can tell Damian that I hope he watches our program." There was nothing wrong with my theology.

It wasn't long after that when Enzo Ciccio stopped me after the Sunday Mass and said he needed to talk to me. I invited him to the rectory and asked him to share my chicken and rice, one of the few concoctions that Luisa, the spying and gossiping housekeeper, was able to fix. She had put it in the microwave earlier that morning before Mass so I could heat it up. As I served him some of the watery stuff that made her so proud, I asked, "What's on your mind Enzo?" I could tell something was bothering him.

"It's Enki. He is telling people of the parish that your ideas are like the revivalist preachers' on television. He is building quite a clique of friends. You better watch him, Padre. I think you should get rid of him. He is dividing the parish." Enzo looked worried as he broke a piece of Cuban bread and spread butter on it.

Because I did not know what to respond, I just thanked him and told him that I would keep a better watch over Enki. "I don't think he means any harm. He is my friend—my spiritual son. Most importantly, he is my administrative assistant, and I rely heavily on him. You know he majored in economics at the University of Caracas. "I always made it a policy never to think evil of anyone, remembering the old saying—evil is he who thinks evil.

Bastits, whom I hired to take care of the ministry of music, was doing a good job with the choirs. Despite the fact that her own voice was dismal, her new methods and techniques delighted the choir. I also noticed that one of the men, a television delivery man, Wolfgang Draper, seemed to be obsessed with her, even though he was a widower and much older than she.

The mission was growing incredibly now with new people arriving every week to the spiritually very powerful English Mass, because Enzo Ciccio continued inviting all his friends and everyone he knew and the Spanish-speaking members brought their English-speaking friends and neighbors. The future looked bright, as everything seemed to be going according to the will of God. Then lightening struck when I was invited to speak at a retreat in a popular parish.

As I was leaving the podium after my appearance, I encountered a strange looking fellow who grabbed my sleeve, stopping me in my tracks. An odd looking man with a full beard, bald head, and a pincenez, he stared fixatedly at me in a nebulous sort of way, and his hand seemed to shake as he pointed to a spot where we could talk out of earshot of others. He was really quite nervous, as he introduced himself.

"Camio Sabnac."

"What can I do for you?"

"I want to talk to you about one of Old Nick Gomorrah's and his wife Lucretia's sons, Focalor whom you may know by his nickname, "Foc.""

"What is wrong?" I had known the family for a long time.

Camio Sabnac—devious, inquisitorial, evil—had a tremor in his voice as he answered. "I am a friend of the family. There have been allegations of improper conduct involving priests."

"So? What does that have to do with me?"

"You are one of the priests being accused."

Shrugging my shoulders and thinking that he was emotionally unstable, I said with finality: "I really have to be leaving now. Good day."

Because I did not pay much attention to what Camio Sabnac said, I was surprised when he phoned me a few days later, asking for an appointment. I refused to see him. As far as I was concerned, that was the end of it.

When Father Damian phoned a few days later about the matter, I knew it was a lot more serious than I had originally imagined. That night I had a nightmare in which I saw a dark demonic figure in a black tuxedo and flowing black cape who, with an evil grin, removed his tall top hat to show me his horns. His eyes were like two burning coals of blue flames that pierced the darkness and terrified me. His hideous laugh still haunts me. When I awoke suddenly in terror, my heart was racing, and I had a hard time trying to fall asleep again.

In the days that followed, I endured much. There were investigations by lawyers, sworn statements by people who knew me, a summary judgment from an ecclesiastical tribunal, and finally peace with Foc Gomorrah, who told me that Camio Sabnac had fabricated these lies to satisfy his own agenda and to destroy my ministry. He signed a sworn affidavit to that effect for the archdiocese.

A few months later, I received a letter from the vicar general, the Very Reverend Damian Babilonia, omnipotent executor of the wishes of His Grace the Archbishop of Rosanada, exonerating me from the allegations communicated by Camio Sabnac. When Foc came to visit me at Santiago and apologized about the entire situation, explaining that Camio Sabnac was responsible for it, I shook his hand and offered him my friendship. Foc began attending Mass at Santiago regularly. One night at a healing service, he came to the altar rail and received Christ as his Savior, appearing to have a genuine religious experience, lingering at the altar rail, deeply engaged in prayer.

One Sunday, he told me, as he came out of the church, walking with difficuty, that he was leaving for Europe, because he had discovered that he was seriously sick from syphilis in its tertiary stages and wanted to get away from his family that was rejecting him because of the disease. He said he wanted to make new friends and overcome his feelings of inadequacy and try to feel like a human being that is worthy of being loved and respected.

Although he found a girl in Europe and brought her back to Rosanada, she only lived with him for awhile, because she discovered that he was homosexual, syphilitic, unemployed and rejected by his family, causing her to return to her former home.

Foc's life was a real tragedy, because his family turned their backs on him and were unwilling to provide the love and support that someone in his condition required. He wound up as a street bum with Father Pompeo helping by giving him a little money, or some food, or clothing. Pompeo told me that Foc, when he became incapacitated and in a wheelchair, moved in with a journalist, Ali Purcell, who offered him a home in exchange for a story for her forthcoming book that eventually catapulted the attack on my ministry at Santiago.

25
Luz

Life at St. Mary Tudor, Queen of England, parish kept Luz busy. As she watched Margie working in the large stainless steel kitchen, she was even learning to cook. One evening when Margie could not be there, she thought she would be able to fix dinner for Msgr. Shamus O'Rourke who succeeded Msgr. Stalker as pastor and ultimately would be the victim of allegations of sexual abuse of minors as determined by the summary justice of a cowardly bishop that was trying to deflect suspicion from himself by casting guilt on O'Rourke. Luz recalled local lieutenants in Latin American towns that behaved much like that bishop. They would practice what they called "defenestration," which means that they would throw someone they wanted to get rid of out a window and inform the press that he had commited suicide. Poor Pastor O'Rourke deserved much better treatment than that. After listening to a lot of clergy gossip, Luz had no doubt in her mind that he was innocent, but the archbishop following his agenda, paid a settlement, and defrocked him in a mock canonical trial that he himself orchestrated in cahoots with the archdiocesan judicial vicar and the promoter of justice, both very well known as gays. "*Summum ius, summa injuria.* More law, no justice."

Luz enjoyed cooking for Monsignor and the other four priests at Bloody Mary's—so many people referred to the parish by this affectionate name that even Luz got in the habit of doing it. She put a roast and potatoes in the oven and prepared a salad. Since Monsignor liked shrimp, she decided to fix shrimp cocktail. She spent an hour trying to remove the shells from the raw shrimp. Later she found out that if you cook them first, the shells come off easily. She also did not know that shrimp cook quickly, and for this reason she boiled them for an hour. When she served them, Pompeo immediately exclaimed: "What did you do to them? They are like rubber." He picked up one out of his dish and started bouncing it on the table. "Look they even bounce!" he quipped and snickered gleefully.

Msgr. O'Rourke glared at Pompeo. "They taste good to me. They are fine Luz. You are doing a great job."

She was glad it was Thursday, for Marco always picked her up on Fridays and took her to Santiago for the weekend where she practiced her new culinary arts on him. No matter what she fixed, he was always appreciative and told her what a good cook she was.

Because she was having premonitions that some evil was lurking around him, she was worried about her son. Just before she fell asleep the night before, it was as if there was a very dark cloud in her room swirling in a vortex above her bed. She seemed to hear a strange and evil laugh coming from it. When she flipped on the light above her bed, instantly it was gone. Frightened she held her rosary tight in her hand for fear it would reappear. She fell into a fitful sleep. When she awoke in the morning the memory of the black swirling cloud was gone. In her heart there was a lingering feeling of apprehension that something was wrong with Marco.

Marco picked her up at 3: 00 p.m. Friday afternoon as usual. As they drove up the river in Marco's new Chevy Cavalier that he had been able to buy recently, she exclaimed:

"I am so pleased with all the wonderful things you are doing. Then she asked what was really on his mind. "Are you all right? Have you been ill lately?" She enjoyed the ride even though the heavy traffic on the road was a bit disconcerting.

"I'm fine, Ma, just a little tired."

When they arrived at Santiago, a woman and a man that he introduced to her as Yo-Lin Sin and Enki Mutante were waiting to see him. As soon as she shook their hands, she had a feeling of evil emanating from them. After they had gone, she asked: "Who are they, Marco?"

"They are a couple of parishioners. She is Yo-Lin Sin, a very devout woman who contributes generously to the mission. He is Enki Mutante my administrative assistant," he explained to her.

"I don't like that woman's looks, nor his either." She looks cheap in her expensive clothing. And she is dressed more for enticing men, than worshiping God. She has bad vibes."

"She's all right, mom. You can't judge a book by its cover. We must not think evil of anyone."

Luz went into the kitchen of the trailer and started preparing dinner—boliche, a Cuban pot roast of beef, with a crown of fresh vegetables. "Tell me about the man who was with her," she said to Marco who was sitting at the kitchen table watching her peel potatoes.

"There is not much to tell. He is a fellow from Caracas. He is a reliable assistant. He and Yo-Lin are good friends. Don't worry, Mom, he's OK."

"When I shook his hand, I felt that he is somehow unclean—that he is involved in something unsavory." She put the potatoes in a pan of water and set it on the back burner of the gas stove.

Because she did not want to worry him, she did not tell him about the presentiments of lurking evil that troubled her. She knew that he too was sensitive to those around him and often picked up their thoughts.

Before the weekend was over, Marco visited with her at the kitchen table after they had lunch Sunday afternoon. Because he seemed to be hesitant about telling her something, she sensed he had something on his mind. "What is troubling you, Marco? I always know when something is wrong with you." She could feel the worry lines creasing her forehead. She reached across the table and laid her hand on his arm. "Tell me about it, please."

"Oh, some crazy man, Camio Sabnac, concocted a bunch of insane lies that I had sexually abused a boy."

She took a deep breath. She simply couldn't believe what she was hearing. "That's ridiculous!"

"Of course, it is, Mom. But it has caused a lot of trouble for me. They had a huge church investigation. The boy himself signed a sworn paper that I am completely innocent."

She sighed deeply. "Well, that should be the end of it then, shouldn't it?" She was relieved to hear that the boy had cleared him. She stood up and put on her apron and started to clear the table of the lunch dishes.

"Yes, it should be. But it isn't."

"What do you mean?"

"The man, he is a man now, is in the last stages of syphilis, and his family has disowned him and rejected him. Some newspaper journalist, Ali Purcell, took him in. She keeps him supplied with all his needs, and she has persuaded him to give her a story for a new book she is writing about pedophile priests."

"*Oh, Dios mío!* Surely they won't write anything bad about you!" She could not believe this was happening to her son.

"I am sure they will."

"I knew it! I knew something was wrong." She told him about the strange experience she had Thursday night when the swirling black vortex hung over her bed.

"I too have a sense of foreboding," Marco confessed to her. "But I don't know exactly what it is, beside the book Ali Purcell is writing. Perhaps we will find out soon."

26
Damian

He was sitting on top of the world—at least that is how he felt. Because Archbishop Melusine had made him vicar general, he now held an intoxicating share of the power in the very affluent Rosanada Archdiocese, as he had always dreamed he would, and could now keep all the priests in line, while building up his own little financial portfolio. With all the new money Renato was bringing to the chancery, he was heavily investing in Wall Street, and had been able to purchase fifty percent of International Woods, Inc., a company that was importing precious woods from Brazil and Central America, making millions, while illegally depleting the rain forests. Soon, he was going to be able to extend his dominion and reach his goal of total control of the archdiocese.

Determined to get revenge on all his enemies and to get rid of people he disliked, he was targeting first and foremost Marco Lamadrid—whom he had envied since their seminary days—and his Protestant-like television and crusades ministries. With an ally like Enki Mutante who was administrative assistant to Lamadrid, he was sure that it would be just a matter of time until he would deal severely with him, and he would silence him as he so much desired to do.

Much simpler than Archbishop Lingam, his predecessor, who ran the archdiocese like a medieval monarch, Melusine was a strange bird. Certainly, no intellectual, he probably did not even like to think, making it easy for Damian to seize control of the archdiocese, as he relieved Melusine of all the dirty laundry bishops have to deal with. Now, all Melusine had to do was celebrate his Pontifical Masses, smile, and greet people, occasionally embarrassed by bouts of uncontrollable flatulence.

In response to Melusine's call for a financial meeting, all the involved department heads of the chancery had assembled in the boardroom—Msgr. Rattlet, the treasurer, Msgr. Toccafondi, the financial director, and Renato Del'Ano, the fireball who kept things humming by raising unbelievable sums of money. Clearing his throat, the archbishop handed out his agenda, while fumbling through his brown, scuffed and worn briefcase, looking for a pen that would write. After he tried three of them, he finally found one that worked.

"Gentlemen," he began clearing his throat again, "I feel in my heart that the campaign we are planning is the life blood of the archdiocese." He paused, waiting for those present to agree.

Filled with contempt by the archbishop's referring to money as the lifeblood of the archdiocese, Damian listened as Renato, exclaimed, *"Bravo! Bravissimo*! Let's make this the theme of our campaign." Immediately, the others seated at the long black mahogany table enthusiastically agreed.

Msgr. Rattlet, the money man and a very discrete womanizer, suggested having a series of dances for the elite at the Rosanada Heights Country Club, while Msgr. Toccafondi opted for fund raising dinners where people would pay premium prices to attend. As usual they bumbled around for two and a half hours doing something that should have required only thirty minutes.

Two weeks later, the money raiser himself, Renato Del'Ano, Melusine's pride and joy, showed up in Damian's office with glowing reports of how his St. Thomas Society was growing, especially since the archbishop had visited their meetings several times and each time had given them inspiring talks, always about fidelity to the magisterium and the papacy. Obviously, Renato's group was the most reactionary of the archdiocese—a throw-back to the days the Inquisition. They stood for the restoration of the "Index" of forbidden books, the excommunication of all re-married Catholics, the midnight fast before receiving communion, the prohibition to eat meat on Fridays, and more than anything else the Latin Mass and Gregorian Chant.

As he took a seat in the white leather chair across the desk from Damian, Renato chortled exuberantly: "I have big news, really big news! I have really pulled a coup. I'll give you a hint."

"Good," Damian replied, eager to hear what Renato had to say. Figuring it was about money, he asked, "Big money?"

"Really *big* money," Renato answered, emphasizing the word big.

"Great! Let's go and tell Melusine. He's bound to be in his private dining room now having lunch."

Renato jumped to his feet and headed for the door with Damian close behind. As they entered Melusine's private dining room located behind his office, the archbishop was sitting at table with a meager sandwich and a glass of milk, as he did every day for his modest *collatio.*

Damian was very confident in approaching the archbishop, for he alone was allowed to disturb His Excellency during lunchtime. Without a moment's delay, Damian said, "Your Excellency, we have great news for you. Our hard working friend Renato here is doing a fantastic job, pumping more blood into the veins of the archdiocese." He was referring to the archbishop's slogan about money being the blood that ran the Kingdom of God in Rosanada.

Putting aside his empty milk glass, Melusine said: "I have always known that this young man has great potential. Tell me what is going on."

Determined not to be upstaged by Renato, Damian, wanting to take credit for Renato's success, said: "I don't have a complete report for Your Excellency yet, but I want to tell you that your campaign 'the Blood of the Archdiocese' is already a wonderful success. In a few days we are going to have the first millions deposited in our bank account." Smiing proudly at the archbishop, Damian waited to be congratulated for raising the money.

"That is really great, young man! Really great! I want to have a special function—a big party—for these people once they make their donations."

Bowing his head slightly as he spoke, in deference to the archbishop, Renato, determining not to be overlooked, said in his most mellow sycophant tones: "Our pleasure, Archbishop, we will be happy to do that."

When Damian learned two months later that ten million dollars had been added to the bank balance of the archdiocese, he was struck by the horrible realization that

Yo-Lin Sin was the Queen of Sex and Drugs and her friends who contributed to the campaign so very munificently were all Mafiosi. There was no way that he could share that information with Melusine, who was demanding a large social gathering to honor them all. Under the circumstances, he did not feel that it was in the slightest disingenuous to keep this information from him.

The bash at the archiepiscopal residence was breathtaking, to say the least—a real extravaganza with Archbishop Melusine, resembling a South American parrot, as he appeared in full regalia wearing his choir robes, covered by the *cappa magna*, a grand purple cope. All the priests who worked in the chancery were there, mostly ogling Yo-Lin Sin who was quite a spectacle in a purple, zircon-decorated Christian Dior original that showed about ten inches of flesh above her knees. Over her shoulders lay a mink fur, open in the front, revealing a choker of amethysts, her décolletage, and plunging cleavage. Although she was of normal height, her open sandals with four-inch heels, made her into a veritable Amazon. To complete her appearance, she had her toenails painted bright purple and decorated with some zircons.

The great irony of the evening—the archbishop hired many off-duty policemen to guard the luxurious cars and the persons of the criminals who were enjoying his excellency's hospitality at one of the most exclusive restaurants of Rosanada. "*La Bastille*," catered the event, providing not only every delicacy that they had at their establishment, but their very own specialty "Canard Guillotine".

It was quite a party, Damian decided, and what the archbishop did not know about his Mafia guests would not hurt him, or so he thought.

27
Renato

Proud of his achievements in successful fund raising, Renato N. Del'Ano, tossed all his belonging into his Lincoln Mark VII, left Pope Julius III Seminary and drove to his new assignment at Saint Portia's Church, a wealthy parish located in the southern part of Rosanada where many drug dealers and their wives attended Mass. Most of them had been reared Catholic, and they were bringing up their children in the Church. Many of the Mafiosi, especially ones from Latin America, are very superstitious. They they like to burn candles before the statutes of saints, wear rosaries around their necks, and even give money to the poor and to the Church, believing that by so doing, God will help them escape being surprised and caught by law enforcement. Well aware of their attitudes, Renato gladly accepted their financial favors.

Dedicated to proclaiming the traditional Catholicism that Renato loved, the Society of St. Thomas had evolved into the Goretti Church Restoration Society that had received permission from Archbishop Melusine to operate in every parish of the archdiocese. Renato was delighted that no pastor could now refuse to let his group into his parish to solicit members and funds.

Pleased to see that Yo-Lin took an active role in the group and seemed to enjoy it, Renato made her one of the board of directors for his society. After she brought some of her collaborators in drug trafficking onto the board, together they converted the organization into an excellent means for laundering money, depositing large amounts of cash into the checking account of the society, a non-profit organization. The money was then transferred to charities in Panama and then to *El Fuego de Yo-Lin*, a dancing club owned by Yo-Lin Sin, who then redeposited the money in the United States in her nude bar, *La Estrella de Amor*, just north of Rosanada, or in any other of her fictitious companies. A fantastic and clean operation! Zing!!! Once again Yo-Lin had another load of money to spend or invest, buying drugs, paying off cops, agents of the law, and even a couple judges who were her friends. Best of all, Renato got a decent cut for the "work of the Lord." Because they contributed generously to the Goretti Church Restoration Society, Renato was glad to have them aboard.

After all, he reasoned, the Mafia would have gotten the money anyhow and laundered it elsewhere. No priest or preacher ever asks where the bills in the collection plate are coming from. So why should he? Since they laundered their money through his organization, large contributions came into the society, a lot of needy people were helped, and, of course, the archdiocese benefited, and he was able to build up his own nest egg. He was sure God did not mind.

Surely, he thought, Damian must have figured out that the money he had raised for the archdiocese came from Mafiosi drug dealers, but since Damian never mentioned it to him, he decided to keep everything running just as it was. However, late one afternoon, when he was getting ready to leave the chancery for the day, Damian stopped him in the parking lot, just as he was about to open the door of his Mark VII.

"Just the person I wanted to see," Damian said as he approached him.

"What can I do for the vicar general?" Renato tried to sound self-assured and confident, even though he had a nervous feeling in the pit of his stomach that Damian was going to reprimand him.

"Be in my office at nine tomorrow morning," Damian ordered abruptly.

Trying to get some idea of what was on Damian's mind, Renato asked, "Anything special? Do I need to bring anything with me?"

"I want to discuss your fundraising with you. I have some serious reservations about it that we need to clear up." That said, Damian quickly walked away to find his own car.

Realizing that his future advancement and career were at stake, panic overcame Renato, making his head spin and his stomach growl. Knowing he was going to be sick, he stopped by the drugstore on the way home and picked up some Imodium and took two pills immediately.

That night, he slept very little, except for a terrible nightmare in which Damian was chasing him through a vast hall of mirrors where he beheld himself reflected, twisted into all manner of grotesque shapes and forms. Suddenly, Damian metamorphosized into a gigantic black and green spider with long fuzzy legs that was hopping after him. Just when the spider caught him, he woke up with his heart pounding and a cold sweat drenching his body. Overcome by feelings of terror, he got out of bed and fixed himself a snifter of brandy—a drink he had learned to relish since he had been in Rosanada. Although, it was only five a.m., he could not go back to sleep. Worst of all he couldn't find where he had put the Imodium that he desperately needed. Because of his nervousness, he kept having awful cramps in his abdomen, and had to run frequently to the bathroom.

When he arrived at the chancery, he was ushered into Damian's office by his secretary and told to wait there at Damian's desk until the vicar general could see him. When Damian finally showed up, he came right to the point.

"I want to speak to you about something very confidential. Above all, I want you to know that for the rest of the world you and I have never talked about this subject. Agreed?"

Damian's appeal to absolute secrecy frightened Renato all the more. "Of course, Damian, of course. You know that my only interest is to serve the Church and to help you, my friend." Renato noticed that Damian's long twisted fingers were fidgeting with a pen on his desk. When Renato said this, Damian dropped the pen, leveled his piercing brown eyes at him and said, "At the moment, Renato, let's leave friendship aside. Instead let's just say that we are brother priests." Damian's eyes were penetrating as they stared fixedly and coldly at Renato.

"You offend me, Damian. I have always considered you my friend," he said in his most ingratiating tone, as cramps assailed him violently. Actually shaking and terrified, knowing that his career was in danger, he got up and headed for the bathroom door in the back of Damian's office. After all laundering money was a federal offense, even if he knew perfectly well that Damian could not expose him for fear of causing the archdiocese a scandal.

Managing to get into the restroom just in time to avoid embarrassment, Renato took care of his emergency. Then to his dismay he suddenly realized that there was neither bathroom tissue nor paper towels left anywhere. In other words he was up the creek without a paddle. But, being a man of ingenuity, he would not admit defeat, and he had to do something, so he pulled the Egyptian cotton handkerchief out of his breast pocket. When he unfurled it, he noticed a little tag on the corner that was embroidered with the following in red letters: "Compliments of His Excellency Archbishop Melusine." It was the handkerchief the archbishop had given him for Christmas. The cheap bastard! That is all the old man gave him! A cheap handkerchief! He wadded it into a ball, made quick use of it, washed it out in the lavatory, wrung it as tight as he could, and stuffed it in his pants pocket. Faking a big smile, Renato rejoined Damian, who was waiting impatiently for him to return.

"It is not my intention to offend you, but I want to make it perfectly clear that I do not want to be involved in any way with your group of people. The entire clergy of the archdiocese have heard that they are engaged in drug trafficking and that is why there is so much money in your society. You must clean up your board of directors." The vicar general's voice rose like thunder as he commanded, "Kick the Mafia out! And do it now!"

"I will see what I can do." Renato answered meekly, feeling about ten inches tall.

"You WILL do it." Damian said with all the force of his office as vicar general.

Limping from the chancery with wounded pride and fears of what this would mean to his career, Renato went home to a very unsettling day and a long sleepless night in which he decided that he had no recourse except to visit Yo-Lin, put the matter before her, and implore her help.

When he arrived at Yo-Lin's condo the next day, he was greeted at the door by her daughter Lin-Yu and her boyfriend, the Puerto Rican doorman. Since Yo-Lin was still in bed, disdainfully nibbling her breakfast, while watching the news on WSAP, Renato rushed into her room and sat down on the side of her bed."

"*Oh Querido*, how nice to see you," Yo-Lin purred. "Come get in bed with me and have something to eat. Anything you want."

The old whore never missed an opportunity to get a man in her bed, Renato mused, but aloud he said, "It is nice to see you, too." Overcoming feelings of revulsion, he bent over and kissed her hand. Then laughing nervously, he very gently sat on a corner of the bed as far away from her as he could. Forcing a smile and chuckling, he said without conviction: "Leave me alone, Yo-Lin, you know I can't tango with you, I am a priest."

Suddenly dropping the appearances of conviviality, she asked him coldly with her eyes narrowing to green slits: "What brings you here? At this hour of the day?"

"I couldn't sleep." He picked up a piece of toast from her tray and began to eat it. "I'd like a cup of chamomile, if you don't mind."

"Colette," she called out to the maid. "Bring Father Renato a cup of chamomile and some more coffee for me, please."

When Renato began sipping the hot beverage, he began talking. "Yo-Lin, the vicar general called me up on the carpet yesterday. He's on to us. He says I have to clean up the board of the Goretti Church Restoration Society. He found out that you are all drug dealers." His heart was beating faster because of the anxiety he was experiencing.

"I don't know what you are talking about," she protested trying to appear innocent.

"Yo-Lin, you have to help me get out of this problem. The vicar general is the most powerful man in the archdiocese. He was very harsh with me. Please, tell me what we can do."

All the usual sweetness and sparkle that characterized her had vanished. Her emerald eyes were callous and unfeeling as she looked down her nose at him.

"Look Renato, business is business and we are talking about millions of dollars. I'm not just a playmate to amuse you for an hour or so. I'm playing for keeps. You are in this as deep as I am. OK, I will take care of the situation for you. In a couple days your archbishop with the baggy pants and the greasy stains on his shirt will have to find himself a new vicar general because this one will have fallen from a staircase or a balcony. Outside of that, to deal with the Church is your problem. You got that clear?"

He was dumbfounded, because for the first time she talked to him, shooting from the hip. With a trembling voice, and trying to control his rising temper, he stammered, "That is not a solution. It is simply not an option. We need to come up with something else."

She finished her cup of coffee and set the cup on her tray.

"All right then. Very simple. Let's have a big religious affair of some sort." She thought a moment and then exclaimed, "I got it. Let's have a big Eucharistic Congress. That may calm Damian down when he sees how people respond to our convocation."

Staring at her intently, he considered what she was saying, as she brazenly sat there in bed in a flimsy black, transparent nightgown that revealed her huge bronze breasts.

"We will invite Old Baggy Pants and he can show up with his miter and fancy funny cape. I will rent a helicopter to bring the Reverend Fart himself to the stadium with the monstrance and the white thing in it. Then you guys can have your processions and your incensations. We'll get all the church officials to come," she continued. "I will bring Enki and get him to help with it".

"That is not going to calm Father Damian," Renato insisted wringing his hands and sighing deeply.

"Renato, you are hysterical. Calm down. Control yourself. Talk to the arch himself as soon as possible to make him commit to coming to this event. That will get Damian off your back for a while, and we can forget the balcony accident—at least for now."

Because Father Damian was implacable with his enemies and would never forget anything important, Renato knew that Yo-Lin was radically wrong about the matter. Anyhow as it turned out, Damian eased up on him, after Yo-Lin sent a couple of her men to work his car over, as it sat in his reserved parking spot one afternoon at the chancery, making him realize that it was dangerous business fooling around with the Hispanic Mafia. After leaving a dead cat on the driver's seat as a reminder of what could happen to him, the thugs smashed the body of his car so badly that it was in the shop for two weeks being repaired. Of course, when the police arrived and began to ask questions no one had seen anything. No doubt Damian wanted to keep on living the same as he did. Realizing that he was more deeply compromised than he had imagined, fear consumed him, and he would do as Yo-Lin instructed.

As soon as Renato told Damian of the great Eucharistic Congress that he and the Goretti Church Restoration Society were organizing, they went to tell the old archbishop, and Melusine, a real dreamer, was immediately very enthusiastic.

"A great idea! Father Renato, a great idea! Of course I will come. I will make it mandatory for all parishes to participate." Sighing with relief, Renato felt he was off the hook, at least for the time being.

They had chosen the 14th of August, the eve of feast of the Assumption for the celebration. Unfortunately, a major thunderstorm storm blew up unexpectedly, preventing the event from ever taking place. In the days that followed, Renato saw the fear that was in his heart reflected in the eyes of Damian. Like Vesuvius, the situation was apt to erupt at any moment.

28
Marco

My dream was to create a Christian community composed of many small groups, meeting in various homes, inviting all to live according to Biblical principles, by which they would share the important issues of life with each other. The first step that I took to strengthen the community was meeting with families two evenings a week, as they gathered in parishioners' homes, usually taking a musician with me to complement my teaching with praise and worship. Drawing upon the members of these groups, I selected people to form my first pastoral council.

Two men who had been faithfully attending the evening Bible classes were the brothers Selkis—Belial and Juan, who contributed generously to support the mission, and on whom I could count, if I needed anything for the church. It was my understanding that the brothers were involved in the purchase of airplanes, and since that did not require much of their time, they were frequently at church activities.

Belial Selkis, the brother who was most active at the church, bought an extensive estate in the mountains a few miles from Santiago that he made available for church activities and me. Behind the sprawling vacation house that faced a two-lane road bordered with magnificent oak trees, Belial built a very spacious gazebo where I could hold talks, conferences, and meetings. It was even enclosed and had heat in it so that we could use it during the cold winter months. I was pleased because we now had a center that we could use to help the ministry grow. Members of the parish quickly named this estate *"Monte Santo."*

From time to time, I noticed, when I happened to be there during the week that a small plane would land on the field behind the gazebo, stay a while and then take off again. Sometimes the Selkis held large parties on the premises, but they always joined in the songs of praise on the weekends, when their wives would also come to *Monte Santo*.

The Selkis had come to us from Renatos Society, having learned about us from him. For this reason, I assumed they were very conservative in their religious views. However, this was not the case.

One day after the Tuesday evening Bible class, a woman parishioner, who seemed quite distressed and agitated, called me aside to talk to me.

"Padre, it's the Selkis."

"Fine Catholic people," I replied always trying to speak well of everyone.

"Padre, you have to open your eyes. These men are members of the Mafia." She spoke confidently giving the impression that she knew what she was saying and was telling me the truth. "Mafia people like to hang around churches and priests—it gives them a feeling of respectability," she added.

"This can't be true. I know them well, and they are very committed and dedicated men." I started to leave.

252

"Wait, Padre. It is true. Someone who works with my husband told him, and he told me. You have got to stop going to their estate."

"I cannot do that without some kind of proof. Perhaps, you could confront them face to face in front of me and some of the board members." I reached for the doorknob and opened the door to leave.

"I can't do that. You know they would kill me and my child, if I did." Horror froze the features of her face, as she contemplated what could happen.

"But, Padre, that is not all." She sighed deeply and continued, "They are spreading Protestant teaching among the church members and telling people that you told them that they were your beliefs. The people are confused." She hid her face in her hands.

"Don't worry. God will take care of us." Hoping I had calmed her fears, I said good night and left.

As I drove home that night after the Bible class, I had a few lingering thoughts about the brothers. Dealing in drugs could explain why they were able to make such large contributions to the mission. But that was ridiculous! Renato surely would not have sent me drug dealers for the mission! Would he?

A few other people told me they were also suspicious of the brothers, but since they could offer no proof, I simply dismissed what they told me as unsubstantiated rumors. A year went by and I decided the people who warned me about the brothers were mistaken.

Finally one day, two men in dark blue suits showed up at the rectory. I noticed that they spoke with a New York accent, as they said, "Good day, Father, we would like to talk to you." As soon as they were inside the rectory, they pulled out their badges and identification papers that showed me that they were from Drug Enforcement. I sensed that they were there because of the Selkis brothers, and I was right.

The older of the two, a man of about fifty, spoke: "Father, we are here to ask what your relationship to the Selkis brothers is. Would you mind telling us?" He stuck his badge back in his pocket and looked at me expectantly.

Stammering, not because I was guilty of anything, but because of the normal discomfort investigative authorities cause, I said, trying to distance myself from the Selkis. "Belial and Juan Selkis are members of this church."

"What do you use their estate for?" The younger of the two inquired, as his piercing glance held me fast.

"We have many activities at *Monte Santo* for the good of the members of this community." I was determined to be noncommittal.

"Have you received money from either of the two brothers?" the older one demanded insistently. Did they give you money in cash or checks?

"Both," I replied.

"Would you show us your records?"

"Of course, I would, if you bring a judicial order. Donations to churches are a private matter."

"Do you know of any other activity which takes place on this farm?"

"Not really." I was beginning to be frightened, fearing that all the talk that I had heard about them was true.

"Father, because we have been investigating you, Santiago, and the Selkis for four months, we know that you are clean, which prevented us from raiding the place until now. But you must know that at this very moment the Selkis brothers are being arrested, together with all their accomplices who worked at their estate. As far as you and the members of Santiago go, there will be no charges made, but we are reporting this situation to the Archbishop of Rosanada." They left as quickly as they had come.

Just what I needed! Another call from the vicar general! It wasn't long in coming. A week later Father Damian phoned.

"There is no way of stopping you from messing things up. I am working full-time to solve your problems. What the hell are you doing now?" His policy of using an iron fist in a silk glove had given away to an inflexible steel fist. Without waiting for me to answer his question, he snapped, "Be here in my office tomorrow morning at ten." He slammed down the phone without another word.

I had a sleepless night, knowing that I had to face the inquisition the next morning. Before I was admitted to his inner sanctum for a third degree examination, Damian kept me waiting in his outer office for thirty minutes, while my anxiety compounded and my blood pressure soared.

After countless questions about the Selkis brothers that I tried to answer truthfully, I candidly remarked, as gently as I could, "Father Renato sent them to the mission. They were members of his society. He knew them and recommended them to me."

Sternly he stared at me with anger blazing in his eyes and said emphatically, "Marco, do not try to deflect responsibility from yourself, and above all do not blame

Father Renato for your lack of discretion and poor judgment." Raising his voice, he continued: "You have come close to placing the entire archdiocese in a very embarrassing situation, by getting the mission involved with those people. You preach on a Protestant TV channel and now you are mixed up with the Mafia! I have many doubts about you! You leave a lot to be desired."

I kept silent, waiting for his wrath to subside.

"You will be here next Monday in the boardroom at 10:00 am. with all your personal bank and credit card statements, as well as those of the church—everything for the past two years. We will find out exactly what your relationship has been with these Mafiosi drug dealers." Damian slapped the palm of his hand loudly on his mahogany desk, forcefully pushed his white leather chair back, and jumped agilely to his feet. In spite of the seriousness of the situation, I could not restrain the desire to laugh, because Damian always reminded me of Groucho Marx with his bushy eyebrows, prominent nose, mustache, and large eyeglasses. Because he was so furious with me, his hairpiece slipped out of place and slid down over his forehead, turning him into a real low brow. Because I knew that I could not shake his hand without roaring with laughter, I just mumbled a polite goodbye and left.

The following Monday, the archbishop, the chancellor, and one of the archdiocesan attorneys were waiting for my arrival in the conference room to hold their kangaroo court. They put me at the end of the large mahogany table with the archbishop nervously seated at the other end—in the seat of confrontation. One of the lawyers for the archdiocese from the law firm of Puck,

Warhol and Associates was seated to my right with the treasurer next to him. Damian was on my left and the chancellor on his left.

"Please give me the documents we requested," Damian demanded without preamble.

He passed the documents I gave him to the attorney who began going through them, and then passed them page-by-page to the treasurer, who handed them to the chancellor. Although Melusine sat in on the meeting like a figurehead, he had little to say, except every once in a while he mumbled an incoherent phrase. As I squirmed on the hot seat, they scrutinized my accounts for an hour and a half.

Finally the attorney, a Mr. Greeb, a weasel-eyed old fellow, said, "Well, I find nothing wrong with anything in these statements. Everything is fine, gentlemen."

Without another word, the lawyer handed me my statements, while they all got up and silently left the room, except for the archbishop who stopped me as I rose to leave.

"Father, I am coming out to Santiago soon. I want to see with my own eyes just what you *are* doing out there."

Ever since I had been assigned to Santiago, I had tried very hard to please the archbishop. After all, I considered him as a successor to the apostles, and I knew that they were not perfect either. Therefore, I attempted to perform all my duties according to the guidelines he issued. It did not take me very long to learn that the only way to make the archbishop happy and to please Father Damian, his omnipotent vicar general and chancellor, was to reach the financial goals they had set, administer the parish income well, send the assigned assessments to their business office, and, above all, have an excellent yearly collection for the archbishop's charity campaign. Sorrowfully, I realized that all that mattered at the chancery was money. Like a Spanish-speaking TV ad said at the time: "All that counts is the cash."

Since the mission continued to grow, I was able to comply with all the financial requirements the archdiocese made on the mission and myself. However, it saddened me, year after year, when the archbishop or one his auxiliary bishops came to Santiago to administer the Sacrament of Confirmation or for a special Mass, that they never inquired if there had been any conversions or miracles of healing, or anything supernatural. They limited their questions to asking about the year's statistics in dollars and cents and about the number of confirmandi. In all my years as a priest, I have never heard a Roman Catholic bishop talk or ask about any spiritual experiences. Either they simply do not care about them or their work in the offices of the chancery has turned them into bureaucrats instead of apostles of Jesus Christ. I have never been able to determine which it is. Their seminary training educated them to believe in a God that should be ignored in daily life. Products of that formation, they pass it on, perpetuating it in the troubled few men that still want to become priests. Nowadays, in order to attend any of their functions one must prepare oneself for a veritable festival of pathologies.

According to the doctrine of the Roman Catholic Church, a bishop is to be the father and teacher of his community and a friendly figure to his priests. To be quite truthful, I have never found a Roman Catholic bishop who was either a father or a teacher to his people or his priests, nor have I ever found one who was a real friend. Instead, to my regret, I have found them to be tyrants, judges, and men concerned about protecting their own interests rather than ministering to the people of God. My experience has brought me to believe that they are the epitome of selfishness.

Because I love the Church, I wanted to bring new life into her. With my preaching and television ministry that had spread over into radio ministry, and participation in conferences, I tried to introduce people to a deeper level of faith and show them how to apply it to daily living.

The solemn and joyful celebration of the liturgy of the Church was one way that I tried to reach the hearts of those entrusted to me. People usually search for God at the altar or in special moments in their lives, especially during difficulties, forgetting that God is present in each moment of their existence in every part of their reality. Trying to bring this truth home to them, I wanted to instill in them my belief in the sacrament of the present moment, knowing that it could completely transform their lives. Being fully alive and deeply aware of the present moment is the most wonderful experience we can have, when we realize that God is with us and within us. With this knowledge we can remember the past with peace and look forward to the future without fear. Of course it takes time to fully develop comprehension of this mystery.

If the Church is going to be meaningful in today's society, I also firmly believe that it has to change. The priesthood should be open to married men and to women, to heterosexual as well as homosexual celibates—provided that they are totally committed to keeping their vows. I entertain these views—not in response to the demands of a materialist society—but in answer to the basic drive of the human being who needs affectionate intimacy and sexual relations. I do not see it as a solution to the lack of vocations or the remedy for the inability and failure of some homosexual priests to keep their commitments, but rather as a call from the Lord to all his children to share in the guidance and direction of His Church.

Unfortunately, a significant number of homosexuals have been attracted to the priesthood, believing that they could either go unnoticed through life or unreservedly live their gay lifestyle behind the doors of lavender rectories, where they could also give full expression to their misogynistic attitudes with impunity. They have little to fear as long as they do not poach on altar boys, because the hierarchy whose members are drawn from the priests—is abounding with homosexuals that close blind eyes to activities of homosexual priests, as long as they are discrete.

I am convinced that most people who attend church, or even just consider themselves to be people of good will, never progress beyond a desire for moral conversion. They make the decision to change their lives and become better persons, usually prompted by attending a retreat, or at the beginning of Lent, or listening to an inspiring sermon. The desire for change lasts but a short time, because moral conversion will not take root in the life of anyone, unless it is accompanied by an intellectual conversion that motivates an emotional change. There must be an emotional response to God, if lives are going to change and transform morally.

Feelings and emotions motivate people when making decisions, despite the emphatic denial that feelings have anything to do with religion that priests like Father Damian make. They regard emotions as a tool simply to move the masses and without any theological basis. They also want to return to the past, not only to Latin chants, but to a morality that would compel couples to have as many children as possible, insisting that any sexual act that was not meant for procreation was a mortal sin that would send the sinner to an eternity of pain and grief. What irony! The Vatican teaches this and at the same time they have owned vast amounts of stock in pharmaceutical companies that manufacture birth control pills, while teaching the laity that purchasing them would bring eternal damnation. Incredible!

In my heart burned a vision of a new and glorious Church, and to me, the old ways shared by Damian, Renato, and Enki were monstrous and odious. The message of Christ points the way to bring everyone to His Father, by cleansing them of sin through the power of His Blood. In the gospels, Jesus was very compassionate to people burdened and downtrodden under the weight of their sins. To teach them to receive His forgiveness and redemption was His mission and should be the mission of the Church today.

Because they do not want to change their lives or express gratitude for God's forgiving love, many simply do not want to be forgiven. As a priest, I have observed that many people actually do not want God interfering in their lives, except to provide them with money and health.

The only thing that is important before God is a sincere heart—one that is surrendered to His will. The root of success in my ministry has always been to explain to people how to live—beyond human traditions and denominational differences—constantly in the Presence of God. I have never been able to comprehend why Rome, in spite of Vatican II and all the conciliar and post-conciliar documents, does not realize that all the Protestant churches are their offspring and to maintain any hostility toward them is a loss of God's grace and human energy. Although, I loved my Church, I still admired all the good things that God did in the Evangelical and Pentecostal Churches. Many times I felt more identified with some Pentecostal pastors than with Roman priests like Fathers Damian and Renato.

Firmly believing in the participation of the laity in the life of the Church, I established councils at Santiago that would help establish our church policies, permitting dedicated laity to make all the important decisions. After all, a celibate caste is not the ideal group to make decisions or write theology books that will affect the lives of millions. There was a lot of truth in the saying that went around in the 1970's in regard to *Humanae Vitae*: "If you no playa da game, you no make da rules."

Granting the laity the right to make decisions is a complete break from centuries of clericalism, where the only opinion that counts is that of the bishop or the pastor. If the Roman Catholic Church expects to continue in existence, it needs to take into account the opinions of its faithful members who are no longer uneducated peasants, but are often more learned and knowledgeable than the hierarchy. Because dedicated laity love the Church and sacrifice themselves for her with their financial support, they must have a say in the selection of bishops, in the appointment of pastors, and in the ordination of priests and deacons. Although the long centuries of clericalism have made the Catholic people rubber stamp all the opinions of the hierarchy and clergy in the past, a new day is dawning in which they demand to be permitted to express their opinions.

I love the Church, and my most intense desire has always been to bring the power of the Holy Spirit to the people, because the Presence urged me to call them to adoration and holiness. Although I did not feel worthy, the Presence spoke to me very clearly saying, "It is you that I have called to this ministry." I have no choice but to accept His call.

The strong calling from God has turned me into a public character, an object of admiration by many and of hate by some. To become a television religious personality with the biggest audiences of all the programs in the areas where they were shown, made me very popular and, at the same time, profoundly envied by a sector of the clergy and of the lay people. The more successful I became, the more enemies I attracted. I did not realize how many people—clergy and lay people—wanted to destroy my ministry, because of their low negative desires. It was only a matter of time until all hell would break loose.

29
Enki

It was Thursday and Enki couldn't wait to enjoy his day off. Just wait, he thought, 'til I tell Yo-Lin the news. Since it was too good to tell her over the phone, he was on his way up the Rosanada River to her nude bar, *La Estrella de Amor*, in the mountains north of the city where she had agreed to meet him since she spent the nights there on the weekends to be close to the business. He knew that if he got there early enough she would still be in bed in her secret room, a huge area behind the stairs, perhaps having her breakfast.

The club was deserted in the morning hours, but Colette was there and let him in. Lounging on a leather sofa with a black man he had never seen before, Yin-Lu was there too. Because he could not stand to watch their cavorting, he carefully avoided looking at them. Rushing into Yo-Lin's room, he found her propped up in bed wearing a flimsy red, see-through night-gown, looking at her face in a small golden hand mirror trying to detect any new wrinkles. Surrounding her, as usual, were piles of pornographic photos of children that she was selecting for distribution, for she never got far from her work. The best ones were to be picked up by two of her most trusted men for processing.

"What brings you here so early? You should have been here last night. I got a couple new nude dancers that I'd like for you to see."

"I have news to tell you that will make you dance and sing!"

"Hurry up! Tell me!"

"The Selkis have been arrested. The Feds caught them with the stuff—cocaine and ecstasy. They wrapped up their whole operation." He felt like the cat that ate the canary as he watched her reaction.

"Great news, Enki. I am delighted that finally they got out of the way. The Feds will not be looking at the church anymore. Now, we will be more secure and will continue at Santiago. Sometimes I feel so dirty that giving away money and helping those poor people there gives me a sensation of cleanliness." She paused, studied her face in her mirror, and added: "Besides it is a good cover." Pushing the breakfast tray away and laying down her mirror, she rose from her bed, pranced across the room in her nightie to a black lacquered dresser, and picked up a hair brush with an ornate goldern handle.

Brushing her hair, she walked over to where he was sitting in an elaborate brocaded chair and bending over kissed him. He did not respond.

"There is still more news," he said gently pushing her away. "Our old friend Renato is the one who sent the Selkis to the mission. I do not know exactly why he hates Marco, and I don't care. He is just as determined as I am to squash him like a bug—a *cucaracha*! Priests and bishops are destroying the Church—well, Marco is one of them with all his charismatic mumbo-jumbo, fuzzy theology, and fake miracles. He is turning the church into a circus that is destroying the piety of the people. His Masses are just a show, not a religious function, because they lack the respect and solemnity of the Church's liturgy!"

She sat down on his lap and put her arm around his neck. "Marco's television ministry keeps growing as does the mission. That should help your career, since you are his administrative assistant, his right hand man. He should be raising your salary as everything grows."

"Yes, I have made contact with Trent Television and Radio Network and they are going to give me a program on their network that reaches around the world. My folks in Caracas are looking forward to seeing me on it. I don't need Marco anymore. He has served my purposes."

"I wonder why the mission keeps growing in spite of everything that happens. How many staff members are there at the mission at this time?

"Well, let's see. Maybe thirty. Besides me, the administrative assistant, there are two vicars—Father Lalo Chochon and Father Falito Joto—guys who came recently from Cuba looking for money. Then there is Luisa the so-called cook and housekeeper who can't even boil an egg right. There is also Pazi the television director and frigid and crazy Bastits the music director. There's a lot more of them. Let me see if I can remember any more. Oh, yes, there is the deacon—Deacon Angel Rios, a good man. I almost forgot Tetita, Marco's secretary. She is a real bitch on wheels. He only hired her because she is a parishioner and was in a desperate situation. I don't think she likes anyone, but I must say Tetita is a titillating dame as far as looks go, but her personality is poison—strictly poison. I would not touch her with a ten-foot pole—if you get what I mean. But I have made friends of all of them. I can count on them all to help me. Luisa spies on Marco and reports to me. There are other employees, and I get along with all of them. You know I can be everything to everybody when needed. Oh, I almost forgot to tell you the biggest news."

"Yes?" She was almost breathless as she waited to hear.

"There is a newspaper woman, one Ali Purcell, and she is publishing a book, *A Church of Darkness* accusing Marco of sexually abusing Foc Gomorrah. And—"

She interrupted: "Foc Gomorrah gave a sworn affidavit that Marco is innocent." She got up from sitting on his lap and retreated to her bed where she propped up on four pillows.

"Yes, I know. But Foc was down and out—his family kicked him out and he was dying of syphilis. Ali Purcell took him in. They shared a bed and he gave her a fantastic story for her book. At least that is the story that his mother is spreading around. In exchange, she took care of his needs."

"He had syphilis and they shared a bed?" She thought a minute and continued" "Of course, there are many ways to skin a cat, as the old saying goes. Not to change the subject, but, Enki, I need to talk to you about something important to me. I *am* trying to cut back on my drug dealing operations. If the capos knew I was working for the Venezuelan government as a double agent, they would send someone to kill me in a flash. So I hope to get out of that and now I am working on another way to make big money." She studied him carefully before continuing. "You could be a big help to me and make good money. I will try to help you with your career. If

Marco lets you sing on his television programs, you will be a big success and someone will give you the break you have been waiting for." She motioned for him to come sit beside her on the bed.

Curious as to what kind of business deal she had to offer, he did as she told him to and started climbing into bed.

"No, silly! She protested. "Take off your clothes first. If you like, there is a man's bathrobe in my closet."

He undressed in the closet and slipped on the posh Luigi Ventoso black velvet robe. As soon as he was comfortably ensconced in the king-size bed beside her, he asked: "So what is the business deal you are offering me."

"I have certain contacts in South America—in Paraguay—that make porn flicks of kids—even snuff. There are some Germans down there, the children of the old Nazi refugees, hidden away in a forest, and they are producing lots of it."

"What's that got to do with me? And what is snuff?"

"For heaven's sake Enki you are such a crybaby. Here am I, a full-grown total bitch having to explain to you a most primitive bisexual pedophile what pornography is all about! Snuff is a porn film in which the victim is killed. Gilles de Rais should have been their patron saint. He used to kill young boys, split their lower abdomen to have an orgasm in their still warm entrails. The Marquis de Sade, which by the way I have never read, states that the ultimate sexual high is killing the victim."

"I don't want to get mixed up in any killing," Enki protested vehemently, pulling away from Yo-Lin.

"No, of course not, you won't have anything to do with that or with making the porn."

"I don't see how I can make any money. Just what is the deal you are making me?" he fretted.

"When you are not busy at the mission, you can come here to *La Estrella de Amor* and help me to edit and distribute the porn, I'll set up an office for you in the room next to mine. You will do your actual work here, but you can take some of the films with you and work on them at Santiago, if you are very careful with them so as not to get caught. I want you to help me distribute them to customers that I have lined up." She took his hand in hers and smiled at him benignly.

"Well, I guess I could do that easy enough. It's a deal."

"OK. Good. I will work out the financial arrangement between us and I will be generous."

He reached out to pull her closer to him.

"Wait, there is something else I have to discuss with you first."

He sighed deeply, frustrated that his desire for her was waning.

She smiled at him sweetly and flashed her sparkling emerald eyes at him.

"It is time for a wedding. You need to be married. What are you waiting for?"

"You must be out of your mind. Yo-Lin, I'll do it, if that is what you want, but it would seem very strange to everybody. You are old enough to be my mother, besides you have never been married and you want me to be your first husband!" He tried to pull her closer. She pushed him away forcefully.

"No! Not me, Dummy. I am not ready yet to get married. I would not even say that in joking. Our relationship is better than marriage. It is very nice, but it is not leading to anything of that sort. I don't want a husband."

"What are you suggesting then," he inquired.

"Think, baby, think. In order to function in the Church, if you are not a priest, you need to be a married man. Marriage gives you respectability and approval from everybody. And I suggest you marry, at least until your musical career is solidly established. You can still continue your relationship with me, helping me in my work and sharing my bed, but you will get married and appear to live like everyone else at the mission. As I always say, anyone who is not married by age twenty-five has a few loose screws!"

"A marriage of convenience! What kind of hypocrite do you think I am?" The very idea of it annoyed him and even angered him.

"Come on, Enki, you are still young—there must be some girl in the choir that you could marry." Indeed he was young; however, in spite of his delicate manners and his Venezuelan courtesy, women were not attracted to him. Because he was too pale, his face badly scarred, his smile uneven, and his black hair too straight and unruly to be well-combed, women did not find him attractive.

"You upset me when you talk like that. Marriage is more than just an arrangement to cover up a situation."

"Enki, in your situation, you have plenty to cover up and hide. Marriage might not be capable of doing it, but if you do not get married you are going to be unprotected and vulnerable."

"And who do you think would be a good wife?" he said sarcastically, while pulling roughly away from her.

"The girl you have been going out with. Espi Cárdenas is the perfect one—shy, naive, has had a lot of boyfriends, so therefore I am sure that she would accommodate you and besides all this, she teaches catechism at Santiago. She is just the girl for you."

"Won't this have an effect on our—uh, uh— relationship?"

"Not in the least, and I will be sitting in the front pew at your wedding." She paused a moment, smiled slightly. and said, "Even more I am willing to pay for the implant?

"What are you talking about now?

"An implant to enlarge your penis."

"You have never complained before." Enki felt really humiliated.

"Forget what I said; let's go on with the planning, but if you wish to consider it, I am open to helping you. You have all the right moves, but you would definitely benefit from the enlargement."

"I'll think about it," he said flatly, as he pulled her into his arms and rolled over on top of her, ready to prove his sexual prowess. This time she did not resist, but gave herself eagerly to him. However the conversation about marriage had a negative effect on him, so after trying all kinds of techniques, they gave up and played a gay porno movie that finally succeeded in arousing Enki.

A few hours later after a lunch of quail and champagne, Enki, dismayed with anxiety and confusion, returned to the mission. Although he liked the idea of the business deal he had struck with Yo-Lin, the idea of getting married made him very uncomfortable. Although his sexual preference ran to young males, he saw the logic of what Yo-Lin had told him. A Catholic marriage would make it possible for him to work for her in his office at Santiago and in the evenings at *La Estrella de Amor* and continue as Marco' administrative assistant, until he hit the big time with his career. He was hoping to hear any day how the big wheels in Nashville liked the recordings he had made in the mission studio and sent to them.

So all considered, he decided to proceed with asking Espi to marry him. After she accepted, he drove her home in his Mustang. That very night he sealed the engagement by impregnating Espi.

As soon as Enki learned that Espi was pregnant, they arranged to get married at the Rosanada County Court House, keeping it as secret as possible. When Enki told Yo-Lin that they were married and a baby was on the way, she was dancing on the clouds for a week, insisting that she was the baby's aunt and godmother. At her age, Enki reasoned, she would more properly serve as grandmother.

With the passing of time, Espi's pregnancy was starting to become obvious. Although he was worried that Marco might fire him, it was necessary for him to tell Marco the truth. Marco would be completely justified in firing him, because secret weddings were forbidden to Catholics and it was a serious violation of Church law that that a civil servant rather than a priest married them. Nevertheless, when they could delay no longer, he and Espi went to Marco's office.

"Father, Espi and I have something to tell you."

"Of course, come in and take a seat" Marco invited very cordially with a smile of welcome.

Enki put on his best face and manners. "Espi and I were married at the court house, because she got pregnant with my child. I know you are a very compassionate person, Father, and that you will understand and help us."

Father Marco's smile turned into a frown. "This is a sad day for me, you were a good example of a Christian engaged couple for all the community. I am very confused by this. You know that Catholics should only be married by a priest. As far as the Church is concerned, you are not married, but merely cohabitating. Since you are both involved in parish ministry, people expect you both to be exemplary Catholics."

"Please forgive us and have compassion on us," Enki pleaded. "We did not mean for things to happen this way. Surely, we can come up with a solution."

Father Marco took his hand and Espi's into his and said, "I understand, we will have a wedding at Santiago asking God's blessing on your union."

Espi managed to hide the already visible presence of the baby by wearing large, baggy shirts, as she prepared for marriage. The wedding, the biggest and most crowded social event of the parish's year, was Yo-Lin's triumph. She ordered nothing but the best from the florists so that the church overflowed with roses, gardenias, and lilies. The bride and groom knelt under a trellis, entwined with orchids and jasmine, that was placed in the aisle before the altar, as friends from all over the area witnessed the marriage.

During a ceremony that lasted two hours with all the music, readings, and testimonies about the goodness of the couple, Enki declared his love for Espi, so convincingly that many of the women present were crying. Even Yo-Lin was shedding crocodile tears—she had slept with him just the night before. Although the members of Santiago Mission were mostly very hardworking, middle-class people, Yo-Lin organized a reception worthy of a king.

After a honeymoon in Venice and other Italian cities, following Yo-Lin's itinerary, the couple returned to Rosanada, and Enki settled down to his new business of helping Yo-Lin with the pornography. After telling everyone that he needed privacy and quiet to work on the parish business, he put a large "Do Not Disturb" sign on his closed office door, so that no one would barge in and discover that he was working on pornography instead of the church's accounts. Sometimes, however, he tended to be absent minded and forgot to put it up.

30
Renato

America really was the land of opportunity! Ever since he had come here, his fortunes had continued to soar. Old Melusine had reached the mandatory age of retirement—seventy-five—and sent the required letter of resignation to the pope. What a relief to be rid of him! His Excellency, the Most Reverend Cecil Anselm l'Abbadon J.C.D., B.S.D., D.D, a typical French Canadian, with good manners, but a true autocrat, arrived in Rosanada determined to rule with an iron fist. His parents, faithful and hardworking French Canadian Catholics, together with their five children, had moved to Rosanada back in the fifties. His father was an airplane mechanic and a bit of a drunk, while his mother was a constant complainer and whiner. L'Abbadon had joined the Kentucky Blackfriars' Priory in his youth, and when that congregation that was heavily into New Age practices collapsed for lack of members, he incardinated in the Rosanada Archdiocese. Archbishop Lingam sent him to Rome where he worked for many years at the Pontifical Institute Antinoo for the Defense of the Rights of the Holy See. He was also the Grand Master of the Equestrian Order of the Most Holy Foreskin, Assistant to the Supreme Pontiff's Throne, Pontifical Chaplain to the Tiberius Caesar Children's Choir, the very best in Italy, and now Rome had sent him back to Rosanada as the new archbishop. Because of his mundane and lackluster family background, he pretended to be a highly sophisticated connoisseur of the arts. A tall man with very fair skin, blotched with freckles, a full head of white hair, he had a very prominent nose, making him reminiscent of Jean Cocteau. Although he had a very deep and mellow voice, it could become quite harsh when he was crossed. Then his facial expression would darken as he clenched his teeth and the corners of his mouth drooped downward. Renato was quick to notice that he had a characteristic facial expression when he was annoyed or stressed—he pursed his thin lips contracting them into a circle. He would do the same when forced to smile without a desire to do so. A friend of Renato's told him that not all faggots smile like that, but whoever does it is a faggot.

It soon became obvious that Archbishop L'Abbadon loved luxury and the finest things that money could buy, because he took one look at the house Melusine had called home, declared that he could never live in such a dump, and immediately hired an architect to draw up plans for a three million dollar home worthy of his office and according to his exact specifications. Meanwhile he lived in the Hyatt Regency in a penthouse suite overlooking the waterfront of the Rosanada River.

To satisfy his expensive tastes, Renato knew the archbishop would be making demands on him to raise more money. Thank God that for the time being he could relax because Melusine had amassed a great fortune for the archdiocese due to his natural stinginess, so that all the capricious desires of His Excellency L'Abbadon could be satisfied. It soon became apparent that the new archbishop liked to spend money as if there were no tomorrow. Just how expensive his tastes would be was indicated by the tall jeweled miter, studded with genuine diamonds, emeralds, and rubies that he purchased for his installation. When the choir sang *Ecce Sacerdos Magnus* he seemed to be eight feet tall, as he proudly walked down the center aisle of the cathedral. He probably would have loved to enter sitting in the pope's own *sedia gestatoria.*

Very skillfully Renato played on the archbishop's cupidity and love of money, arranging for the millionaire members of his Goretti Society to visit L'Abbadon and impress him with the high opinion they held of Renato. This ploy was successful. Six months after his installation, Archbishop L'Abbadon began to shuffle all the personnel in the chancery. Renato rejoiced to see Father Damian Babilonia demoted, made a simple pastor in one of the large parishes that was not especially affluent, and given the title of monsignor as a consolation prize. Sadly, Damian died of liver failure shortly after being demoted. All Damian's friends and protégés were similarly ousted.

Obviously impressed by his ability to raise money, the archbishop promoted Renato to the position of Sub-Secretary of His Excellency, and Renato felt it would only be a matter of time until he would be elevated to the episcopacy. Having reached a position he had so long desired, Renato was not impressed by L'Abbadon's arrogant expression and eloquent words. All that mattered to him was that the archbishop trusted him, and Renato was certain that he could manipulate him to his liking.

To celebrate his promotion, Yo-Lin Sin held an intimate soirée with dinner catered by one of the best restaurants in North Park. Jumbo shrimp, steak tartar, Norwegian smoked salmon, and French *paté de foie gras* proceeded the Beef Wellington and broiled lobster that were accompanied by an exquisite 1964 Chateau de Sade wine—Yo-Lin's favorite. For dessert Renato chose the tiramisu, while Yo-Lin had a mango cheesecake.

After all the other guests had left—there were just of a few of her Mafia friends invited—Renato braced himself, because he knew that she would try to seduce him. The woman was an insatiable nymphomaniac, but she held no interest for him, even though she slipped into her most seductive Issey Miyake nightgown, for she simply turned him off.

"Let's talk, Yo-Lin. You know I am not interested in sex." It was money that motivated him and he knew it. He simply was not interested in the Queen of Drugs and Sex.

"What do you want to talk about?" she asked impatiently with frustration.

"I want to talk to you about Marco Lamadrid, his ministry, and the Santiago mission." Now that he was close to the archbishop, he planned to stop Marco in his tracks and put an end to his preaching on television, his healing services, and his exorcisms.

"What do you want to know?"

"Everything!"

"Well, everything he touches is a great success. His television programs in both Spanish and English are bringing people from all over the county to Santiago. Marco welcomes everyone, including traditional families, but also the divorced, alcoholics, drug addicts, convicts, homosexuals, and just the plain curious. He insists that

Jesus came to seek those that are lost and that they are all welcome at the mission—everyone who has a problem gets an open door. He tells everyone that Santiago is their second home."

Renato merely nodded and said, "Tell me more."

"He is going to Montevideo this weekend to preach to a stadium full of people. Some one phoned him from down there inviting him to come. He declined telling them that he already had other plans. When they told him that an Evangelical preacher had been there last weekend and that now the Catholics decided they would fill up the stadium this weekend, but they had no one to preach. Marco agreed to go. He is spreading his vision for an effervescent Church everywhere—just like the Protestants. As you know, he has done away with piety and formality, and at the same time, he has become the most popular priest in the area, and some people even think he is a saint."

Yo-Lin went to the kitchen and fixed herself a drink—a Fantasia brandy cocktail. Because he had already had enough for the evening, and he wanted to keep his wits about him, he declined.

"Look Yo-Lin, he is no saint, believe me. I have known him since I met him in Rome, years ago. I want you to get close to him and learn all you can about him and report to me. I need to find a way to get him out of ministry. How is Enki taking Marco's success?" He sat back in his chair, kicked off his shoes, and propped up his feet on the ottoman.

"Enki hates him and would do anything to destroy him."

Good! thought Renato. He knew how to make use of him. Now that he had the power and his good friends, Yo-Lin and Enki, were close to Marco, all he had to do was pull the strings and watch him fall. He had a score to settle with Marco Lamadrid. Anger boiled up in him, as he recalled the evening that he had invited Marco out to dinner and then took him to his condo afterwards. Marco's good looks appealed to him, and he had hoped that in spite of their theological and liturgical differences they could have become close.

When they arrived at his condo, Renato excused himself, saying he was going to put on something more comfortable. He put on his best Italian silk pajamas, his finest Serge Matta silk robe, and a pair of soft leather slippers. When he returned to the living room, Marco was sitting on his over-sized contemporary sofa, sipping Cardenal Mendoza, a Spanish brandy that Renato bought especially for him, from one of the Murano crystal glasses Renato acquired to celebrate his promotion to sub-secretary of His Excellency. Renato could not help admiring Marco's handsome and sexually appealing features. He was glad that he had been to the salon and had all the hair waxed off his body just a few days before, so that he now appeared at his best. Indiscreetly and with evident curiosity, he stared at Marco's crotch and said, "Wow! You are really something!"

"Why do you say that?" asked Marco naively not understanding Renato's meaning.

Sitting down in a chair opposite Marco, Renato thought to himself that Marco was either stupid or wanted to play stupid, but he said: "I just meant that you are so well proportioned." Leering at him, he continued: "You really fill out those pants—quite a bulge!"

Ignoring his comments, Marco changed the subject adroitly by discussing the latest appointments in the archdiocese. When that subject was exhausted, Renato went to the bookcase at the opposite end of the living room and returned with a handsomely bound book. "I want to show you a copy of my dissertation for my doctorate in liturgy that I wrote at the Saladin's Pontifical Institute of Saint Desiderius Erasmus." After handing Marco the book, he sat down close beside him on the oversized black velvet upholstered contemporary sofa.

As Marco began thumbing through the volume, Renato let his robe fall open and began unbuttoning his pajamas. "I think the brandy is making me hot!" He really wanted to show off his fancy feminine underwear that he had put on for the occasion. Jumping to his feet, he dropped his pajama pants to the floor and stood there before Marco wearing a padded bra of black lace and a matching black lace thong panty that revelaed his bare, flaccid, and pimply ass in the rear and a very modest bulge in the front that was discretely covered with black lace. Although he noticed that Marco eyed him rather quizzically, but did not react negatively, he sat down beside him on the sofa and snuggled closer to him, hoping that Marco would respond to his overtures. A pang of fear raced through him, as he considered the possiblilty that Marco would not find him appealing.

Deciding to press his advantage, Renato laid his hand on Marco's thigh.

Instantly and forcefully pushing his hand away, Marco jumped to his feet and exclaimed, "I really have to be going now. I have stayed too long already."

Humiliated, Renato saw that he had completely misread Marco. There were so few heterosexual priests in the archdiocese that he felt sure Marco would yield to his propositioning him, but instead he was shocked by what Renato had done. Nevertheless, Renato was not worried that Marco would report him to the chancery, because no one would believe him if he did. Renato felt quite secure in his position with the archbishop.

"I'll see you to your car," Renato offered, trying to compensate for the incident and make their parting seem gracious.

"No, thanks. I can manage by myself."

Several months had passed since that evening. "Now we will see," thought Renato, "how well you can manage by yourself, now that I am ascending to prominence and power. I will show Marco Lamadrid what it means to reject and humiliate me!"

31
Enki

It was simply incredible how Marco's ministry kept expanding. He had even opened an office of International Evangelization in Montevideo and was beginning to expand to the rest of the Latin American countries. It was disgusting! And it was really weird.

The episode in Virginia looked like it was destined to silence Marco Lamadrid once and for all. It all began when Marco converted Chuck and Steve Carter, a couple of Protestant Pentecostals from Virginia, with his ideas of a new vibrant Catholic Church. He made Chuck youth minister! A Protestant convert! Converts will never be real Catholics—they have not been brought up in the faith, and they have no idea of what the true Church was like before the insanities of Vatican II. So he made this Chuck Carter with his Protestant ideas youth minister. Well, it backfired on him. It served him right. Enki laughed as he thought about it, relishing Marco's abasement.

It all began when Chuck—a real redneck—got the idea of organizing a week long retreat at a state park in the Blue Ridge Mountains of western Virginia. Marco insisted that Enki tag along with them, because Marco wanted him, as his administrative assistant, to help run some of the events of the retreat and be in charge of all the financial arrangements. Although he tried, he just couldn't get out of it. The park of almost four thousands acres was nice enough with two lakes, a camp-ground, rustic mountain cabins, meeting facilities, and lots of activities. They said it once was the home of the Algonquin Indians. The view of the mountains above Lake Lenape was a pretty site but could not compare with the mountains surrounding Caracas.

The cost of the retreat was low enough for parents from Santiago and neighboring parishes to send their kids for a week, since the event was partly funded by the church and it was slightly off season at a time when few other people chose to go there. Consequently, the retreatants had the park mostly to themselves.

Although Marco did let Enki sing, and the kids seemed caught up in the worship of God, obviously enjoying his singing, Marco would not let him preach. Rather, he let Chuck with his Protestant and Pentecostal ideas preach to them, while denying Enki the opportunity.

After Chuck's preaching a hell and brimstone sermon, Marco gave an altar call, just like the Protestants do on TV, and all the kids came forth in doves to accept Christ into their hearts and to renounce the devil and all his deceits. One girl—her name was Patricia—was so fired up she claimed she had a vision of the Sacred Heart. Later on, she said perhaps she had just imagined it.

Enki just couldn't believe the kids were really going to give up all the worldly things they said they would—lying, cheating, indecent dancing, and using drugs. He knew the boys would never go for the clean-cut look, and the girls would never stop wearing those tight miniskirts and jeans that reveal every curve of their anatomy.

Things went from bad to worse. When Chuck called for everyone who wanted deliverance to come forth, Enki could not believe his eyes. It was a very dark night as Chuck stood in the circle of the campers who were gathered around a big bonfire. It was a quite a sight. The flames of the bonfire were rising high into the blackness of the night, creating an almost eerie atmosphere, as one after another of the young people began to clamor for deliverance from evil. When Marco laid his hands on the head of one youth, he roared like a tiger. Another got down on the ground and began writhing and undulating like a snake. Then Chuck Carter stood over him commanding the evil spirit to leave him. A chill ran up Enki's spine as a group of bats began to circle the campfire and a large hoot owl began his plaintive and mournful dirge. It was as if all hell had broken loose! Some of the young people were chanting in a language that he had never heard before, in a strange uncanny and unnatural sound.

All one hundred and thirty of the young people were caught up in some unusual supernatural experience, such as Enki had never before witnessed. He couldn't wait to get back to Rosanada and tell Renato what had happened. Surely, the archbishop would reprimand Marco severely for this shameful occurrence.

Deciding the news was too good to keep, Enki phoned Renato on his cell phone. "Marco and Chuck are doing exorcisms! It is disgusting. Kids are screaming and rolling on the ground. You have to do something about Marco and his weird practices and ideas." Renato thanked him, making him feel really favored as he considered how he was ingratiating himself with the chancery and how they would reward him. More importantly, however, they would silence Marco Lamadrid sooner or later!

When the kids returned home and told their parents that they had been converted and did not want to listen to rock music and watch sexually explicit and obscene programs on television any more, they were furious. Renato told him how the parents had complained to him saying that Marco had turned their kids into religious fanatics. Why they had even cleaned up their language and never said the bad words that teens commonly used to talk to each other and shock their elders! Gleefully, Enki heard that the parents were demanding an investigation of Marco whom they considered to be inflicting harm on the young with his exorcisms and fanaticism. It was incredible! Marco thought he had done the parents a big favor by converting the kids, but they did not see it that way, nor did the chancery. Exorcism is forbidden in the Catholic Church! Somehow they all seemed to forget that until recent years every priest was solemnly ordained as an exorcist. Besides, Marco was not doing exorcisms, but deliverances.

Enki was delighted to learn that Renato, whom he knew hated Marco with a passion that dated many years back, had scheduled an archdiocesan tribunal to examine all the complaints the parents had brought against the priest. It was really unfortunate, Enki thought, that after careful examination, they were unable to find any fault with them. However, they did insist that Marco placate some of the parents who were most indignant and demanding some recourse.

Talking to his own parishioners was relatively easy for Marco, but Enki watched him sweat the night he went with him to nearby St. Gertrude Church where the pastor, Father Elton, and a group of about twelve couples were waiting to rip him to shreds. Even Marco's humility as he faced the irate pastor and his parishioners sickened and appalled Enki. No man could be that humble as he answered them in a quiet tone that calmed their tempers and deflected their wrath. Once again Marco had escaped, but he, Enki Mutante, would find a way to destroy his ministry!

It was really good news when Chuck decided to pick up and move back to Virginia. Now, Marco was left with little support among the members of the parish staff.

Enki could count on Bastits Koldwall, the music director, to help him stop the spread of Marco's ministry. Great Bastits! She was only about thirty, but seemed much older with her holier than thou ways and her cold and frigid attitudes. An ugly woman—hair dyed platinum blonde, face covered with blotches of acne and its residual scarring, she was short and fat, ungainly, stumbling over her own feet, and just plain clumsy and awkward. Furthermore everyone agreed she had a voice like a fog horn, and that she badly needed a man to subdue, dominate, and possess her.

He had befriended Bastits, although she had no other male friends. As the director of the choirs, she developed a possessive attitude toward Father Marco, resenting his attempt to talk to anyone else when she was present. Utterly ridiculous, she followed at his heels like a cocker spaniel bitch with every step he took, as he went through the parish hall consulting with various employees. So to take care of business, he had to ask her to step out of the room. She became so controlling and overprotective that she developed the habit of spraying perfume around her office, when she knew he would be there.

It was interesting, thought Enki, how she could turn on Marco when she felt he ignored her, defaming him bitterly to any and all who would listen. Knowing that she would be useful to him, Enki would simply say when she complained to him of Marco's indifference: "You are so right, Bastits. He does not care about anyone, except himself." Comforting and ingratiating himself with Bastits, he would wait until the time was right and then use her to discredit Marco. Although the woman was sick and completely lacking in emotional balance, she would suit his purposes admirably.

32
Bastits

Enki convinced her that she needed to get out and have fun. "You are too confined, Bastits," he had said, "spending all your time on the music ministry several nights a week. Marco doesn't appreciate your sacrificing yourself the way you are. He only cares about himself." Always supporting her position vis-á-vis Marco, Enki was a good friend, but it was very difficult for her to understand how Espi, a fairly good-looking woman, had married him, because he had absolutely no sex appeal with the ugly scar on his face and his unruly black straight hair. It must have been for his courtesy and manners that she found pleasing.

Although she felt no attraction for any of the men her own age in the parish, she decided to take Enki's advice and have more fun. She invited Wolfgang Draper, the television deliveryman, out for dinner for his birthday. Even though he was generally disliked by most of the staff at Santiago—they all called him Wolfbane—she thought he was a nice man who would not try to take any sexual liberties with her, because he was fifty years old. At the Green Mill she insisted that he have a drink before dinner.

"I can't drink," Wolfgang protested. "I am a recovering alcoholic. I still go to AA every week. "He looked at her admiringly. She could see in his eyes that he found her appealing.

"Just one little drink won't hurt, will it?" she cajoled.

To please her, he acquiesced and ordered a "Devil's Tail", a mixed drink with Vodka and Rum, and sipped it very slowly. After that, he drank two more, because she insisted that he have another drink every time she ordered one. When they left the restaurant, he was in high spirits.

"I'd like you to come to my office at Santiago," he invited. "I want to show you the pictures of my family. My wife died ten years ago and I have two grown sons who live in Rosanada Meadows."

She smiled at him and replied, "I would be delighted to see pictures of your family." Suddenly, as she surveyed him, noticing that he had honest looking, calloused, strong hands with short stubby fingers, she realized that this slightly paunchy middle-aged man was probably very lonely. Yes, she felt she could trust such a man not to come too close to her.

When they arrived back at Santiago and were comfortably seated on his office sofa, he handed her a stack of photos.

"This is my wife," he pointed to an attractive woman in the photo standing under a large pine tree with two boys about fifteen years of age." She was a small woman with jet black hair and a charming smile.

"You must miss her very much."

"All the time. That is why I decided to do church work and give my life—what's left of it—to God." He took the photos from her and put them back on the bookcase where he kept them. "The pay is certainly nothing to brag about, but I feel like I am doing something worthwhile."

When he returned to the sofa, he slid closer to her. Flustered by his nearness, she jabbed him in the ribs with her elbow—one of the many protrusions of her clumsy and awkward body.

"Oh, I'm sorry," she exclaimed. Then trying to change the subject, she began telling him how she was going to start singing at the English Mass on Sundays.

"You too are going to sing?"

"Of course, don't you think I can?"

"You will do a beautiful job. You are so nice looking"

He slid a little closer to her on the sofa. Again she jabbed him with an elbow. As she felt his arm encircling her shoulders, she was nonplused and terrified. Flustered, she began speaking very rapidly telling him that she liked the way he worked so hard for Santiago—anything to distract him from her body. How could she explain to him that she was frigid? Suddenly, he grasped her to draw her to himself to kiss her. She felt his teeth gnash against hers and was instantly repelled. When she pushed him away, his hand fell from her shoulder and landed on her knee.

"Masher!" she yelled, pushing him away so forcefully that he fell off the sofa and hit the floor with a thud.

Jumping to her feet, she ran from his office and sought the safety of her Cavalier in the parking lot and quickly sped away in a cloud of dust.

Without wasting a minute she drove to the home of Teresa Valdés, the president of the Pastoral Council. She would know what to do, for she could refer her to a ministry where the leader would be an expert in abuse, having been the victim of incest in her childhood, consequently growing up to be an alcoholic, and spending many years in rehabilitation with Alcoholics Anonymous. When she entered the Valdés home, Bastits was disheveled, her long stringy hair was in disarray, and her skirt was torn by one of her spike heels that had damaged it as she had jumped from the sofa when Wolfgang had tried to kiss her. Gasping for breath, she told Teresa of how that horrible Wolfgang Draper had attemptted to rape her.

"My dear, you must calm down, you are hysterical and hyperventilating. Here lie down on the sofa while I get a bag."

She could hardly breathe—she was gasping so hard for air.

Teresa returned with a brown paper bag and had her place it over her face and breathe into it. In a few minutes, her breathing returned to normal.

"I can recommend a good psychiatrist for you," Teresa ventured.

"I'm not crazy! I don't need a shrink! A man tried to rape me!" Teresa did not try to push a psychiatrist on her anymore. Instead, she advised, "Go see Father Marco in the morning and tell him what has happened. You can stay here overnight if you want to."

She went home determined to see Father Marco early the next day. She would make Draper pay dearly for what he had tried to do to her!

33
Marco

I greeted the new day with enthusiasm. The chancery was off my back and the ministry was flourishing. Although there were always new problems, I would cross those bridges when I came to them. No doubt, I was getting pretty good at crossing hazardous bridges, but I certainly wasn't expecting what happened when I arrived at my office. Standing at the door waiting to see me was Bastits Koldwall—her face contorted like those of some of the insane I had seen when visiting hospitals. The smile on my face froze into a frown upon seeing her. Here comes trouble, I said to myself.

Just as I figured she would, she broke down into hysterical sobbing when she entered my office.

"Padre," she gasped between sobs. "Padre, Wolfgang Draper..."

"Pull yourself together, Bastits. I can't understand a word you are saying." I poured myself a cup of the coffee that Tetita always put on my desk each morning. "Would you like some coffee, Bastits?" I said, hoping to calm her down.

"No! He tried to rape me!" she cried with a fresh burst of tears.

"Who?" I asked in bewilderment.

"Wolfgang! Of all people!" A scream came bursting from her throat loud enough to wake the mummies of Egypt.

"Calm down and tell me about it." I offered her a chair across the desk from my own.

"I took him out for dinner to the Green Mill for his birthday and then we came back here. He wanted to show me photos of his late wife. We were sitting on the sofa in his office and he…he…"

"Yes, go ahead," I urged.

"He tried to kiss me and I pushed him and he touched my knee and fell off the sofa onto floor with a thud. He wanted to rape me, I know it, but I ran out of his office and went to see Teresa Valdés. She knows all about it. She told me to come to you." A tremor shook her body as the sobs sub-sided.

"So he kissed you? That's all? And you pushed him on the floor and on the way down his hand fell on your knee?" I suppressed the desire to laugh at the ridiculous situation, as I pictured a surprised Draper, picking himself up off the floor.

"That's enough! He wanted to steal my virtue…my chastity…my virginity—and he's an employee of the church. To placate the woman, I said, "I'll talk to him. Don't worry. I'll take care of it."

Anger contorted her features and the acne on her face became scarlet, except for scars that remained almost white. "You must report him to the archbishop, or somebody down there in the chancery. If you don't I will, and I will tell them that you were an accomplice by refusing to report him." She was furious and demanded immediate action. "You know that all sexually inappropriate conduct must be reported to the chancery."

OK, I will send them a letter and send you a copy, so you will know that I took care of it."

Reluctantly, I sent the letter to the chancellor downplaying the incident, certain that they would ignore it for what it was—a fantastic scenario contrived by an unstable woman. Much to my surprise, they took immediate action by phoning Bastits to get the details from her. I figured they did not have very much to do in the chancery, since they were wasting time on this. They also called Wolfgang Draper and made him come into the chancery for one of their kangaroo courts in the boardroom. Consequently, Draper lost his job and could never get another one in any parish in the archdiocese. They even reported the incident to the Rosanada police, because they did not want to face any liability in the matter, and they always liked to look like law-abiding citizens by reporting the people they did not care about. If one of their own did something unseemly, they covered it up, but poor Draper got the full treatment. Bastits went around the parish condemning Draper for his lack of moral responsibility, convincing everyone that she was his pitiable victim in his plot to deflower her.

Being a victim was one of Bastits' favorite activities. To feel misunderstood, abused and rejected were specialties that characterized her. Furthermore, in some part of her subconscious, she wanted to be an object of mockery—otherwise she would not have tried to sing solos at Mass. I was horrified when a few days later, she told me she was going to sing at the Mass on the following Sunday. Although she was good at directing the music, she personally had a very unpleasing voice. Although I wanted to forbid her to sing, I didn't have the heart to do so after the Draper affair.

The next Sunday she appeared at Mass wearing a long white dress that she tripped over repeatedly. Because of her buxom and generously proportioned body and her shaking hands, and her husky raucous voice people remembered her ever after as the "Fog Horn." Although people mocked her to her face, made negative comments, or exchanged knowing smiles behind her back, nothing—absolutely nothing would stop her singing and believing that she was rendering God and the people of Santiago a great service.

When I went to Uruguay for the crusade, Bastits came along as the music director. A few minutes before the evening service was to begin, I was on stage checking out the sound system, when I was completely abashed as she appeared on the stage in a long pink dress with fake white flowers on her left breast ready to sing for six thousand young people.

"No! Bastits. Not here!" I spoke as forcefully and emphatically as I could. She made a terrible scene, shocking the local organizers of the crusade. Then instead of withdrawing quietly, she pitched a big tantrum right there on the stage, wailing so loud that one of the local organizers went over to her and asked, "What is the matter, Sister Bastits? Are you sick?"

Amid outbursts of sobbing, with big tears rolling down her ruddy cheeks, she screamed, as only she could scream: "Father Marco will not allow me to minister as God wills me to do."

At that moment I saw Enki approach her and put his arm around her shoulder. Intentionally and loud enough for me to hear him, he snapped: "What has the son of a bitch done now?"

"He told me I can't sing!" she started sobbing again. "Please help me." Pitifully she looked to Enki as her protector.

Turning to me, Enki yelled disdainfully: "Who do you think you are? What right do you have to prevent the most talented person in our group from ministering her songs?"

I had had enough! "Common sense, Enki. We must stop being clowns and do things right. She will not sing on stage tonight or ever again."

I could see the fury and hatred in Enki's face as he yelled at me: "This is inexcusable."

I shrugged my shoulders, turned and walked away. In spite of this unpleasant episode before the crusade started, wonderful things happened that evening—many accepted Jesus Christ as Lord, others were healed of physical ailments, still others renounced the use of drugs and alcohol, and many families were able to heal their broken relationships. It was a marvelous evening!

I loved Uruguay—the traditions of the people, the smell of food wafting through the streets, the simplicity of the people, and the genuine affection that the members of the local ministry expressed for us. There was one black cloud—one of the locals, a Father Amando Pichin, a Peruvian singer who came to the crusade in order to use our equipment to record a few songs—showed up with a very effeminate man with whom he was staying in one of the local hotels. He was a well-known singer in his native

Peru who was going to tape his music for me to use in future crusades. The two days he taped were torture for the crew from Santiago. Father Amando always showed up very late, prancing in like a star in a large theatrical production. His companion Emelio T. Ensarto danced around him while combing his hair, touching up his makeup, applying an astringent to remove the bags from under his eyes, and carefully smoothing the wrinkles out of his suit so he would look good on TV. Father Amando was a good singer, much better than Enki—a fourth rate singer—who was obviously envious of the priest's talent.

I returned to Rosanada knowing full well that I could no longer rely on Enki and Bastits, both of whom were important to the success of my ministry. They were two venomous vipers, lying in wait to instill their poison.

34
Enki

Upon returning from Uruguay, Enki locked himself up in his office, working on some new child porn movies that Yo-Lin had given him. He would carefully guard them, review them, and then return them to *La Estrella de Amor* and spend time working more freely there. Always careful not to keep any of the porn in his office for any length of time, he had to review the films so that he would be able to recommend them to clients according to their tastes and preferences. Convincing everyone that no one was more serious, spiritual minded, or dedicated than he, Enki insisted to Marco and the others that he needed solitude in his office to concentrate on his work, paying the bills and balancing the accounts for the parish.

Striving to create a circle of supporters around him, Enki was given over, body and soul, to a counterfeit phony, sugary holiness at all times during his working hours. It was easy to fake holiness. All he had to do was quote a few words from the Bible, roll his eyes heavenward, and speak with a mellow voice trying to be gentle to people.

Because of his reputation for saintliness, many people actually sought him out to help them solve their problems. Although a constant flow of people kept interrupting his work with the porn, he enjoyed his reputation as a counselor and even delighted in building up a following.

By contrast, Father Marco never sought to have a lot of followers, insisting that Enki should not get involved with counseling, for he had no qualifications whatsoever in that area, neither as a therapist or a theologian. Besides Marco's opinion regarding spiritual advising was very simple; he felt his job was to put people in contact with God and with his Word so that in Him they would find answers. He maintained that it was very pretentious to give counseling for half an hour or even an hour, thinking that a person's problems could be solved in such a short time, very much aware that unless God would perform a miracle the difficulties, incomprehension, and lack of love that take years to develop, also need time to heal. Because of Marco's attitude, it was easy for Enki to build up a following of people who wanted the instant and immediate solutions he provided. In ministering to these people he was gaining ascendancy over Marco and still had plenty of time to go to *La Estrella de Amor* to help Yo-Lin with the business, while pretending to be taking care of church affairs or errands. After all, he had taken some business courses at the university, had a lot of business ability, and with Yo-Lin's capital behind him, he was able to keep on the rise, while at the same time being careful to promote his reputation for holiness.

From various places in Latin America, Yo-Lin was able to obtain films of children's orgies that were far better than his greatest dreams. Because these items were very difficult to come by in the United States, Yo-Lin was able to turn them over with incredible profits, since the most violent flicks brought in thousands of dollars.

Money kept rolling in—Yo-Lin provided him with all the money he could spend—beyond his wildest imaginings. The movies also became a sexual obsession to such a degree that watching the films of pre-pubescent boys and girls having sex with each other and with adult males was all he could think of day in day out. Faced with this visual bombardment of sensuality, the pleasures his scrawny wife offered were more revolting than appealing. He dreamed of actually being possessed by a thirteen-year-old boy, or maybe being able to force a fourteen-year-old girl to have sex with him.

His pleasure in watching the films increased to such a point that he lived for them, neglecting his work and his family, spending as much time as he could at *La Estrella de Amor*. When he had to do anything else, all he could think of was the moment when he could return to his world of sexual fantasy.

Spiraling hopelessly and floundering, he finally decided it was ridiculous for him to be content with just watching videos. Why not have the real thing? In a local teen hang out, he met a boy who was about fourteen, dazzled him with some twenty dollar bills, and arranged to take him out one night in his car and drove him to Rosanada State Park on the river. He had a marvelous time. All the porn he had seen prepared him for the unbelievable moment when he had sex with the boy—the first of many contacts. All he could think about was sex!

35
Pazi

Pazuso Masterna, television director for Father Marco, rose early because he wanted to see Marco about some materials he needed to purchase for the ministry. Jumping into his Honda Civic, he drove straight to Santiago. Although he did not look forward to seeing Marco who had never been really friendly toward him, he nevertheless felt that he needed to inquire about some matters to make sure of doing things right.

As he approached the pastor's office, he thought about the encounter he would have with Tetita and Leona, the two watchdogs who guarded the door to Marco's inner sanctum where no one could go, unless they passed by these two women. It was said that Marco referred to them as Scylla and Charbydis for they were very skilled at turning away people who tried disturb the pastor needlessly and without an appointment. However, the classical allusion was over Pazi's head.

Because Tetita always tried to pick him for gossip, he hated talking to her. One thing he hated was gossiping. He had learned when he worked for the secret service to keep his lips zipped. Marco was tough to deal with—just like his captain had been. When he gave an order, he expected and demanded that you carry it out. He really ran a tight ship and expected everyone to fall in line. Pazi respected him for that.

When he arrived at Marco's outer office Tetita and Leona were exchanging salacious tidbits about someone. When he got closer they got very quiet. He didn't like the way Tetita eyed him. She stared at the muscles in his arms, and once before when he came to her office, she even reached out and patted them and squeezed his arm. As if she were undressing him in her thoughts, her eyes wandered over his entire body. He knew she was crazy about anyone who wore pants.

"Good morning, Pazi. What brings you here?"

"I'd like to have a few minutes with Padre Marco." He remembered that her favorite saying was: "Do it and then think about it." She always repeated this with a knowing look on her face and a bit of a leer.

Leona, the younger of the two and the more active one who was eager to run everything, looked up from her computer and said, "He is not seeing anyone this morning. He is quite busy."

Because she always treated him with the respect due to him, since he was the pastor's television director, Pazuso Masterna, never minded talking to Leona. Even though, because of his greasy hair and shabby clothing, he did not look at all elegant or deserving of respect, she respected him, and he always thought she was a fine woman. Pazi had worked hard to reach his position in the television ministry, and convincing his wife, a mulatto who was a real bitch, that he was a man to be respected and admired was not an easy task, because she browbeat him at every opportunity.

When he turned to leave the office, he was surprised when some one reached down and pinched him on his rear. As he turned in indignation, the two women laughed hysterically at him. He couldn't figure out whether it was Scylla or Charbydis that pinched, but he was sure he was going to have a black and blue mark that he would have difficulty explaining to his unbearable wife.

36
Marco

Always when everything seemed to be going well, something invariably happened to dishearten me. When my mother came to spend the weekend at Santiago, she brought with her some bad news. Mínimo had told her, almost jubilantly, that Ali Purcell's book, *A Church of Darkness*, had been published and had shown her a copy of it that he had bought at the Rosanada Mall.

"If he is your friend, why is he savoring that awful book? He came to the rectory yesterday looking for Pompeo and came in the kitchen where I was fixing lunch. He had that Onan Wilde with him. He has that kid with him all the time and people constantly talk about their suspicious friendship. Together they were snickering over the lies that Purcell wrote about you. I think he is perverse or crazy...or both. I wouldn't trust him, if I were you, Marco. He is no good." She shook her head and started setting the table for our lunch. "His aura is almost completely black. That is a very bad sign." My mother had always been able to perceive people's auras ever since I could remember.

"What color is my aura now, Mom?"

"Right now it is ivory...looks almost like a halo." She smiled and patted me on the top of my head like she had done when I was a little boy.

"Of course, Mom, that is what you always say about me!"

The news that the Purcell book had actually been published and was being read by people in the area was devastating news. I felt as if a knife blow had been dealt me and was absolutely horrified to think that my parishioners and my television audience around the world—the program was now able to be viewed by up to five hundred million people—could have doubts about my integrity and believe the calumnies concocted by the mentally unbalanced Camio Sabnac, Foc Gomorrah, who had died of untreated syphilis, his dysfunctional family, and the fame hungry journalist Ali Purcell.

Although I drifted off once or twice, I could not sleep that night, but had nightmares that were so vivid that they woke me up with heart palpitations and a cold sweat soaking my T-shirt. In my dreams a colossal black monster with a hideous leer was chasing me through a deep, sinister forest. In the darkness, by the light of a crescent moon, I beheld gargantuan snakes crawling through the trees of the woods where I was running, trying to escape with my life. I fled the woods into a patch of tall grass where I came upon a grizzly bear that began to chase me. When the bear opened his jaws and reached to seize me with his paws, I awakened with a start, trembling from fear. I got very little sleep that night and for many subsequent nights.

The pain I experienced was agonizing and insufferable. If I walked into a room of the parish hall and one of my vicars was there, he would quickly leave the room without greeting me. Wayne Creasy, an investigative reporter for the The Rosanada News, wrote column after column, smearing me with the lies that Purcell had promoted with her slanderous inclusions about me. Every time I turned the television on, I saw myself being defamed and slandered by the media. It was an excruciating experience, such as none that I had ever experienced before in my life.

Although there were very few people on my staff that I could rely on, the vast majority of my parishioners stood behind me, refusing to believe the calumnies. Many of them knew that Foc Gomorrah had of his own free will recanted his allegation and wrote not only an affidavit but a hand-written letter to the archbishop stating that I had never sexually abused him. Furthermore, the archdiocese had exonerated me from any wrong doing in regard to him. The media never mentioned any of this.

I knew that Purcell's book was the fruit of Foc's desperation, for at the end of his young life as he died of syphilis of the central nervous system, he was without family or anyone, except Ali Purcell to help him. In exchange for providing for his needs, she had succeeded in getting him to make infamous accusations against Pompeo and me. Although I thought my life was going to fall apart, my parishioners proved to be more faithful than ever, and I also began to get support from groups that I would never have imagined.

One night, accompanied by a seminarian—Cletor Delsapo, I met with all the members of my pastoral council to explain to them the difficult situation I was facing. As a seminarian, the archdiocese had sent him to me to gain practical parochial experience as part of his education. For this reason, I took him to the meeting so that he could experience the working of the pastoral council during a crisis. It was good training for him. He lived at the rectory and was responsible, among other things, for patrolling the grounds and locking up the heavy metal gates at night so that the criminal element of the neighborhood could not enter the premises, for I had built a high iron fence around the entire property. It was also his responsibility for opening the gates in the morning and preparing the offices and rooms for the work of the day.

"Father Marco," Cletor said sincerely, "I want to tell you that I know that you are totally innocent. You can count on me." A tall man—almost six feet tall, he came from Bolivia and had that distinctive appearance people have when they are of mixed Spanish and Indian ancestry. Although he often lacked the necessary style and grace that I hoped he would acquire with the completion of his education, he demonstrated the possibility of making a good priest. For this reason, I had suggested that perhaps he should study a year at Fagiola University of Andorra to broaden him and teach him something of European charm and graciousness. He eventually did go to Andorra, where he got a degree in Sanskrit that made it possible for him to compose long and elaborate homilies that were the bane of his parishioners' existence, causing some even to wear earplugs to church. Nevertheless, he returned to the United States the same old Cletor Delsapo that he always was.

"Thank you, Cletor. I knew I could count on you."

When we entered the meeting, all the members of the pastoral council rose to their feet and applauded me, greeting me with warm smiles. I was overwhelmed by their support, as I explained to them that I was innocent.

"Never in my life have I suffered such humiliation—to have my name smeared in the newspapers and on the television is a real crucifixion for me," I told them quite honestly. "I thank you for your support and with the help of God we will defeat the plot of the devil to destroy our ministry." I looked around the circle of faces and saw that one face—the face of Enki Mutante—was smirking at me. He seemed to be enjoying my misery and debasement.

"Let us pray now for God's guidance and mercy." When I ended the prayer and said "Amen," I was astonished to hear Enki yell out with his voice echoing through the room, "Justice, Lord! Bring justice!" The idea of God bringing justice did not bother me. I also yearned for justice and to be cleared of these horrible accusations. However, for Enki to call for it publicly at that time suggested to the other members of the pastoral council that he believed I was guilty. I fully expected all members of the council to believe in my innocence. Enki had stood up with great arrogance, knowing that he had the support of Renato Del'Ano, the sub-secretary to the archbishop, and humiliated me in front of my parish council. It was more than I could take.

No one seemed to notice what Enki had done. All the rest of them left the meeting determined to defend me and to do everything necessary to continue forging ahead, taking care of the mission that had been entrusted to them. To defend my honesty and decency was for each one of those that was at that meeting, except Enki, a solemn duty. They told me so as one by one they came and shook my hand before leaving the room, attributing the denigrating accusations to the work of the Evil One who was trying to destroy the work of God being manifested through his prophet. Many times in the past, we as a community had experienced strong attacks of evil, but this was the most forceful and compelling one.

That night when sleep eluded me and the shadows of night surrounded me, I feared that my life—my ministry—would come to an end, but the Presence flooded my being with feelings of security and comfort, consoling me, and confirming that a new state in my life was beginning. Advising me to be prudent and discerning, He enveloped me in His love and renewed my spirit.

37
Marco

The ministry and the mission were growing so fast with such large numbers attending that all our Masses were filled to capacity and only those people who arrived a full hour before the beginning of the celebration were able to find a seat. It had become time for me to do something about this, so I presented my plans to build a new sacred space to the pastoral council that responded wholeheartedly to my idea of building a contemporary church, utilizing all the developments of modern technology. The architect I consulted shared my dream of glass ceilings, a myriad of lighting effects, fountains with splashing water—one in the sanctuary and several in front of the building—live plants in the sanctuary, and a sound system that would permit everyone to hear perfectly the voices of the speakers and the choir. When I presented the plans to the archdiocese, I then waited anxiously to get a response. Although Renato Del'Ano was openly speaking out against my building plans at every opportunity that he could find, arguing that we did not need mega-churches like the Protestants have in our archdiocese, I knew that if God wanted me to build a church, it would be done. When the response finally came from the archdiocese after weeks of waiting, I was disappointed. Although I got the approval to build, they had scaled back some of my more adventuresome details—no glass ceilings except for the glass roof of the cupola that rose high into sky over the sanctuary. Since we were located in a high crime area and to protect the altar vessels and the Sacred Hosts in the tabernacle and the consecrated Holy Oils for the sacraments in the ambry, I designed the building to have no windows at all and very sturdy doors—so that vandals or thieves could not break in. With the techniques of modern lighting, I was able to devise a method of making it appear that windows were in the walls. The parishioners were enthusiastic about building the most modern church in the archdiocese and supported the building project so that in a relatively short period of time, we were able to raise the two million dollars needed to begin construction.

From one end of the property to the other, I worked to bring beauty and order, determined that every detail would reflect the glory of God. At the entrance of the mission I placed a large earthen jar surrounded by the palm trees that to me symbolized my native land, in such a way that one would have a taste of Cuba before arriving at a breezeway that recalls the Spanish missions of California. At the end of the breezeway rises the magnificent temple of God.

Every plant, every detail of the new Santiago spoke of the love I felt for God and His Church. I never had time for golfing, or fishing, or any other activity that my priest friends engaged in, and I always declined their invitations when they suggested I accompany them. Once a week, I usually spent some time with Pompeo with whom I had studied in Rome, even though as the years passed, he grew a lot crazier and I found him boring as he always repeated the same stories about the past and was obsessed with movies and magazines. Santiago and my parishioners were my family—wife, children, and my life—my entire existence revolved around Santiago and my people.

Giving myself to my parish community and to the international family that God created for me though the evangelization ministry in Latin America and the United States, I put my love into all the pastoral events and activities. Happily, I spent all my time working for the Kingdom of God and my life was totally consecrated to His Holy Presence. Everything I did was to extend the Kingdom of the One who had given His life for me. Some people said I was a fanatic—even priests said this. Others said I was riding too high. As for me, all I wanted to do was to speak God's message to an aching, hurting world.

I never imagined how difficult it would be to build a four million dollar church, not to mention a complementary parish hall and rectory, which would have to wait until later. Sometimes it seemed to overwhelm me; there were new challenges everyday. People constantly complained—some said the new building would be too small, others said it should be smaller. Everyone complained about the dust and having to park farther away and walk to the old building for Mass. A number of people tripped and fell over misplaced rocks and bricks. One elderly man who did not see very well fell into a construction hole.

As the construction progressed and the church began to take shape, I began planning the ceremony that would consecrate it as a place of worship. I dreamed of a moment when heaven and earth would come together and be as it says in the Scripture: *"Terribilis est locus iste."* The ceremony had to be majestic and worthy of the Presence. I made sure that Archbishop L'Abbadon himself would preside, with all his auxiliaries attending, as well as all my priest friends and parishioners. When I set the date for the inauguration, I was confident that I was allowing the contractors plenty of time to finish all the details. The choirs practiced for weeks to get ready for our big celebration that was scheduled to last for an entire week.

A week before the scheduled event, I was frenetically concerned that the building would not be ready and everyone would arrive to find the place in a state of disarray. As the time got closer, a feeling of panic overcame me, when only two days before the event, Santiago looked like a disaster area. The morning of the inauguration, we were still not sure that we would be ready, but at the last moment everything fell into place. At five that afternoon, the procession came in as solemnly as I had desired it to be. The music of all the choirs singing together was celestial, making the entire atmosphere joyous. The new church was overflowing and the latecomers had to be seated in the old church—the new parish hall—where the inauguration was being transmitted via closed-circuit television. With five Masses on the weekends, we could now accommodate over twenty thousand worshipers. L'Abbadon, who never liked me, remarked during his sermon that Santiago looked like a theater, not a church, and also complained that the sound system, as expensive as it was, did not do a good job. He ended his homily by giving me very tepid congratulations.

Another sour note came from Archbishop L'Abbadon at the reception for the dignitaries from the chancery and for my priest friends and members of the parish board and the staff of Santiago. After the Mass we adjourned to the old church building that I was refurbishing as the new parish hall, where the women of Santiago had prepared very tasty canapés and some kind of green punch made of ginger ale in which they floated lime sherbet. I knew that the archbishop would have preferred a Manhattan.

The archbishop, still wearing his jeweled miter studded with diamonds, emeralds, and rubies and his golden chasuble with the elaborate embroidery, raised his cup and said,

"I propose a toast—to Santiago Church, its pastor and staff."

"Hear, hear!" cried Mínimo to everyone's astonishment. The auxiliary bishops glared at him and I think he realized that he had acted out of order, for I didn't see him any more that day, perhaps his problem arose because he had spent a couple of days without his usual heavy tranquilizers. Being pastor at St. Henry VIII's Church took its toll on Mínimo, eventhough it was a nice parish that had as its motto, "Where relationships count."

The archbishop ignored Mínimo's outburst and repeated for all to hear. "With all your four million dollars spent on your new church, it still winds up looking like a theater."

I was not about to take that insult. Immediately I spoke up so that everyone in the room could hear me. "It may resemble a theater, but it surely is a place of worship. We just had a beautiful ceremony in it." Not accustomed to having anyone contradict him, L'Abbadon was glaring at me. I glared right back at him and he averted his eyes.

After the reception, all the priests and deacons moved to a special tented area where we had a bountiful dinner for all our special guests, and the archbishop imbibed so much booze that his secretary had to guide him back to his limo.

As I was circulating among the guests, my two vicars at this time, Fathers Stanki Yorhiney and Poly Grande cornered me and called me aside. I never liked to get very close to Stanki, a big strong Ugandan, because he just plain smelled bad—his skin was very oily and he seemed to have an aversion to bathing.

Father Poly Grande, an arrogant, mentally unbalanced Cuban with a bad attitude, and uncouth manners, acted as speaker for both of them.

"Nice party. Marco. I am sure it cost a bundle. So I know you won't mind giving us a bonus now that you have the new church and all the money flowing in." He got right up in my face.

"I am already giving far more than the diocesan allotment for assistants."

"Damn it, we know that there is money here—lots of it," Stanki's purple lips trembled as he drew closer to me, blowing his offensive breath in my face. I stepped back from him.

I had expected that these priests would congratulate me for the success of Santiago; instead they were trying to browbeat me for more money. When they saw that I was not inclined to give them more than I already was, their voices rose, getting louder and louder, until people were beginning to stare at me. I finally agreed to give them a bonus for their cooperation.

Stanki Yorhiney and Poly Grande were a trial for me. The Ugandan never listened to orders or advice, much less hints, but always followed his own will. I felt he was headed for trouble. Poly was a cleanliness freak and a pea-brain, and I always thought he purchased his theology degree at Wal-Mart, for no serious institution would ever approve him. He took care of having the kitchen spotless, helped the housekeeper, and thought that nobody could beat him in humility. He usually scraped and bowed in an attempt to patronize me. Unfortunately, his past as a drug dealer and addict, and his mental problems betrayed him. Money was the ultimate goal in his life, yet he liked to appear absolutely selfless in that regard. When he washed the dishes after dinner, he would insult and even calumniate anyone, including the pastor, and would act, as if he had great charity. His specialty was gossip—he knew everything that was going on in everyone's life—from the altar servers to the archbishop. It amazed me how anyone could know so much who never cracked a book in his life.

One of the worst trials in the priesthood was the poor quality of the priests the archbishop sent me as vicars. Santiago started as a mission for migrant workers—it became a church of migrant priests. A priest from Uruguay, who was a vicar of the mission, and the superior of his congregation in the area, was justly accused of being involved with three different women at the same time. Another one was accused—and he confessed to it—of caressing the breasts of a young girl during the Sacrament of Reconciliation. A third one was accused of having a girlfriend during his stay at the mission. There were others, like Father Morgan LeFey, an old Cuban fag who would go crazy over good-looking American boys. But the real champion, the one who caused my biggest headaches, was a Venezuelan who lived in El Salvador and because of a psychological crisis was sent to the United States. Father Rodolfo Sanabria proved to be the lover of a parishioner and also went to bed with the woman's daughter, and then later with the daughter's boyfriend. A prowess worthy of medieval times which, of course, cost him expulsion from the archdiocese.

Worst of all, I had to report all these happenings to the chancery. Then, I would have to follow up on my report and lose a priest who should have helped me. The priest shortage drove Archbishop L'Abbadon to give faculties to any South or Central American priest that wanted to escape from his bishop and kick up his heals in dollarland. The most thoughtless case of all was that of a priest from Honduras who decided to take a girl boating on the river and offered her a beer. He had forgotten the small detail that in the United States you must be twenty-one years old to drink alcohol. He too was thrown out of the archdiocese.

Nevertheless, despite all the trials and hardships, I lived in His Holy Presence—people were converted, healed, and delivered. In spite of everything my life was filled with joy. To move in the supernatural world was a normal thing in my life.

38
Bastits

What happened in Uruguay was utterly inexcusable. Marco was not going to treat her that way and get away with it. She had made Wolfgang Draper pay, and now she was determined that Marco would also pay—pay in full for the despicable and abominable way he treated her. With this thought uppermost in her mind she stopped by Enki's office.

"I have been doing a lot of thinking, Enki. The television ministry has become so vast that I don't think Marco should be in charge of it all by himself."

"What's on your mind, beautiful?" he chortled while smiling at her intently. She was seated safely across from him with his computer and oversized desk between them.

"I think the television ministry should depend on God, not on a man." As she poured a cup of coffee from the decanter on Enki's desk, a sly grin crept across her face.

"I couldn't agree with your more!" he exclaimed with enthusiasm. "So what do you think we can do about it?"

"Let's turn it over to Archbishop L'Abbadon."

"That's impossible," he protested. "It is an independent ministry, Sister. There is no way we can turn it over to the archbishop."

"Trust me! Woman power gets things done that you men only dream of doing. I know exactly what to do so that Marco will lose it and it will wind up in the hands of the archdiocese," she alleged convincingly.

"If you have a plan, you can count me in. I am willing to do anything to screw the son of a bitch." Bastits knew that Enki had been waiting for a good opportunity to double-cross him.

"It might take a little time, but I am certain I can do it. I am going to take away his ministry." She rose to her feet, set her coffee cup down on his desk with an air of finality and marched out of his office.

With a hearty laugh, Enki called out to her. "In the name of God."

"Amen," she replied with fierce determination.

A few days later, Bastits returned to Enki's office to discuss further plans for taking the television and radio ministry away form Marco.

"Well, ever since we discussed it the other day," Enki said, "I have been thinking about it. I think I have the answer. It is perfectly obvious what we have to do. I will call the attorneys for the archdiocese and ask them to draw up the transfer documents. The secretaries for the ministry corporation trust me implicitly as the pastor's administrative assistant. All I have to do is to get them to sign without realizing what they are signing."

"Brilliant, Enki! You are a genius! Believe me, it is only matter of time before Marco will be without his ministries. Go ahead and phone them right now!"

Bastits watched eagerly as Enki contacted the legal department of the archdiocese, reaching Vily Puck, Esquire who was famous for some of the most notorious failures in the history of the Church in the entire state. Although his father, Fylgiar Puck had been very successful in negotiating real estate deals, he was ignorant of everything else. Known in legal circles as "a loser with a tie," Vily surpassed his father in ignorance. Sometimes he did not even wear the tie.

She listened as Enki explained to Puck their plan to donate to the archdiocese a ministry, valued at one million dollars—an offer he surely could not refuse. After a few seconds, Enki hung up the phone.

"Well, what did he say?" Bastits asked almost breathlessly.

"He insists that in order to make the transfer, a majority of the board of directors would have to vote in favor of it."

"Well, let's think about it and talk about it more tomorrow," Bastits suggested.

The next day when Bastits returned to Enki's office for plotting and planning, his office door did not have the "Do Not Disturb" sign on it, so she knocked briefly and entered without further ado. She did not know who was more surprised, she or Enki! Obviously in a state of sexual arousal, judging from the protrusion she saw in his slacks, he was deeply engrossed in looking at photographs of naked children. He had a big stack of them in his hands. Noticeably flustered, he jammed them in his desk drawer.

"Just some poor orphans that I am trying to help with my donations for their support. The poor things—they don't even have adequate clothing. As you are aware, the Scripture says: 'Religion clean and undefiled before God and the Father, is this: to visit the fatherless and widows in their tribulation: and to keep one's self unspotted from this world,'" he commented while looking up toward heaven and piously folding his hands, as if in prayer.

"I think it is wonderful that you help poor children in need. God bless you, Enki, and reward you for your charity. You are a good man." She spoke these duplicitous words in an attempt to hide her own desires that came from seeing Enki's tumescence. She could not understand what was happening to her. Ever since Wolfgang Draper tried to rape her, strange urges came unbidden to her, upsetting her emotional equilibrium. She could not understand her deepest feelings. She was a good girl and a virgin and determined to keep her virginity intact at all costs. Now looking at Enki's male organ fully protruded made her feel like kneeling down before him and adoring her true god, by placing it in her mouth and servicing it as long as needed. Torn and twisted by conflicting desires and emotions, she dropped down in the chair across from Enki.

"So what is your problem?" he asked as if nothing was out of place or unusual.

"How are we going to donate Marco's television ministry to the archdiocese? If we have to have a majority of the board members approve the transfer, I guess we are beaten." Dejection was written in her face, as she slouched despondently. "I guess we just have to give up." She shrugged her shoulders and sighed deeply, while her eyes kept wandering to Enki's intriguing bulging protrusion.

"Don't ever say such a thing. 'Greater is He that is within you, that he who is in the world,'" he said very devoutly, "That is from the gospel." He did not know where the quotation came from, but that did not matter because he was sure Bastits wouldn't either.

"Oh, you are so intelligent, Enki! You know so much. What can I do? I want to see the bastard suffer." She smiled at him timidly. Although she was obsessively in love with Marco who ignored her, she was overcome simultaneously with intense hatred for him.

"Let's approach Marco himself. He might even like the idea. Tell him that it would please Archbishop L'Abbadon—all priests want to get in good with the archbishop. Tell him that the archdiocese will value the ministry more if it is part of the archdiocese. He might just swallow that." Noticing that Bastits was staring at him with a strange lustful expression on her face, he carefully folded his hands in his lap, hiding his troublesome appendage.

When she returned two days later to discuss the matter further with Enki, she was wearing her most seductive red miniskirt and a very snug white shirt. Carefully knocking on his door and waiting for him to invite her in, Bastits, taunted by the remembered image of his tumescent organ, experienced a strange and unfamiliar sensual awareness that aroused her making her wet, causing her to feel a sense of conquest and giving her the realization that sex and power are intimately related. Trying to control her wayward emotions and her physical responses to them, she smiled at Enki and said,

"I did what you suggested, Enki, I asked Marco about transferring the ministry to the archdiocese, telling him how much it would please the archbishop if we did. I reminded him that it would give us more status in the archdiocese, if the ministry belonged officially to it." She could see that Enki was delighted with her activity.

"What did Marco say to this?" he asked eagerly.

"He said I would have to submit the matter to the board to decide."

"I am surprised to hear that he even suggested proposing the transfer to the board!" Enki replied. He thought a minute and toyed with the pen that was on the desk before him. "I have an idea," Enki exclaimed enthusiastically. "You can make it work, Bastits! All you have to do is get the corporation secretaries to sign the transfer by using a double document proposing to change the name of the ministry adding the word Catholic and, in the second document that the secretaries would not be able to read, the ministry would be transferred to the archdiocese." Enki leaned back in his chair and propped his feet on his desk proud of the Machiavellian plot he had devised.

"Enki, you are a real demon!"

"Just like you. I am determined to make him pay! I think that you and I can keep the ministries and run them ourselves. We can get Pazi, the television director, to work with us. I am a fantastic administrative assistant and can preach as well as Marco can any day, and you are a great music director. The archdiocese would not interfere with what we are doing. The ministry will be ours!"

At the board meeting Enki sat next to Bastits and gave her moral support. What a disappointment it was when once again the plot failed dismally. The board simply rejected the whole notion. They had no desire to add the word Catholic to the name of the ministry.

39
Enki

The Trent Catholic Television and Radio Network invited Enki to be the commentator for one of Sister Labra's special Sunday programs, when she, sounding like an archbishop, pushed her elderly audience—most were over seventy—to clean up their lives because the day of final judgement was close at hand. Ironically, she sternly forbade these old people to have abortions or to use contraceptives, and encouraged them to write their congressmen to defend life in the womb.

Because Sister Labra really liked Enki's speaking voice, he took advantage of his opportunity while with them in Texas to inveigle from them an invitation to have his own half-hour weekly program on their network discussing various Biblical subjects. Although he had never taken a course on Holy Scripture, he had a good commentary and could easily cobble together enough material to make ten shows in the studio at Santiago and send them to the network with the help of Pazi, the television director. Up until this time he had only sung on Father Marco's program, and Bastits had made an appeal for funding at the end of the show. Now he was going to have his own show. Just being an administrative assistant and a singer was not living up to all his capabilities and talents.

With head held high and gloating over his success, Enki proudly went to see Father Marco in his office to tell him that he had now arrived at having his own television program on the Catholic channel that had rejected Marco, saying his ideas were more Lutheran than Catholic. When he arrived, Marco was busy preparing his talk for his program on *Vision Hispaña*, a national Spanish language TV channel. More and more channels and networks were opening their doors to him. His success was disgusting! Now, Enki felt he was successful also, for he had been invited to make a program for the Catholic network, and they had rejected Marco.

Deliberately interrupting Marco—a thing that always annoyed the pastor—Enki pushed himself forcefully past the secretaries into Marco's office in the parish hall.

"What can I do for you?" Marco asked him brusquely.

"Oh, I just wondered if you had seen me on the Catholic channel, when I appeared on Sister Labra's program." He was hoping to glean a few compliments from Marco and make him envious.

"I never watch that channel. My cable company does not carry it."

"Oh, well, they have invited me to make a series of ten shows with them."

"That is very strange," Marco replied coldly. "They have not contacted me about it. That is the proper protocol. You are an employee of my church and they have to request my permission before they can contract with you to make any programs with them. Any deal you make has to be made through me. Tell them to get in touch with me," Marco responded with an air of finality, as he resumed working on some matters at hand in an attempt to dismiss Enki.

"It's not that easy," Enki protested.

"Are you definitely transferring with them or do you want to continue with us?"

"You know, Father, that I am not planning to change my place of work, but I would like to expand my own ministry."

"Your own ministry? I thought that we worked in the same one! I hired you as my administrative assistant."

"Of course, that's what it seems like, but you already know that I sell my own music and my own productions."

"Could you tell me when and where you plan to film your programs for that Catholic channel and where you make your music CDs?" Marco's tone was becoming very authoritarian.

"Well, I do it whenever I can," Enki bristled and looked at Marco defiantly.

"I understand how you feel, Enki. However you are an employee of this ministry, and you cannot expect to use our time and our studios to create your productions. There is a very definite conflict of interest involved here. I am sure you understand what I am telling you."

Knowing that the priest had a reputation for being resolute and unyielding, once he had come to a decision, Enki could see that Father Marco was adamant and could not be persuaded to change his views.

"That is a very selfish way of looking at things!" Enki was shouting.

"On the contrary," Marco contradicted him, "my way of looking at things is the just one. You are the one who takes advantage of a privileged situation, where you have little supervision and do what you please."

Enki had raised his voice so loud that Tetita, Marco's secretary came to see what the commotion was all about.

"It is all right Tetita, everything is under control." He rose to his feet and towered over Enki. "Mr. Mutante is just leaving." To Enki he said in parting: "Look, my decision is very simple. From now on, you *will* work exclusively for us and whenever you decide to leave, we will remain friends. Good day!"

In an exceedingly foul mood, Enki drove home and slammed the door, yelling: "Espi, you can't believe what that son of a bitch has done to me now!"

Immediately his wife came running. "What's wrong?" she asked when he poured a double shot of brandy.

"Marco won't let me make the show for Trent."

"How can he stop you?" Espi was pregnant again.

"He can fire me. I think I will quit! I am sick of him and all his alleluia shit!"

"I agree with you a hundred per cent, Enki. The man is just impossible. He makes me sick, too." She sat down beside her husband on the bed, where he had thrown himself in desperation.

"However, you can't quit right now, the new baby is on the way." She patted her bulging abdomen that was in the advanced stages of pregnancy. "You don't have a degree—you dropped out of the university before you graduated—and your English is not the best. With two children we can't make it, if you quit. And I certainly don't want your getting involved in Yo-Lin's business operations. Besides," she asked, unaware of all the money

Enki received from Yo-Lin, "who else is going to pay you so much money?"

"Well, OK," he reluctantly agreed, "but you might start looking for a job, as soon as the baby is about two months old. We might need more money. I'll keep working there for now, but I promise you that priest is going to suffer for this." He sat up in bed and gulped down the brandy that was in his glass. "Be a good girl, Espi and pour me another."

Unable to sleep that night, Enki lay awake dreaming up schemes to destroy Marco. Meanwhile he would spend as much of his time as he pleased at the mission on Yo-Lin's porn business, while being careful not to leave any evidence of it in his office. Furthermore, he would continue to make and sell his music CDs behind Marco's back. He'd be damned, if he were going to take orders from him. Still unable to sleep, he got up from bed about two in the morning and watched some porn on his VCR. Before he finally fell asleep about four, he decided that he was going to use all the time he could, working on Yo-Lin's porn operation, because he needed the money. And he would not rest until Marco was ruined.

40
Marco

Bastits' behavior in Uruguay was inexcusable. I had no alternative but to discharge her. When I gave her the news there was wailing and gnashing of teeth.

"I've given the music ministry the best years of my life," she screamed hysterically.

"That is not the point, the only issue here is the good of the ministry, and for that I have to let you go. I really can't risk another scene like the one you put on in Montevideo."

When she saw that her tantrum would not persuade me to keep her as an employee, her wailing turned to fury. Yelling obscenities as loud as she could, she rushed from the parish hall to her car. Knowing she was an enemy, I felt safer with her off the premises of Santiago and out of the music ministry.

That very next night, about eleven, when I was getting ready for my night prayers, the phone rang and a muffled voice that I did not recognize said: "We don't like the way you are treating Bastits, you miserable priest. If you don't give her her job back, get ready for a huge scandal."

Disregarding the threats, I hung up the phone without saying a word.

Continuing to receive threatening calls, which even came at the office, I was disturbed when one day Leona informed me that I had received calls from unidentified men—one of them called me a sex pervert and the other one a faggot priest. If she received any more calls like that, I instructed her to hang up immediately. No one was going to force me to compromise my ministerial life.

On my day off while visiting my mother at her house, I was sitting beside the swimming pool, talking to her about the days long ago, when I was a child in Cuba, reminiscing about my father. Although she was still in her fifties and a number of men had been attracted to her, she told me often that she would never marry again. She still loved my father very much.

As the sun sparkled on the waters of the pool and reflected onto her face, I noticed that she was getting some wrinkles and that patches of gray were visible in her long black hair that she put into a very becoming and youthful French twist.

"I am worried about you, Marco. I have these dark premonitions and dreams. I had a nightmare just last night—in it, you were being surrounded by snakes that kept crawling closer and closer to you. Just when they were about to sink their fangs in you, I woke up screaming…"

When the newspaper boy threw the *Rosanada News* into the yard, I went over and picked it up. Opening the paper, the headlines struck my attention." I couldn't believe what I was reading.

The Queen of Sex and Drugs Yo-Lin Sin
Arrested in Raid
By Wayne Creasy

Last night the state police raided La *Estrella de Amor*, a nude bar located on State Road 69 five miles north of Rosanada, and owned by Yo-Lin Sin, aka the Queen of Sex and Drugs, who was arrested for trafficking in child pornography. Large quantities of child pornography were taken from the premises of her posh bar, famous for its spectacular nude dancing girls. Ms. Yo-Lin Sin, pal of the notorious drug king, Lon Chiang, now serving a ten year term in a Venezuelan prison, was arrested and released after her friend Enrique Mutante, administrative assistant to Father Marco Lamadrid at Santiago Mission, arranged her bail for $500,000.

So that's the kind of people Renato sent me! The Queen of Sex and Drugs! A nude bar! Pornography! So that's where she got the money for her large donations! I studied the photo that accompanied Creasy's news item. It was a photo of the nude bar, some women in scanty attire, the police putting handcuffs on Yo-Lin, and there with her was Enki Mutante! I had no choice but to fire him and find another administrative assistant to replace him.

The ringing of my cell phone distracted me from the *News*. Because I could never rely on the vicars the archbishop sent me, I did not turn off the phone when I went out, wanting to be always available to my parish.

Leona was on the phone. "Father, please come immediately, she said calmly, but I could tell she was shaken and that something had happened that needed my immediate attention.

"Why Leona? What is wrong?"

"The police are here going through our office files and examining our computers."

"I can't believe it! What has happened?"

"Please Father, come! We need you!"

"Tell the police I will be there in fifteen minutes. I'm on my way."

When I arrived, I found all the employees cornered in a room, while a task force from the police was rifling through the contents of every office."

I walked over to the police officer in charge. "What seems to be the problem, Officer? Do you have a search warrant?"

He flashed the warrant before me. "I'm sorry to bother you, Father, but for several weeks we have been observing the activity of all the members of your organization, because we have caught one of your parishioners, Yo-Lin Sin, and arrested her for trafficking in child pornography. Since she was a close friend of Mr. Enki Mutante, we came here to see if she was using Santiago in any way for her porn racket. We have searched your premises and all your computers and there is no evidence of any wrong doing here at Santiago. Sorry to have bothered you."

Because Enki always appeared to be very devout and dedicated to the ministry, I couldn't believe what I was hearing. The police officer must have realized the impact his words were having on me, for he continued speaking sympathetically. "Don't take it so hard, Father, we have found so far nothing that would incriminate you. In the beginning we thought that your whole organization was a child pornography network. Consequently, we observed the behavior of all the people that work here or have contact with you."

Unable to imagine that Enki with all his piety could be involved with such a woman, I was at a loss for words. "Thank you, Officer, for checking this out. You can count of me for my complete cooperation."

As soon as the police had left, I went to the TV studio where all the members of the ministry were huddled and wondering what the police were doing at Santiago. After summoning all the employees of Santiago to join us, I began addressing them.

"Please, be patient," I told them trying to appear as calm as possible. Briefly I explained to them why the police were ransacking our premises, as I saw the bewilderment in their astonished faces. As soon as I began speaking, Enki slipped from the room, went into his office, and closed the door.

Although I hated confrontation of any kind, I would eventually have to face all the employees of Santiago, the media, parishioners, and the chancery. After I explained to all the employees that had gathered to receive an explanation from their pastor, some people were very sad that Enki had been photographed at *La Estrella de Amor* with Yo-Lin Sin at the time of her arrest. The music director Corwin Monroe very indignantly exclaimed: "This is intolerable behavior in a church! Enki should be fired! We need a new administrative assistant! I have four kids and I would not want him ever to get around them."

A priest from Honduras—someone filling in for Poly Grande—contradicted him saying. "No! We must give Enki support. We are his family and he needs to feel our support."

Corwin snapped back "I don't consider myself family of that degenerate, and I don't want this Church to be identified with him."

Seeing that it was not a good idea to prolong this meeting, I concluded by saying: "At this time the important thing is to remember the reason for our ministry—the spreading of the Kingdom of God under the Lordship of Our Lord Jesus Christ. Let us therefore keep our eyes on Him and not let these events discourage us. You are free to maintain a relationship with Enki, if your love for him prompts you to do so. Christian love looks for the redemption of the sinner, not for his damnation. None of you are under suspicion and neither am I, so let's get back to work."

I was crushed under the weight of opprobrium that Enki's association with Yo-Lin Sin had put on Santiago. Soon I would be hearing from the chancery, and I dreaded going before one of their asinine sessions once again. Magnus Peter, the spokesman for the archbishop, phoned later the same day. In his overly refined and saccharine tones with which he could articulate the most agonizing and lethal news, as if he were doing the listener a favor, he told me: "Father Lamadrid you are to distance yourself from Enki Mutante. He is no longer part of your community. Above all make no statements to the media. Do not even acknowledge to anyone any relationship you may have had with Ms. Sin. Is that clear?"

It was perfectly clear. Puck, attorney for the archdiocese phoned me with a similar directive. "Enki has become a liability for the archdiocese, therefore, do not talk to anyone about him, nor mention his name at the Masses. If you need to say or do anything regarding him, call us, and we will tell you what to do. Is that clear?"

"Crystal clear." I had no choice.

How could I explain to the parishioners that Enki, my right hand man, whom they were accustomed to see working in the parish with me, was involved with *La Estrella de Amor* and Yo-Lin Sin, its notorious owner? I could delay telling the community what had happened until the Sunday Masses, but I had to share the debacle with the pastoral council.

At the council meeting, I found solidarity and support. Although many of the members were friends of Enki, they could not defend his behavior. However, Teresa Valdés, a tenderhearted woman with liberal tendencies, spoke up for Enki: "We must have compassion on him. We can't be judgmental. We have to be tolerant and forgive him." A few others murmured their approval. Obviously, they had forgotten how when Ali Purcell's book *A Church of Darkness,* accusing me of being a pedophile was published, Enki had loudly exclaimed "Justice! Justice, Lord!"

Facing the staff of the TV ministry was a more difficult task. Accompanied with Deacon Angel Rios, a very good man and a real friend, I met with them in the TV studio.

Crispín Galíndez, one of the cameramen, was immediately unusually aggressive. "Padre, all Enki needs now is our unconditional love. You have always taught that we must love people with an unconditional love. I, for one, intend to do just that. How about the rest of you?" He glanced at the members of the staff—people who had known Enki for years. I saw that quite a few of them were agreeing with Galindez who was already developing a faction that would oppose my authority, even using my own teaching to do that. However, Deacon Angel Rios took my position and defended me boldly.

"Wait a minute, hold it," he protested lifting both hands up in front of him, as if to stop them. "You are failing to understand padre's teaching on unconditional love."

"Yes," I said softly but firmly. "Unconditional love means having a personal relationship with a person that you accept and love with all that makes up their reality, including their faults and sins. In no way does unconditional love justify or hide that which is wrong in that person. Because what Enki has done is public knowledge, we cannot hide it or dissimulate about it in any way. We have to acknowledge it and go on from here."

The camera staff was not convinced. I could hear most of them mumbling and expressing their disagreement.

The hardest task lay ahead of me. I still had to meet with Enki and his wife. Because of his embarrassment, he had left the church and gone home for the day. When I arrived at their home, they were both expecting me.

Because Espi was obviously a powder keg ready to be ignited by my first word, I began the conversation as gently as I could, knowing that it was going to be a difficult meeting.

"I am very sorry, Enki and Espi, but I will have to let you go, Enki. I cannot have one of the major members of my church, my right hand man and administrative assistant, involved with Yo-Lin Sin and her nude bar. I am prepared to provide you and your family with the usual salary check for the next six months." They seemed to take this kindness as their due and voiced no thanks.

"I insist that you keep this matter a secret," Espi said intently, as she advanced toward me and stood with her face in mine. She had not invited me to sit down. "I don't want people to know about this. I want it kept hidden from our children. You simply have to keep it secret." Her face was hideous with rage. A tic was playing at the corner of her left eye.

"Espi," I tried to be as patient as I could, "there is no way I can keep it secret. It was on the front page of the *Rosanada News*. Everyone in Rosanada knows about it now." I could see that she was beyond reason.

"All the members of the ministry are pledged to help him and me," she insisted, refusing to hear what I was saying.

"You must realize that by associating with Yo-Lin Sin, a known pornographer, and the owner of a nude bar, where he was photographed, has placed our entire church in a very bad light. Why he even took care of her bail bond for her! Moreover he has even tied my name and the name of the mission into the sordid affair." When I said this, her fury increased even more.

"Leave," she screamed, "get out of here! I curse you! May the Lord in His Providence give you a hundred times more pain than you have given my husband!"

A faction developed around Enki and continued to grow. The more I tried to make them realize that what Enki had done was very wrong and had compromised us all, the more they rallied to his defense.

Because I had no desire ever again to see this man who had betrayed my trust so abysmally and placed the work of God in great jeopardy, I sent a priest to minister to him. There was nothing else I could do for him. Trouble continued to foment in the parish from the opposition that had arisen to defend Enki—trouble that would engulf me and Santiago in an impossible quagmire from which there seemed to be no escape.

41
Enki

Although Enki had arranged bail for Yo-Lin Sin, he was very despondent that he had lost his job as administrative assistant at Santiago Mission. Unemployed, with no prospects of finding another job, because of his association with the pornography ring, he remained at home seeking sympathy from his wife and the large number of friends who rallied around him. Because he and Pazi Masterna, the television director for Father Marco, had never been friends, he was surprised when Pazi came to his house offering support.

"Welcome, Pazi. It is good to see you." Enki said extending his hand to Masterna who took the big armchair in the living room and settled down to talk to him.

"I had to come—I felt it my duty. It is terrible how the pastor has fired you," Pazi said very sincerely. "Although you and I have never really been friends, you can count on me to help." Pazi said while pushing up the long sleeves of his flannel shirt.

"I'm innocent—totally innocent. I just happened to be at *La Estrella de Amor* when the police came and arrested Yo-Lin Sin. I didn't do anything wrong. It is not a crime to watch a few nude dancers is it? I just arranged the bail bond for her—I though it was a nice Christian thing to do." Enki saw that Pazi was nodding his head in approval. Because many members at Santiago considered Pazi a saint who like Saint Francis was always the champion of the poor, he was so glad to have Pazi on his side.

"Let me tell you what Marco did to me a while ago," Pazi said very seriously.

"I am listening." said Enki.

"He had the audacity to oppose my friendship with you and the support I am offering you. I am fed up with him! I'd like to get rid of him and get a new pastor at Santiago. I think the best defense is for you to go on the attack."

"So do I. Don't worry, he will pay for all he is doing. He should have forgiven me and kept me on as his administrative assistant. Instead he got rid of me!"

"Do you really think he could keep you as his administrative assistant after this bad publicity?"

"With God, everything is possible," Enki said piously rolling his eyes heavenward.

"I agree. He should be forgiving you."

"Since he won't forgive me and reinstate me as his administrative assistant, I am going to get even with him and trigger his downfall. As the old saying goes, "The bigger they come, the harder they fall.""

"How can you do that? His position is very solid."

"Don't worry. I have been thinking about it a lot. All we need is for someone to accuse him of child abuse, like so many priests in Boston have been accused."

"And how can we get someone to do that?"

"Very easy." Enki said. "All we need is to contact some guys and let them know that they can make a lot of money by accusing Marco of sexual abuse. It is being done very successfully in Boston. The Church is paying off everyone that makes an allegation of sex abuse against a priest."

"And you don't care that they are not true?" asked Pazi.

"The only thing that matters in this case is to finish with that son of a bitch."

Grinning and showing his crooked teeth, Pazi said, "OK, I agree. What can I do? He really annoys me. He never appreciates anything I do. No matter how much I do, it is never enough!"

"Start contacting, one by one, some of the youth that have had contact with Marco in the past and remind them that they can easily become rich. Get Bastits to help you. She will do anything to nail the bastard. Ever since he fired her, she hates him with a purple passion!"

"I'll do it," Pazi agreed, as he shook Enki's hand and left.

Now that they were going to begin searching for people to make allegations against Marco, it was time for Enki to phone Monsignor Del'Ano to tell him that the thing he had so much longed for was about to take place. He would use Renato to help him destroy Marco, even though he and Renato were not the best of friends. However their relationship had improved since he dropped out of his society.

"Monsignor, this is Enki Mutante."

"How are you? Nice to hear from you. Is Yo-Lin out of jail?"

"Absolutely, I got the bail bond for her. She is out on parole."

"Oh yes, I did read that in the *Rosanada News*. Well done. I am glad."

"And now I am calling you to let you know that we, with the help of Yo-Lin, are going to put together Marco's downfall. We are looking for people who will accuse him of sex abuse. He will die just like I have."

"That is better yet! Count on me for whatever you may need."

"I will call you as soon as we have something definite."

"Ciao," said Monsignor Del'Ano, "Give my best wishes to Yo-Lin."

"Talk to you soon," Enki answered.

Consumed with the desire to destroy Marco, Enki had no scruples. Before he was photographed at the nude bar and had arranged bond for Yo-Lin, he pretended to be a holy man, but now no one would be taken in by his mock pieties. His only desire now was to see Marco humiliated by having him accused of pedophilia. Guilt or innocence did not matter! All that mattered was to see Marco suffering just the same as he was suffering. Backed by Renato, Yo-Lin, Pazi Masterna and Bastits, Enki was convinced that it was only a matter of time until he got revenge on Marco and destroyed his ministry and his life.

42
Renato

Renato kicked off his shoes, sat back in his easy chair, and reminisced. He had come a long way from Torricella! Although he had climbed high in the clerical ladder, he wasn't finished yet. If only Don Giorgio Bandi could see him now! He laughed to himself. The old buzzard had tried to keep him from becoming a priest. What a pleasure it would be, if he could only see him now! In another hour he was going to drive up to the church of St. Francesca Romana in the adjoining archdiocese to visit the confessional of a certain Father Bob Salito whom Fr. Randy Horn had recommended to him. He and Randy had had a close relationship for the past several months and Father Bob was, Randy said, tolerant of the gay life style. Well, he would try him out and find out for himself.

When the time came, he entered the confessional box where he could remain anonymous, rather than the reconciliation room where he would have to face the priest. When the priest opened the sliding door on the grill and blessed him, Renato began his confession.

"It has been a year since my last confession."

"Go ahead."

"I had sex with four young men. I failed to say my breviary many times. I neglected my spiritual life. I lied about someone so I would get ahead in my career. I told serious lies about him so I could get his position." He paused to think what he would say next.

"Is there anything else?"

"I have been living in a relationship with another priest for about six months." From what Renato had heard, this confessor would understand.

"Since you have been in a relationship with this priest have you been faithful to him or are you still involved with other men?"

"We have a stable relationship and I have broken off with the others, Father."

"That is good. I don't see any harm in what you are doing, provided you are in a monogamous relationship and you both care for each other. However you must be very careful not to give scandal to anyone who might not understand what you are doing. Promiscuity is very bad and there are many priests with Aids today." He paused before continuing, and then concluded with some platitudes about the spiritual life, recommending that he make it up to the person he had hurt. "As your penance, say three Hail Marys."

He gave him absolution and that was all there was to it. Renato left with a much lighter heart, believing that God had made him gay and now he was sure that He understood and blessed his life style with Randy.

When he got back home, a message was waiting for him on his telephone answering machine. When he pushed the button to retrieve the message, he immediately recognized the voice of Archbishop L'Abbadon.

"Hello, this is the archbishop. I was hoping you could come to my house for dinner tomorrow night. I will send my car for you."

Immediately Renato returned his call, saying: "Of course, I will be there." He said to himself, "I wonder why Queen Victoria is inviting me for dinner?" He always thought it was funny that many of the priests referred to the archbishop as the Queen. When he asked them why, one priest said it was because his imperious demeanor and feminine mannerisms reminded them of Queen Victoria or perhaps Margaret Thatcher. Another priest told me he thought the archbishop looked more like Edith Piaf singing "*Je ne regrette rien.*" Renato knew that the favorite phrase of His Excellency was, "I don't care." No matter, Renato was going to have a chance to see him in his habitat and discover for himself what the old coot was like. He had never been inside an archbishop's world before.

"He will pick you up at your place at seven. I won't take no for an answer. Ciao!"

Perhaps this was the big moment he was waiting for. Perhaps the monsignor had displeased His Excellency and he could take over his position—perhaps there was a new opening at the chancery and he could become a department head. In any event, he intended to make the most of his opportunity. He didn't care if the old guy looked like the Queen of Sheba! Renato had heard from the clerical gossip circle all about this archbishop's secretaries. His first one was an intelligent, handsome, athletic young priest born in Poland with blonde hair and blue eyes. He quit after a few months, because he said he had not come as a priest from Warsaw to this country to write letters all day, chauffeur the archbishop's limo, carry his luggage, and fix drinks without being permitted to even taste them. To get revenge against the priest for quitting, the archbishop assigned him to the most infamous section of the city. Frustrated, he ended up as a bartender in a gay bar.

Archbishop L'Abbadon replaced the priest who asked to be transferred with another handsome young priest, Reverend John N. Bugumil J.C.D. Coming from a Slovak family, he belonged originally to the Byzantine Catholic Church and was actually bi-ritual. Renato had heard that he was also bi-cultural and bi-sexual. This very outgoing, jovial, and happy-go-lucky traditionalist must have served the "boss" very well for in a short time he received a variety of ecclesiastical titles and other dignities that are usually accorded to older priests. There was a lot of gossip in the chancery and around the archdiocese about Monsignor Bug who had big hazel eyes, a captivating smile, and the composure of Farah Diva, the last wife of the dethroned Shah of Persia. The young canon lawyer was a real asset for the institution. According to the most vicious priest's forked tongues he was canon lawyer by day and an impaler by night. They say he made a mean Manhattan and an even meaner Long Island Iced Tea and wrote letters that would throw fear into the most intrepid priest that managed to cross the archbishop. Such was the driver that picked Renato up and drove him to the three million dollar renovated archiepiscopal residence that was even more grandiose than he had heard.

The first thing Renato noticed when the long black limo delivered him on time at 7 Coziness Lane in Champs des Bauchery was that the mansion was located on

Rosanada River and had a nice-sized yacht moored at the dock that ran the full length of the property behind the mansion. Later Renato learned that it was a 40 foot Apreamare 12 with 480.00 hp with a spacious salon, a complete galley, two staterooms and two heads, each with a separate shower stall. The interior was made of beautiful mahogany and decorated in Luzl prints.

When Renato arrived with Monsignor Bug, he was escorted into the main salon and told that His Excellency would join him in a few minutes. As he waited for the archbishop to appear, Renato drank in the opulence of the salon. Heavy brocaded drapes, imported Oriental carpeting, and black lacquered Chinese furniture, all indicated that the best decorators money could buy had furnished the room. The crystal chandelier looked like a museum piece. In the center of one of the walls was a portrait of Archbishop L'Abbadon that reached from floor to ceiling. A pair of three branched golden Florentine candlesticks stood with one on each side of the portrait, giving the appearance of a sacred sanctuary or shrine. There he was in his entire formal magnificence—Cecil Anselm L'Abbadon—black cassock with cape all piped in violet, with matching violet buttons and brilliant violet-fringed sash. He was even wearing violet socks to match and had a violet beretta on his shaggy gray head. His pectoral cross hung from his neck on a fine gold chain. Renato had never before seen such a splendid cross as the one His Excellency was wearing, studded as it was with four diamonds, four rubies, and four emeralds—a stone for each of the twelve apostle, he later learned. His archiepiscopal ring matched his pectoral cross—being also of yellow gold and set with matching gems. Carefully arranged on a chair beside the archbishop in the painting, but made to look as if it had been casually placed there, was a miter resplendent with many jewels—emeralds, rubies, and diamonds—His Excellency's favorite gemstones. Beside it were a glorious violet floor-length cope and a mahogany crosier with a golden crook bearing his monogram comprised of emeralds, rubies and diamonds. Spotlights on the ceiling illuminated the portrait so that whenever anyone entered the room, their eyes were immediately attracted to the painting. His Excellency himself stood in all his glory, with one hand folded inside the other, and a big smile on his face, as if he were simply delighted with all his munificent magnitude.

After about twenty minutes, as Renato stood gazing at the portrait, his host entered the room and greeted him, holding on one arm a miniature white French poodle that he introduced as Pigalle, saying: "Pigalle, say hello to Renato."

Confused, Renato did not know what to do, so he silently watched the little dog that was wearing a rhinestone collar and a big pink ribbon to keep its hair out of its eyes. L'Abbadon placed the *beau monde* little dog on the floor and then shook his hand. Pigalle paid no attention to Renato and ran upstairs where the archbishop explained he loved to sleep in his bedroom.

As the archbishop drew closer Renato noticed that he exuded a fragrance that resembled absinthe. Later, Renato learned that the archbishop always wore cologne that reminded connoisseurs of perfumes the fragrance of *Mystique*—a word that perfectly described his spiritual leadership. Although the cologne was redolent with the fragrance of absinthe—some swore that it was *Lolita Lempika au Masculin Fraîcheur*, while others insisted it was just plain absinthe or wormwood oil. Whatever it was, Renato soon learned that the archbishop wore it to cover up the odor of Manhattans that always clung to his breath. When they shook hands, Renato could not help notice how smooth, soft, and well-manicured his hands were, bearing an almost unperceivable gloss, suggesting that a manicurist had just recently lacquered them. The archbishop was casually dressed in white linen slacks and a classic piqué Lacoste Polo in lollypop pink, such as Renato had looked at and considered buying recently at a boutique on the Boulevard.

Since His Excellency was dressed in casual elegance, Renato felt uncomfortable in his black, imported Italian suit. Very discretely, L'Abbadon glanced at his Rolex and said, "Well, Renato, let's have some drinks and then dinner."

The chair Renato sat down on was covered with a tapestry made of predominantly gold and red threads that created a magnificent Chinese dragon. Although Renato had always heard that many Roman Catholic bishops and archbishops lived like medieval princes, this was the first time in his life that he had ever been invited into the private world of such a man. Everything from the star sapphire—his episcopal ring—down to the well-manicured toes in his Italian sandals showed that he had spent hours on his grooming.

"Fix us a pitcher of Manhattans, Monsignor Bugger," he said jokingly in buttery tones and watched as the monsignor hastened to do his bidding.

As they sipped their drinks, Renato commented, "You have a magnificent home. It is really a tribute to your good taste, Your Excellency."

"Just call me Archbishop. Relax and make yourself comfortable. Drink up, Renato, and I will give you the grand tour."

Renato set his glass down on the black lacquered cocktail table, rose, and followed as the archbishop led him upstairs and into his private chapel where a gilded archiepiscopal throne stood proudly to the left of an altar of black mahogany that the archbishop had imported from Brazil. Renato wondered why anyone would need a throne to sit alone in the presence of God. Tall golden candlesticks flanked the gold tabernacle on the altar. Unfortunately, no one except his friends, his household staff, and his executive secretary were able to see these splendors.

The archiepiscopal bedroom boasted a king-sized mahogany bed, likewise a Brazilian import. Heavy lavender brocaded draperies cloistered the windows, shutting out the hot summer sun. Renato was amazed to see that the bedroom ceiling was made of Venetian mirrors shipped over from Italy. The mirrors permitted His Excellency to observe himself as he lay abed, reclining in such posh surroundings. Carved into the mahogany headboard of the bed was the monogram CAL—Cecil Anselm L'Abbadon. It was embossed in gold and was also embroidered on his lavender bedspread of moiré silk—also an oriental import. As he proceeded through the house, Renato noticed that the archbishop's monogram was everywhere, just as it was at the chancery where he usually signed his memos simply CA. He also noticed that Monsignor Bug's bedroom adjoined the archbishop's and was decorated in the same lavender color as the master bedroom.

As soon as they had returned to the living room, L'Abbadon looked at his watch and exclaimed. "You can see more later. Dinner is now being served."

To go from the living room to the dining room, the archbishop led him around the large decorative and illuminated pool and fountain that lay situated between the two rooms. A fountain in the pool was gaily cascading and splashing jets of water that changed colors from a very deep purple, to lavender, and pink, reminding Renato of similar indoor pools and fountains he had seen in Rome.

Dinner was served in a dining room that was large enough to accommodate about forty people. The service was exquisite. Nothing but the best for the successor of the apostles, as Roman bishops like to be considered—Limoges china and Waterford crystal—every piece monogrammed in gold. A butler and a maid served the meal and poured the champagne. After all he was a member of the most exclusive club in the country, the National Conference of Catholic Bishops. Monsignor Bug was conspicuous by his absence.

After the dinner, they retired to the archbishop's den—a room that was more designed for intimate conversation.

"Have a cigar," His Excellency invited.

"I don't smoke, thank you."

Very carefully L'Abbadon snipped off the end of the cigar with a special tool he had for that purpose. Soon a large cloud of smoke surrounded his head.

"You are Italian. I went to school in Rome, but I was born in Canada. I really feel at home in Rome and with Italian people—like you."

Remaining quiet, Renato listened to what he had to tell him, merely agreeing from time to time saying, "Uh huh." The archbishop seemed to be really warming up to him. In fact, he even seemed to admire him. Renato had always felt disadvantaged because of his somewhat feminine characteristics, but the archbishop seemed to like him. Some men seemed to sense that he was gay and were repelled by that. He couldn't stand big, tall, strong men who towered over him and considered him to be in someway inferior to them because of his sexual orientation.

As the evening progressed, and the archbishop consumed another couple of cognacs, he began to get mellow. "Listen Renato, the reason I invited you to dinner tonight is because I have a proposition to make to you." He looked at Renato and studied his face carefully as he rounded his lips, a facial expression he assumed when contemplating some action he was about to undertake. "Monsignor Bug is going to be transferred to a parish up the river, and I would like to have you move into my house with me and be my executive secretary. Does that appeal to you?"

"Very much. I am certain I can serve all your needs very well," he said emphasizing the word "all." It will be my pleasure to do everything you wish."

"We will announce your appointment tomorrow and you will have three weeks to move over here. You can have Monsignor Bug's room right next to mine. We are going to have a wonderful relationship. Now, I will get

Monsignor Bug to take you home so you can get your things together and come on over again tomorrow. I'll take you for a spin you will never forget."

Renato looked at him in bewilderment, uncertain of what he meant by his remark.

"A spin on my yacht on the Rosanada River."

As Renato was leaving the archiepiscopal residence, he was impressed by the large swimming pool behind the house and the big yacht—one of the archbishop's many toys. He couldn't wait for the archbishop to take him for a ride on the river.

As soon as he arrived home, he phoned Randy who was not there and left a message on his answering machine:

"Hi Randy, Renato here. I went to confession and I have decided that it is best if we don't see each other any more. Anyhow I am going be very busy now that I am the new executive secretary to the archbishop. They say he is very demanding when it comes to executive secretaries. Sorry! Ciao!"

43
Enki

"*Hijo de la gran perra!*" Enki snorted to his wife as she dressed to go pay a call on Pazi Masterna, the television director, at his parish office. "Marco's days are numbered now—no compassion in that man!" He quickly downed a shot of brandy.

"Don't worry; I'll take care of it. Then I have to go to Dewacco Swamps for a couple hours. I'll be back about six and then tell you what Pazi plans to do to help us." She quickly applied lipstick and ran a comb through her long stringy hair. "I'll pick up the kids at nursery school and take them with me."

Because he felt certain that Pazi would do everything he could to help him, for he was always the champion of the afflicted, downtrodden, and oppressed, Enki was glad that Espi had an appointment to see him. There were lots of people besides Pazi who would help him. It was just a matter of organizing and Pazi was good at that. His thoughts were interrupted by the doorbell. Although he really did not want to see anyone, he peaked through the little hole in the door provided for such purposes to see who was calling. Yo-Lin!

Instantly he threw open the door. "Yo-Lin! How wonderful to see you," he lied. He did not want to see her, but he badly needed her help. With her money and Mafia connections, she could do a lot of damage to

Marco. He had never saved any money; he threw it away as fast as he got his hands on it. If he didn't Espi would. Because he needed money from Yo-Lin, he knew he would have to perform in bed and try to satisfy the insufferable old bitch, who was insatiable.

"I came to thank you in person for getting the bail bond arranged," she said in sugary tones. It was so sweet of you to help me, when I needed it.

"I was glad to help, Yo-Lin, but I did lose my job because of the bad publicity." He knew he could count on her help now.

"As I always say, what are friends for, if they don't help us when we are in a tight spot? I'm sorry you lost your job, and I understand that you want to make Marco pay for firing you and damaging your chances of getting another job with the Church. Don't worry, Enki Baby, I'll take care of you—and Marco. I am not worried in the least. I have the judge in my pocket. He is going to give me a bench verdict of not guilty. All it takes is money and I have plenty of that."

Enki was delighted to see that Yo-Lin was apparently not concerned in the least about her arrest for trafficking in kiddie porn. Her confident attitude lifted his spirits.

"So what have you been up to today?" he asked.

"I went shopping and bought some new living room furniture for a poor family I met at Santiago."

"Oh, have you been having nightmares again with the dancing devils taunting you with their pitchforks? Don't you know modern theologians don't believe in Satan and his devils anymore? You don't have to worry like that," he said trying to console and help her.

"Well, I feel better when I do things like that for people. I also went shopping in a cute little boutique on the Boulevard and found this great outfit." How do you like it?" She spun around so he could view her from all angles.

"Purple—your favorite color—it always looks so good on you!" She was dressed in a deep purple low-cut miniskirt that clung to her body just below her naval in which she was sporting a large amethyst. The top part of her outfit was a very low décolletage affair above which her large melons peaked out in an attempt to be coy, but failed dismally. Her shoes with stiletto heals were also purple with open toes revealing her purple painted nails. Physically Yo-Lin repulsed him, but he knew what he had to do, if he wanted her to help him destroy Marco Lamadrid.

After she finally had enough, they got up from the bed and Enki quickly tried to smooth out the bedspread, so that Espi would not notice that it had been disturbed by an alien presence.

When he heard Espi and the kids drive up in the car in the driveway beside the house, he noticed that Yo-Lin's face was flushed. "Go in the bathroom, fix your face and spray some of Espi's perfume around. The place smells like a bordello!

After bursting breathlessly into the house, Espi quickly went to the bedroom and then came back and joined Enki in the living room. "Where is she? I saw her car in the driveway. She must be here some place." Obviously Espi was suspicious of him and Yo-Lin. In the future, they would have to be more discrete."

"She is in the bathroom," Enki replied gently. "She has come to help us. And God knows we need all the help we can get."

"Wait 'til you hear what I have to tell you," she said dropping down on the faded brown sofa.

"What's new?" asked Yo-Lin who was returning from grooming her face and applying perfume.

"I saw Pazi. He was wonderful. He is adamant in fighting Marco! It was really wrong for him to treat you the way he has—firing you and giving you some meager alms and effectively terminating your ministry forever."

"Great!" Enki exclaimed. "Does he have any ideas what I can do to fight back?"

"Yes! He is coming to our house tonight about eight." Espi took one of the Egyptian cigarettes that Yo-Lin offered her, went to the bar at the far end of the living room, opened a can of beer for herself, and poured some *aguardiente* for Enki, and some scotch and soda for Yo-Lin. Actually, the Johnny Walker black label had been a gift from Yo-Lin at Christmas.

After finishing the remaining drops of whiskey in her Waterford crystal—also one of her presents to Enki and Espi, Yo-Lin rose to her feet and excused herself, saying, "I have to go now, but I'll be in touch. You can count on me for all the help you need. And don't worry; the situation is going to get better. I am certainly not worried about my arrest, because I have what it takes to get out of this." She held up her purple purse and shook it slightly and smiled.

As soon as Yo-Lin was gone, Espi exclaimed with excitement. "I almost forgot to tell you. Today I saw Marco—*ese marica!*" Anger twisted the features of her face, making her look grotesque. "When I was leaving Pazi's office, I ran into him in the parking lot. I didn't speak at all, just rushed by him."

Espi fixed a light supper and put the children to bed before Pazi arrived at about a quarter to eight.

Enki always thought of the "Little Brothers of Jesus"—a congregation that worked among the poorest—when he saw Pazi in his faded and frayed blue jeans that even had a few holes in them. The friend of all who needed help, he tended to be a bleeding heart liberal, but that did not matter to Enki now. His main concern now was to get himself out of the impossible situation in which he found himself. So he welcomed Pazi like a good friend, even though in the past they had never really been friendly to each other.

"I told Marco off today," Pazi, said, declining the drink Espi offered him.

"That makes me happy!" Espi yelled with a smile. "Tell us all about it. Every detail." She lit up a cigarette.

"Well, today after you left, Espi," he glanced at her, "Marco came into my office and I confronted him before he could say a word. I said, 'You seem to have forgotten that Enki and Espi are also your parishioners.'"

He snapped back at me: "On the contrary, Pazi, I have them on my mind constantly; consequently I am doing what I have to do to keep peace in the community.'"

"Then, I let him have it," Pazi said with a smug smile, 'There will be no peace until you reconcile with them, Marco.'"

"Would you believe what he said next?" Pazi asked contemptuously. "He said: 'In my heart I am already reconciled.'" Pazi shook his head in disgust.

"Hell will freeze over before I ever speak to him again," Enki said slapping his hands on his thighs emphatically.

"Then, what happened?" Espi asked eagerly.

"I told him that he was lying—that the doors of our church have been closed to the Mutante family. He denied this and said that you, Enki, need to find peace in another parish, because the harm you have done to Santiago is incalculable. I told him that obviously he has not forgiven you, Enki, and that his heart is full of resentment."

"What did he say to that?" asked Enki.

"I didn't give him a chance to say anything. I reminded him that in this country a person is innocent until proven guilty, and you, Enki, have not been proven guilty of anything. To defend himself, he said he saw your photo in the newspaper, that you are the one who brought Yo-Lin to Santiago, and you are the one who bailed her out of jail, and the one who caused the mission and him to be dragged into the sordid mess. I reminded him that we do not know why you were at *La Estrella de Amor*. Perhaps, I suggested, you went there to try to help Yo-Lin spiritually. He does not know what your relationship with Yo-Lin has been. I told him I figured you were ministering the gospel to her."

Enki and Espi were enthralled by Pazi's brash confrontation with the pastor, eager to hear every detail.

"Now comes the real clincher!"

Enki moved closer to Pazi savoring every word that fell from his mouth. "Then the bastard told me that our conversation wasn't getting us anywhere and that there was no room at Santiago for anyone who opposes the pastor."

"He really said that? I can't believe it," commented Enki. "He was always so agreeable and willing to avoid friction! He never interfered with my projects."

"Then I really let him have it," Pazi said folding his arms across his chest and cocking his head defiantly.

With bated breath, Enki asked, "What did you tell him?"

"I said that, if that was the case, then there is no room for me at Santiago."

"Wow!" exclaimed Enki. "You really blasted him! "I don't see how he can run Santiago without both you and me. Are you really going to quit?"

"I have already requested a leave of absence, and I never plan to return to Santiago again."

"Great! Together we will destroy Marco and his grandiose plans," he replied with much enthusiasm. "Do you have any ideas how we can proceed?"

"Well, I have had some success in looking for men to accuse Marco of sex abuse when they were young. Bastits is helping with this and has someone lined up. I'll let you know how that develops, but what I would like to do next is hold a prayer meeting here at your house tomorrow night. We will round up the troops and start our campaign to utterly destroy him."

"You are a true friend, Pazi," Espi said as he left for the night.

When Pazi arrived the next evening about a half hour before the prayer meeting was to start, Enki was elated to tell him that he had taken the first step in fighting the pastor.

"I talked to my attorney who is handling my case and he got in touch with a lawyer, Jonathan Snodgrass, who specializes in filing sex abuse cases against the Catholic Church. Snodgrass is anxious, ready and willing to take any case he can—it means big bucks for him. So we are arranging a meeting with the Gomorrah family immediately. You know the one that Ali Purcell wrote about in that book, *A Church of Darkness*." Enki was feeling better now that help was on the way.

"But," protested Pazi, as he laid his Bible on the table in front of him. "Foc died of a venereal disease. He can't file a lawsuit."

"No, but his parents can for moral damage and for the suffering caused by their son's abuse and subsequent death."

"Brilliant!" Pazi exclaimed. "Marco will be getting just what he deserves!"

"His ministry will die—just like mine has! I am really going to fix him. Totally destroy him!"

"We can get a lot more than just the Gomorrahs." Pazi said with determination. "Bastits has found somebody, and I know of someone I think I can talk into it. He was at St. Ellen's parish when Marco was there years ago. I met him some years back at the auto races. I've seen him from time to time. As a matter of fact, I saw him recently; his name is Frido Sodomat. He is not very bright. He teaches judo to children, but he is not doing too well financially, and if I tell him how much money he can make with a sex allegation lawsuit against Marco—well, I think he might be just our man. I will get in touch with him. I think we can find at least six or seven people to make allegations. All over the country, people have been accusing priests and getting paid large sums of money without ever having to go to court. The bishops are so anxious to deflect suspicion and guilt away from themselves that they gladly pay."

"Pazi, you are a genius!" Enki threw his arms around Pazi and murmured "A true friend—a faithful Catholic helping the Church get rid of people like Marco."

Soon Bastits and members of her choirs began arriving with so many crowding the house that they could not all fit in. Yo-Lin welcomed them to the yard behind the house, where Pazi had strung up speakers so everything that took place in the house during the prayer meeting could be heard in the yard.

When the music began, shouts of "Alleluia!" and "Praise the Lord!" rang out. Bastits was ministering with songs like "Victory in Jesus," and other similar hymns designed to rouse the audience to action. Then Enki spoke delivering the message for the evening, concluding with the following deceitful comment, lying unabashedly: "I am innocent," he declared, wide-eyed, looking heavenward. "It is always that way with true servants of God. We are always persecuted, but God will uphold me and justice will be done."

When he finished speaking the audience responded with feverish and enthusiastic applause, contributing most generously when Pazi had some of the men pass a basket to raise money to help Enki.

Confident that the prayer meeting had been a tremendous success, Enki slept like an angel. Marco would certainly hear about the prayer meeting the next day—Enki would make sure of that.

A few days later when Yo-Lin phoned, saying she was bringing Renato Del'Ano, the new executive secretary to the archbishop, over to see him, Enki was simply delighted, but was surprised that such an important person would take the time to come to visit him. The reason he was coming was very simple. Renato did not want anyone to see Enki at the chancery office chatting with him; neither did he want to be seen with someone associated with the Mafia at a restaurant, so he invited himself to Enki's home. Since it was midday and her guests had not yet had lunch, Espi made them welcome with some sandwiches and a goblet of wine.

"I am glad to see that you are doing well, Enki," Renato said with the gravity due to his position in the archdiocese. We understand the difficulty of your situation." He emptied his glass of *Chateauneuf du Pape* and Espi filled it again with the wine she rushed out and bought when she heard that he was coming to their house.

"Thank you for your understanding at this trying time," Enki said to the archbishop's secretary. "We are really going to nail Marco. After we get done with him, he won't be confusing Catholics anymore, by not adhering to the magisterium, just to please the audience of that Protestant TV channel where he likes to preach."

"We have to work to rid the Church of people like him who want to destroy traditional values and make us just like everybody else," Renato said encouragingly.

Although Yo-Lin was sitting across from Renato and kept flashing her ponderous breasts at him like a couple of headlights, Enki could see that her melons did not titillate him.

"You can count me in," Yo-Lin said. "I want to get back at Marco for what he has done to Enki. And Monsignor, you can tell His Excellency that my friends and I will continue contributing to his charities as usual."

"I will be praying that many people will be benevolent toward you and help you," Renato assured him. "Not to worry! "I also want to see Marco's ministry ended for what he has done to you, Enki. Remember that I have the ear of the archbishop all day long."

"Some days, I am very worried and afraid," Enki confessed while toying with his key ring. Then he stuck the keys in his pocket and said belligerently, "What they have done to me in the Church is unforgivable. They won't let me return to my job, and they have stopped paying my salary. And it is impossible for me to get another job in any parish."

Apologetically, Renato said: "You know, Enki, that those orders come from the top. But there is hope for you. Don't give up. As it says in the Scripture, 'All things work together for good...'"

Espi served a dessert wine with the French gateau she had bought to please the palate of the guest of honor. And at the end of the meal they were all mellow when the topic of Father Marco again was mentioned. Enki was surprised and quite pleased when Monsignor Del'Ano asked: "How long will it take to carry out your project?"

Now he knew that the archbishop's secretary was just as anxious to get rid of Marco as he was, and that the archbishop was probably entertaining the same dispositions.

"Don't worry, Monsignor. There are many of us working on that." Enki smiled smugly, confident that with the help of the executive secretary of the archbishop on his side, he could not fail. "Marco and his ministry will succumb in a horrendous sex scandal, just like I did."

44
Marco

Life was replete with sublime moments when I preached, prayed for the sick, and was graced by the awesome Presence that continually sustained me, but I still had to deal with the traitorous people who were deceitfully trying to harm me. Enki and Bastits were grievous trials for me, but others like Tetita, the secretary who had a doctorate degree in animosity, Diddle Henpeck, the ministries receptionist, the degenerate Maculata Stromboli who worked in adult education, and finally Ira, the perverse parish floor cleaner—all of them in one way or another undermined the work of my ministry. While the work of God was being attacked on all sides, God poured grace into my life and work. The more God blessed me, the more Satan seemed determined to annihilate me. Some of the worst people that I had ever known in my life had come together at Santiago Mission, forcing me to work, minister, and pray with people who seemed to be utterly faithless. What they were doing in the Church was a mystery to me. The only answer I could come up with is that, like the Lord said, an Enemy has sewn weeds in His field, the Church.

Because I believed that God could do wonders in any open heart, my hope was that with the passing of time solutions would present themselves and people would improve. Sometimes problems do vanish in time, but at other times they only get worse.

Speaking at conferences kept me busy and I was usually the main speaker at most of the events that I attended in this country and abroad. In almost every South American country where I preached, I received a grand reception with thousands of people in attendance.

My mother, who had become an excellent cook, always spent the weekends at the mission, so during those two days I was spared Luisa's usual concoctions. Going out of her way to make life pleasant for me, my mother knew how to be helpful without meddling. Since I could always go to her for truthful advice, I saw her as my guardian angel and spent my days off at her house. Knowing how to be helpful without ever interefering, she only gave me advice when I asked her, and also she knew when to console me, and when to leave me alone to face my own doubts and problems. An expert at prayer, probably because of the years she spent in prison where she had learned to rely of God in the face of great difficulties, she prayed for me constantly.

Some people that you would expect to be committed to God and the Church are the first ones to fall when an occasion arises that tests their mettle. Such was Pazuso Masterna, my television director.

Early one morning shortly after Enki had appeared in the photo on the front page of the *Rosanada News* in the Yo-Lin pornography affair, I was surprised to see Espi Mutante, her face grotesquely distorted by anger, leave Pazi's office, rush by me in the hall without speaking, and slam the door as she left the parish hall.

In an attempt to bring peace and cohesion to the community of Santiago, I decided to pay a call on Pazi. Entering his office as a peacemaker, I was met by stringent and inflexible confrontation. Pazi, a bleeding heart liberal, attacked me for not ministering to the Mutante family, demanding that I be reconciled with them. I explained that I was reconciled, but that he was confusing two different concepts, failing to understand that it is one thing to forgive Enki Mutante, and another to pretend publicly that I did not care about what he had done.

When Pazi protested that Enki was not guilty of anything, I balked at that, because I had seen Wayne Creasy's article and the incriminating photo on the front page of the *News*. It was ridiculous for Pazi to insist that Enki was at *La Estrella de Amor* to minister the gospel to Yo-Lin and the nude dancers! Arranging her bail bond and identifying Santiago mission with the affair by dragging my name into the papers with Yo-Lin Sin's could in no way be construed as an act of charity.

Because I had had enough, I told him plainly that there was no room at Santiago for anyone who opposed the pastor. The following Monday, I received a letter from Pazi in the morning mail, informing me that he was taking a leave of absence immediately. "Make it a long one—a very long one," I thought to myself. I was better off without him, or so I thought at the time. How could I have known that my worst enemy had just been turned loose on the streets to plan my destruction?

Time passed, gossip died down, and everything seemed to return to normal, except for the threatening phone calls that Leona kept receiving, saying: "We are going to squash that sex pervert Marco Lamadrid." Obscenities and hilarious laughter followed the threats, but Leona always hung up as soon as she realized what was happening. One night I even got a call from Frido Sodomat threatening me with sex allegations. I could barely remember the acne scarred youth that I had briefly known years before, when his parents invited me to see their sleazy television station and took me out to dinner in several cheap restaurants. I couldn't understand why he was phoning. Recalling that intelligence was not his forte and that, on the contrary, he was rather dull, even stupid, I simply hung up the phone in disgust as soon as he reached me, or refused to take his call as soon as my caller ID gave me his number. I was not going to be intimidated by some dimwit.

With great sadness I read in the *Rosanada News* and heard on the television that Cardinal Law of Boston had made a court filing in June of 2001 that he had assigned a priest as parochial vicar, even though the priest had been accused of sexually abusing seven boys. How could he do such a thing? How could a cardinal archbishop be so contemptible as to assign such a priest to a parish where he would be in close contact with more children?

In a short time, I learned that Cardinal Law had a history of protecting pedophile priests by moving them from place to place. Then reports of sexual allegations against priests nationwide began to be big news in the media. It was incredible! How could the bishops have permitted a scandal like this? What was worse, they were paying large sums of money to anyone who made allegations, because they did not want to be dragged into court and have the laity and the general public learn of the dastardly way they had dealt with pedophiles. Pedophilia is a crime in the United States and the whole world; the bishops by protecting the pedophiles became accomplices to their crimes. No wonder they were afraid to go to court.

On the other hand, the bishops had no clue as how to proceed with false allegations made against a priest. At one of the meetings of the United Conference of Catholic Bishops in Dallas, one bishop even spoke, saying that some priests would have to be sacrificed to save the establishment. It reminded me of what Caiphas said referring to the death of Jesus that it was better for one man to die, rather than that the nation should perish. I could not believe that the bishops were accepting the allegations as fact, making absolutely no attempt to defend priests, but instead paying off the accusers, making it seem as if the bishops believed that the priests were all guilty. We priests soon found that our bishops had taken an adversarial stance toward us driving a huge wedge between them and us.

In April of 2002, I got a message on my cell phone that Father Pompeo dell'Anitra, with whom I had gone to school at the Pontifical Dionysian University, wanted me to phone him immediately, as soon as I got his message—anytime day or night. I punched his number in my phone and in seconds I heard him raving and ranting about some newspaperman—Wayne Creasy—of the *Rosanada News*. Because Pompeo was so upset, I could barely understand him. He has a reputation for talking circles around everyone, and when he is agitated he gets even worse.

"Slow down, Pompeo." His frequent complaining was wearisome to me. "What's the matter now?"

"Wayne Creasy sent a fax to my secretary inquiring about my sex life and my relationship with the Gomorrah kid—Foc," Pompeo spat out the words, as if they were poison.

"Was my name included in the questionnaire?" I asked with great apprehension.

"Yes, it was!"

A few minutes later, Leona phoned me saying she too had received the same fax from Creasy and the *Rosanada News*. I was hurt and frightened. How could the *News* dig up that old story about Foc Gomorrah, when he had clearly recanted his allegation? It had been dealt with years ago, and was dismissed because of lack of credibility!

The annual Confirmation at Santiago was scheduled to begin in thirty minutes, and I was faced with the appearance of an article in the newspaper attacking me. In addition to dealing with that, I had to entertain the bishop who had been sent to do the Confirmation by Archbishop L'Abbadon—aka—Her Majesty the Queen.

The next day I learned that the parents of Foc Gomorrah—Old Nick and his wife Lucretia—had created an estate for their son who had died of syphilis, after completely losing his mind, and it was suing me, Father Pompeo, and the archbishop for a large sum of money, alleging that Pompeo and I had sexually molested the boy, and that the archdiocese had covered up the abuse. What a nightmare! Once again, I had to summon all the members of the staff and tell them that the Old Nick and Lucretia Gomorrah family had filed a lawsuit and was asking for a seven-figure settlement. No one could understand, least of all me, how it was possible. Little did I know then that the nightmare was just beginning! Newspaper and television reporters arrived in droves with their cameras clicking every time they could catch up with me. Leona, a strong person, able to deal with the press effectively and politely, while denying them access to me and sending them away firmly, was a great help.

That weekend, I read a statement at all the Masses, explaining the Gomorrah allegations and attesting to my innocence. *The Rosanada Sunday News* carried Wayne Creasy's version of the Gomorrah lawsuit on the front page. Every time I turned on the television, there was Lucretia Gomorrah weeping and sobbing that she had suffered greatly because of the abuse that Pompeo and I had inflicted on her son, not realizing that the real criminal was a person very close to her—her husband, a known homosexual, guilty of incest and pedophilia.

Never in my life had I expected such a nasty situation. The week was a constant challenge to my patience and courage, because just when I thought I had reached my maximum denigration, another news clip would hit the media, spiraling me lower and lower.

All my attorney Guli Sasa would say was: "Zipped lips are your best protection. A closed mouth always avoids trouble."

45
Yo-Lin

"I will never forgive that wretched priest that fired Enki!" Yo-Lin fumed. Revenge would be sweet. She would see to that. Now her days of being known as a good Catholic and a parishioner at Santiago were over. Well, no priest was untouchable—least of all Marco Lamadrid. Not only would he suffer for firing Enki and destroying his ministry, he would also pay because he had repeatedly rejected her attempts to seduce him.

So far in the past year, she had slept with four young priests and wore them out. Of course they ended up being "blessed" financially by her generosity, as she hoped simultaneously to erase both the sin and the great age difference between them and her. She enjoyed particularly the favors of a very handsome and sexually appealing seminarian, Marco's cousin, who was young enough to be her grandson. To show her gratitude, she paved his way into her bed with gold.

A funny little priest from South America had paid her the tribute of calling her "pansexual." Remembering how he had spent the week with her and returned to Chile completely exhausted, after experiencing a lot of her anal nights, she laughed out loud. She had heard someone say that hell has no fury like a woman scorned. Marco would soon know what it meant to scorn her!

Now that Pazi was helping Enki by searching for men to file lawsuits alleging that Lamadrid had sexually molested them when they were minors, she was sure Marco would be destroyed. Because he fired Bastits, even she was helping to find people to accuse him of sexual abuse. When he fired Enki, her reputation as a virtuous woman was demolished, but she was determined to tear his ministry down forever. Never again should he be able to preach or even minister the sacraments. The latest man that Pazi had found to accuse Marco was Nakki Laflamboy. He did have a criminal record and was even arrested for soliciting sex in the vicinity of a school, but Jonathan Snodgrass, who had already filed a number of cases against the Archdiocese of Rosanada, had assured Enki that the bishops in the United States had the hidden agenda of paying all claims without really investigating and demanding proof of the allegations, because they themselves were eager to bury the putrefaction, as soon as possible, in order to avoid being sucked into the controversy by the law or the media. Rather than risk losing their prestigious positions, as Cardinal Law had lost his, and being debased and perhaps even defrocked, they would let the priests suffer for their neglect in dealing with pedophile priests and for moving them from parish to parish, rather than reporting them for their criminal activity, as the law required. After all, most of them did not have the large sums of money required to slide under the table to oil the machinery of the Holy See and the various cardinals in Rome in order to obtain a respectable position at the Vatican. Besides, it took extreme finesse to make the payoffs, and, if you botched the job, you could end up in the Church's equivalent of Siberia.

Ransacking her jade green purse—the one with the neon green sequins—she searched for her cell phone, while accidentally dropping her Beretta semi-automatic pistol on the floor. Picking the gun up, she checked the combat-style trigger guard to be sure it was in place and then stuffed the pistol back in her purse, patted it affectionately and thought, "Never leave home without it!" Carefully, so as not to chip the emerald green polish from her nails, she punched in Enki's number, almost certain that he would be at home, since he was so overcome by the publicity in the media that he did not want to leave the house.

"Hola!" Enki answered almost at once.

"Poor baby! How are you today?" she purred.

"Much better now that we keep finding men who are willing to file lawsuits with Jonathan Snodgrass accusing Marco of sexual abuse. Nakki Laflamboy will testify that he spent the night in a hotel with Marco many times and was foully and grossly abused by that disgusting, despicable excuse of a priest that thinks he is God's gift to the world."

"Wonderful news, Enki! If you need anything, just holler! Ciao!

46
Marco

Vacation time was fast approaching. To get away from the all the gossip, rumors, and accusations that were swirling around me, I was planning to fly to Liechtenstein. Faithful to God and to me, my parishioners were wonderful. Believing that I was innocent of the hideously, despicable and mendacious accusations made against me, they did everything they could to let me know that they stood with me.

Faithful parishioners are the Church—the true bride of Christ, not the hierarchy with all its pompous, arrogant, and oppressive clericalism. No matter how corrupt its leaders might be, the gates of hell will never prevail against the holy Church of God. Someone, who visited Rome during the Renaissance at the time of Rodrigo Borgia, better know as Pope Alexander VI, stated very correctly and astutely: "I know the Church is a divine institution, otherwise it could never survive the corruption I see in Rome." Alexander VI, known for his infamous life, one day while sitting in a chair in his Vatican apartments had the floor break open from under him and he fell, crashing violently down into the room below. He cleaned up his life—for one year. When he died, his corpse was so repulsive that no one would touch it, and they had to tie a rope around his foot and drag him out of the Vatican.

Some episodes in the history of the Church are just beyond comprehension. In the tenth century, the distinguished Marozia became part of the history of the Church as the daughter of Pope John X and his mistress Theodora. Years later Marozia became the mistress of Pope Sergius III and eventually saw her son by him elevated to the papacy as John XI. She is the only woman in the history of the Church who was the daughter, the mistress, and the mother of a pope. I smile when I hear that women have no power in the Church. Marozia was more powerful than a pope, because the Church was under her control for two pontificates.

Another and more recent powerful woman in the Church was La Popessa, Sister Pasqualina Lehnert, friend, confident, and housekeeper of Cardinal Eugenio Maria Pacelli, who became Pope Pius XII. While in Menzingen on holiday, he met her and she returned with him to Munich where he was papal nuncio for Benedict XV. She remained with him for the next 40 years as his housekeeper.

An interesting story and one that is most apropos for our time is that of Julius III, for it is one that has been repeated in the lives of many contemporary clergy. We have seen members of the hierarchy elevate unqualified men to high positions just as Pope Julius III did with Innocenzo. This pope, born Giovanni Maria Ciocchi del Monte in 1487, became an expert at canon law and was one of the three co-presidents that started the Council of Trent. After he was elevated to the papacy, he supported Michelangelo as the architect of St. Peter's, and was the pope of the Council of Trent. Nevertheless, a great scandal whirled around him for a large part of his career, because, when he saw a fifteen-year old beggar named Innocenzo fighting off a pet ape, he became enamoured with him to such a degree that Julius made this beggar boy a cathedral provost. Later when he was elected pope in 1500 taking the name of Julius III, he persuaded his brother to adopt Innocenzo. Then, amid great protests from others in the Church, he named his beggar boy-lover a cardinal and made him his chief diplomat and political agent, although he had absolutely no qualifications for the job. The Romans of that time referred to the boy as "Ganymede," the boy beloved by Zeus in Greek mythology, while the ambassador from Venice insisted that he shared Julius' bedroom and bed. Because Julius doted on Innocenzo excessively, he gave him so many benefices that his income exceeded that of the Medicis. After the death of Julius, the succeeding popes were embarrassed by Innocenzo whom they called the "Cardinal Monkey," because of his licentious and profligate lifestyle. His body and that of Pope Julius III rest today in the Church of San Pietro in Montorio in Rome.

One of the most bizarre accounts in the history of the papacy involves an event known as the Cadaver Synod when Pope Stephen VI, made pope in 896, ordered the exhumation of his predecessor, Pope Formosus, to try him for alleged crimes against the Church. Although Formosus had already been dead for about nine months, Stephen dressed his corpse in full papal vestments, sat it on a throne, and provided a counsel to defend him, as required by canon law. Presiding over the trial himself, Stephen, of course, found Formosus guilty. As a consequence, they cut off the three fingers on Formosus' right hand, with which he swore oaths and gave blessings, and declared that all the ordinations he had performed were invalid, causing chaos among the many priests involved. They dragged his rotting remains through the streets of Rome and eventually threw them into Tiber. However, later the tide turned and Stephen VI was punished for his disgraceful behavior when he was stripped of his papal insignia, imprisoned, and strangled to death!

The wheat and the tares will exist side by side until the Lord comes with justice and retribution—and He will come! Then the tares will be burned up and the good wheat of God collected and put into His barns. There will be justice for all the priests who have been unjustly accused of sexual abuse and have been abandoned by their bishops who are more interested in preserving their bishoprics than ensuring that justice be served and the innocent protected and defended.

Distressing beyond belief was my humiliation from all the accusations that Lucretia Gomorrah was making about me to Wayne Creasy and the television reporters. A totally dysfunctional family, they regarded the Archdiocese of Rosanada as a fat cash cow to be milked to their satisfaction, and were taking advantage of the frenzy the sex scandal was causing throughout the entire country, with fearful bishops ready to reward financially anyone who came forth with an allegation against a priest. Old Nick and Lucretia Gomorrah were simply opportunists looking for a way to get rich at my expense.

One night when I was scheduled to minister at St. Colon Parish—I often ministered at other parishes—I was met by the usually passive pastor—Father Billie J.

King—in the parking lot as soon as I pulled in. When I stepped out of my car, he confronted me cruelly and viciously: "We don't want the likes of you here." Then pointing at my car he added: "Get out of here and never show your face around here again."

Crushed in my spirit and silently without a word, I got back in my car and drove the ten miles back to my rectory at Santiago. My God, I cried, what humiliation! I couldn't sleep that night except for a few minutes of tormented sleep in which a nightmare plunged me into a black pit in which jeering voices pierced the darkness shouting, "Accused! You have been accused!" In the midst of this torment, an angel of light came and stood by my side, banishing the darkness and the jeering voices and restoring peace to my troubled spirit. Then the Presence came to me advising me that I would have a terrible fight with the powers of darkness, but that He would be with me through it all.

The final weekend before my vacation was scheduled to begin, I bid my people goodbye at all Masses, telling them that I would be on vacation in Liechtenstein for a month. My last Mass that Sunday—the 11:00 am Spanish Mass was very special. The Gifts of the Holy Spirit were abundantly manifested, and I felt God's Presence within me stronger than I ever had before in my life. I knew that I was doing His will and speaking for Him when I ministered to the people.

The next morning my faithful personal assistant Leona, phoned me while I was still in the rectory, as I was preparing to go to the airport. Usually a calm and level-headed person, she seemed troubled. As she stammered to express herself, I said:

"What's wrong, Leona?"

Catching her breath, she stammered. "Oh, Padre, there has been another allegation. Wayne Creasy from the *Rosanada News* just phoned, saying that the story of another man who claims you abused him is coming out today in the paper and on the TV."

Stunned to the core, I said softly: "Thank you, Leona." I could not believe what I was hearing. So many afflictions! Another accusation! It was my Gethsemane, and I prayed asking God to help me: "Blessed Father, I have ministered so many times in your Name. So many times I have felt your Holy Presence. So many times I have administered your sacraments and now I find myself humbled and confused by my enemies. Rise up, O Lord, and defend your servant. I don't believe this to be Your will and I also believe that our community does not deserve to be damaged by those who hate me."

When I phoned my mother, explaining to her about the latest accusations, she advised me to go on my vacation and that she would hold me in constant prayer.

The flight to Liechteinstein that was almost full seemed interminable, besides I had to fly to Zurich and then drive to Vaduz, the capital of the principality. After the stewardesses finished serving dinner, they started a movie, but I couldn't concentrate on it, because the events of my life were much more compelling than any movie and my mind kept reviewing everything that had recently happened. Just before I left home, Wayne Creasy of the *Rosanada News* phoned my office and asked Leona for an appointment to interview me; she explained that I was unavailable and on vacation for a month.

The new accusation being made by Frido Sodomat, whose family I had known at St. Ellen's, was a real surprise. It made me very uneasy, especially since it came right on top of Old Nick and Lucretia Gomorrah's announcement that they were filing a lawsuit against the Archdiocese of Rosanada, my old schoolmate Father Pompeo, and me, because of the supposed suffering inflicted on their family. All this had been narrated in *A Church of Darkness* and when the Purcell book came out, I erroneously thought that I would never again have to face that kind of infamy. Now, years later, I was being forced to relive that horrendous experience, but now it was even worse, because it involved the legal system. In addition, Frido Sodomat was threatening me with still another lawsuit.

Suddenly in the midst of my preoccupation with my problems, a stewardess came with much solicitude and asked me: "Do you feel all right?" Surprised that someone could so easily notice my distress, I replied—stretching the truth a bit—that I was, and asked for a Scotch on the rocks, while I continued meditating on the events of the day.

The flight seemed neverending. I had hoped that the Scotch would make me sleepy, but I continued to feel wide-awake. Through my window, I could see the first light of dawn. Little by little, the stars of the North Atlantic that lighted the night gave way to the sunrise, but still I could not sleep, although most of the other passengers were sleeping and once in a while I could hear sounds of snoring.

As torrents of rain swept through the streets of Vaduz, the overcast and somber sky, with its ominous dark clouds, reflected the way I felt, when checking into a hotel far from the city center where I did not think reporters could find me. I was attacked, persecuted and also condemned by the press that seeks to try people and find them guilty, before they even have a chance to defend themselves. Shortly after I checked into my room—the hotel was dark and dingy too—I received a phone call from Monsignor Zagan, the vicar general.

"Father Lamadrid, another accusation has been brought against you in a news conference held by Jonathan Snodgrass, a local attorney. Therefore, the archbishop is putting you on administrative leave effective immediately. You cannot exercise your duties as pastor of Santiago any longer, you can no longer refer to yourself as a priest, nor can you wear clerical garb. You can only say Mass in private. We have contacted all the television people that carry your programs and have advised them that you are no longer allowed to preach the gospel. Archbishop L'Abbadon is appointing an administrator today, Father Maximo Bello entrusting him with the pastoral care of your parish. And we want you to return to the archdiocese immediately." Giving me absolutely no opportunity to ask any questions of him, he ended the conversation, once he had delivered his message.

It was clear that L'Abbadon faithful to his motto "I do not care," just wanted to get rid of me as soon as possible. Obviously, they had completely ignored canon law, which has certain procedures that should have been followed, prior to taking this action against me. They had no time to investigate the charges made against me to see if they were credible or not, as canon law required. They simply jumped on the opportunity to strip me of everything that made up my life. I am a priest, called by God, a pastor of a community—and with one phone call all this was taken away from me.

When I opened my suitcase to find a change of clothes, I discovered that someone had spread about three dozen condoms on the top of my clothing. Because I had packed the suitcase myself the previous day, I knew that one of the staff members at Santiago had tampered with it, trying to create a scandal and embarrassment to me, when I opened it going through customs.

The following days were dismal. Although I searched unceasingly for the consolation of the Holy Presence of God, I could not find it. Emptiness, loneliness, contradiction, and infamy were my constant companions. Would I ever minister the word of God and His sacraments again? What would become of me? I was only fifty-seven years old and the best years of my ministry lay ahead of me and I was robbed of them. What would I do? What could I do?

47
Renato

La dolce vita! Life in the archiepiscopal residence was sweet! He had moved in the previous evening, but did not see His Excellency who was locked in his room all night. Now the maid Ella, a kindly Central American woman with indigenous facial features and a heavy Spanish accent, a recent immigrant who probably had no permit to work in the country, was bringing him breakfast, just as he ordered it—a pot of espresso, Eggs Benedict with extra hollandaise sauce, and some real prosciutto that a delicatessen on the Boulevard imported directly from Italy. Renato thought the maid would probably be much better at making *tortillas* and *frijoles*, but he would not like such a meal. When he was just starting to enjoy the morning, he was rudely interrupted and jolted by a voice coming out of the intercom speaker near his bed. At first, he thought it was a local radio station, and then realized that it was the archbishop.

"Renato, come here," His Excellency commanded. "At once."

He put down his cup of espresso, and slipped into the thick cotton terrycloth bathrobe that the maid provided him. It too had the monogram CAL emblazoned on the breast pocket. As he tied the sash, the door that separated his room from the archbishop's flew open and there stood His Excellency, having just stepped out of the shower—in all his naked seventy-two-year-old infamy, milk-white skin, sagging buttocks, hanging breasts and protruding belly covering a diminutive and almost invisible cork-sized penis.

"Renato, get one of my suits out of my closet and lay it on the bed. Find my gold monogrammed cufflinks and a shirt I can wear with my vest and Roman collar. Get me a pair of boxer shorts out of the dresser over there." He pointed to a highboy dresser with a dozen drawers.

Renato began to open the drawers of the dresser frantically and continued until he found a droopy pair of boxer shorts and handed them to the archbishop who was standing there expecting to be waited on. "I'll also need my Borsalino hat that I bought in Italy on my last *ad limina* visit to see the pope. I have a very important appointment this afternoon. I'll wear my black crocodile loafers—also in the closet."

Finding it incredible that he, Renato Del'Ano, his executive secretary, was expected to help him dress, Renato, nevertheless, assembled all his clothes and then handed them to him piece by piece,

"As usual I have an appointment at eleven and the second of the day at three. You will take me to the chancery and stay with me until I am ready to come home at four. That is the schedule we will follow most days. When we get back here to the house, I expect you to make a pitcher of Canadian Club Manhattans. After we get home, I will give you your instructions for the evening. Most importantly I want you to draw me a hot bath using my favorite French bath salts at ten o'clock tonight. After that—well after that—we will see. Perhaps, we can play a hand or two of gin rummy. I like to play gin every evening before I go to bed. Do you play gin?"

"I have never played it."

"Well, I will teach you. You are a fast learner. It's a great game."

As Renato drove him to the chancery in the limo, he decided it was a good time to tell him about the latest allegations against Marco Lamadrid and Pompeo Dell'Anitra. Because he was now certain that Marco would be finished in the priesthood, he was elated by the news of the Frido Sodomat lawsuit.

"What can you tell me about this Sodomat fellow?" the archbishop asked, as he sat in the back seat fiddling with the *Rosanada News*. "Wait a minute; it says here that he is suing the United States Congress as well as us, charging that Marco Lamadrid and Pompeo Dell'Anitra were running a prostitution ring to service visiting congressmen from Washington." His lips pursed into a tight circle as they always did when he was troubled. "I'll probably get a phone call from Ratzinger today asking me what the hell I am doing over here! Tell him I am out of the office when he calls."

"Of course, Archbishop."

"I'm not going to wind up like Bernard Law who got kicked out of Boston and moved to Rome for his stupidity. Tell Puck I want to settle this case as soon as possible." He folded the newspaper and laid it beside him on the seat. "Have you talked to Lamadrid and the other one?"

"No, Msgr. Zagan did; Lamadrid is in Liechtenstein, but he left a number with his secretary so I was able to tell Jan how to reach him." Renato could see in the rear view mirror that the archbishop's forehead was furrowed with wrinkles. "I know that Zagan is not the best choice for any task, but he is the vicar general."

"Did you do as I advised every time an allegation is made against any of our priests?" He leaned forward and spoke almost in his ear.

"Of course. He was put on administrative leave and his faculties taken away, except for celebrating Mass privately. He was ordered to come back here right away. I myself wrote the letter to take Pompeo Dell'Anitra out of St. Giordano Bruno as pastor and put him on administrative leave."

"Did they conduct any investigation of this matter at the tribunal?"

"Of course not, Archbishop, you are the only judge in this archdiocese!"

"Good, good! At eleven this morning I am meeting with the architect who has finished construction on Casa St. Popola. It looks great and is ready to move into. I am setting it up as a home for priests of the archdiocese who need a place to stay. Monsignor Zagan will live there also and be the head of the household. Bishop Morales would like to live there; we will give him one of the best suites. Furthermore, I want Bishop Sinew to retire immediately and then we will have to house him there too. His brain lymphoma is slowly getting worse, so today, write him a letter asking for his resignation. He will give it freely at once, or I will contact the Congregation of Bishops in the Vatican and have him removed."

Renato dropped the archbishop at the impressive entrance of the chancery on Wanton Street not far from the archiepiscopal mansion. He left his attaché case in the car, expecting him to carry it in for him.

About one o'clock, Enki Mutante phoned to tell him that they had found another man who was willing to file charges, alleging that Marco Lamadrid had also molested him—one Nakki Laflamboy. That phone call really made his day. He inquired about Frido Sodomat and learned that his family ran a third-rate Spanish television station in the city. Frido was in financial difficulties and was eager for a cash settlement.

When at four o'clock, right on time, he pulled the limo up at the front entrance of the chancery, the archbishop came immediately, and they went home. Renato had never before in his life made a Manhattan, but it seemed simple enough. He wasn't sure exactly how it was made, but he thought it had olives in it. So he poured sixteen ounces of Canadian Club whiskey and an ounce of dry vermouth in a large shaker with ice. Later he learned that a Canadian club Manhattan requires much more vermouth than that. He took the pitcher of Manhattans out to the outdoor pool where the archbishop was swimming.

After climbing out of the pool, His Excellency sat in a lounge chair that accommodated his tall six-foot frame. When Renato served him the Manhattan with the two olives in his glass, he looked at the drink rather strangely and then took a sip. "I don't like dry Manhattans! In fact I can't stand dry Manhattans! I want a sweet Manhattan with cherries in it!" He jumped up and began stamping his feet, as his voice raised an octave higher. He was like an hysterical woman as he yelled, "Go and make me a decent Manhattan with three cherries in it and a twist of orange peal and put in more vermouth, and don't use dry vermouth, use sweet vermouth!" As Renato stared at him in disbelief that he was actually having a tantrum to get what he wanted, he yelled "NOW!"

When he returned with the drinks, the archbishop had calmed down. However, when Renato tried to pick up one of the drinks that he had made to drink it himself, he reprimanded him harshly, "No, you can't have any. I might decide I have to go out this evening. You can't have alcohol on your breath when you drive the car. What a scandal it would make—archbishop's chauffeur DUI."

In amazement, Renato watched him drink, one, two, three Manhattans. When the butler announced that dinner was served, the archbishop could barely walk. He leaned heavily on his arm as they walked to the dining room. In astonishment, Renato watched as the archbishop had several glasses of wine with dinner and a glass of Port afterwards.

"I'm very tired this evening," he stammered in blurred speech. Please help me up to my room, Renato." As Renato put his arm around his waist to steady him, they headed for the elevator to the second floor. When they arrived in his room, he asked him to draw his bath water, which he did. On unsteady feet and with Renato supporting him, His Excellency managed to get into the bathroom. Suddenly he threw up all over Renato and then collapsed in a drunken stupor on the bathroom floor, urinating at the same time, soaking his trousers. Renato was able to rouse him, get him up on his feet, and undress him. He held him under the shower as the warm water helped him to come to his senses. The odor was almost more than he could bear. He reeked of whiskey and all the rest he had consumed. With difficulty Renato managed to get him into his bed, pull down his monogrammed covers and tuck him in. As he went into his own room, locking the door behind him, Renato suddenly realized that the archbishop planned to stamp his monogram also on him. Was the price of success really worth it?

48
Marco

Still reeling from the vicar general's news putting me on administrative leave, I booked the first flight I could to Rosanada. My world had come to an end! Everything that I held dear had been ripped from me! I was a priest without faculties—I could neither preach nor administer the sacraments. The vicar general had actually phoned all the television people that carried my programs to an audience of up to five hundred million people and cancelled them, telling them that I was no longer permitted to preach the gospel of Jesus Christ. And he did this without even taking the time to investigate whether the allegations about me were even credible. If the people I worked with did not believe in my innocence, how could anyone else?

Across the nation and the world, newspapers everywhere wrote that Pompeo dell'Anitra and I ran a prostitution ring for visiting congressmen from Washington! How could anybody in his right mind believe that? To all the millions of people who believed in me and the gospel I preached, televisions around the world blared the story that I was an incredibly evil priest involved in the grossest sins of the flesh. My life's work was being irreparably destroyed and I was helpless and unable to do anything to stop it.

Priests that I considered friendly to me no longer wanted to have anything to do with me. I was a pariah—a *persona non grata*—expelled from life, as I knew it. I was even excluded from attending clergy activities and other archdiocesan events.

No longer permitted to live in the rectory I had built, I picked up my personal belongings and vestments from Santiago and moved them to my mother's house. Almost as soon as I was back from Liechtenstein, Pompeo phoned me and invited me to come to see him at the Casa St. Popola where he was now living, since he had been evicted from his rectory at St. Giordano Bruno's Church where he was pastor. When I arrived, he was even more wound up than I had imagined he would be. Forced to live in Popola, with all the pedophile priests who had nowhere else to go, Pompeo gave the impression of being on the verge of a nervous breakdown.

Casa St. Popola, the building L'Abbadon erected to house homeless clergy including his vicar general and two of his bishops, was a modern, but very plain, apartment style building of ten suites and eight large bedrooms. The building was of Colonial design made of frame and stone with a large stone chimney. Inside the furnishings were of exquisite taste, as was everything chosen by L'Abbadon. The furniture was Scandinavian, very plain, but highly sophisticated. Due to the very modern altar appointments, the private chapel appeared to have been designed by a European architect.

The dining room, where Monsignor Zagan, the vicar general, presided at the head of the long blonde table, was solemn and impressive. In fact, the whole house spoke of the dignity of the present administration of the archdiocese, except for the atrocious paintings and prints that pretended to decorate the walls that were all painted a light cream color. The furnishings were mostly a harsh shade of yellowish green. Pretentious as it was, there was certainly none of the luxury that the archbishop built into his own residence. Actually, it was a nice version of a roach motel.

"Come on in," Pompeo welcomed me. As he led me into the living room where there were several other priests that I recognized from attending clergy conferences and retreats, I could see instantly that he was totally distraught. Then I spotted Bishop Sinew, wearing blue jeans and a plain T-shirt, as he came strolling through the living room with a tall purple miter on his head.

"Good afternoon, Bishop," I greeted him.

"If you want to talk to me," he replied firmly, "you must get an appointment with my secretary." His vacant stare and bizarre attire told me that his brain tumor was taking its toll on him. I knew that he had been an excellent slave of Archbishop L'Abbadon who had elevated him to the episcopate. Besides that he was a yes man, without any opinion, avoiding all confrontation, and never contradicting the boss. He was just what L'Abbadon wanted. It was said that the main reason the archbishop had built Casa St. Popola was to provide a home for people like Bishop Sinew and other archdiocesan officials. The archbishop always tried to cultivate the impression that he treated his friends well, so as to garner support from the priests of the archdiocese. Nevertheless, the majority of the clergy detested him.

"Thank you, bishop. I'll take care of it." He seemed pleased with my response and pulled a rosary from his jeans' pocket and began reciting it out loud, disturbing a bishop wearing a silver pectoral cross who was sitting by the large bay window trying to read the *Rosanada News*. I glanced at Pompeo who shrugged his shoulders and started leading me to his room. Walking through the corridor, we passed a priest coming towards us—a Father Carmichael that Pompeo told me was accused of pedophilia and was under house arrest waiting for his trial for pedophilia to begin. Because the person that claimed that he abused him was only ten years old, the statute of limitations did not apply, and the case had to go to trial.

There was another priest we encountered on the way to Pompeo's living quarters—one from England, also accused of sexual improprieties, a Father Leo Boudoir, who called out to Pompeo and me: "I can't stand it! I can't stand it here! I don't understand why Her Majesty, the stupid queen and her *cage aux folles* at the chancery are doing this to me. Raising his voice so that he was almost shouting, he said, "Everyone knows that the vicar general is a flaming queen, the archbishop's secretary Renato is L'Abbadon's lover, and the judicial vicar looks like a woman!

Hearing this Pompeo merely smiled and nodded in agreement. Once we were in his room with the door shut, we relaxed in comfortable leather chairs by the window, discussing what had happened to us both. His room was plain, resembling a cell in a monastery. There was a single bed with a crucifix on the wall above it, a small desk with writing materials, a bookcase furnished with traditional Catholic books that the archbishop thought were appropriate reading for priests and that Pompeo vehemently despised, preferring books of a more worldly nature. A plain brown carpet on the floor completed the décor.

"L'Abbadon knows we are innocent yet he presumes we are guilty! The allegations of Sodomat are contemptible inventions of that pothead—that crack addict. I never liked him with his double face and forked tongue." Pompeo bent over and couched his face in his hands. I could see that he was close to collapse."

"He is actually suing the US Congress!" I said unable to fathom the depths of the depravity of his mind.

"I don't think he will get very far with that," Pompeo replied as he looked at me with his face betraying the despair that was in his heart. "Congress is out of the jurisdiction of our local Circuit Court. They have sued them just to get the media's attention."

"He says I molested him when I had not yet even arrived in this country. I was still in Rome during the year he accused me of sexually abusing him! He also claims I molested him on the third floor of the rectory at St. Ellen's. When I lived at St. Ellen's, the rectory did not have a third floor. They built a new rectory since then that does have a third floor. Can't they figure those things out at the chancery? You don't have to be a genius to understand that!"

"There is no way I could have molested him either. I also checked the dates of his alleged molestations—he was no longer a minor!

"I suppose you heard that some Nakki Laflamboy has also filed a lawsuit, alleging that I spent many nights in a motel with him. Very conveniently he does not remember the name of the motel, simply because it does not exist. Since he claims he does not remember the name, he cannot be expected to produce motel records verifying that we were there. And he also claims he spent the night many times at the rectory. You remember Father Cletor Delsapo—a seminarian at the time—who was assigned to Santiago to gain experience. He did all kinds of chores and was in charge of security, locking up the gates at night and prowling the grounds looking for intruders. He and all the staff at that time have sworn in affidavits that Laflamboy never spent the night on the premises of Santiago and…"

Pompeo interrupted my account about Nakki Laflamboy. Because he was not a party to the suit, he was not interested in hearing about it. Pompeo had a hard time putting up with any conversation in which he was not the center. However, Cletor Delsapo *was* a subject that interested him:

"Are you still a friend of that son of a bitch Delsapo?"

"Yes" I replied.

"You are making a big mistake. That Bolivian with the Indian face is nothing but a worm that deserves to be stepped on."

"Come on!" I said, hoping his comment was not true. "How is Mínimo these days," I asked to change the subject.

Pompeo immediately warmed to the subject of Mínimo.

"I want to tell you about Onan Wilde and Mínimo. Do you remember Onan?"

Recalling what my mother had told me about Mínimo spending much of his time with him, I answered: "Yes, I remember him. He brought sexual abuse allegations against Mínimo several years ago, and still they continued to be friends. A very strange situation. I have never really had any association with him. He seemed like a criminal type and I avoided him, which seemed to irritate him."

"I don't care for him either."

"Why does Mínimo continue to befriend him then? A priest should be more careful about the people he has as friends."

"Well, as you know Mínimo lost his faith years ago, if he ever had any to begin with. That was way back, when we were studying in Rome. You remember how he left and went to Holland and got a job as a sacristan for a while. I never told you the whole story about that. He spent two years in a mental institution because of his violent schizophrenic disorders. After that he worked in a brothel in Amsterdam as a domestic servant. They called him a "malemaid," and made him wear a ridiculous costume like theirs. All the girls there were dressed up to look like pussy cats with very brief, black body suits that were cut high exposing two inches of flesh above each hip, and their legs were clad in seductive black mesh hose. To make them look like cats, they had large velvet catlike ears fastened to their heads and long black velvet tails fastened to their bottoms that they swished around as they flirted with their customers, trying to attract them into their private cubicles. Mínimo was dressed like a Tomcat—the same tight body suit as the girls, and a long black tail with big black velvet ears fastened to his head. His costume did not include the mesh hose, so his hairy legs and knobby knees made his appearance utterly ludicrous. Because that was the only job he could get, I felt sorry for him. He was so mad at society that he joined the communist party. Then he got in trouble with the Dutch police for living with an under age Austrian boy without his parents consent. They say his neighbors notified the cops, and they investigated the matter, and he escaped to the States. I think Onan might have something really serious on Mínimo. He keeps demanding money from him, and Mínimo keeps giving it to him. He has given him thousands of dollars so far. He has come after me for money, and I do not know what to do about it, because he can be pretty intimidating."

"Well, I certainly would not give him any money," I replied with emphasis. "By the way, who was that bishop that was sitting reading the *Rosanada News* downstairs here when I came in? I have never seen him before. Is he a new bishop here in Rosanada?"

"Oh, him. He is a friend of L'Abbadon from a diocese in the East. He had nowhere to go and so L'Abbadon brought him here. He is mentally unbalanced ever since he was raped by three gerontophiles."

"Gerontophiles? What's that?"

"You know. Like pedophiles except they don't prey on kids—they pick on old people, like the old bishop downstairs. Poor old bishop, if you had looked closer you would have seen that he was holding the newspaper upside down that you thought he was reading. He sits there everyday with the same newspaper, holding it upside down."

I rose from the chair. I had had enough of Popola. "It is getting late and I'm getting hungry."

"I wish I could invite you to dinner, but today is Saturday and the cook doesn't come in on Saturdays and Sundays. We have no food available. I usually go out—there is an inexpensive restaurant a couple blocks from here…"

"What happens to Carmichael on the weekends? He is under house arrest and can't go out."

"He goes hungry or else opens a can of tuna fish. Bishop Sinew is worse off. He is so senile that he cannot even feed himself. Rosa, the cook, spoon feeds him when she is here, and when she is not here—he just goes hungry, unless his sister shows up to feed him."

"Unbelievable! I thought he was L'Abbadon's good friend?"

"Yep!"

"That is how he treats his friends?"

"Yep!"

"Can't some of you priests that are staying in the house feed him?"

Abruptly, Pompeo changed the subject. "Let's go to the restaurant now," he said, as he headed for the door.

Downstairs in the living room, Bishop Sinew was muttering to himself and staring off into space. He did not even see us, as we walked past him. The old bishop who was holding the newspaper upside down glanced over at me and said, "Be careful when you go outside. It is not safe out there. There are vampires roaming around this time of day."

I was glad to leave Casa Popola and decided that I would never visit it again. I also renewed my determination to have nothing to do with Onan Wilde. He was bad news.

49
Marco

The *Rosanada News* was filled every day with sex scandals, accusing priests of molesting children. All the news channels on the television talked on endlessly about the victims. What began in Boston quickly spread throughout the United States, as reports of sexual allegations against priests snowballed. Cardinal Bernard Law had to resign in December of 2002, because of the magnitude of the sex scandal in the Boston Archdiocese. Faced with more than 500 accusers, Boston was forced to sell off property worth a hundred million to make settlements and prevent bankruptcy. All around the country bishops were settling cases for large sums of money. Rumors had it that at the semi-annual meeting of the United States Conference of Catholic Bishops, they decided behind well closed doors, that they would pay all claims, settling out of court, and in this way escape from testifying on the witness stand under oath how they had protected and hidden pedophiles. Besides, going before a court could bring to light some other offenses and a variety of peccadilloes that they were hiding. They did not seem to realize that the more settlements they made to accusers who never had to prove their accusations, the more accusers would show up at their doors with their hands out. Completely ignoring the church's law that requires a case to be investigated prior to action being taken against a priest, the bishops adopted a zero tolerance policy that meant that anyone who was accused was immediately removed from his parish and could no longer function as a priest, or even wear clerical garb.

Having decided to defend myself all the way, I got an attorney who had been a friend since my youth, a second one who was a friend of his, and a criminal lawyer who was a devout Jew who had the reputation of defending only innocent people. It meant a lot to me that he believed in my innocence and was eager to defend me.

After the judges, afraid of losing popularity among the voters, rejected the motions to dismiss the flimsy cases against me that had absolutely no substance, all the attorneys—the archdiocese's, Pompeo's and mine, began the discovery process, taking the depositions of people who had accused me and Pompeo of abusing them. It was a slow and painful process. Although I was not present at the depositions, I received copies of them and painfully read them—filled with all their contradictions and lies. I looked forward to being able to give my deposition and clear my name, but I was denied this opportunity. Although the accusers began by suing the archdiocese and me, they dropped me from the suits, when I retained as counsel an excellent defense lawyer Hugh F. Brighton, Esq, because they did not want to be subjected to his searching cross-examinations. Because they dropped me from the cases, I was unable to fight them, for I was no longer a party to the lawsuits. The archdiocese was the one with the deep pockets, not me. If I had remained a party to the suits, then I could have given my testimony and told the truth to counteract their lies. They had excluded me completely, and there was nothing I could do about it. I did not have the money to sue them for slander and libel, although I was confident that I could have won those suits, if I had had the funds to pursue them. Unfortunately priests do not make a lot of money. So I was unable to tell my side of the story.

A fourth person, one Ian Dagon, whom I could not even remember accused me of molesting him under nebulous circumstances. He told some fuzzy story that made absolutely no sense. It was filled with contradictions so that anyone could see he was lying. Obviously he did not think straight, being on heavy medication for schizophrenia. Furthermore, he had accused another priest many years ago to a vicar in the parish, and at that time, he never said anything about me, when he had ample opportunity.

The Roman Catholic Church has one of the oldest legal systems and codes of law in the world. I read it and saw how egregiously my rights under this code of law had been violated. The code of canon law was good, but it had one great deficiency—there was no one to enforce it and no one to whom I could appeal. Moreover, canon law came into existence as the means to protect the rights of the organizational Church and not those of the people. I found a canon lawyer and hoped that he would help me defend my rights and return me to my parish from which I had been illegally, according to Church law, evicted. Although, he was a very good priest, he just did not have enough time for me, so I sought help in another direction. Since there were so many canon lawyers occupied with sex abuse cases across the country, it was hard to find one that had the time to help me. I paid a Catholic organization seven hundred dollars for them to provide me with the name of a canon lawyer that they said was "one of the best." He was an utter disappointment. I had to write my own defense and petition for the CDF—the Congregation for the Defense of the Faith, formerly known as the Inquisition, that had been placed in charge of all cases relating to sexual abuse, asking them to transfer my case to Rome and to provide me with a canonical trial there. According to canon law, I had a right to have my trial held in Rome. In time, I learned that canon law has absolutely no meaning. Bishops run roughshod over priests and when they appeal, they have no recourse. The good old boy clerical network of bishops and archbishops does whatever it pleases without regard to canon law. In actual fact, every diocese is a feudal possession of the archbishop where he, as lord of the manor, does as he pleases. In turn every pastor in a diocese is like a Mafia "don" who has his own little operation and will be in good standing as long as he pays his dues. Furthermore, since the Vatican runs on US dollars, American bishops are given *carte blanche* to do as they please.

Although Hugh Brighton, my civil lawyer, told the archdiocese that none of those who had made allegations against me had any evidence, and we could easily prevail against them in a court of law, they paid all of them generous settlements. By paying off these accusers without their having to prove their cases, the archdiocese made me look guilty. This was one of the bitterest fruits of this entire affair for me. I knew that I had no hope of getting a fair canonical trial in Rosanada, run by L'Abbadon. There was no way he could find me innocent after he had paid off all that money to the accusers. In the eyes of the laity and of the Vatican, he would have looked ridiculous and stupid for having paid off the accusers, only to find that I was innocent and that he had given the money to liars and thieves.

My canon lawyer, Aloysius Fairmont, phoned me one day and informed me that the current promoter of justice, Rev. Paul F. X. Linde G.G.G., of the Rosanada Archdiocese was going to arrange for a canonical trial to be held locally. Paul had hated me as far back as I could remember. There was no way that I would let him put me through a trial, judge me, find me guilty to please the archbishop, and unfrock me. An active homosexual—he was known for the sexual relationships he had had with various priests, violating his commitment to chastity. He and the director of vocations were known gay activists and friendly only with members of their clique.

I simply could not stand trial in the archbishop's kangaroo court. There was no way he would permit me to prove my innocence. He wanted to get rid of me, and had paid off my accusers, so that he would not have to testify in court, laying bare his actions to the scrutiny of the legal system.

My canon lawyer was naïve enough to encourage me to stand trial in Rosanada. Because canon lawyers earn their way in the Church by working for the bishops, it was my impression that he was a slave of the system. There was no way that Aloysius Fairmont would confront my bishop and provide an adequate defense.

Since I still had not received word from the Congregation for the Defense of the Faith, formerly known for 800 years as the Inquisition, in response to my request to have my trial transferred to Rome, where I thought I would get a fair trial, I contacted an old friend in Rome and asked him to help me find a canon lawyer there. He put me in touch with a friend of his, a man who taught canon law at one of the pontifical universities of Rome, and who was a Roman Rota lawyer. The Roman Rota is the supreme court of the Roman Catholic Church and anyone who receives the recognition of being permitted to practice law before the Roman Rota can work in any court in the worldwide Church.

I flew to Rome and engaged him as my canonist and was encouraged when he notified me that he had gotten my case transferred from Rosanada to Rome, and that I would have a canonical trial there. I was very optimistic when I received this news and felt that it was only a matter of time, until I would be reinstated as pastor of Santiago. However, there was one problem, my Roman canon lawyer made it clear to me that he would not do anything to help me that would in any way have a negative impact on his clerical career.

When I founded the television ministry, I did not take a salary for approximately the first five years. I also gave the ministry the profits from the sale of my teaching tapes. For more than ten years, I had been taking a salary from the ministry and that together with the money I was paid as pastor, even though I was on administrative leave, made it possible for me to survive. Thank God I was not forced to live in Casa Popola as Father Pompeo was with the demented bishop, the vicar general, and Father Carmichael who finally plead guilty to charges of pedophilia and was sentenced to three years of house arrest there.

Firmly believing that prayer can conquer all obstacles, I continued prayer meetings three nights a week with friends who knew I was innocent and rallied to back me up.

Although I suffered from the pain and humiliation of the rude treatment I received from people who only knew what they read in the papers about me, things were going along fairly smoothly. Although, I had many sleepless nights, the Presence of the Lord consoled me. Then, came the letter from Father Colon Olid, a bad friend and a real shame to the gospel, informing me that as administrator of Santiago, he was discontinuing my stipend from the television and radio ministry, valued at over a million dollars that I had created. How could I survive on the pittance the archdiocese was paying me?

50
Renato

"Renato, fix an extra pitcher of Manhattans this evening," the archbishop requested. "Jan is coming to dinner. We will make it a working meeting and after we get the business taken care of, perhaps we can play a few hands of poker in the den."

Renato welcomed the chance to get friendlier with Monsignor Jan Zagan, the vicar general of the Rosanada Archdiocese. Since he had been living in the archbishop's residence, he had learned that the vicar general was a long time friend of His Excellency. They met years before when L'Abbadon went to Rome with Archbishop Melusine to a Synod of Bishops, where they enjoyed slipping out of the meetings and going to St. Johnny's, a gay bar just off the Via Veneto, not far from the Piazza da Spagna, where they used to drink Canadian Club Manhattans together. Because of their old friendship, His Excellency gave Jan Zagan the second position in the power structure of the archdiocese, despite the fact that he was not capable of handing the job. The archbishop was well aware that his memory was almost non-existent due to the cumulative effects of his using alcohol in all its potable forms. With no common sense or basic intelligence for daily living, he resembled a person who had had a lobotomy. As one of the pastors in the southern end of the archdiocese used to say, he had the agility of a turtle, the grace of an ostrich and the sincerity of a snake. For good reason, L'Abbadon was dissatisfied with his performance, but because of their friendship, and perhaps because of all he knew of the archbishop's secret life, he retained him as his vicar general. Renato had heard rumors about how in the past Zagan had been an *aficionado* of Rosanada's gay bars and that some sexual allegations had been made against him, which the archbishop hushed and covered up. Perhaps in time the archbishop could be persuaded to replace Zagan. After all, he had gotten rid of Damian Babilonia. "*Vediamo*," Renato whispered to himself as he fixed the Manhattans.

Monsignor Jan Zagan arrived promptly on time. Renato watched from the kitchen window as he parked his Porsche in the driveway next to the house and came in the back door unannounced, as one who was familiar with the house and its routine.

"Good evening, Monsignor," Renato welcomed him while extending to him a C.C. Manhattan. Zagan eagerly took the drink and sipped it avidly.

"Good for you, Renato. You make a damn good drink."

"His Excellency is waiting for us in his den. We can work there until dinner." They walked into the dining room where the table was already set with sparkling Waterford crystal, solid silver, and Haviland china, then around the indoor pool into the living room past the grand portrait of L'Abbadon, and into the den on the far side of the living room.

Seated at the head of a mahogany table, L'Abbadon had before him a pile of papers, a few photos, and a gold pen that bore his monogram. Very deftly Renato managed to seat himself in the position of honor at the archbishop's right. Zagan sat down beside him and across from L'Abbadon.

"I brought us together, because I need to discuss with you these pedophile accusations that have been made against a number of priests in the archdiocese. Here is the photo of Gustavo Adamo who has just filed a lawsuit today against us, alleging that Father Bocchino Martinelli abused him over twenty years ago. He claims that he has repressed memories that have just reemerged." He handed the photo to Renato who looked at it briefly and passed it on to Zagan.

Renato watched Zagan as he took the photo and scrutinized it briefly and was startled when he made the inane comment: "Father Martinelli does not have very good taste."

They both laughed at the remark and then L'Abbadon said, "We are not here to discuss Father Martinelli's taste; we are here to dispatch Martinelli. I want you, Jan, to put him on administrative leave effectively immediately tomorrow morning," L'Abbadon ordered.

"But," Zagan protested, "canon law requires that we investigate the claims before we remove Martinelli from his parish."

"Canon law!" L'Abbadon exploded, "I am the law in this archdiocese!" His face reddened with anger that anyone would even think thoughts contrary to that. Just do as I said and remove him from his parish at once."

Renato watched Zagan's wrinkled face as he rubbed his bulbous nose and thought of a proper response to what the archbishop had just said. A blank stare glazed the features of his face as he slowly shook his bull-like head. Finally he said, "Of course, Cecil, You are right, I will do it tomorrow."

"Now there is another new matter. Perhaps you can give me the correct details on this case. It seems that someone made sexual allegations about Mínimo Tabrón. We gave him a generous settlement and then I understand he came to you Jan, and said that he had lied—that Mínimo was innocent. Is this the way it was?"

Renato could see that Zagan had probably been a handsome man when he was younger, but now he was overweight and clumsy. Short in stature with a large bull-like neck, when he stood next to L'Abbadon who was quite tall, the two of them reminded Renato of Mutt and Jeff in the comics that he had learned to enjoy since coming to America. Zagan's face bore the ravages of the overindulgence of his sensual appetites. Moreover, his mind seemed to be constantly in a fog.

"I tried to get him to sign a statement that he had lied, but he refused. I think his lawyer—Jonathan Snodgrass—must have told him that we would prosecute him, and he would go to prison, if he reneged on his story. No doubt Snodgrass did not want to lose his cut of the settlement. Then what happened? The next part of the story is confusing to me."

Renato listened carefully as he watched the inner workings of the archdiocese.

"Then some low life by the name of Onan Wilde came to my office, insisting that Mínimo was innocent and that he should be reinstated in his parish. I just ignored him and sent him away. He was a degenerate if I ever saw one. I didn't want to talk to him. He looked like he didn't have two dollars to his name. Slovenly and uneducated, he spoke very vulgar English. He is definitely trash." Jan paused and then asked, "Can I have another drink? I'm very thirsty." He sighed and took in a deep breath.

Renato looked at the archbishop to see if it was all right to give the vicar general another drink.

"Not yet, Jan, we still have business to take care of," L'Abbadon said denying his request. "What happened next? The story is confusing."

Wilde wrote a note to Magnus saying that Mínimo Tabrón was willing to back him up in his allegations, and he is going to accuse and file lawsuits against ten of our priests! To make matters more confusing, we must remember that he accused Mínimo of sexual abuse about ten years ago."

"Ridiculous," snorted L'Abbadon. "Incredible!"

"I almost forgot there have been two new allegations about Pompeo Dell'Anitra. Both of these men making the accusations have criminal records. I think we could win against them in court, if you would like to try that," Jan suggested.

Once again the archbishop lost his temper and his voice went up a full octave as he said, "How many times have I told you, I am not going to go on the witness stand in any court. I don't care who they are, arrange with Puck to pay them off. The case that really upsets me is the Marco Lamadrid mess."

Renato listened closely as the name Lamadrid was mentioned. Marco was on administrative leave and he intended to do everything he could to keep him there.

"Well, Puck is in the process of making settlements with all the plaintiffs!

Anxious to hear more about Marco, Renato said, "Lamadrid is terribly guilty, and I will be glad when we get rid of him. So many accusations!" Although he knew that Enki and Pazuso had found the accusers and enticed them to make their allegations in hopes of getting big settlements, he would not divulge that information to the archbishop.

"No! On the contrary," said L'Abbadon pursing his lips. "He is innocent. You know that too, don't you Jan?" The archbishop waited expectantly for the vicar general to answer.

"Of course, he is innocent. Why he is not at all like us!" Realizing his statement did not sound quite right, he added, "Well, you know what I mean!"

"You got it!" the archbishop said explosively. "I don't care!" Then setting his jaw defiantly, he added, "I am not going to court to defend him. Better him than me. Let him take the heat. I will not." He slammed the palm of his hand down on the table for emphasis. "I don't care how much money it costs the archdiocese. Pay them all off and get rid of them and the accused priests!" He pursed his lips as he always did when considering something serious and then suddenly declared, "That reminds me, it is time to get the Charity Campaign running. We have spent millions in payoffs to all those who have accused priests of sex abuse. I told the media and the laity it was only eight million, but it has been much more. We need cash flow and we need it now." Turning to Renato, he said, "Organize the campaign; you are good at raising money. Tell the people in all the parishes that we need them to give sacrificially for the poor. Be sure to tell them it is for the poor. Above all, I don't want them to think I am making settlement payments with their money. I want everyone told that they are been paid with the insurance company's money".

Zagan thought about that a minute and commented, "People know that even if it was insurance money, we pay the premiums with their donations."

"People cannot think that much, Jan! Now let's go to dinner."

Our genial host, genial now that business was dispatched, led us back through the living room past his huge portrait that seemed to wink at me as I sauntered by it.

"I always liked that picture of you, Cecil," Jan remarked. "You look so jovial that no one would know that you rule this archdiocese with an iron fist—all they see in the picture is the velvet touch that you so elegantly master. I have a lot of faith in you Cecil! I always knew you would get to the top. You had the faith—you had the faith—no, you had the determination to do it. Now they should make you a cardinal." Jan was walking along the side of the large indoor pool that shimmered a bright blue as it was illuminated with blue lights.

"You are right, Jan. Faith has nothing to do with it. It is power—sheer raw power. I'd take power any day over faith."

"Can I have that drink now, Cecil?" the vicar general asked impatiently. When L'Abbadon handed him the pitcher of Canadian Club Manhattans that he was carrying, he quickly filled his glass and gulped down the drink and refilled the glass and took it with him as they made their way to the dining room.

After dinner we can play poker and drink some Port." L'Abbadon commented in an overbearing manner.

"I don't like Port, you know that, Cecil." Jan whined. "How about some nice LouisPhilippe cognac after dinner or a Hennessy?

The archbishop ignored Jan's requests as they sat down to the dinner table. The service was elegant, the food superb. Renato watched as Zagan greedily stuffed himself, spilling food, without seeming to be aware of it, on the linen napkin that he had placed on top of his Lacoste sport shirt. Actually, Renato decided, the vicar general was a drunk—an uncouth, soft mannered drunk.

Renato observed that Zagan had had so much wine at dinner that he had difficulty rising from the table. Nevertheless, he still picked up a cognac that the butler had brought to the table. He was unsteady as he walked towards the den where the butler had set up a card table.

Renato watched with amusement as the two of them—Mutt and Jeff—the archbishop was more sober than the vicar general—walked arm in arm in an effort to bolster each other up—along the large indoor pool on the way to the living room. Suddenly L'Abbadon lurched, whether on purpose or inadvertently, Renato could not determine. The result was that Zagan was catapulted into the pool. Violently thrashing with his arms flailing, he was floundering helplessly and crying out: "Help, help, I can't swim."

Renato looked at L'Abbadon for some direction as to how they were going to get the vicar general from the pool. It was incredible, the archbishop was doubled over and laughing hysterically at his friend who was thrashing the water in terror.

When Zagan went down for the second time, Renato decided it was time for him to act. After kicking off his shoes, he jumped into the pool and swam to the terrified vicar general who was quickly sobering up. When he tried to get a good hold on him to pull him to the side, the man fought him desperately, so that Renato thought he would pull him under too.

Finally the archbishop, who seemed to be thoroughly enjoying watching his friend and his chancellor wrestling in the pool, threw a flotation device to them. Renato managed to get Zagan on it and pushed to the side where L'Abbadon pulled him out. As soon as he was safely on his feet and away from the pool, Zagan collapsed in a drunken daze.

"Help me, Renato," L'Abbadon ordered. We will get him upstairs and into the bed in the room across the hall from yours and mine. Although Zagan was a short, but fat man, the two of them managed to get him in the elevator and up to the bedroom.

"We will have to take his wet clothes off," snapped L'Abbadon. "We can't put him to bed soaked like that. It would ruin the bed."

They pulled off his shoes, his shirt and his slacks. Renato was surprised to see that Zagan's baggy boxer shorts bore the monogram CAL.

51
Marco

Several months went by, during which time I kept sending material to Rome for my canon lawyer to help him prepare my defense. I was confident that, if I my case was heard in Rome, I would have a fair trial and would be reinstated as pastor of Santiago and would resume my national and international television ministries. Nothing very eventful happened, until I received a phone call from Pompeo. More agitated than I had ever heard him previously, he insisted on coming to my house to see me.

"It is urgent. I have to talk to you at once."

"Sure, come on over." Because his nervous agitation and worry always disturbed me, I really did not want to see him, since he seemed to have a way of transmitting his anxiety that I found very disconcerting. Nevertheless, he was at my house within the hour.

His ashen faced, disheveled hair, and wrinkled clothes told me that he was really in a vortex of confusion.

"What's on your mind, Pomp?"

"Don't call me Pomp. You know I don't like that," he whined.

Ok, Peo, what's your problem? Take it easy and have some faith!"

"Do not call me Peo either—I hate that even more! Faith! I got faith; I just believe that I have to defend myself and so should you! Nothing is working for good in my life."

"So what brings you here today?" I was beginning to wonder if he was ever going to come to the point."

"First, could I have some coke and cookies?"

"You have come to the wrong place! I am into low carbs—trying to lose weight." I'll get you a glass of ice water or a diet chocolate shake if you prefer."

"Oh forget it! The trouble is Onan Wilde. As I told you, Mínimo has been paying him large sums for years. A month or so ago he came after me for money. I gave him what I could. Now he has asked me to deliver a message to you." Pompeo fidgeted nervously twirling the ends of his mustache in his fingers.

I couldn't imagine what Wilde would have to say to me. I had never befriended him. Actually, I had always tried to avoid him. So I said nothing and waited for Pompeo to explain.

"Onan says that he needs money, and if you don't give it to him he is going to file sex allegations against the archdiocese, accusing you. He made the same demands on me, and I paid him off, and I think you should too. You know he charged Mínimo with sexually abusing him about ten years ago." Fearfully, Pompeo glanced at me. I could see that he was being consumed by fear.

"You can tell him to go to hell! I am not about to give him any money. I have no money to give. My income has been cut in half, and my bills keep mounting—lawyers, canon lawyers, all sorts of expenses. Even if I had the money, I would not give a cent to that scumbag! That is all I need at this time. I am calling the police and notifying my lawyers immediately. By the way, why are you bringing me this message?"

"Because Onan said he would charge me with sexually abusing him, if I didn't." His eyes evaded mine as he squirmed uncomfortably under my gaze.

"You are making yourself an accomplice to his crime of extortion!"

"No, I'm not doing that. I am just delivering a message," Pompeo protested, but his denial sounded hollow.

"Would you be willing to go with me to the police right now?

"I would never do that. Remember, I am his friend."

"You are a coward and a poor friend. Do you really think that because you delivered his message to me that he won't say anything against you?"

"Yes, he promised me—gave me his word—that he would not."

"You believe the word of that man?" I could see that Wilde had so addled him that he wasn't thinking straight. Because his left leg kept twitching, I decided that he seemed to be on the verge of collapse, as we talked.

"He is going to sue the archdiocese alleging that ten priests and a layman molested him."

"That's incredible! He would have had to be pretty stupid to make himself available to ten priests. What's he claiming—a big orgy?"

"No, just ten of them one after another in different places at different times." Terror was consuming Pompeo as he twisted and turned in his chair, unable to sit still.

"No one will believe that."

"Oh, yes, and he is even accusing Monsignor Damian Babilonia of sexually abusing him."

"Damian is dead now—has been for quite some time."

"Sure, that makes it easier for him to get money from the archdiocese. Damian is not around to defend himself. Two of the priests he is accusing are dead; the others are pastors in this area. He figures that since so many allegations have been made against you, and the archbishop has paid them all big settlements without their having to prove their allegations in court, it will be easy for him to collect on you too."

"It was stupid of the archbishop to pay off all those who made allegations without demanding proof. Now more and more people will come forth demanding easy money." I said emphatically and Pompeo agreed.

"Well, the archbishop has dug himself into a hole and fallen into it. Rumors going around among the clergy have it that he is either going to retire or get another archdiocese—that he wants desperately to leave Rosanada. I have heard that he is hoping to go to St. Louis. They say he took a lot of money to Rome to pass out among the Curia when he went on his last *ad limina* visit."

"He doesn't have enough money to buy St. Louis. If Rome knew how badly he has mismanaged Rosanada, they would send him to some backwater diocese where he would never be heard from again."

A short time later the *Rosanada News* carried the story that Onan Wilde was suing the Archdiocese of Rosanada, alleging sexual abuse by ten priests. It would take an extremely large sum—well over a million—to buy him

421

off. The worse part of it was Mínimo was a witness for Onan against me and the archdiocese, supporting that scumbag and his vicious lies and allegations. There was only one explanation, greed; or perhaps they were lovers—Onan being some sort of an expensive hustler, or both. Who knows? How was Pompeo involved in this? The last I heard of Mínimo his next assignment took him to a home for the elderly at 7 Oblivion Lane in the very center of Daftmarsh, a withering little town near Rosanada.

The same weekend that the Wilde story broke, Archbishop L'Abbadon asked the parishioners of all parishes to give sacrificially "for the poor." Was the archbishop so crass and obtuse as to think that people would believe him when he came asking for money in the name of the poor?

When I thought that things could not get any worse, I was hit like a lightening bolt by the news that my case had been bounced back from Rome and my canonical trial would be held in Rosanada. Perhaps my Roman canonist found that it would impinge adversely on his career, although canon law plainly stated that I had a right to have it heard in Rome. On the other hand, L'Abbadon may have made a couple of phone calls to the Vatican and had the case returned to Rosanada. Canon law exists only on paper; the autocrats do as they please. Their favorite word is dispensation. They dispense arbitrarily at their will, whenever it is convenient for them or the institution. That simple word could and actually does erase all 1500 and some canons. Furthermore, the pope has his papal authority that is above every law. The pope can, and has, annulled the verdicts of canonical judges around the globe. Additionally, a very ill pope like John Paul II would stamp his seal on any documents his assistants would place in front of him. To get some idea of the use of dispensation, consider how really serious the autocrats in the Church sound when they defend the "sacredness of life," yet in Africa they will grant a dispensation to nuns to take an abortifacient in case of rape.

When Monsignor Zagan phoned me and informed me that he was already beginning to arrange for my canonical trial in Rosanada, I knew that my chance of proving my innocence was non-existent. There was no way they could find me innocent after they had paid large settlements to my accusers unnecessarily.

I searched my soul to find what the Lord wanted me to do. He had called me to serve him in the Roman Catholic Church and I was a priest without faculties, without a parish, and without hope of being reinstated. There was no point in continuing the canonical charade they were planning for me. The promoter of justice, Monsignor Paul F. X. Linde, a barhopping and dancing, gay priest, popular and famous for being a flaming queen, was eagerly waiting to prosecute me. The Church had abandoned me and thrown me to the lions. No one in the hierarchy gave a damn about what happened to me. They just did not care.

Strongly aware of the Presence who assured me of His future plans for my life, I picked up the phone and called the vicar general.

"Zagan here," he answered.

"This is Marco Lamadrid. I have decided to retire."

"Good! Good! I think that is the best thing for you to do. It will save you and the archdiocese a lot of trouble. Send the archbishop a petition requesting retirement."

"I thanked him and hung up. I faxed my petition for retirement and almost immediately, the archbishop accepted my retirement as being immediately effective.

That night I went to sleep, but I was not able to rest well. So I got up, went to my computer, and wrote notes to a few friends. "Men of God" had deprived me of my church, my ministry, and my money. I felt really overwhelmed. Then I returned to bed—just to find out that God—the Father of Mercies was ready to do a great work in me. In the morning people, could not see me or find me, because I was immersed in the Divine Light and surrounded by His grace that guided me all my life and would continue to lead me until the end of my days on earth.

52
Renato

Renato heard the sound of a car in the driveway of the archiepiscopal residence, while the archbishop glanced out the window to see who was arriving.

"Make an extra pitcher of Canadian Club Manhattans, Renato. Msgr. Zagan is coming to dinner tonight," the archbishop ordered regally as Renato busied himself at the bar in the dining room.

"I'll have them ready right away," Archbishop. "He put the Canadian Club and a touch of vermouth into the shaker. Then he turned toward the archbishop and asked, "Do we have some work to do tonight?"

"Yes, of course," replied the archbishop. "Business as usual."

About the Author

Son of an American mother and a Spanish father, Josué Raúl Conte, a native of Andorra, a principality in the Pyrenees, was born in 1969. After his early education with the Jesuits, he enrolled at the Opus Dei University of Navarra in Pamplona, Spain where he received his doctorate in medieval philosophy and literature. During his years at the university, he became a member of the Neo-catechumenal Way, but later was very disillusioned with the stringent constraints of ultraconservative Catholicism and adopted a more moderate approach to his faith and left the Way. Having taught at various colleges and universities, he is now a free lance journalist, living in San Francisco with his second wife Alicia and Ivan, their Russian wolfhound. He is also author of The Chancery Murders. In the coming year, his latest work, Rosanada Requiem, will be forthcoming. For more information about him and his works, please visit www.contebooks.com.